D0444115

"An intriguing, multifaceted plot peopled with believable, authentic characters. There's a lot more to this story than just bringing down the bad guy."

—SUSAN MEISSNER, author of *Widows and Orphans*

"Once again, Amy weaves a suspenseful tale of intrigue that will leave you begging for more. *Healing Promises* is heart-wrenching and powerful. The chase to stop a killer kept me turning the pages, and Clint and Sara's story broke my heart and kept me cheering for them right to the last page. Whether you want an emotional story straight from the heart or a suspense full of twists and turns, *Healing Promises* delivers it all."

—WANDA DYSON, author of *Intimidation* and *Why I Jumped*

"In *Healing Promises* Amy Wallace does what so few writers are willing to do. She looks down the gun barrel of reality, and she does it without flinching. This novel is so real, it nearly breathes on its own. I highly recommend it."

—BRANDT DODSON, author of the Colton Parker Mystery
series and *White Soul*

"*Healing Promises* was one of the most compelling stories I read this year—full of spiritual depth, rich with authentically drawn struggles, yet also packed with hope. Amy Wallace humanizes the typical heroic character in a powerful way. I identified with Clint's battle as his own body betrayed him and with Sara's journey toward trusting God even when it hurt too much to hope. I couldn't put the book down and left the story encouraged and inspired."

—SHARON HINCK, author of the Becky Miller books,
the Sword of Lyric series, and *Symphony of Secrets*

"From page one, *Healing Promises* captures your attention—and your heart—and doesn't let go until the deeply satisfying end. Amy Wallace has crafted another must-read."

 —MARK MYNHEIR, homicide detective and author
  of *The Void*

"Amy Wallace is a master of heart-tugging suspense. She has a gift for creating realistic characters struggling with haunting life situations, even as they battle bone-chilling villains. This book satisfies on multiple levels."

 —JILL ELIZABETH NELSON, author of the
  To Catch a Thief series

"Amy Wallace's greatest gift as a writer is her unflinching honesty. Her characters are individuals who wrestle with the thorniest questions a Christian can encounter: Do I trust that God is truly working out all circumstances for my good? Is the source of my joy and hope found in the circumstances of my life or in Christ alone? Is His grace truly enough for me? The answers to these questions don't come easily or comfortably, but the end knowledge is worth every moment of the struggle."

 —HEATHER NATIONS, cancer survivor

"Amy Wallace does an amazing job of bringing to life the conflicting feelings of cancer patients and their families—fear, worry, and anger fighting with faith and hope. At the same time, she weaves in the agonizing search for a child killer who could strike again at any moment. You won't want to put the book down."

 —RENEE KOSTER, cancer survivor

HEALING
PROMISES

DEFENDERS *of* HOPE, BOOK TWO

HEALING
PROMISES

A NOVEL

AMY WALLACE

MULTNOMAH
BOOKS

HEALING PROMISES
PUBLISHED BY MULTNOMAH BOOKS
12265 Oracle Boulevard, Suite 200
Colorado Springs, Colorado 80921
A division of Random House Inc.

Scripture quotations or paraphrases are taken from the following versions:
King James Version and the Holy Bible, New International Version®. NIV®.
Copyright © 1973, 1978, 1984 by International Bible Society. Used by
permission of Zondervan Publishing House. All rights reserved.

The characters and events in this book are fictional, and any resemblance to
actual persons or events is coincidental.

Song lyrics for "I Know That Jesus Loves Me," quoted in chapter 5, are by
Nathan Phillips and are used by permission of Nathan Phillips.

ISBN: 978-1-60142-010-7

MULTNOMAH and its mountain colophon are registered trademarks
of Random House Inc.

Library of Congress Cataloging-in-Publication Data
Wallace, Amy, 1970–
    Healing promises : a novel / Amy Wallace.—1st ed.
       p. cm.—(Defenders of hope ; bk. 2)
    ISBN 978-1-60142-010-7
    I. Title.
PS3623.A35974H43 2008
813'.6—dc22

                                        2007049253

Printed in the United States of America

2008

10 9 8 7 6 5 4 3 2

In memory of Kenneth Alan Whaley.
You showed us in action
that even when circumstances don't go the way we prayed,
God is on His throne and He is very, very good.
Always.

And to the Whaley family.
I will never forget your beautiful example of grieving with hope.
You've given us a glimpse of Home and abundant grace
that nothing on this earth can steal.
Thank you.

ACKNOWLEDGMENTS

Writing *Healing Promises* required so much of my heart and challenged my faith on so many levels. But there were scores of incredible folks who held me up in prayer and practical ways and kept me going with their love.

My awesome family has continued to wash, cook, clean, inspire, pray, encourage, and love me anyway. Thank you, David, for being my first and biggest fan and for turning my eyes again and again to our heavenly Daddy who satisfies each and every need. Every time. Abundantly. Steven, Clint, and Michael are who they are because of your example and love.

Thanks to my precious princesses too. I'm so honored to be your mommy. And very thankful for the twinkle in your eyes when you tell the world your mommy is an author. As you continue to grow more and more beautiful inside and out and use your incredible imaginations to dream big, always remember that Aslan isn't safe, but He is good. I pray the amazing plan God has for each of you will keep you forever between the Lion's paws. Know you are loved—to infinity and beyond.

Mom, Heather, Renee, Chris and Tiff, and Joe, you looked cancer in the face and held on to Jesus. Thank you for allowing me to mix my tears and prayers with yours and be pointed back to Jesus every step of the way.

Mom, Dad, Josh, Heidi, Zack, and the Wallace clan, thanks for loving me well. I love you each more than words can convey. Linda, thank you for the myriad details on Blacksburg that helped bring those scenes to life and for being my sister-in-law and friend.

Special thanks to the incredible team who has prayed me through: Ane, Anna, Cheryl, Cindy, David, Elizabeth, Heather, Jen, Jennifer,

Julie, Kelly, Kristian, Laurie, Meg, Melissa, Michelle, Pam, Patty, Sally, Stephanie, Susan, Tiff, Tricia, and Vicki. Your prayers and encouragement are Jesus's arms and words of love.

A world of thanks goes to the entire team at WaterBrook Multnomah. Julee, Anne, Kelly, Tiffany, Allison, Melissa, Liz, Leah, Jan, Stuart, Teresa, and many more, you continue to be a gracious part of making dreams come true. Thank you for everything!

So many wonderful people gave of their time and expertise: retired federal agent Jack Branson, Corporal Lou Gregoire, Tiff and Chris Colter, Heather Nations, Renee Koster, Deb Kinnard, Dr. Ronda Wells, Dr. Michael Andrews, Ronie Kendig, amazing counselor and songwriter Nathan Phillips, and photographer Sherri Winstead. Thank you. My life is richer and my work far easier thanks to all of you.

My crit partners extraordinaire, Jen Keithley and Meg Moseley; The Threshing Floor ladies, Jen, Mary, and Staci; the Writers of Remarkable Design group; truth teller and loving journey buddy Sharon Hinck; CRAMM friends Cindy, Rachel, Meg, and Marci; and the amazing ACFW folks are some of the greatest gifts and joys on my writing path. My words are better and my heart fuller because each of you has shared the journey. Thank you.

Finally, to my holy and perfect Abba. You have both given and taken away. On the pathways of pain and the mountaintops of peace, blessed be Your name.

The LORD gave, and the LORD hath taken away;
blessed be the name of the LORD.

JOB 1:21

M ost days, Clint Rollins loved his work.

Most days. But not today.

He leaned back in his swivel chair and listened to the hum of voices, computer keys, and his partner's detailed explanation of a new case. Only a week back to work, and he already needed a quiet weekend to rest.

"You listening, Rollins, or still suffering from vacation withdrawal? Maybe it's just too early on a Friday morning."

Steven Kessler's ribbing jerked Clint back to the reality of working in the FBI's Crimes Against Children Unit. Another child missing. No easy cases.

"I'm listening." Clint rubbed the back of his neck.

Too bad criminals didn't care if cops were up to snuff or not. His head still ached from a nasty cold that'd been dogging him for weeks. According to his physician wife, he needed a vacation to recover from his unprecedented two-week vacation. But no one in DC stayed home with just a cold. So he was back on the job in mid-January, doing his second favorite thing.

Putting criminals in jail.

He'd still rather be hanging out with Sara and the munchkins.

"One of Baltimore's finest is heading our way—point cop for the kidnapping case." Steven handed over a new file. "The suspect was spotted with the child at a hotel outside Blacksburg less than an hour ago. His license plate matches the one given in the AMBER Alert. Local cops are keeping watch to be sure no one leaves, and there's a Learjet ready and waiting. We'll head out as soon as Sergeant Moore arrives."

At his partner's no-frills tone, Clint flipped through computer printouts and watched his quiet weekend disappear. "Why aren't the Baltimore or Virginia field offices handling this one?"

"Because we're the best." Steven grabbed paperwork and motioned for him to follow.

Clint checked his Glock and stood. "Cute. More details. Real ones."

"We are the best. But you're right. The reasons go deeper. The boy's mother is Ben Dickson's girlfriend."

"Dickson." Clint frowned. "The Baltimore police chief?"

"Yep. And Dickson's an old pal of Unit Chief Maxwell."

"Interesting queue of string pulling. What else do we know?"

"Wes Standish went missing from the playground after school yesterday. Babysitter called Dickson's girlfriend to say she'd lost him, and a missing-persons report was filed right away. So lots of cops went to work round the clock, and Dickson breathed down Quantico folks' necks to get their data inputted and analyzed."

Clint flipped through the file again as they walked. "They know who snatched Wes?"

"Mom says the ex-husband. A community college professor in Christiansburg named Ed Standish."

"So Mom and the chief want us involved to get a federal conviction when we catch the guy."

Steven shrugged. "Likely. But according to eyewitness accounts, Dad's not the kidnapper. A few people saw Wes leave with a tall, young-looking blond man. Dad's middle-aged, balding, and average height." Steven stopped and held out a second file, this one much thicker. "What makes this case top priority for us is ViCAP flagged three cold cases with a similar MO and victim profile."

Clint grabbed the file as adrenaline shot through him. "A serial?"

"Could be."

Clint scanned the info from the FBI's violent criminal database. "So we have January kidnappings from parks, boys ages five to six, brown hair, blue eyes. No ransom and no bodies. But this one looks more like a domestic, a disgruntled dad who lost custody."

"Whether it's the dad or not, we need to bring Wes Standish home and nab this suspect."

Clint froze midstep, staring at pictures in the file. "Any of these boys could be James's twin."

Steven's jaw clamped tight. "Coulda done without that."

"Sorry. I should've kept quiet."

They continued in silence. Steven's six-year-old son had been injured in a school shooting in October. His girlfriend, Gracie, had been kidnapped in November. And last summer, they'd been too late to save a little boy named Ryan and a teenage girl named Olivia—failures that still haunted Steven.

They both needed more recovery time. But work wouldn't wait. Wes Standish needed to come home. Today.

Steven answered his phone as soon as it buzzed. "Stay where you parked, and we'll meet you there. I'll drive to the airstrip."

Pulling up short in front of the outside door, Steven narrowed his eyes at Clint. "Let's make sure we bring Wes home before he ends up looking like Ryan. I don't want any more rescued kids never leaving the hospital."

And that was that. For both of them.

※　※　※

The condescending cop seated facing him grated on Clint's nerves. Even the high-end business plane couldn't make this trip pleasant.

He usually managed to keep away from the local and federal ego dances. But this officer was a piece of work, smirking at the Learjet's fancy mini-conference-room interior and acting like his department had every right to claim the glory when Wes made it home.

"Even before you Feds got on board with our hunch about Standish, we knew we'd be bringing home a prize today." The over-forty officer crossed his beefy arms and flashed them a blinding smile.

Steven crossed his arms in return. "Enlighten us as to your reasoning."

Clint rested his throbbing head on the Learjet's leather seat, rubbing his temples as Steven and the cop locked wits. He tried to pray, but the cabin's August-in-Texas temperature dampened his concentration.

"You up for this, Rollins?" Moore's curt question bristled. "You don't look so hot."

Steven stifled a chuckle.

Everything in Clint wanted to rattle off how they'd recently taken down an international kidnapper and solved a three-person cold-case murder. Not to mention that all the events involved people he loved like family. But he refrained. "I can handle it."

Moore cleared his throat. "After we found out about the cold cases, Chief Dickson ticked off a list of Standish's favorite gambling places. Said his girlfriend always kicked her estranged husband out after the holidays, and he'd be gone for weeks each time. It's why he lost his job at the University of Maryland last year. They separated after that, and he moved back home to Christiansburg, got a job at a community college. She finalized the divorce this January in honor of their history. That's obviously what set him off."

Steven shrugged. "All circumstantial. And there are other—"

"Look, the guy's a world-class loser. A sleazeball with a Ph.D. Him rotting in jail would be the best thing for his son. But since you can't connect the dots, here's one for your superior profiling. Standish has been teaching early childhood education courses at a community college near where his brother lives in Blacksburg. We're heading to Blacksburg. All the missing kids fitting the same MO for Wes's case match Wes to a T, and they all disappeared in January when Standish was on his benders. And as the chief mentioned to the agent at NCAVC, Standish used to sit in a dark room, watch the kid sleep every night. Guy's a pervert. Case closed."

"Hardly."

Even if the folks at the National Center for the Analysis of Violent Crime agreed that Standish fit a violent pedophile's profile—and Clint wasn't convinced of that—Moore's speech sounded more like gunning for a promotion than good investigative skills. Good thing they had federal jurisdiction and this Baltimore officer didn't. And thank the Lord not all police they worked with were like Moore.

The Baltimore cops were clearly trigger-happy when it came to Standish's guilt. Just thinking about the other possibilities increased Clint's headache a million points on the Richter scale. He closed that mental file and watched the plane come in for a landing.

Steven's arm punch got Clint's attention. It smarted more than he wanted to admit. "What?"

"Got your picture in place?"

"Always." He slapped his vest under layers of winter wear. "The family Christmas photo is right here."

Steven grinned. "Got mine too." Steven might be the CACU's head coordinator, but he still tended to follow Clint's lead, just as he'd done since Quantico. In most things anyway.

A Blacksburg cop was waiting for them with a car at the Virginia Tech executive airport. Moore took the front seat. "Got an update for us?"

"My sergeant just radioed as y'all were landing. Shots were fired. Suspect tried to leave but opened fire when our guys approached."

"He's gone?"

"Nope. Still out there shooting. They can't get close to the car."

Clint met Steven's hard look. "Let's do this fast and careful so we can get home before midnight."

Minutes later, they eased into a run-down hotel's parking lot and stopped behind two squad cars. Unsnapping holsters, all four exited the car and crouched behind the nearest vehicle.

Clint flashed his credentials, and the local sergeant nodded. "Manager called in the tip, said our suspect checked into room 102 early this morning. When he tried to leave, we moved in. He just dumped the kid in the car and took off into the woods. We've been dodging bullets ever since."

Shots punctuated his report.

Two of the local cops returned fire.

Moore's neck veins bulged. "The boy still alive?"

"No way to tell. He wasn't moving, and we haven't been able to get to him. Backup's slower'n Christmas."

Moore's eyes locked on to the tan Impala's open trunk and grew wide as his face got red. "You shot up the car?"

"No." The officer stayed in firing position, gun trained on the woods, too busy to care that he'd just been insulted by a big-city cop. "Those were from his last volley before y'all arrived."

Clint studied the car. Tangled trunk metal and busted taillights said their kidnapper wasn't a sharpshooter. He moved to the front of the patrol car. "I'm going to check on the boy." He caught Steven's gaze. "Pray. And cover me."

With his heart pounding out of his chest, Clint crawled along the black asphalt faster than he'd ever done at Quantico. Reaching the Impala, he paused to listen. Nothing. His back to the tan metal, he reached for a door handle.

Opening the door a crack, he felt inside.

When his hand touched a heavy down jacket, he swerved to face the car. The boy lay unmoving, hands bound with duct tape, a black hood over his head. Clint stripped it off and felt clammy flesh, a flickering pulse.

This boy needed medical help. Now.

Clint's hands shook as he pulled the boy out of the car and onto his lap, then gathered him into his arms.

Shots rang through the metal behind him. But he had to keep moving. He was ten feet from safety.

He held tight to the boy and lunged toward Steven.

Searing pain ripped through his left arm.

Then everything went asphalt black.

2

"Dr. Rollins, we can't thank you enough for listening to all our research."

Sara Rollins smiled and tucked a lock of her unruly red curls behind her ear. Across her cherrywood desk, Joseph Holmes and his mother, Claudia, sat waiting for her verdict on their newfound miracle cure. No such thing existed for Joseph's rhabdomyosarcoma, but saying so was a tricky matter. At thirteen, Joe embodied determination and courage; Sara rebelled against dampening that. But Claudia needed to move past the stage of fighting her cancer fears with reams of computer printouts. It was time to ease into acceptance of proven clinical procedures and trust God with the outcome.

"I welcome your active involvement in Joseph's care, and I agree that naturopathic remedies can be valuable supplements to our treatment regimens." As long as they followed prescribed protocol in the end. "I'll consult with Dr. Silverman, our alternate-therapies expert, about the Essiac tea, and we can discuss options before you leave this afternoon."

A knock at the door interrupted her thoughts.

"I'm sorry to bother you, Dr. Rollins, but Steven Kessler is on the line with an urgent message."

"I'll call him back after my appointment. Thanks, Laurie."

The Benefield Cancer Center's beloved manager didn't budge. "He's left messages on your cell and has called the switchboard three times. It's about Clint."

Sara couldn't swallow past the tightness in her throat. She checked her watch. "Claudia, Joseph, I hate to rush out before we've had a chance to pray together, but I need to take this call."

Joe cleared his throat. "It's okay, Doc. We'll pray at the beginning and end next time." He and his mom stood to leave. "See ya in three weeks."

"I'm praying, Joe."

Laurie escorted them out, closing the door behind her. Sara jerked the phone and punched the flashing hold button. "Tell me he's okay, Steven."

Loud whooshing noises answered her. "Sara? Are you there?"

"Let me talk to him."

"Can't. He's unconscious. There's been an…incident."

That she'd figured out. There'd been calls like this before. But how bad was it? Her teeth ached with tension as she struggled to hear.

"…said concussion on top of the GSW…med-flighted into Alexandria Community. ETA five minutes."

Her stomach turned over. Another gunshot wound. "I'll meet you at the ER." She disconnected the call and made a beeline for the rest room to take care of her queasiness before heading into the adjacent hospital.

Dr. Marilynn Richards met her right outside the physician's lounge. Her best friend's light brown hand closed around Sara's bicep and stilled her forward charge. "Hold on a minute."

"Can't talk now." Sara tried to dodge around her friend. "Something's…something's happened to Clint."

"I know." Marilynn's stocky frame still blocked her way. "ER called. He's here. But the ER personnel are not going to let you in there as a doctor or bow to that Irish temper of yours. You understand that, right?"

Sara could only nod as they speed-walked out of the Benefield Cancer Center and across the walkway into the main hospital building. Switching between her roles as oncologist, FBI wife, and mommy to Susannah and Jonathan was always a challenge. It never happened seamlessly. But Marilynn was right. Charging in there barking orders wouldn't help Clint at all. "Did they say who's treating him?"

"I believe it's Peter Greer." Marilynn's quick smile creased her face as they reached the elevators. "Your husband is a hero, Sara. Remind him of that. I'll be praying."

Sara's feet switched to autopilot as she left her friend at the elevators. She ended up in the ER without another coherent thought.

A mass of people filled the waiting area. She swerved around them and walked toward the ER doors. The busy receptionist put a caller on hold and stopped her. "May I help you?"

Sara flashed her ID badge. "My husband, Clint Rollins, was transported here by Med-Flight."

"That good-looking Texan with the deep chocolate eyes?"

"Yes."

"He's being treated now. Sure made a fuss about not being allowed to walk in." The girl chuckled as she flipped through the papers at her station. "You definitely have a strong one there, even if he couldn't strut in the way he would've liked."

Sara fiddled with her ring and smiled. Clint's alertness was a good sign. The girl could look all she wanted.

The young woman shuffled her paperwork and glanced at Sara's ID badge again. "You work at the cancer center?" She nodded toward the ER doors. "You can go on back—fourth room on the right."

Sara charged through the ER doors, possible scenarios flipping through her mind. Clint had been shot before, but never knocked unconscious at the same time. A male voice from behind stopped her from entering Clint's room.

"Sara? Hang on a minute."

She looked up and met a familiar pair of gray blue eyes. Peter Greer. One of the best ER docs she'd ever known.

"Hey, Peter." How surreal to be on the patient side of polite conversation like this.

Pointing toward the small, doctors-only area past Clint's door, Peter motioned for her to join him. "I'm glad I caught you before you went in."

Her heart drummed against her ribs. "Is Clint okay?"

"Well, his gunshot injury is relatively minor. Would have been far more serious if he'd not gotten such fast medical attention." Peter ran a hand over the black stubble covering his narrow chin.

Sara blinked. Something in Dr. Greer's expression unsettled her. "Does his concussion complicate matters?"

"Yes. He was still vomiting after arrival." He took a deep breath. "We got him stabilized quickly, but I'd like your help in convincing him to stay overnight for observation and let me run a few additional tests."

"Do you think—?"

He held up a hand. "Initial films, a blood workup, and a head CT will tell us more, but it'll be a while before those get processed. Might want to make yourself comfortable." He motioned to the hallway. "Why don't we head in to see your husband?"

They walked back down the busy hallway in silence, and then Dr. Greer opened the trauma room door for her.

"Hey, honey, I'm home before midnight." Clint tried to stand but immediately leaned back into the exam table.

"Glad to see you haven't lost your manners, cowboy." Their familiar banter comforted her even as she and Peter maneuvered her husband-turned-rag-doll back onto the table.

"I'll start the paperwork and call for a room." With that the doctor disappeared into the hall.

"What's going on, Clint?"

"I'm okay. Just a little lightheaded from the fall."

"A concussion with persistent vomiting is more serious than that."

"I think I met the pavement right after the hit. Don't remember much else. Steven says I owe him big for the mess he had to clean up in the copter." Clint chuckled.

Sara didn't feel like laughing.

A knock on the door silenced further questioning. "Come in."

Steven poked his head through the door, looking like a little boy whose baseball broke the neighbors' picture window. "How much trouble am I in, Dr. Sara?"

"You said you'd keep him safe." She crossed her arms and sighed. "But I know it's part of the job. Come on in. I won't rip you to shreds."

"Wasn't too sure about that." Steven wrapped her in a bear hug, then raked a hand through his light brown hair. "You know how he is about being a hero. He got a kid out of harm's way and nearly made it back to cover before anyone else figured out what to do."

Clint smirked. "Like you didn't think about being the big tough guy."

"You told me to cover you."

"So you're admitting I'm faster than you, even in my old age." Clint leaned back against the wall and yawned.

She couldn't help but laugh at the testosterone filling the room. These two had kept that level way over the top for as long as she'd known them—almost eleven years. For once she appreciated their friendly rivalry. It kept Clint awake, which gave her a chance to assess his vitals and get a good look at his eyes.

She concurred with Dr. Greer. Instinct said staying overnight was a good idea.

"I'm not your patient, Sara."

The room grew hot. Caught again. She turned to Steven. "Is the child okay?"

"He'll be fine. Most of his recovery will be on the emotional side." Steven's face clouded. "Clint got him to safety uninjured. He's just now coming to, though."

"Drugged?" Clint asked.

"Yes. It'll be a while before we know what he used."

A look passed between the two men. Sara knew not to ask, but everything in her wanted to know. "Did you get the guy?" She needed to hear that the person who could drug a child and shoot her husband was behind bars.

"Of course."

Clint broke in. "Was Moore right about it being Standish?"

"Yes and no."

Sara leaned against the table. She knew better than to try to decode their shoptalk.

Clint sat up straight. "Come again?"

"The actual perp was a college kid named Billy Raeford, but he ID'd Standish as the money and brains behind the scheme. That's all the intel I have right now."

Translation: They'd talk later when a civilian wasn't listening.

A gray-haired nurse poked her head in the door. "X-ray's on the way, and they'll have Mr. Rollins's room ready after that."

Sara rested her hand on Clint's knee. "Thank you."

Steven gave her another hug. "I'll check in with you tomorrow." He slipped out and shut the door. Clint's shoulders sagged as he gave in to fatigue.

"Tough case?" Sara watched his eyes.

"Could be. Which is why I gotta get out of this home for white coats and help Steven chase some leads."

"You have to mend first. Even top cops need recuperation time."

"I have a serious criminal to lock up. Possibly a serial. Which means other kids are in danger."

Sara sighed. It wasn't worth the argument. Clint would be back at his desk long before she approved. At least he'd get one night of forced rest, and she could make rounds and tie up today's loose ends.

What happened after that was out of her control.

3

I t always astounded him how one so small could be so heavy.
Guess that's why they call it dead weight.
The child's brown hair flopped with every step as he carted the limp form through the woods early Monday morning. Instead of a hindrance, the recent rains would provide a welcome abridgement of the backbreaking work ahead. Not only that, he loved the fresh smell of wet earth tinged with frosty predawn air.

Now that the hellacious pressure was appeased yet again, he could enjoy the endorphin rush that followed. The feeling of power and well-being far more potent than casino glitz and winnings.

He wouldn't get caught.

No one would ever uncover his secret place.

Finding his normal section of the park had become a game. Ten slow, sliding steps down the hill, fifty more to the east, then a straight shot south for about a mile.

The weight in his arms grew heavier than his favorite shovel. Looking over the boy's now-silent features, he let the memories come. His first kill had been somewhat of an accident. And a revelation. He'd become the man parents warned their children about. Only smarter and stronger, because he could bridle the urge. Until life spun out of control once again. Then the demand for release proved irrepressible.

But a quick snap of a boy's neck always ended that problem.

Once a year was all it took.

And if all went according to plan, soon everything else in his life would be set right again.

Taking a deep breath, he reveled in how the experience allowed him the instantaneous rush of redefining an old wound. Now all the power and timing remained in his control. Strange how easy and routine the whole endeavor had become. No outbursts of rage anymore. No sleepless nights afterward. Just taking care of business so he could concentrate on the important things in life.

It fascinated him how no one had an iota of a clue about his handiwork.

He stopped to rest and listen to the forest sounds. Owls hooted, searching for a meal to devour before dawn. Checking his watch, he realized he had only a few more hours before the covering of darkness disappeared.

"Ah, here we are at last."

Setting the child down in the grassy mud, he busied himself with the task at hand.

Scoop. Thud. Another shovelful of damp earth and small rocks hit the ground above him. What a satisfying sound. This part always reminded him of burying the school bully's old dog in the backyard. How sweet his childhood revenge had tasted. The dumb mutt had followed him home without anyone seeing them disappear. In fact, the only glitch in the plan had been their neighbors' claim of hearing whimpering that woke them in the middle of the night.

But they'd never seen him. And he'd become more skilled after that.

He finished his digging and scrambled out of the deep hole. Without any fanfare, he lowered the young boy into the blackness and began shoveling dirt back into place.

One more added to his collection.

4

I t's not what you think. Trust me."

With a low bow, Steven presented Clint's Wednesday lunch in a gray-domed hospital tray. Agents Michael Parker and Lee Branson chuckled behind him as they removed their overcoats. Steven tossed his on the nearest chair.

"Why do I not feel comforted?" Clint scowled as he sat up in bed and tucked a stack of papers far under the covers. Steven noted the furtive move with interest. It wasn't his best friend's style to hide. But six days in the hospital could do strange things to a person.

"What gives with hiding stuff from your brothers?" Lee reached for the white hospital sheet.

Clint grabbed Lee's dark arm and held it fast. "Don't."

"Okay, bro." Stepping back, Lee raised his hands in surrender. "Hospital life does not agree with your usual Pollyanna personality."

Steven studied his partner. He would visit this topic later, but for now they had work issues to address. He nodded to Michael and Lee, and they all pulled tan hospital chairs close to the bed.

Clint shut his eyes for a second and then mumbled an apology. "They don't let you sleep much in this place, and they've kept me five days too many already."

Michael leaned forward and rubbed his blond Marine buzz. "For a GSW? That is a bit of overkill, isn't it?"

"Complications with the gunshot wound. An infection and some other medical mumbo jumbo." Clint pointed to his IV. "They're loading me up with antibiotics. Doesn't help that Sara is armchair quarterbacking everything." Switching focus, he raised his eyebrows and placed the food-service container onto his lap. "Care to tell me why the FBI is delivering my lunch today?"

"Can't a guy do a simple good deed anymore?" Grinning, Steven nudged the container.

"Not likely."

"Just lift the lid and see. Besides, we have some work to do and need your indispensable input."

Clint lifted the gray dome with slow precision…until the scent of fresh-baked pizza with all his favorite toppings filled the room. Then his stomach growled a loud thanks.

"Your favorite personal pan pizza with extra cheese, hamburger, and black olives." Steven bowed again. "Straight from Gracie's kitchen, because we aim to please."

"Pass along my thanks for the pizza, and that Gracie made it instead of you. That girl's a keeper. Good thing you're proposing soon."

"That's the plan. One of many reasons why you need to get out of here pronto."

Clint bowed his head quickly, then made short work of the pizza. While he was eating, Steven passed case files to Michael and Lee. "Under the circumstances, I thought it best to meet here instead of the office. After this, Lee has a video conference with Chief Dickson's team about phone records and a credit card trail on Ed Standish. They're dealing with warrants and keeping us updated as they sort through the mass of data."

"Good thing too," Lee grumbled as he flipped through the paperwork. "I was already buried in stuff before this case hit. Got a domestic kidnapping nightmare with unlawful flight to avoid prosecution and a child support recovery case the U.S. attorney's office tasked to the CACU."

Steven wished they could trade workloads. But that wouldn't have lessened Lee's notorious complaining.

"Everything in Christiansburg is moving slower than Christmas, with jurisdiction issues and red tape for warrants." Michael tapped the keys on his computer. "Locals can't find Jim Standish either."

"That's the brother, right?" Clint wiped his hands with a napkin. "The one who lives in Blacksburg?"

Michael nodded. "Something about him being on a bow-hunting trip. They're keeping watch on both residences, though preliminary searches turned up zilch. I'm out of here as soon as the guy turns up. I'm itching for a good interrogation."

Clint cocked his head but kept quiet.

"We need to find Standish yesterday. He didn't report to work on January fifteenth, just days before Wes was snatched. Since then, he's dropped off the radar. And take a look at this." Steven handed Clint the file on their newest case. "A maroon truck registered to Jim Standish was spotted near the park where Mattie Reynolds was abducted on Sunday, and eyewitnesses reported sighting a balding, baby-faced man alone at the park before Mattie disappeared. Locals are coordinating search efforts with the Virginia field office."

Lee shook his head. "And we have three cold cases to add to the mix. That makes five kidnappings. One child recovered, three likely dead, and one that's growing colder each day."

Clint pushed himself up with his IV arm, his movements slow and weak. Not good. Steven made a mental note to call Sara on his way back to the Hoover Building.

"Y'all are lumping all these cases together with little beyond similar MOs. There are two different suspect descriptions and no linked motive." Clint shrugged. "I must be missing something."

"I'm hoping you can help us decipher a motive. Standish's hired gun matches the cold cases' young blond abductors, and he named Standish, so we know Standish is involved in Wes's case." Steven walked over to the large hospital window and concentrated on the thick gray clouds outside. "The fact that Standish paid someone to do his dirty work ups his threat level. Then we have a possible link between Standish and Mattie's abduction, which takes him out of the parental-kidnapping category and makes him a more likely suspect for the other cases."

"All four of the missing boys match Wes's features. Brown hair, blue eyes, age about the same." Michael looked up from his laptop. "That's a red flag for a serial."

Clint shook his head and grimaced. "But why go from snatching other kids to kidnapping his own son?"

"Maybe he's a sicko like the Baltimore cops said, but he hurt other kids to keep from harming his own. It's been known to happen. Then he gets divorced, loses custody rights, and that shakes him up. So he switches from having his partner nab Wes look-alikes to trying to get his son back."

"So why take Mattie himself?"

"His partner's in jail, and he's desperate for a hit of his drug of choice." Lee shrugged on his coat. "I gotta head back to the office. But here's what I think. Perverts love computers, so once we get into Standish's computer we can verify or refute Chief Dickson's pedophile hunch. And if we can get Billy Raeford to start talking again, we might slam-dunk this investigation with personal testimony and physical evidence."

"There goes my ride." Michael packed up his laptop and grabbed his coat too. "I need to push on getting the computer data expedited." He turned to Clint. "I'm not sold on Standish being our cold-case perp, but I think we have enough to check it out. There's a possibility we find Standish and give a lot of grieving parents closure."

"Get better soon, man. We need you back pushing papers with us." Lee's chuckle followed him and Michael from the room.

Steven sat down again. "Talk to me. I need your sage advice."

"That's rich for a man only two years younger than me." Clint leaned his head back on the bed. "But my gut says y'all are doing a little too much speculation. I'm all for solving cold cases, but what does Wes say about his dad? And how's he doing, by the way?"

"As good as can be expected. He's a strong kid. Smart like James and just as personable. He'll make it. His counselor said there's some natural hero worship for his dad, but nothing to suggest abuse. Lots of physical contact and that weird bit about Standish watching him sleep every night, otherwise nothing really suspicious."

"Which makes the pedophile angle—"

A young nurse with a huge smile interrupted to check Clint's vitals. Steven took the opportunity to pack casework back into his briefcase, surreptitiously watching for the nurse's assessment results.

"So you ready for the big day tomorrow, Mr. Rollins?"

Clint worked his jaw like the girl had accused him of stealing drugs. "I'm fine. Thanks, Lauren." He didn't even meet the nurse's eyes as she worked, looking straight through her to the potted plants and balloons filling his room.

Her face twisted into confusion. She finished and left with a quick nod.

"It's not like you to snap at people like that. What's up?"

"Nothing. I just want out of here. Only time I didn't hate hospitals was when I was in the Houston ER, with my favorite resident's red curls and green eyes making me forget all about my broken wrist."

"Tell me you didn't try that as a pickup line on Sara back then." Steven adjusted his University of Louisville basketball tie.

"I pretty much babbled incoherently."

They both laughed.

"So what's Sara have to say about all this extra pampering?"

"That I'll be home soon."

"Good. I need you at the office after the shortest amount of sick leave possible."

Clint avoided his eyes. "Keep me in the loop on the paper trails and computer data. It'd be good to see evidence backing up all this speculation."

"Why don't you get better and show the rest of us how it's done? No more falling down on the job."

"Ha-ha."

Steven slipped on his overcoat. "Seriously, I haven't worked without you for any length of time since our stint with the Hostage Rescue Team. Don't intend to do it now."

"Yeah, you've been riding my coattails ever since. All the way to the CACU."

"Except I moved to CACU first." Steven walked to the door.

"We'll have plenty of work waiting for you, so enjoy the downtime while you can."

"I'll do that." The look clouding Clint's face made Steven's shoulders knot. His partner obviously wanted back in the game, but there was more to Clint's foul mood. Something connected with the papers he'd shoved under the sheets.

What it was, Steven had no idea. But he'd find out. Soon.

※　※　※

Some doctors had the bedside manner of an ice cube.

Clint's first oncologist was a primary example. He could still hear the young doctor's disinterested, clinical words. *The biopsy shows diffuse large B-cell lymphoma. Stage four. Best-case scenario, forty- to fifty-percent survival rate.*

Clint set aside the pages and pages of Web site information one of the nurses had printed for him, his brain aching from all the possibilities. Sara kept sidestepping his attempts to talk about what was happening. Probably because of guilt over not diagnosing his symptoms when they started two months ago. But he'd never told her about the elevated temps and night sweats or the swollen area in his throat. He'd just assumed it was the flu.

His mistake. He picked up the papers and started reading again about how cancer affected the mouth, hair, and sleep. Chemobrain and memory loss. Blood-count numbers that made his head spin, and descriptions of all the tests he'd have to endure over the next five months.

He wanted to throw his pillows across the room. Or pound his fists into a punching bag. Except his gunshot wound would make that impossible for a few more weeks. But he'd have to thank Wes Standish one day. Saving that kid's life might well have saved his own.

As long as he could live through a little thing called chemotherapy. No telling what that would do to him.

He had to fight. Fight the cancer. Fight the changes.

Fight to survive.

The doctors had said he might return to work by the end of February. Five weeks. Way too much time away. But at least the sick leave would help him avoid Steven with his cancer diagnosis until after Valentine's Day. Steven had big plans to propose to Gracie then at her parents' house in Georgia. No way was Clint gonna risk messing that up.

Looking at the IV, he tried hard to count his blessings. His CT scan was normal. The headaches were gone. His children loved him. His friends depended on him. He'd even had the opportunity to talk about Jesus to a few of the nurses.

But starting tomorrow, all manner of horrific stuff could happen. Mood swings. Vomiting. More ER visits. Doctors, needles, and more doctors.

He already hated the miserable port deforming his chest just below his right collarbone. Who cared if the implanted device made filling his body with toxic chemicals easier? Two days, and he still couldn't look at the thing.

"Mr. Rollins? I need to check your vitals again." Lauren walked toward his bed with her head down.

Clint took a deep breath. "I'm sorry about before. I…I'm not ready for my partner to know about the cancer."

Lauren's face returned to her usual smile. "I thought I'd done something really wrong." She strapped the cuff around his right arm. "And I totally understand about not wanting everyone to know. I've heard patients talk about all the awful advice they've been given from everybody and their brother."

"That leaves me a lot to look forward to."

"Oh." Lauren's face turned bright pink. "Sorry, Mr. Rollins. I need to keep a better watch on my tongue." She finished her assessment. "But it'll be fine. You'll see. The doctors in the cancer center are great. Especially your wife."

"Not sure I like doctors anymore."

"I hope that doesn't include *all* doctors."

Clint turned toward the familiar voice and met the beautiful green of his wife's Irish eyes. Pushing back the covers, he attempted to stand.

"Hi, Dr. Rollins." Lauren exited after a smile from Sara brightened the girl's face.

"Keep your seat, cowboy." Sara's calming voice loosened the vise grip in his chest a notch. "I'll settle for a smile and a kiss."

Clint tucked his wife's body close beside him and kissed her with desperate passion. He never wanted to let her go.

Sara pulled back to catch her breath. "Slow down, handsome, or I'll have to lock the door."

"Wish you could." He moved her white clinical garb out of the way and kissed her neck before she scrambled off the bed. A week was far too long to go without couple time.

He noted again the red in her eyes and the little lines that had appeared overnight after the biopsy results came back positive for cancer. The stress was getting to her. She'd totally lost it when his first oncologist, a new addition to the Benefield Cancer Center, told Clint he'd be dead in three months without immediate treatment. After raking the poor guy over the coals, she'd demanded that Dr. Silverman take over Clint's care.

He held out a stack of papers. "Wanna talk about this yet?"

After a quick glance, she threw the papers in the trash. "I wish you'd stop looking up all the side effects. You've talked everything over with Dr. Silverman and have all the information you need. Obsess over it, and it'll steal your hope." Her voice cracked as she turned toward the window.

"Is that what you tell your patients?"

"I tell them God hears the prayers of His people and He still does miracles." The words came out clipped and hollow.

Clint ran a hand through his thick, dark hair. Soon it'd be gone. "Don't you believe that?"

Sara faced him but stayed by the window, out of reach. He wanted to hold her, to kiss away the fear in her eyes. But it wouldn't work.

She knew the statistics.

She'd watched patients die.

"I want to believe, Clint. I want you home. I even want you to go back to work facing off with bad guys." She wrapped her slender arms around her waist. "But I don't know what to think or believe anymore."

"The truth."

Watching his wife shut down, he strengthened his resolve. He'd show her that he'd make it. They'd spend their golden years just like they'd planned—hiking and fishing with grandkids someday.

"Will I get to meet any of your patients tomorrow?" He shifted in the bed.

Sara's voice and eyes softened. "Yes. Frank Wells will be there. He's still praying for everyone he talks to. That man has such a pastor's heart."

"I'm glad I'll finally get to meet him. I know he and his wife have done a lot to keep you sane the past few years when you were ready to quit your job." He held out his hand, and she came to him. "You have a gift, Sara. You love your patients. You give them hope. Don't lose that because of me. We'll make it. I know we will. Especially if we start praying about this together."

With a nod her only response, she checked his IV bag. "I'll bring the kids up after rounds."

"Good." He hated for them to see him in a hospital bed. But he hated not seeing them more.

"Erica's going to bring them to my office after dinner. We'll come over right after."

Keeping hold of Sara's right hand, he reached for the picture on his nightstand. He rubbed his thumb over their most recent Christmas photo. One month ago they had no idea what January held in store. Susannah's six-year-old smile and Jonathan's big two-year-old dimples were full of energy and joy. "Erica's been a big help this past week."

"Yes. She's been a godsend."

Clint squeezed Sara's hand three short times.

She smiled and returned the gesture with four squeezes. "I love you. Bunches."

"We'll make it, Sara. You'll see."

She took a deep breath. "I need to go make rounds. See you tonight." With that she shot out of the room. But not before he saw the tears.

He had to beat this disease. There was far too much to lose if he didn't.

5

Michael took another swig of gas station coffee as he listened to Kessler talk on the phone with his sister.

"Everything on my end is a go." Kessler sat straight up in the passenger's seat. "You're going to do what after the engagement party?"

Even with the distraction of figuring out the one-sided conversation, Michael's legs ached. They'd already stopped once this morning to top off the boring black Bureau car and get coffee. He could use another break. Even better, the hour run he'd had to skip earlier.

Driving the Bucar to Charleston, West Virginia, on a cold Thursday in January hadn't been his transportation preference, but the planes were engaged on higher priority business. They'd have to interview Mattie Reynolds's mother and pull a ten-hour round trip like rookies. But being on the road sure beat pushing papers. And as much as he missed Clint's diplomatic presence at work, if his friend were up to par, Michael would be drowning in donkeywork.

"What I still don't understand," Kessler switched the phone to his other ear, "is why you want to do it now, after all these years of us asking you to come. It's not that we won't love having you in Alexandria. James will be thrilled, and Dad and Sue will love having you around to pamper. But something's off with this impulsive decision. Care to explain? With some real details."

Michael shook his head and chuckled. Leave it to an agent to interrogate family. Clint had talked about how close Steven and Hanna were, how Steven played the big-brother bit to the hilt. From pictures at Kessler's house, he'd seen Hanna's girl-next-door appeal and understood the protective impulse. Unfortunately, Michael's former wild days were still too clear in Steven's memory. No doubt hades would freeze before his boss let him ask Hanna out.

At least Kessler believed Michael had changed. Unlike Dad, who made no attempt to hide his skepticism concerning Michael's recent about-face toward religion. No surprise there. Nothing he did ever pleased his father. Instead, he'd found acceptance in the arms of beautiful women.

But not anymore.

He hadn't even had a date since New Year's Eve, when he'd gone to a small party with Clint's kids' babysitter, Erica. That hadn't worked out too well, what with them being the only not-serious couple there. After an awkward, no-physical-contact night, they'd agreed a relationship wasn't in their future. So really, his last date had been Kessler's birthday party months ago.

On days like today, he missed his old life. The new-date-every-weekend scene had dulled the ache of loneliness and fended off questions about him settling down. Questions everyone would no doubt start hounding him with after Kessler got engaged, leaving him the lone unattached male on the team.

"What about your boyfriend? Craig somebody?"

Figured she had a boyfriend.

"Why's he out of the picture? No, I'm not going to butt out. Okay. Yes, I know you have to get to work. Dad's coffee shop would cease functioning without you."

Michael would give anything to hear Hanna's comeback. She'd obviously rankled her big brother.

Kessler said a quick "love you, good-bye" and shot him a look. "No comments."

"About what, boss? I'm driving and minding my own business, thinking about our cases, and getting ready to uncover that key piece of evidence that will lead us straight to Mattie Reynolds." Okay, maybe not, but it sounded better than where his thoughts had gone.

He flipped the blinker and changed lanes to speed up. Federal car or not, he couldn't stand driving like a grandpa.

"My sister's decided to move to Alexandria."

"And that's bad?"

"No. It'd be great to have her closer. She's awesome with James, and I know Gracie would love to have her around. Hanna would enjoy running with Gracie and her dog, Jake, too. Even the job transfer is simple. She'll move from managing one of Dad's coffee shops in Louisville to his new one in Union Station."

"The problem?"

"My sister hates change. A big move isn't like her. And she won't give me a good reason for it. First Clint and now Hanna. I'm about done with people hiding things from me."

"I could talk to her."

"Over my dead body, Parker."

That settled that. No use shaking things up with Kessler. For now, they needed to decide between talking to the local cops or Samantha Reynolds first. He leaned toward Ms. Reynolds. She might offer a clue about Standish that hadn't made it into the report.

And they needed all the help they could get. Every tick of the clock diminished recovery stats.

❈ ❈ ❈

Another roller-coaster day, ready or not.

Sara stared past her sage-colored curtains into the darkness. All she wanted to do was hold the sun down and never let this day start.

Clint's first day of chemo.

Not ready to face that reality, she concentrated on the tasks at hand. Like brushing her teeth. In the bathroom, she further distracted herself with redecorating ideas. New furniture. New colors. Maybe an updated cherry bedroom set with seaside blue on the walls and white and yellow accents. She'd talk to Clint about doing it for their ninth anniversary gift to each other.

Sara glanced at her watch. Time to get everyone up.

Today was here, whether she wanted it or not.

"Susannah. Come on, sweetie. Erica will be here shortly to take you to school." She hustled her firstborn past the wonderland-cottage doll-house Clint had built when Susannah was a toddler and into her bathroom, covered in whimsical purple pansies and sunny yellow stripes.

"A mommy's little-girl dream, with some help from her little girl." That was how Sara had explained her daughter's bedroom to Gracie the first time her new friend had taken the house tour. That'd been only four months ago, but it felt like a lifetime.

Susannah washed her face and dressed without a word.

Clint was probably awake in his hospital bed, wondering if she'd even show up. Her body ached to hold her husband and return to their normal life. One without cancer. Or at least without cancer that touched her family. Being an oncologist took its toll, but she'd learned years ago how to leave work at the office.

That had all gone out the window with Clint's gunshot wound and cancer diagnosis.

And in had come more guilt than she'd ever known.

Now life would never be normal again. Not that living with an FBI agent was ever normal. Watching him strap on his bulletproof vest, knowing he'd be gone for days without any word of where he'd disappeared to or when he'd be home, had proven a challenge early in their marriage. But they'd adjusted.

Could she do it again? Even if Clint never strapped on that vest another time?

What if he never watched Susannah and Jonathan grow up?

And what if she'd diagnosed the cancer earlier? Two months could make a vast difference.

She pushed those thoughts into the little padded cell at the back of her mind. Into that place went all the funeral announcements of former patients. All the morphine drips she'd had to order because pain broke the strongest of wills.

All the cancer statistics.

In over a decade as an oncologist, she'd never faced fear this strangling.

"Mama, can you sing me that song about Jesus you used to sing?"

Susannah's wide-awake green eyes cut straight to the heart of Sara's problem. She'd forgotten the simplest truth. Jesus loved them. No matter what storms hit, that truth should be an anchor.

Today it wasn't. Knowing and believing were two very different things. But she couldn't let Susannah see that.

"Yes, my little songbird, I can sing you that song. It'd be good for me to hear too." Sara grabbed the yellow hairbrush and skillfully detangled Susannah's thick red hair.

"I think Daddy is going to have a good day today and come home soon."

"Really?" She hadn't mentioned Clint's treatment plan around the children. They didn't know about the cancer. All they knew was Daddy got hurt at work and would come home from the hospital when his headaches went away.

"Yeah. Daddy said he'd bounce me on his leg and hold me with his good arm in just a few days. He told Jonathan he could have a horsy ride soon too."

Sara braided her daughter's hair as fast as her fingers could move. She needed a real distraction.

"Are you going to sing, Mama?"

Deep breath. She could do this. She had to. *I know that Jesus loves me. He died to save me from sin. That's why He's my Savior. I wish the world would let Him in.*

"Mama!" Jonathan's cheerful voice carried through the walls. He had two volumes—loud and asleep. Hearing him now brought a much needed smile.

Twenty minutes later they hustled downstairs and hurried through their organic orange juice and whole-wheat bagels. As if all that health food had done Clint any good.

Buttoning coats and tying scarves around her children, Sara knelt in front of them on the wooden floor. She caught the vanilla-spice air freshener scent and inhaled deeply. Not long enough to relax though. Erica's knock would sound any minute. She scrambled to her feet and hunted for Susannah's backpack.

"Pway, Mama. Like Daddy." Jonathan's little-boy request stopped her in her fast-paced tracks. Clint had always bucked law-enforcement tradition and spent both quality and quantity time with his family. Every day he was home, he'd pray for the kids before they left for school.

Sara avoided Jonathan's request by peering out the front bay window, watching for Erica's car. The college senior loved Susannah and Jonathan and had passed Clint's background check with no problems. Thankfully, Erica's schedule allowed for frequent babysitting duties. Her car pulled in right on time.

"Erica's here." Susannah hopped up and down. "Pray quick, please."

No way to get out of this without a scene. Clasping two small mittened hands, she said her first prayer in days. "Lord, we ask You to watch over us and protect us in all we do today. Put Your angels round about us, and bring us home..." Her voice caught in her throat. "Bring us all home together soon. Amen."

She opened the front door and forced a smile.

"Hi, Erica! Bye, Mama!" Before hurrying out the door, Susannah gave her a quick hug.

Jonathan planted a wet kiss on her lips and then took Erica's hand. "Bye-bye, Mama. I lub you."

"Good morning, Dr. Rollins." Erica tweaked Jonathan's nose. "See you this afternoon."

"Thank you again for taking on school-taxi duty too." She watched and waved until Erica's red car disappeared down Northern Spruce Lane.

She checked her watch again. Unless she hustled inside the Beltway, she'd miss her eight-thirty appointment with Frank. And Clint's first chemo.

Climbing back into her bed felt like a better idea.

* * *

They parked in front of the old Victorian estate, and Steven climbed out to stretch. The chilly West Virginia air felt good. But he'd rather be here with good news. Not more questions.

Paperwork he could handle. Occasional hostage rescues provided the ten percent of his job that meant adrenaline-rush excitement. But talking to the parents—or parent, in this case—of a missing child was one of the most excruciating aspects of working in the Crimes Against Children Unit. Even when he had police reports, he preferred doing his own interviews and studying body language, responding to minute cues with additional questions. Any extra little detail could help.

He shot up a quick prayer.

A white-haired, sour-faced woman opened the door before he had a chance to knock. "Special Agent Kessler?"

They hurried up the steps to greet her. "Yes ma'am. And this is Agent Michael Parker."

"I'll have you both know my daughter is quite fragile. And the Charleston police officers and Virginia FBI agents who have been our unwanted companions for the past four days have done nothing but upset her." The matriarch stepped aside and pointed him into a formal parlor that looked like a set from *Gone with the Wind.*

"I appreciate your willingness to see us." Steven waited for the woman to sit. "Our primary goal is to return Mattie to his home as soon as possible. Any small piece of evidence can help us do that, ma'am."

Her eyes softened at her grandson's name. "Please, call me Frances." She pointed to a high-backed white chair. "Have a seat. I'll go call my daughter."

Watching the snow flurries outside made him even more grateful for the blazing fire in the ornate fireplace. Gracie already hated all the traveling he had to do, but the promise of a vacation together in three weeks had taken some of the tension from her hazel eyes. Especially since the details were top secret and his beautiful girlfriend loved a good surprise.

Okay, maybe not, but he did.

"Agent Kessler?" A young, petite brunette slipped into the sitting room.

He stood. "Yes. This is Michael Parker."

"I'm Samantha," she said as Parker reached for her hand first. Taking a seat on a dark green–patterned Duncan Phyfe couch, she fixed her watery blue eyes on him as he and Michael sat back down in their chairs. "Do you have any news about Mattie?"

"No, Ms. Reynolds. I'm sorry. But we're doing all we can to bring him home." He leaned forward. "What can you tell me about Sunday?"

She studied the hardwood floor. "I…we were at the park right after school. Mattie asked to go to the rest room." She looked up. "Since he started first grade, he's wanted to be a big boy and go alone. I figured he'd be fine…"

Steven waited, thoughts of his own six-year-old son coming to mind.

"He hasn't had much male influence, and I wanted to encourage his independence."

He nodded. "I understand. My son is Mattie's age, and he'd rather go alone too." Not that Steven would allow it, but James would ask, just as Samantha's son had done.

"Mattie was only gone a minute or two. But when I went in to check, there was no one in the bathroom." She grabbed a Kleenex from the end table and sniffled.

Michael cleared his throat. "Did you see anyone near the rest room when your son went in?"

"No." She inhaled a shaky breath. "But there was this guy at the park. I didn't see him talk to any of the kids there. He just sort of walked around and watched them." Samantha blushed. "I thought he was going to ask me out or something."

"Did you speak with him?"

"He said hi and asked about the weather."

"Any accent?"

"No. Well, a little bit of a mountain twang, but lots of people talk like that around here." She stood and walked to the window, wrapping her arms around her waist.

Steven shook his head at Michael. Rapid-fire questions weren't the best option here. "Can you remind me of his physical description? Maybe what he was wearing?"

Samantha shivered as she turned around. "I see him in my night-mares all the time. He was shorter than you. You're what, six-one maybe?"

"Yes. Good guess." Steven smiled, hoping to make this recollection easier.

"Thanks. He was five-eight or so."

"You told the first officers you thought he was young, but then changed that to older."

"At a distance I thought he might be around my age, twenty-three. He didn't have much hair, but he did have one of those baby faces. Then, when he talked to me...I don't know. He seemed older, more wrinkles. I didn't remember what he was wearing when the other officers questioned me. But this morning I was flipping through a clothing catalog and remembered the guy was dressed sort of like Mr. Rogers. He had on this button-up sweater under his coat."

Steven scribbled a few notes on his small steno pad. What Samantha had just given him meshed with what they knew of Ed Standish from the search of his house. He had a thing for dull sweaters. And tons of products for reversing hair loss.

So far, all indications continued to point toward Standish as their primary suspect.

Bad news for Mattie and his family. Because a serial kidnapper was far more dangerous than a father enmeshed in a custody battle.

❈ ❈ ❈

Traffic proved mercifully light, and Sara had five minutes to spare before Frank and June Wells arrived. She scanned her office, refusing to look at Frank's files again. Thirty was just too young for him to...

She threw that thought away and walked to the window. There were times when she could still smell the fresh paint from her first day on the job. Alexandria's brand-new, state-of-the-art Benefield Cancer Center had embodied her idealistic dreams. Simple dreams. Make the world a better place. Make cancer not hurt as much as it had for her grandmother.

She'd lived that dream in Alexandria, treating patients from all over the world, for six years now.

Today she'd have to face the last run of a favorite patient's cancer battle and watch her husband start his. All in the space of one hour.

She paused at the window, wishing again that she could go back two months and catch the signs of Clint's cancer sooner. Or that she could still feel God's presence the way she had before. "God, where are You?"

"He's on His throne, Dr. Rollins. Where He's always been."

Sara spun from the window and met Frank's million-dollar smile. The smile that had tugged at her heart for the past four years. Even on a face swollen with the side effects of Interleukin-2 injections, it lifted her heart.

Frank and June took their normal seats on the emerald and maroon couch. She joined them. They'd never sit by the cherrywood desk in the comfortable armchairs. Frank preferred the little sitting area with a cup of tea to talk like old friends catching up.

She wished that were all today held.

"Before you start, we've heard about the reports." Frank squeezed June's hand. "I know what you're going to say."

She'd consulted with Dr. Richards and Dr. Silverman on the best course of treatment for Frank. Their suggestions were all she had left to offer. But she couldn't bring herself to say the words.

"Frank, June, I…I think we should revisit some naturopathic options and discuss an additional surgery to see if the surgical team can get the last of the femoral tumor."

"We're okay, Sara. We understand what the next step is, and we're ready to take it." The peace on Frank's face was incomprehensible. His thirty-going-on-eighty eyes held more wisdom and faith than hers ever had.

With shaking hands, Sara handed over the brochures Marilynn had given her. *"They'll take the absolute best care of Frank. You'll see."* Sara had balked at the idea but put the awful, cheerful pieces of paper in Frank's file.

"Yes, in-home hospice care is what we've been praying about." Frank handed the information to his wife. "I think it's the perfect choice."

June burst into tears. "I can't, Frank. I can't watch you give up like this. I know I said I was okay with it, but I'm not." She ran from the room.

Frank's smile faltered for the first time since they had arrived. "I'm sorry. I'll go talk to her. We'll be back in a minute."

Sara stared after them. June would be a widow in less than a month. There was no good way to assimilate that fact. She transferred reference texts back to the bookshelf behind her desk, too numb with her own circumstances to pray for them. Minutes later, Frank returned. Without June.

"She's going to stay in the chapel. It's…this kind of reality isn't always easy to face. Well, I guess you know that."

She avoided his eyes. "Please tell June I'm here if she needs to talk. I can give her some numbers for support groups as well."

"Thank you. Our church has been great, really rallied around us. But other people in our situation might help June see she isn't the only one struggling with warring emotions. We've appreciated your prayers so much…"

Another wave of guilt. Over the years Sara had been deeply thankful for her work in a cancer center where prayers were a daily accepted occurrence. Now she couldn't even utter a simple one for her favorite patient.

She only wanted to hide and pretend today wasn't happening. In her dreams, Frank and June would have the kids they'd planned for years ago. Clint would soon kiss her awake and then go make the world a better place. And all her patients would triumph over the beast of cancer.

This day was only a nightmare she'd wake up from and forget.

If only that were true.

6

Apersonal visit from the big boss was no way to start Clint's day. "Rollins, I okayed this time off for you because of the concussion and gun nick." Maxwell paced at the foot of Clint's hospital bed. "But it's Thursday. You should be out of here already. You're not returning my calls. And seeing you makes me wonder if you're coming back to work at all. I want to know everything. Now."

The short, balding CACU unit chief placed both meaty hands on the bed, leaned forward, and stared a hole through him.

"I wanted to make it through the chemotherapy today before I talked to you." Saying the words made Clint's hands quake. He clenched his fists under the sheets and waited.

"Chemo? You have cancer?"

"Yes."

Maxwell's eyes grew wide, but he crossed his arms and slipped into interrogation mode. "What's the prognosis? What are the doctors saying about your return to work?"

"Fifty percent cure rate. But I have the best doctors in the country, so I'm hoping to return to desk work the end of February."

"Not likely." Maxwell narrowed his eyes. "Good thing we have your sidearm. A lot of agents in your place would end it fast."

The words sliced Clint. That was harsh, even for Maxwell. Clint knew agents who had chosen the quick way out. Knew the temptation would come. But hearing the words from an unflinching superior registered like a defeating slap-down.

Maxwell coughed, a deep smoker's hack. "Look. I know your religion keeps you from things like that. Which is good. Kessler and the rest are drowning under a recent deluge of cases, and I need you back at work. Even desk duty will help. You put those best-of-the-best doctors to work and beat this."

Clint nodded.

Maxwell started toward the door, then turned. "Does Kessler know?"

"No." Clint shifted in his bed.

"Then I suggest you pray to that God of yours and get back to work ASAP. Or I'll need to look into transferring more agents over." With that Maxwell nodded and escaped through the heavy brown door.

No warm fuzzies there. Not that Clint had expected any. But the knots in his stomach tightened a notch. Concussion. Gunshot wound. Chemo. Now his job and his God were on the line.

Father, I could use some big miracles here. Heal me. Help me do my job and catch the man who took these kids. Keep Mattie Reynolds alive. Nothing looks good right now, but I'm trusting You. Help me hang on to that.

There wasn't an answer, exactly. More like a gentle reminder. God had given him work to do, a family to care for. A thousand reasons to fight the cancer and win.

For now, that was answer enough.

He would beat this thing…or die trying.

※   ※   ※

Clint's dreams haunted him. Murky images of little brown-haired boys like Jonathan and case-file pictures swam together. Then all at once there were body bags. Images of his time in the Army. Nothing made sense.

Waiting for his first chemo appointment, he slipped into yet another round of half-asleep, half-awake nightmares. Ryan's bruised and beaten body. The sound of leaves crunching underfoot. Tiny skeletons. Susannah crying. His funeral.

He shook himself fully awake. An agent's life offered plenty of fodder for nightmares. But he'd always been able to pray his way through them. Pray for the families. Pray for wisdom. Pray for peace. Now even his waking thoughts kept sliding into nightmare territory.

He reached up to rub his temples as a teenage orderly loped into the room. "I'm here to take you to chemo."

Clint eyed the wheelchair. "I can walk just fine."

"Sorry, man. Hospital rules. And we need to get a move on or it's my neck." The young man looked like he'd been on a twenty-four-hour rotation for days.

"Not having a great day?" Clint eased himself into the chair.

"Better than you are, I suppose." The kid took off toward the elevators at breakneck speed.

Under normal circumstances, he would have stood tall and reminded the self-absorbed teen what the word *manners* meant. He'd done it for years teaching students at church. His height alone earned him some respect. But now he was in a wheelchair, heading toward chemotherapy and not at all the FBI poster boy Steven ribbed him about being.

A smiling, well-dressed woman met him when the elevator doors opened. "Welcome to the Benefield Cancer Center, Mr. Rollins. I'm Laurie Denny, the administrative manager. I wanted to meet you and personally give you the royal tour. Although I'm sure you're already familiar with it. Marc, could you—?"

But the orderly had already disappeared without a word, leaving Clint stranded in his wheelchair.

"Kids today," she huffed. He smiled. Laurie Denny looked like a kid herself, although she had to be a good six inches taller than Sara.

"Is he new here?"

"No, Marc's been around awhile." Laurie got behind the wheelchair and sped it down the hall. Clint was impressed by her strength, though it rankled him that he couldn't do much to help. All he could do was watch the community hospital's white corridors morph into the rich earth tones of an upscale office. The attached cancer center didn't even smell like a hospital anymore. He hadn't noticed that when he'd stopped by to meet Sara.

Laurie rattled off her spiel about the cancer center's history. He missed most of what she was saying, though he pushed himself to remain polite and attentive. They negotiated a long hallway and rolled past the cafeteria, where people smiled and waved. Omelets and hash browns—all organic, from what Sara had told him—made the place smell like a country kitchen.

The next hallway sported a few plants and a large clock on the wall. He noted they were ten minutes early and figured he was getting the full tour to take his mind off what would happen today. Fat chance of that.

"Well, here's Dr. Silverman's office now. He'll be right in to see you." Laurie put a hand on his shoulder and smiled after positioning him by his new doctor's enormous window. She left him to view the bare trees, gray skies, and curved walking paths outside.

Not an encouraging panorama.

Where was Sara? She'd said she'd be here to talk with Dr. Silverman before he got hooked up for his all-day adventure.

"Clint. It's good to see you out of that hospital room." Dr. Paul Silverman crossed his office in five quick strides and shook Clint's hand. His oncologist was a good six foot three. Bald, but he looked more like a baseball player than an old man. He wore the cue-ball look better than Clint would.

"Feels good to fly the coop every once in a while." Clint refused to complain about his aches and pains. He didn't want anything to stand in the way of getting his chemo started and finished ASAP. If all went well, he'd be home before the weekend.

"Sara should be here any minute. She's meeting with a patient and said she'd slip in when she got free." He scooted an old-fashioned rocking chair over next to Clint's wheelchair.

Clint raised his eyebrows.

The doctor chuckled. "It was a gift from a patient. She said I needed one so she could rock her grandbabies in it when she brought them to visit."

Clint nodded. This place was like none of the other cancer centers he'd read about online. If you had to have cancer, here was definitely the place to be.

"In a few minutes, we'll get some blood drawn, check the numbers, and get started with the chemo." Dr. Silverman nodded when Sara opened the door. "I wanted to sit down with you two first and make sure there were no last minute questions or concerns."

Sara pecked Clint on the cheek and then leaned against the window. He wanted nothing more than to pull her onto his lap and make the world go away. But she had on her stoic doctor mask. Even his favorite tan skirt, which perfectly hugged her curves, couldn't erase the reality confronting them.

"You know all about the water you'll have to force today. I want you to try and eat too. It'll make things go much better." Dr. Silverman motioned over to his desk. "One of Sara's patients dropped off a basket of muffins, healthy Chex mix, and some other snacks."

Clint tried to catch Sara's eye, but she kept hers locked on Dr. Silverman's necktie.

"You've already had your prednisone with breakfast, right?" Sara looked at his shoulder.

"Yep."

His oncologist leaned forward. "Anything you want to ask before we get started?"

"Nope." Better to get moving and get it all over with.

❈   ❈   ❈

Surprising, how cold his eyes had become.

Early Thursday morning, the bathroom mirror revealed how much this month's activities had taken their toll. He'd survived another blow to his precise and perfect plans. That's what he got for relying on someone who wasn't up to the job. Because of that one mistake, life was turning into hell.

Thus far he'd managed to maintain the facade, keep control.

But it was starting all over again.

The pressure that had vanished after burying the boy Monday night began crawling across his shoulders and worming its way through his abdomen.

Too risky to attempt another abduction this close to the last one. No. There had to be another way.

He splashed ice-cold tap water onto his face. Three years running should have made this January end with more sense of accomplishment, more pride in a job well done. But this infuriating setback had stripped it from him.

The anger surged, and his need matched it. He focused on the future to regain control. First, he needed to cover his tracks and reconfigure his options.

Stay one step ahead of the law while he took care of his other business. If anyone could achieve his plans, he could.

He'd learned long ago to keep up appearances. That education would serve him well again. It had to.

Unless something messed it up and everything disintegrated in one wrong move.

He turned off the tap and listened to the sounds in the next room. Cartoons blaring with nonsensical, stilted dialogue. Childish laughter.

The need assaulted him again. He gripped the sides of the sink and stared into his own eyes, willing himself to be strong.

Not now.

Not yet.

※　※　※

Nothing could have prepared Clint for his first date with chemo.

The scene before him looked like a bad *E.T.* outtake. Technicians in gloves and gowns mixing toxic chemicals under a chemistry-class hood. Needles injecting that stuff into his port, the thing sticking out of his pecs and making him feel like a freak.

All around him, people hooked up to similar lines read or slept or played board games. Like a drug party his buds in organized crime had busted a few months ago, except these partygoers had far less hair. Seeing so many bald heads threw him more than the TV news about kidnapping cases he hadn't been a part of. And that was saying a lot.

He longed for a cold night of surveillance or even Quantico's harsh training schedule. He wanted to be anywhere but here.

But what he really wanted was to hit something.

He choked back the bile gathering in his throat and closed his eyes. Rage at a perp who'd abused a child was nothing new. But this? He couldn't identify the root of the emotions stirring in his gut. He couldn't think past the confusion. Heavy eyelids won, and he drifted off to sleep again.

And woke with a start.

"Been asleep for a little while, yes?" An older gentleman ambled over to sit in the recliner next to him.

"Guess so." Clint wiped his mouth and hated what he must look like. No suit-and-tie impression, no holster or vest, just old college sweats and a button-up shirt. He couldn't even stand to his full six foot five.

This sucked.

"Name's Ted. Want to play some cards or chess? I'm here all day like you." The man motioned over to a doorway. "We can get you moved into the other room. It's a bit more comfortable in there where most of us all-day folks hang out." He threw Clint a sly look. "Even the old ladies will cheer up staring at your…how do you say it?…'buff' chest."

Clint guffawed. Sara should hear this guy. Not many people could make him laugh like that. Not these days. And not with a comment about his chest. He hated how after a week's worth of missed workouts, his muscles had already lost definition. And then there was the ever-present port deformation. He had to look downright awful.

Vanity didn't sit right. Neither did the loss of control over his body. Not working out. Not even getting to wear his boots, jeans, and favorite Stetson.

He sighed. "Sure, Ted. Chess sounds like a good way to pass the time."

Ted hustled as fast as grandpa legs could go and got a nurse to help them both relocate. The larger room looked like a hotel lobby. It even smelled like a hotel filled with plants and books and snack food. The

Benefield Cancer Center sure knew how to make a body forget what a hospital felt like. Or almost forget.

Ted set up the chessboard and within a few moves had exposed Clint's rusty game.

"Hey, handsome. It's good to see you awake." Sara's voice made him try to stand up. Her soft touch reminded him to settle back down.

"I checked in on you awhile ago, and you were sound asleep. Everything okay?" She looked him over with a wife's appraisal. It felt good, like he was human again and not some medical experiment. Maybe his chest didn't look so horrendous after all.

"Better now that you're here. I missed you." His voice sounded hoarse. He grabbed his hoss of a water jug and took a swallow.

"Dr. Rollins is your wife?" Ted nodded to Sara and moved his rook to a square that meant an inevitable checkmate. "The luck of the Irish is with you then, eh?"

Only a grandpa could get away with the appreciative glint in Ted's eyes. Even with a few years of maturity under his belt, Clint didn't take kindly to people flirting with his girl. But Sara's laugh made him like Ted even more.

"More like the goodness of God, wouldn't you say?" A young man stepped into their group and held out his hand. "I'm Frank Wells." His Kentucky twang beat Steven's nondescript Louisvillian accent. "It's nice to finally meet you, Clint."

Clint motioned toward a chair next to Ted. "Join us?"

Sara's eyes clouded, and she seemed spooked. His gut tightened. Trouble always followed this particular look of hers. He'd learned to trust it well.

"Sara?" He placed a hand on her waist, nudging her toward his chair. She stiffened. Then looked him straight in the eyes.

"I love you. I'll be back in a bit." She kissed his cheek and waved to the other patients in the treatment room. Then she disappeared around the corner at a fast clip.

"Clint." Frank's quiet voice broke into his thoughts. "She had to talk about hospice with me today."

The words were a sucker-punch to his ribs.

"I don't know what to say. I'm sorry. For you and June. And for Sara. She loves you both."

Other patients in the room had stopped their diversions and were listening in, some misty-eyed. Frank was an obvious favorite, his faith and friendliness apparent even at first introductions. According to Sara, the man was a pastor who'd grown a struggling little church into a thriving community. And he obviously hadn't done it by reading dry theology books.

"Don't talk like the man's dead." Ted's words sounded gruff, but his eyes moistened. "He's too young to die now."

Frank smiled. "Ted's right. I'm not gone yet." He kneaded Ted's shoulder like a longtime friend. "But I'm going. I'm gonna meet Jesus before too long. And I'm ready."

Frank greeted other folks nearby and asked about their families and prayer requests. Some wanted nothing to do with him. But that didn't dissuade Frank. Clint wasn't nearly as open about his faith these days. Maybe he needed to make better use of his time here.

"You still with us, Clint?" Frank's lighthearted jab jerked him back to the present.

"Sorry. Just thinking."

A few of the ladies scooted their chairs over to the growing group. "Aren't you the FBI guy the nurses were talking about?"

He held back a chuckle. Worldly or not, he could use the ego boost. Steven would get a kick out of it too.

"Yep, that's me. But I always let my partner tell the good stories. He's a little more theatrical than I am. I'll have to get him down here." His smile faltered. To do that, he'd have to tell his partner why he was walking into a chemo ward.

Steven's visit would have to wait.

He didn't want to tell FBI stories anyway. He wanted to talk to Frank, ask him how he could be so confident facing death. And what he'd done to take care of June. Clint had to consider those things.

"You've only got a forty percent chance of beating this. Even with your

superb physical conditioning." His first oncologist had seemed bent on making things look as bad as possible, which infuriated Sara. She'd said he was jealous of Clint. Among other things. She'd learned years ago to keep her Irish temper in check, but every now and then it exploded. She wasn't a redhead for nothing.

Questions and conversations swirled around him, and he tried his best to clip the answers short so he could get back to Frank and the chess game.

"No, I can't discuss that TV report."

"Not sure about that, but you can find a plethora of tip sheets on the FBI Web site."

"Been an agent nearly eleven years, happily married for the last eight." He bit back a grin at the disappointed face of the twenty-something girl who'd asked that. They used to check for a wedding band first thing.

"Almost nine years, isn't it?" Frank stepped into the conversation. "Sara mentioned your anniversary was coming up. Agreeing to a Valentine's Day wedding must have earned you some brownie points."

"You know my wife. She's a hopeless romantic at heart." He'd have to remember to make some phone calls for gifts to be delivered. He wouldn't be up for the legwork this year.

He forced himself to drink more water and took one of the muffins Frank offered. The thought of throwing it up later almost made him reconsider.

"Eat. It'll help." The voices chorused around him. These folks were veterans whose advice he needed to heed.

Clint nodded his thanks, peeled back the paper liner, and took a few tentative bites. It already tasted metallic. One of the side effects he'd read about. But he ate it anyway. Sara would be proud.

"You doing okay, Frank?" His new friend's eyelids were closing fast. Fatigue? Or he could have been praying.

Frank's eyes slowly opened. "Just losing steam is all. Need to rest. The tests and doctor visits drain me. June said she'd be back to get me by three." He looked at his watch. "It's past time, but I'm guessing she's in the chapel praying. I should probably go find her."

But Frank stayed fixed to his seat. He watched Ted's winning chess move and then looked straight into Clint's eyes. There was a fire there that made Clint squirm.

Frank leaned forward and spoke in a low voice. "Clint, before I go, I want to leave you with a piece of advice."

He leaned in close. "I'm listening."

"Don't let the fear win. Remind Sara of the promises. They'll help you both focus on the truth." Frank stood and put his hand on Clint's shoulder. "God is good. Always. Remember that."

Frank waved a small farewell and trudged out of sight.

Clint couldn't shake the sense that he'd had his last conversation with Frank. His new friend and Sara's favorite patient was stepping into a future with limited days.

But Frank held his head high. Clint respected that. Longed to follow Frank's example.

Because he didn't know how many days were in his own future.

7

H ey, Sara. Clint awake?" Steven leaned on the door frame and looked over her shoulder. No sign of Clint. His best friend hadn't returned calls since coming home last Monday. A week of silence warranted a stop on Steven's way out of town.

She didn't budge from the doorway. "He's still asleep, Steven. And not quite ready for visitors."

"Why? Does he have the flu?"

"Something like that." She looked down at her tennis shoes and picked at her sweatpants. Strange attire for a workday. "I took a couple of days off to play nurse. And I really don't think you want to be catching anything, what with your big engagement plans only a week and a half away."

Steven surveyed the bleak early February landscape. Bare tree limbs groaned in the wind. He pulled his coat tighter and checked his watch. He needed to get on the road. And Sara was right. He didn't have time to get sick. Too much work to do before his upcoming vacation.

"Tell him I'm headed to Kentucky for a few days, doing some digging into the first cold case."

"You going to see Hanna too?"

"Of course. I'm taking her out to dinner tonight, after my interviews. We'll hammer out the last few details of the engagement party."

"Steven, about the party." She swallowed hard and clenched her jaw. "You know Clint and I want to be there. But…I don't think we'll be up for a trip to Georgia and staying with Gracie's family."

"Clint's flu is that serious?"

"He's still weak from the gunshot and the infection. We just need to be extra careful."

Something didn't sit right in his gut. But there was no arguing with Sara once she set her mind to something. He'd keep calling and try to convince Clint to let him come over before the weekend. Maybe even lean on him a little to change Sara's mind about joining them in Georgia.

"All right. You win, Dr. Rollins. I'll leave the doctoring to the professionals. Just tell him I'll stop by again soon."

"Bye, Steven." She closed the door before he could return the pleasantry.

Steven started the Bucar and pointed it toward Lexington. The sooner he hit I-64 West, the better. But his upcoming interview with the Davises loomed in the distance like a thunderhead. He had no answers for them, just more questions. And the distinct possibility they could help find their child's abductor, but not their child.

At least not alive. After three years, little hope of that remained.

He wished once more that Clint were with him. His partner handled this kind of interview better. But he was on his own. So he shot up a quick prayer for Clint and the family he'd soon interview.

But he couldn't shake the notion that his prayers for Clint were far more urgent than this case.

❅ ❅ ❅

Michael sat on the metal table in the Blacksburg PD's interrogation room late Monday afternoon. Across from him a short, wiry man squirmed in his chair.

"So you want to tell me how a garage owner can afford to take a two-and-a-half-week bow-hunting trip?"

"Business was good last quarter." Jim Standish picked at the grease under his nails. Hard to believe this rustic's brother was a college professor.

"You or your friends catch any deer?"

"Naw. Pickings was slim."

"Convenient. Let's go back to your truck. It was supposedly stolen while you were on your trip, but you didn't report it missing until this morning."

"Got in late, figured there weren't no way of getting it back now, seeing as I'd been gone so long. What's the rush?"

Michael leaned closer. "Did you know your brother's partner died in jail? Seems those surfer good looks and being in for kidnapping a young boy made him a prime target. Prison justice takes care of perps like that in record time."

Jim blanched. "Billy's dead?"

"Yes."

"Billy weren't no partner or perp. He was just a friend of Ed's, one of his students a long time ago. He followed my brother down here from the big city. They hung out, did things together."

"Like gambling?"

Standish studied his muddy boots. "I dunno."

"I have credit card receipts that place Ed at Keeneland racetrack in Lexington three years ago January and at the Argosy Casino near Cincinnati two years ago January. And I have kids in those very cities missing right around the time of your brother's trips."

Plus eyewitness accounts of a blond kidnapper who could easily have been Raeford. But Billy hadn't confessed anything beyond Standish paying him to nab Wes and taking him along on some gambling and hunting excursions.

Jim blinked rapidly. "So Ed likes to gamble a little. Not a crime."

"Kidnapping is."

"Ed ain't like that. Sure, he played the field before his divorce got made final, and he likes to bet on horses and play slots. You still got nothing to prove he did something illegal."

"Your truck was spotted near where a young boy was kidnapped in Charleston, West Virginia. A kid who looks a lot like Ed's son."

Jim shrugged.

"You've had some run-ins with the law, huh?"

"Nothing big. Pot and a few brawls. Why?"

"Your big brother always bailed you out."

"So? Our parents died when I was in high school. Ed looked out for me."

Michael stood and looked back over his notes. If only Ed's computer had been analyzed already. Then he'd have more to back up the pedophile angle. Some things took way too much time.

"Tell me about Ed's girlfriends."

Jim shrugged again. "He likes 'em young and pretty."

"Did any of them have kids?"

"Yeah. I think the last two or three did. Boys, mostly."

Michael sat in the chair across from Standish. "You don't find that a little odd, considering he's a prime suspect in his son's kidnapping and the disappearance of another young boy?"

"He ain't some little-boy lover or whatever you call them freaks."

"How do you know?"

"He never bothered Wes, did he?"

Standish had him there. According to counselors and Wes's own testimony, his father had never made any sexual advances. Neither had he molested any of his former girlfriends' children, at least not the two Michael had talked with earlier this afternoon. Still, pedophiles were known to lurk for years without acting. Until something set them off. Something like losing a job. Or a divorce becoming final.

Adding to that speculation, they could prove Ed Standish was involved in his son's kidnapping, and they'd placed Standish at two of the cold case sites. Jim's truck connected Ed to Mattie Reynolds's disappearance. All of that together pointed to a serious threat...and a shrinking possibility of finding Mattie alive.

What they needed now was another AMBER Alert sighting or tip. Then they'd find Standish. Maybe Mattie, too. With no bodies linked to this case, there was hope that Standish or whoever would keep the kids alive for a stretch of time. Maybe even like the case in Missouri where the pedophile kept a kid he'd nabbed five years earlier.

"Can I go yet?" Standish pushed back his thinning hair. "I mean, you got nothing to hold me."

Michael left the room to regroup. He needed to check his computer for any case updates. If nothing turned up soon, they could only keep tabs on Jim and pray Standish contacted his brother via traceable means.

So far, nothing in the phone records implicated Jim in a lie about Standish's whereabouts.

He needed a drive in his Mustang to clear his head. Too bad it was back in DC and he was stuck out here in Podunk, Virginia.

Interviewing Jim had yielded less than nothing. They needed a break. Otherwise any hope of finding Mattie Reynolds alive would disappear without a trace.

※　※　※

Steven finished his interview at the Davises' home with a pounding headache. Before hitting the road to Louisville, he stopped at the Starbucks on Versailles for a double espresso and a quick review of his handwritten notes.

Five-year-old Luke Davis had been missing from his modest Lexington home for three years. Having to dredge up painful family memories and look at pictures of a child near his son's age—a boy who was probably long dead—had done nothing good for his heart. One drawback to getting serious about his relationship with God was that he'd lost the ability to remain aloof to others' pain. He couldn't show as much as he felt. But what he felt, he couldn't shake either.

Until he prayed.

Really prayed, sitting in the Bucar in the Starbucks parking lot. For the family he'd promised to keep informed about the investigation. For Clint. And for the time with his sister tonight before he headed back to DC in the morning.

That was the one part of this trip he looked forward to. Not the interviews. Or the gray sky and freezing weather. Or even his necessary trip to the cemetery.

Dinner with Hanna and making plans for her move to Alexandria got him back on the road again.

Less than an hour later, he pulled off the Waterson Expressway and onto Dixie Highway. A few short turns, and he stopped to pick up a bouquet of roses before heading toward Louisville Memorial Gardens. It didn't take long to find the old oak tree that sheltered his mom's gravestone.

He'd not been here in years even though he still missed his mom something fierce. He wasn't the type to stand in a graveyard and cry. And today wasn't a day for tears anyway.

It was a day to rejoice.

He was getting married. Again. And this time, he felt sure Cynthia Kessler would approve. She'd have loved Gracie as her own daughter. Unfortunately, his mom's cancer had taken her away long ago.

"It's been almost nine years, Mom. I miss you." He bent down and touched his mother's name on the stone, forcing a smile to ward off the waterworks. "I wish you could meet James. And Gracie too. She's his first-grade teacher, and hopefully soon she's going to be my wife." He placed the dozen white roses into the attached vase and dusted off cobwebs and dead grass. "Not sure why I'm telling you all this. I suppose you already know. In fact, I'm pretty sure you do. There are times I feel your prayers for me, just like when I was little."

Remembering the nights his mom had knelt by his bed to pray brought a lump to his throat. Even when he was a teen, they'd prayed together. His parents' love had been fierce and insistent when most of his friends' parents had resigned themselves to surly teens and grunted answers.

Not Mom and Dad.

Not until he'd walked away from all they'd taught and married Angela.

What a mess that had turned out to be. But it was getting better. At least the custody battle was over and Angela was continuing with rehab. During the supervised visitation agreement they'd worked out, neither he nor James had seen her take a drink in months. And the frostiness between him and his ex-wife had thawed into an amicable semi-friendship, as long as Angela's current husband—the man she'd left him for—stayed in the background.

Steven still couldn't figure out what the squirrelly law professor had that he hadn't. Maybe Angela's husband influenced his instinctive dislike for Ed Standish. If so, he'd have to keep personal and professional lines more clearly drawn.

"I miss you so much, Mom."

He swallowed back the rest of his words, and a few tears escaped. "Hanna's helping me with the engagement party." He pulled out his wallet to look into Gracie's hazel eyes. Clint was right; he had it bad. "I'm proposing on Valentine's Day at her parents' house in Georgia. Gracie thinks it's just a vacation. But everyone's going to be there."

Except Clint.

Thoughts of his partner's hospitalization and the unreturned phone calls tightened the knots of tension across his shoulders. All he could do was pray. And that didn't always help. God hadn't healed his mother's cancer, no matter how much he'd prayed. But God had healed his mother. Just not in a way that was easy to understand. Or accept.

Forcing his mind back to the present, he prayed for Clint's recovery, his quick return to work. Getting back on the job would be good therapy. Clint lived to love God and his family and share that big heart of his by returning kids to their parents and runaway teens to their homes.

And putting away creeps for good.

A nudge in Steven's spirit made him reconsider his last thought. He stood and pulled his coat closer, pacing the silent cemetery aisle. Other agents would have said worse without a second thought. But labeling people didn't fix things. The men and women his team put away needed consequences for their crimes. The citizens of the U.S. needed those people behind bars and not hurting kids anymore. But he had no right to judge them. He hadn't walked in their shoes.

Not that he really wanted to. He could study the profiles, look at the backgrounds, and try to understand their motivation. But only enough to capture them. Not to live inside their heads. Doing that could drive an agent crazy. And it didn't always help.

He had no desire to plumb the depths of suspects like Ed Standish any further than necessary. Everything in the ViCAP report meshed with his knowledge of serial murderers in long-running cases. Middle-aged. Intelligent. Street smart. Having a means to afford what it took to lure and destroy. He had patterns, time lines, and theories, but no bodies. Very little physical evidence. And no verifiable motive. Even what they could prove made little sense. Just because a guy was abused as a child, had his parents die young, or snapped because of life circumstances, nothing ever fully explained how someone could hurt a child.

Or children. Four of them now, not including Wes Standish. Probably more. All five- or six-year-old boys with brown hair and blue eyes, like his son.

Steven shook away the memories of crime scenes and case files. He didn't want bodies to deal with. Not yet. Not until they'd found Standish. And hopefully Mattie. Alive. Then they'd secure both a confession and the physical evidence they'd need to put this guy in prison for good. With the perp behind bars, the families could then have closure.

But judging from his interviews today with the Lexington police and the Davises, that capture could be a long time coming. With few leads and everything growing colder by the day, he needed their suspect to make a telltale mistake. Just one.

Steven stopped at his mother's grave and looked around to make sure no one had slipped in unnoticed. It did seem strange, even to him, to be working a case while pacing in a graveyard.

Glancing at his watch, he realized Hanna would be here soon.

He sat down on the cold earth and rested his head on his knees. Case details, memories of his mom, worry about Clint, and Valentine's plans collided, fighting it out in his head.

"Valentine's Day just needs to get here soon."

"You're quite a sight, pining away for February fourteenth, you know." He jumped at the sound of his sister's voice. She slipped around a few grave markers and snapped a picture with her ever-present camera. Her wispy blond hair blew in the wind.

"I'll title this one 'longing for love' and hang the print in Dad's new store. Your FBI buddies will love it."

He enveloped Hanna in his arms. "Ha. No on the picture. And stop sneaking around. It makes me look bad that my baby sister can surprise me like that."

"Always could and always will. FBI badge or not." Hanna poked him in the ribs. "Ready to go eat, big brother? Your stomach sounds like it needs a good steak and potatoes dinner."

He smiled. To his kid sister, he would always be the big brother. Always a hero, even when he failed.

The older he grew, the more that meant, and the deeper he understood how much family mattered. Dad, Sue, Hanna, and James. Gracie. How close he'd come to throwing it all away less than a year ago just to shoot the man who'd tried to kill Gracie. A shudder crawled down his back.

Hugging his sister tighter, he pushed everything else away. "So you're sure about moving to Alexandria and letting me find you a good husband? Lots of great guys at my church."

"What, now you want to find me a date?" Hanna stepped away from him and stooped to finger the white roses on their mom's grave. "You were the one who chased off every prospect when I was in high school. Don't change your stripes just when I've finally figured you out."

Adjusting the lens on her camera, she nodded toward the car. "Let's head out. I'm ready for a lighthearted dinner with my obnoxious big brother."

"Yeah. I can hear your stomach begging for that tiny salad you'll call a meal."

They walked to Hanna's Equinox, poking each other and playing like two kids at a park. He held the passenger door open for his sister. "We'll come back and get the Bucar after dinner. They don't lock up until eight, I think."

"It's my car."

He smiled. "Yep. And I'm driving like I always do."

They exited Memorial Gardens in silence. Driving through the gates like he'd done the day of his mom's funeral always made it hard to think past the lump in his throat.

"You'll help me find an apartment near you, right?" Hanna brushed bangs from her eyes.

"You know I will. Though I still think this whole thing's a bit sudden."

"It's getting awful lonely over here with you and Dad and Sue in Alexandria. And all my friends are having babies and way too busy to spend time with me." She turned in her seat to face him. "My photography work can be done anywhere. And Dad's new coffee shop is set to open next month. It's the perfect time."

"That sounds like a good plan, Sis. Of course I'll help." Something still bugged him about the whole deal. But moving closer to family made sense. And he recognized the longing in his sister's eyes. He knew it well. "Sure you'll be ready to move so soon?"

"I'm almost finished packing and tying up loose ends here. Which means I'll move after Valentine's Day, like I told you on the phone. Dad said I could stay with them until I find a place of my own, so I won't be in your way."

He stopped at the traffic light and scrutinized his sister. "You want to fill me in on what happened with you and Craig?"

She wouldn't look him in the eyes.

"Hanna?" He gripped the steering wheel. Kessler blood ran thick. If that guy did anything...

She shook her head and touched his arm. "I've already handled it. I'm just ready to move on and be closer to family."

His shoulder muscles relaxed. A little. Her explanation, or lack thereof, left him with a few unanswered questions. But it'd be good to have her in Alexandria. Easier to protect her from people like Craig. "Think you can handle having two big brothers close by?"

Her laugh filled the car. "Clint? Yes. If I can handle you, I can handle him."

True enough.

Too bad Hanna couldn't help him find Mattie or Standish. Even off duty, he had cases bouncing around in his brain.

Unfortunately, his trip to Kentucky hadn't provided any helpful leads. They had mounting circumstantial evidence on Standish and a growing pile of other important cases. A traceable clue could make all the difference. If they got it in time.

Lord, keep Mattie alive. Please.

8

Sara's stomach rebelled with every move. More evidence of the toll stress exacted.

For sanity's sake, she'd reduced office hours on Fridays to allow more family time. But instead of relaxing, she ran interference for Clint by screening calls, turning away visitors, and making him rest as much as possible.

She grabbed another Clorox wipe. So much to clean before the kids came home. Following prescribed protocols like a good patient's wife, she scoured the main floor of their Mount Vernon house. Door handles, light switches, and computer keyboards received a perfect spit and polish.

"Do you have to do all that? I've been home almost two weeks, and all I see you do is clean. You're becoming compulsive about germs." Clint adjusted his loose blue sweater and waited for an answer.

Deep breath. Big smile. "What do you say we spend our date night tonight looking at decorating books and then watching some basketball? We need to be prepared for March Madness brackets."

"Fine. But you didn't answer my question."

Throwing the last wipe in the trash can, she joined Clint on the couch. "I'm just doing what I recommend to my patients. Keeping everything disinfected really does help, especially with little ones at home."

He leaned his head back and closed his eyes. Her husband had aged a decade in the last three weeks. More wrinkles on his thinner face. And his arms had lost much of their sinewy definition.

She turned away. Even the kids had noticed the changes. Up until now, she'd gone along with Clint's insistence they only know about the gunshot wound. But their questions were growing more intense, matching the level of whining about what Daddy couldn't do anymore.

"We need to talk to the kids about your cancer. Susannah knows people don't have to wash up or sleep so much just because they were in the hospital."

Clint worked his jaw muscles. "I said no. Case closed."

"This is ridiculous, Clint. I've been patient with helping you get past the shock and adjust to the diminished energy level. But I'm worn out. And I can't talk to any of my friends at church or my parents to ask them to pray for us. Some meals delivered by our Sunday school class would be a huge help. So would the prayers."

She paused for a breath and charged ahead. "I'm working full time, single parenting, and helping you. I can't keep this up."

"Then cut back on your work hours more."

"What?"

"You won't pray with me about anything. So if you can't handle our life, decrease your responsibilities. And forget about your stupid redecorating project. I don't want my bedroom changed anyway." He grabbed his massive water bottle and took a gulp.

"Clint, the furniture is already ordered. We agreed on this."

"I don't remember agreeing to anything. This was all your idea. And if you can't manage work and family, your projects have to go."

Hot tears threatened to spill over her eyelids. She stood, wanting to shout that he never remembered anything anymore. That her projects gave her something to look forward to beyond the next chemo round. That work and talking to her friends helped her hold on to a small thread of normalcy.

"Your pride is out of control."

Red rage spread over Clint's face. "I have cancer! I didn't ask for this."

"Neither did I."

"You don't know what it's like to be awake all night staring at the ceiling or to taste nothing but metal. You get up and go to work. I can't. I fall asleep in the middle of the day. Everything is out of my control." He stood on shaky legs, anger raising his volume with every word. "I won't have the world show up at my door with their pity gifts and stupid advice. I can control this one issue, and I will."

Her voice was little more than a whisper. "The kids should at least know."

"Know what? They already see what a wimp I've become. As soon as you tell them I have cancer, they'll think I'm gonna die. I won't do that to them."

"Clint—"

"Did you hear me? I said no!"

Stalking out of the room like a charging bull, Clint slammed the basement door.

The sound echoed through her shaking limbs. She'd never before experienced how chemo and steroids could turn a loving man into a raging bully.

Where are You, God? Why are You doing this?

Silence. She didn't really expect an answer. Maybe it'd be better if she quit trying to pray altogether.

First God and now Clint. Who would be next to turn a deaf ear to her cries?

❈ ❈ ❈

"Can't this prop fly any faster?" Michael adjusted his headset and watched the Shenandoah River snaking below. The pilot, an agent with the Bureau's flying cadre, ignored him. "Mattie's alive and we need to find him before Standish makes him disappear again."

"We're doing all we can." Kessler's eyes stayed focused out his side of the six-seater. "Maxwell expedited the paperwork and handled the arrangements with the Virginia State Police as soon as our tipline took the call."

"The VSP will just wait for us at this Big Spring airstrip in the middle of nowhere?"

"Airport's on their way." Kessler leaned back in his seat. "Besides that, we're lead on this case."

"What if Standish bolts before we can get there?" Michael didn't want to be the one to tell Samantha Reynolds they'd arrived too late. "How can you sit there so calmly?"

Kessler raised an eyebrow, and Michael shut his mouth. He'd better back down before he pushed his boss too far. Insubordination wouldn't earn him Kessler's respect.

Two officers awaited them when they touched down near Luray, Virginia. Michael shouldered his laptop bag and strode across the tarmac. "What's our ETA?"

A young lanky redhead stood by his cruiser, squinting in the late afternoon sun. "I'm Brady. Hop in, and we'll get there faster." Michael liked the guy already. He rode with Brady while Steven took shotgun in the other cruiser.

"The cabin's 'bout ten minutes from here. Not that all-fire secluded, but a ways away from any real traffic. Good place to hide out." Brady pulled away from the other cop, letting his lead foot shave off a few vital minutes. "You Feds sure made good time. Twenty minutes is 'bout the same as we'd have taken to get on-site."

Michael watched the winding river fly by and tried to make small talk. After a few hairpin turns along the mountainous road, they pulled onto a grassy car path that might have passed for a gravel road in its heyday.

"Here's the rental office." Brady parked by the front stoop of a lone cabin with a sign out front. Kessler's car pulled in behind them a minute later.

Michael pounded on the front door of the rustic cabin-turned-office while Steven looked in the window. The loud TV clicked off. Seconds later, the door flew open.

"You the FBI?" A man with salt-and-pepper hair stepped over the threshold, wiping his hands on his red flannel shirt.

They both flashed their credentials. Kessler spoke first. "Yes sir. You're Mr. Dean, the rental manager?"

"Sure am. I saw that Mattie Reynolds's picture on the TV. Right after they checked in this afternoon, I called. Sure did. An I jus' got back from talking to Mr. Jones—that's the name he gave anyway—a little while ago. Them two are all snug in for the weekend at one of my old hunting cabins. Doesn't much look like a cabin though. It's more green siding and all."

"Can you give us directions?"

Mr. Dean pointed up the gravel path. "It's a mile north, set back from the road apiece. Right on the Shenandoah River. Can't miss it." Dean puffed out his chest. "He's still driving the maroon truck too."

"We appreciate your call." Kessler was already halfway to the cruiser.

The old man waved. "Glad to be of help, I am. Sure glad."

They left quickly but pulled over as soon as the cabin came in sight.

No signs of life near the river. No other cabins nearby. They walked through the woods to come in behind the green one-bedroom shack.

No movement inside. No vehicles either.

Kessler and the cop he rode with circled around front. Michael and Brady flanked the back door. At Kessler's whistle, they kicked in both doors.

Nothing but run-down living room furniture and an empty kitchen.

No sign of Mattie anywhere.

Gun ready, Michael stood by one closed hallway door, and Steven stood across from him by the other.

Michael nodded. Charging through the door of what turned out to be a tiny bathroom, he growled and slapped the dingy shower curtain.

"Nothing. Bedroom's empty," Kessler called. Michael wanted to curse. So close. They'd come so close.

Everyone met in the musty bedroom and holstered their weapons. Brady spoke first. "We looked all around outside after you cleared the living room. No sign of anyone hiding in the woods."

"My guess is, the rental manager spooked Standish with the extra attention." Steven pointed to a mess on the floor near the closet. "In his hurry, looks like Standish left the clothes Mattie was last seen in."

"And fast-food containers for two." Michael touched nothing.

Steven turned to the officers. "We need to get an APB out and let all surrounding police departments know Standish is in the vicinity. We also need an evidence team out here so we can collect everything and verify these are Mattie's."

"I'll radio the sergeant." Brady left with his partner.

Steven ran a hand through his hair. "We know Mattie's still alive. That's something."

Not enough. Sweat dripped down Michael's back. The PlayStation game wrappers said Standish was keeping Mattie well entertained.

God only knew what else.

9

Valentine's Day red screamed at Sara from every corner of Target on Tuesday afternoon. Not in the mood to shop with two excited little ones, she reminded herself that celebrating the holiday together would give them all a much-needed sense of normalcy. They'd always done special days up big. And after a month of unusual stress, her family deserved a party.

A twinge of guilt hit as she thought of the missing child Steven and Michael hadn't returned home last Friday. Steven's terse phone message and Clint's refusal to discuss the situation communicated the grave plight of this kidnapped child.

Clint had prayed for the little boy before he fell asleep last night. And she'd slipped out of bed to kiss Jonathan and Susannah one more time, hoping God wouldn't ignore Clint's desperate pleas for Mattie's life.

"Mama, let's get Daddy this humongous box of chocolates." Susannah held up a heart-shaped container that filled her six-year-old arms. Jonathan clutched an equally large M&Ms doll he was convinced Daddy needed.

An array of choices. Nothing she wanted to purchase. "We already ordered some chocolate for Daddy, so let's choose something else."

Their four o'clock pre-Valentine's shopping spree had sounded like a good idea this afternoon. She'd left Clint sleeping to pick up Susannah from Hope Ridge Academy and Jonathan from the nearby day care he adored. But now the bright lights and sugary-sweet chocolate smells everywhere only intensified her pounding headache and the queasiness in her stomach.

They meandered to the bed-and-bath section to find towels for her newly redecorated bathroom. She and her interior-decorator friend, Linda, had spent the whole weekend transforming the master suite into a beach retreat. Light blue walls with a white chair rail, sunshine accent pillows, blue and yellow curtains, plus an elegant seashell border and coordinating accessories for the bath. Though Clint still grumbled, the updates brightened everything, including her outlook.

She felt only a tiny bit guilty for skipping church to work on the renovations. Clint wouldn't have gone with her anyway. He'd hidden in the basement watching sports all weekend while Erica took the kids for a sleepover so she and Linda could paint and paste uninterrupted.

Remembering Clint's sulking took all the fun out of shopping for the house. She gave up on finding towels and directed the kids to the toy section. "Choose one little toy each."

Susannah clapped. "I think I'll get a new doll and maybe a board game for Daddy." Her green eyes danced with delight. "He'd like that, won't he, Mama?"

"Yes." Sara wanted to suggest the Pretty Pretty Princess game. Last year, Clint would have roared with laughter and donned the silly jewelry with his little princess. This year? Not worth finding out.

She adjusted her pink sweater and wiped sweaty palms on her low-rider jeans. She had no idea how Clint would react to anything anymore.

Loneliness infiltrated every cell of her body.

Susannah hummed as she studied each doll with a critical eye. That child had Clint's analytical bent to a fault, while Jonathan pushed the buttons on every Elmo toy and danced with the high-pitched Sesame Street character, totally engrossed and carefree.

Sara smiled. Between watching her children and thinking about their anniversary tomorrow, her spirits lifted a little. They'd have steak and potatoes for dinner. With candlelight. The kids thought candlelight was such a treat. *"Like a starry night in Bethlehem,"* Susannah would say in breathless wonder. Where she got her dramatic flair, Sara didn't want to know.

After the kids were tucked in bed, she'd give Clint the Godiva chocolates she knew he'd enjoy. Well, hoped he'd still be able to enjoy. The vincristine part of Clint's CHOP protocol did awful things to taste buds. She'd slip into her new silk pj's and try to talk Clint into putting on the black-and-red boxers she'd ordered for him. And then, maybe, they'd create a little drama of their own.

Nine years. They'd celebrate nine years of married life on Valentine's Day, and Sara refused to let chemo steal that from her or Clint. Because even with the stubbornness, the mood swings, the physical changes, Clint remained the man she'd fallen for eleven years ago. Her larger-than-life tough guy with a gentle heart.

"Here, Mama." Susannah's eager voice broke into Sara's thoughts. "Let's get Daddy the red-and-white-heart checkerboard game."

Sara grinned at the gaudy heart-covered box. "Yes. I think he'll like that."

Susannah placed it in the cart with a satisfied nod. "We can play it tomorrow when we're home."

"We 'tay home?" Jonathan's sweet brown eyes begged for a hug.

Picking him up, Sara snuggled close. He looked so much like his daddy's baby pictures, it made her heart ache. "Yes. You and Susannah are staying home from school tomorrow. We'll decorate and have some special fun with Daddy."

They'd make this the best Valentine's Day ever.

※　※　※

"Fifteen minutes. Great. I'll be there." Sara flipped her cell shut and fastened Jonathan into his car seat. He and Susannah would be happy and quiet with their new books while she drove to pick up tonight's supper. She had zero energy to cook, so carry-out would have to suffice.

Slipping behind the wheel of their silver Range Rover, she fastened her seat belt and then popped in her favorite Celtic CD. They headed south toward Murphy's, her favorite place to eat. Clint complained the food wasn't organic. But healthy Irish food was hard to come by, and she salivated over Murphy's menu. It was easy enough to overlook that their

Irish stew and soda bread couldn't compete with her mom's generations-old recipes.

A sudden longing for her mom's strong hands kneading her shoulders and her father's easy laugh almost took her breath away. She missed her parents something awful. Especially now. They had spent the winter traipsing through Ireland. And she was too stubborn to call them home before their dream vacation ended in April. That would be soon enough for them to know about Clint's cancer.

Maybe there'd be good news to share then. She longed for the date circled in red on her office calendar: May tenth. Clint's last chemo. The date when normal was supposed to return.

Thirty minutes later, with food in hand and hungry kids clamoring for dinner, Sara weaved her way through the garage toys and into the kitchen. "Wash your hands well, both of you." While the kids cleaned up, she hid the Target packages in the laundry room and hauled the dinner boxes to the cooking island.

The grandfather clock in the living room chimed six. Hustling through dinner prep, blessedly minimal with takeout, she and the kids set the table in the breakfast nook for their evening meal.

"Susannah, remember, no telling Daddy about our Valentine's surprises." Sara got down on her knees to look into Jonathan's eyes. "Holiday secrets are the only ones we keep. Right, buddy?"

Jonathan nodded with his finger popped in his mouth. Bedtime would come early tonight.

"I'm going to wake Daddy for supper. Why don't you all choose some wrapping paper from the craft room downstairs and lay it out on my worktable?" That would keep them occupied for a few minutes. She held Susannah's arm to prevent her running full speed ahead. "Nothing else, understand. No scissors. No stickers."

"Yes ma'am. Just the wrapping paper." Susannah smiled her loose-toothed grin. "Can we play some pool if it takes you awhile to wake Daddy?"

Heat trailed up Sara's neck to her cheeks. Unfazed, her two little ones ran to the basement stairs and disappeared. Did Susannah know why waking Clint from a normal Sunday nap used to take awhile? No, she was too young to have a clue.

Fat chance of such an intimate time tonight, though. Clint needed to save his energy for tomorrow. A cavernous longing for an anniversary night like the eight before tightened around her waist.

She remembered Clint's strong arms wrapped around her. His searching lips kissing her fingers and palms. She shuddered. How long until she didn't have to think how many days it had been since chemo? How long until she could look at her husband and see his body strong again, his eyes shining with power instead of need?

She climbed the stairs, holding on to the wooden banister to drag herself forward.

Clint lay tangled in the blue and yellow sheets, sweat beading on his forehead.

Her stomach clenched. She felt his forehead with her wrist, then went to retrieve a thermometer from the bathroom.

He continued to sleep, so she placed the instrument under his arm like she did for Susannah and Jonathan. Clint didn't stir.

Seconds dragged like hours. *Please don't be sick.*

"Sara, what the devil are you doing?"

Clint's voice made her jump. The thermometer fell to the floor.

"Checking your temperature. You felt hot."

His eyes flashed like a bull's before a red cloth. "I am not a baby! Don't doctor me, Sara!" He pushed the covers back and stormed into the bathroom, shoving a T-shirt over his shoulders.

Her eyes watered as she picked up the thermometer. Ninety-eight point six. She should have left well enough alone.

As she studied the closed bathroom door, hot tears spilled onto her cheeks.

Given this mood, dinner was sure to be a raging success. But she'd done the right thing. So why did she feel like a failure?

Because she hadn't diagnosed Clint's cancer.

Because she couldn't manage being wife, mommy, doctor, and caretaker.

Guilt snaked through her insides and planted its fangs deep. What would she mess up next?

❋ ❋ ❋

The shrill ring of the phone stirred Sara from fitful sleep. She reached for Clint and felt nothing but cold sheets and pillows. Where was he?

She hugged her arms tight around her to ward off the chill and padded to the bathroom, ignoring the phone. Without the lights she found her white robe and slipped into it as she returned to the bedroom and stared at the handset. She didn't want to see the caller ID. The digital clock said enough. Anyone calling at two in the morning wouldn't have good news.

She considered not answering. She wasn't on call in the evening anymore.

Then she remembered her parents traveling in Ireland.

And Steven and Gracie heading to Georgia.

She grabbed the phone on the next ring. "Dr. Rollins."

"Sara? It's Marilynn. Were you asleep?"

She nodded. Then remembered her best friend couldn't see her. "Uh, yeah." She listened for Clint's footfalls. "What's wrong, Marilynn? Two in the morning is not the time to chat."

"No." Marilynn sniffled.

Stiffening, she sat on the edge of the bed, fighting with her stomach to keep dinner down.

"I wanted to be the one to tell you… This is so hard, Sara."

Now anger fed on the fear, and she found her voice. "Tell me what's going on, Marilynn."

"Is there any way you can come over to the office? I can't… I can't get ahold of anyone to cover my shift, or I'd come over there." Marilynn's voice faltered.

Bile burned her throat.

"Sara? Who are you talking to?" Clint's voice boomed in the dark silence, and she jumped to her feet, dropping the phone.

Her stomach wouldn't wait for her to answer. She ran to the bathroom, barely making it to the tile floor. The pain in her middle section and the smell of her partially digested dinner made her head swim. She had to get out of here. But she had to clean up the mess first.

She rinsed out her mouth and spat into the marble sink basin.

Clint's now faraway voice spoke to Marilynn. Sara refused to think about the unfinished conversation.

Grabbing the Clorox wipes, she managed to scour the floor quickly and rinse her hands in the garden tub. She washed over and over with the vanilla soap. It didn't help.

"Are you okay?"

Clint's presence filled the bathroom, but she couldn't meet his gaze. Didn't want to hear what he had to say.

"I'll be fine."

"That was Marilynn on the phone."

She nodded and stared into the tub.

"She's worried about you, thinks stress is getting the best of you." Clint put his hands on her shoulders. "You're shaking."

He lifted her up and wrapped his strong arms around her.

"That's not why she called at two in the morning."

"No."

Sara buried her face in her husband's chest. It was Valentine's Day.

"Sara." Clint tipped her head up and kissed her forehead. She tried to look away. "Don't. I need you to look at me."

She had no strength left to fight, so she obeyed.

"Marilynn was calling to let you know that Frank… Frank's with Jesus now."

She wanted to scream. To run. To do something. Anything. But her legs wouldn't hold her up. She slumped onto the bathroom floor.

"No, Clint." She shook her head against his kneeling form. "Not Frank." Her sobs drowned out any other words.

Not Frank, God. Not now.

How could June handle becoming a widow on Valentine's Day?

10

"Mama, Daddy, wake up! The sun is high in the sky, and it's Valentine's Day." Susannah's drama-queen pronouncement jerked Clint out of an unusually sound sleep.

Fuzzy memories from yesterday, especially the news of Frank's death, hit him like a sucker-punch. Sleep had only been a temporary escape.

Now other memories blared like an alarm. Today was their anniversary. Vaguely recalling that he still hadn't sufficiently apologized to Sara about the redecorating argument, he tried to focus his thoughts on how to make it up to her.

"We 'tay home, Daddy."

Clint squinted over the side of the bed. Jonathan's morning breath alerted him to reality; his son's excited face wasn't a sweet dream.

Sara didn't stir beside him.

He scooted out from under the covers, glad he'd started wearing a shirt to bed in addition to shorts. Whispering, he drew his two little morning birds close. "Let's go get ready quietly." He nudged them toward the bedroom door.

Once safely outside the master suite, Clint looked down at the kids. They were still in their red pajamas. "What do you say we make Mommy a special breakfast?"

Susannah nodded.

Jonathan jumped up and down. Clint picked him up, rubbing his stubbly chin over Jonathan's tousled head. A burst of giggles rewarded him.

They tiptoed past Jonathan's nautical-themed nursery. Remembering how Sara had worked herself sick making it perfect caused his chest to tighten. Not to mention his bladder.

"Hey, can you two stay in here quietly a minute? I'll be right back." He didn't wait for an answer. But when he returned, they were stretched out on the floor looking at books like two tiny angels.

"So what should we make for breakfast?" He had no idea. His growling stomach reminded him he still needed to push water and get food in there. Tomorrow the abominable chemo drugs would disrupt his life again. Not to mention the prednisone, Zofran, Prilosec, and Tylenol necessary just to feel somewhat human.

Susannah's green eyes twinkled as she grabbed his hand and pulled him downstairs to the kitchen. "Let's make Mama some heart-shaped pancakes!"

"Cakes! Cakes!" Jonathan chanted as he hopped around his big sister.

Staring at the kitchen appliances, he felt like a fish out of water. The wall clock read nine, which meant eight o'clock Texas time. Mom would be finished with breakfast and busy caring for the animals she fostered. But maybe she could manage a quick tutorial on heart-shaped pancakes in between medicating a sick puppy and bottle-feeding an orphaned goat. Or whatever needy critter was currently in residence.

"You two get plates and silverware out while I call Grandma."

Susannah giggled. Jonathan shrugged and followed his sister into the pantry.

Dialing the eleven digits required thinking, a fact that raked his emotions. But he didn't have time to sulk as he dropped into a dining room chair. Two rings…"Hi, Mom. Happy Valentine's Day."

"Clint?" Sure enough, he heard puppy yips in the background. In his mind's eye he could see his parents' old ranch house, the one his dad had grown up in. Bright yellow kitchen. Mom always fixin' something for someone.

"Yep, it's me. Got a question."

His dad picked up the extension. "Hey, son. Happy anniversary."

"Thanks. Let's hope it turns out happy in the end."

"That doesn't sound like you. You okay?"

Clint's abs tightened. He needed to get food in his stomach before dry heaving started. Gunshot wounds he handled better than retching from the chemo side effects.

"I'm fine, Dad. The GSW is healing. But I had a question about how to make heart-shaped pancakes for breakfast. Is Mom still there?" Susannah was getting out Sara's griddle and mixing bowls. She seemed to know what to do. Maybe he shouldn't have called his parents.

"Clint, I'd like a real answer to my question. We know something's not right." His dad's voice sounded old. Tired. They must have dragged the truth from Sara already.

"You know?"

"We know Sara's hiding something for you. And we want to know what it is."

"Not right now, Dad. I'm trying to—"

"Clint Walker Rollins." All the miles in the world couldn't hide him from his mom when she used his full name. "Enough of this. Tell us the truth. All of it."

"I didn't want to tell you on the phone. I'd hoped to have y'all come visit in a month or so and tell you then."

"On your birthday, you mean?" Mom's words pierced him.

"I hadn't considered the timing." He watched Susannah shove a chair to the freezer and scrounge around. She hauled out a huge Ziploc.

"Look, Daddy. Pancakes. All we have to do is cut them." She nearly burst with six-year-old pride.

His eyes watered. One more sign of weakness.

He swallowed hard, nodding to Susannah. She grabbed a table knife from the drawer and started cutting lopsided heart shapes from the pancake circles.

"I can't really talk right now." He moved to the snack shelf by the fridge. Nothing but the organic crackers and a few boxes of those healthy cookies he'd insisted Sara purchase. Pigskins and a Hershey chocolate bar sounded better at the moment.

"What's wrong, Daddy?" Susannah stopped cutting pancakes.

"Nothing, honey. I need to have some grown-up talk with Grandma and Grandpa for a minute." He grabbed a whole-wheat bagel from the breadbasket on the counter and stepped into the dining room. The healthy circle tasted like cardboard. Just like everything else.

"Does Steven know?" Martha Rollins loved Steven like a second son. At least Clint hadn't told his partner before he told his parents. That had to count for something.

"No."

"You know, we have the Internet down here in Texas too. I can do some research for you." He could hear his dad already clicking away on his office keyboard. "Son, just tell us what we're dealing with."

Clint sighed. "It's cancer, Dad. Diffuse large B-cell lymphoma." He gagged on the bagel and grabbed the now warm water he'd left on the table. It tasted like tin. "The lymphoma's at stage four. A few small lung nodules and some enlarged nodes in my chest and abdomen."

Mom gasped but said nothing.

"But everything's under control here. The Benefield Cancer Center is the best in the country, and my doctor is confident we can lick this. I'll be back to work by the end of the month." He hoped. Judging from his weak muscles and chemobrain, though, it might be even longer.

"Are you taking the rituximab and a G-CSF drug?"

"Dad, get off the computer. The Internet is great, but you'll drive yourself crazy on there. Please don't."

He'd already done enough research for all of them. Enough to understand what was in store. His heart tightened another notch. Now his parents knew.

Soon he'd have to tell Steven. And the kids. Then the whole world would take front-row seats for his deterioration.

His insides pitched. "Mom, Dad, I'm sorry you had to find out over the phone. But things are all right here. What I need more than anything is your prayers." Jonathan's whines caught his attention. "And right now I've gotta get back to the kids and make breakfast. We'll talk soon about a visit. I love you."

Within ten minutes, he had the whining stopped and four semi–heart-shaped pancakes in the toaster oven. "Jonathan, why don't you tell Mommy to rise and shine?" His son's eyes and grin nearly filled his face. "See if she'll close her eyes to come into the kitchen." Jonathan bolted for the stairs.

"Mama will be so surprised!" Susannah hauled the orange juice and milk out of the fridge and then climbed onto her chair to fetch breakfast glasses. "Are we gonna do presents at breakfast?"

He nodded, watching his daughter set the table and bounce around the kitchen getting everything ready. He gripped his water jug, arms aching as a fog of fatigue encompassed him.

Helpless *and* useless didn't sit well at all.

Trying to focus on something besides his miserable body, he thought of his partner. He and Gracie should be on their way to Georgia right now. And before the day was over, Steven would propose.

No doubt his best friend would tie the knot soon. And he had to be there to see it…even if he hadn't been much of a friend lately.

After the messages Steven had left on Friday, he should have called. He could call now, but he didn't want to risk putting a damper on Gracie and Steven's day. He'd try to check in later.

For now he just sent up a quick prayer.

And a heartfelt hope that nothing would interfere with Steven's best-laid plans.

❄ ❄ ❄

Steven yawned as he filled up the Explorer's gas tank and watched the sun rise just past Richmond, Virginia. They'd left at four in the morning to make it to Georgia on time for the big party. He could easily imagine a better way to spend two twelve-hour blocks of their short vacation than sitting in a car. A pickup game of B-ball. Swimming with Gracie and James. A real nap. But he hoped this road trip would help replace bad memories from last November with better ones.

He stretched his neck muscles, trying to push away the unpleasant thoughts this section of interstate conjured. Last time, Clint had been driving. They'd raced to rescue Gracie from a man who'd kidnapped her to cover his killing her family in a drunk-driving accident. Even now, remembering it, Steven's body constricted in anger.

But they'd survived. Gracie's kidnapper was in jail, awaiting trial. And the rest of them had come so far in the last three months, thanks to amazing trauma counselors and a huge helping of grace.

Now, in just a few hours, all of Steven's plans would come together. One grand surprise for the woman he wanted to marry yesterday.

As he pulled back onto the road, James stirred in his booster seat but stayed sound asleep. Gracie woke up and rubbed her eyes. "Have we passed that awful place yet?"

"Almost." He maneuvered around a semi and took exit 51 to I-85. "Why don't you catch a few more *Z*s, and I'll wake you when we're in Greensboro."

Sleepy eyes and an adorable grin answered him before she fell back to sleep.

Gracie would be a beautiful sight to wake up to this summer. If she said yes, that is, and agreed to an early July wedding. With both Gracie and James out of school, the timing would be perfect.

For a long time, he kept himself awake praying for the day ahead and going over all the details he'd covered with Gracie's parents last night on the phone. Then thoughts of his ex-wife crowded in. How would Angela take the news of his upcoming wedding?

Not that her reaction would alter his plans. He just hoped it wouldn't reverse how far they'd all come. Once Angela's rehab was complete, she and her husband would be flying in from Kentucky once a month for an overnight visit with James.

He hoped the arrangement would work well. He still disliked seeing Angela's husband, and there were plenty of awkward moments. But after six years of single parenting, Steven was glad for James to know his mom. And to his surprise, Angela had turned out to be a truly loving parent.

Gracie and James woke around eleven but were happy reading out loud and waiting on him to stop for lunch. His plan required their arrival in Atlanta by late afternoon. He'd let a few more exits slip past before stopping.

When Gracie finished reading James a few chapters from *The Lion, the Witch, and the Wardrobe,* she turned her attention to Steven.

"Need me to take a turn at the wheel?"

"Nope. Got it covered." Out of the corner of his eye, he noticed her biting her lip. "Something you want to ask?"

"No. Just wondering what's up your sleeve for this trip." She leaned across the console and patted his jacket. "Or in your pocket."

They all three laughed.

"I know what it is!" James beamed into the rearview mirror.

Steven shook his head slightly.

James nodded.

Steven grinned. "It's not another locket."

Gracie smiled and fingered the gold heart-shaped locket around her neck. The Christmas gift she'd first thought an engagement ring. It'd been fun watching her reaction. And then receiving a very nice kiss.

Now it was time for a gift of a different sort.

No lockets in his pocket today.

Gracie cleared her throat. "Since I don't want to spoil your big secretive surprise, how about we change the subject?"

He nodded with amusement. She'd obviously figured it out long ago and was playing along for his sake.

She fidgeted with her red-and-white polka-dot dress. The one she'd insisted on wearing despite the long drive. She glanced around at James, who was busy with one of his Dr. Seuss books, then spoke in a quiet voice. "Is Clint going to be all right?"

"Good question. I'm praying he's better soon." Sara's excuses bothered him. But with Clint still not answering his phone, he'd had no choice but to accept they weren't coming.

"Sara said it was the flu?"

"Yeah. Clint's a big baby when it isn't a life-threatening thing. He'll be back to his old self in no time."

"Flu can be serious, though. And a gunshot wound is a big deal."

He looked back to make sure James wasn't listening. This topic required careful treading. "You're right. But I know Clint. He'll be back to work as soon as the good Dr. Rollins lets him fly the coop."

"I hope so. Seems with the two of you, no bad guy stands a chance." She smiled and reached down for her tote bag of lesson plans. Getting to know Gracie had taught him that even first-grade teachers put in plenty of overtime.

No bad guy stands a chance. If only that were true. The cases his unit tackled were rarely open-and-shut, done-in-a-week deals. Especially cold kidnapping cases almost sure to be homicides. Or active cases with disappearing perps and a victim who couldn't be found.

Pushing those thoughts aside, he adjusted the ring box in his left pocket and watched Gracie out of the corner of his eye.

She knew. Of course she knew. But the fun wasn't just in the surprise. It'd be in hearing her answer. And the kiss that was sure to follow.

❈   ❈   ❈

Hanna stood right inside the Thompsons' front door, watching out the large window, camera ready.

The happy couple and her adorable nephew looked syrupy sweet chatting as they made their way up the sidewalk.

Steven paused at the door and pulled Gracie close to him. "You may think you know why we're here, but remember who you're dealing with. Think lockets, like at Christmas, and maybe I'll throw in some fancy toe rings."

Oh, bother. Hanna rolled her eyes as the door opened and everyone chorused. "Surprise! Happy Valentine's Day!"

Gracie froze in the entryway. A perfect shot for the wedding slide show, with the red and white streamers providing a festive backdrop. Hanna snapped away as Gracie's parents enveloped the new couple in hugs. Hanna's dad and stepmother, Sue, joined in next. Aunts, uncles, cousins, and friends all crowded around. Hanna did her best to blend in and capture the moments. Candid shots beat stoic poses any day.

"Coming through, folks." She maneuvered around the knot of

people by the door. "Gotta preserve the memories on film." The camera was digital, actually, but the old saying died hard.

Gracie's sister, Beth, and her wiggly twin boys planted slobbery kisses on grandparents and Gracie. Tears started flowing, and Steven had yet to do his deal.

This was only the beginning.

Hanna did her best to focus on the strong scent of chocolate cookies and the vast array of homemade dinner fixings in the kitchen. Anything but the emotional scene playing out in front of her. She'd learned long ago to distance herself during weddings and new-baby photo shoots. If she allowed herself to absorb and really participate in the joy around her, she'd break into little pieces.

She'd never have a white wedding day. And her biological clock had never even started ticking. This was no world to bring kids into.

But what could a photographer do? Shiny, happy occasions helped pay her bills. They supplemented her coffee-shop manager's income and provided valuable experience for when she opened her own studio.

This shoot wasn't a professional obligation, though. She wouldn't have missed it for anything. Not with an FBI brother capable of tracking her all the way to Antarctica.

She snapped an excellent picture of James tugging on Steven's leg. That photo would be incredible in black and white. "Now, Daddy?" James's giggles made everyone stand back.

Finally, a good angle to capture the big moment.

"Steven?" Gracie's face was a glowing shade of bright pink. Hanna's stepmom had indicated that was Gracie's normal color around Steven.

Gag.

Hanna didn't care for bashful, blushing types. In this case, though, she was probably just jealous. What she wouldn't give to be in Gracie's position right now. But Craig had foiled that hope.

Stop. Don't go there. Focus on Steven's big day. He deserves this.

Looking through her telephoto lens, Hanna watched Steven take hold of Gracie's hand and drop to one knee. James followed and knelt right beside him.

What a photo. Tears blurred her vision, her carefully cultivated distance gone. She snapped pictures anyway.

"We would like to know if you'd be interested—you might need a moment to think about it, and that's fine—in becoming a part of our family?"

Gracie blinked, and a few tears trailed down her cheeks. Hanna captured it all, every perfect moment.

James tugged at Gracie's skirt. "Please? We both love you a lot."

Everyone laughed.

Steven raised an eyebrow.

Gracie nodded and wiped tears away, smiling all the while. "Yes."

Still kneeling on the hardwood floor, Steven pulled a little blue box from his pocket and opened it. The marquise diamond surrounded by deep green emeralds popped against its velvet case.

"Gracie Ann Lang, will you marry me?"

More tears. Another humongous smile. "Yes."

James wrapped his little arms around Gracie's leg, and when she bent down to return the hug, he kissed her wet cheek. Then he ran to Hanna's side. "We're gonna be a family, Aunt Hanna."

The room filled with sniffles and cheers.

Hanna gave James a quick thumbs-up and raised the camera again.

Steven placed the ring on Gracie's trembling hand, then stood and enveloped his fiancée in a hug. Her brother had never looked so dashing.

The normally reserved Gracie pulled back slightly and then, in front of everyone, laid a passionate kiss full on Steven's lips.

The room erupted in cheers and laughter once again.

Ignoring all the surrounding noise, Steven deepened the kiss until Hanna thought he'd pass out from lack of oxygen.

As they finally drew apart, she was close enough to hear Steven whisper, "Wonder if I'll always be able to make you blush?"

"It'll take you a lifetime to know for sure."

With knowing smiles, the crowd dispersed to the Thompsons'

kitchen. Hanna remained, unable to pull away from the captivating scene.

Steven held Gracie close. "I'll take that challenge, future Mrs. Kessler. And raise you a kiss for every time I succeed."

Steven bent down and collected on the first of what would likely be a long lifetime of sweet experiences.

11

Steven's annoying phone drew him away from a rousing game of Cranium. He stepped into the foyer but could still hear triumphant shouts and exaggerated moans as various family members battled it out.

"Hate to bother you on vacation, the day after Valentine's Day and all, but you know how it is." Parker's voice registered defeat. Not finding Mattie had hit the twenty-eight-year-old agent hard. He needed to get some distance, or he'd burn out fast.

Slipping into a light jacket, Steven stepped outside Gracie's childhood home. Georgia's mild February weather bested DC's frigid temps. Blue skies, family, and a beautiful fiancée waiting for him—nothing Parker had to say could ruin the day.

"What did you need?" Steven held the phone close to his ear.

"We got a call from a ViCAP analyst about skeletal evidence that could match one of our cold cases. If so, it could throw a wrench into our investigative matrix."

"Where was the skeleton found?"

"At a construction site in Louisville, Kentucky. The unidentified remains were submitted to ViCAP by Louisville Metro PD. That's all I know at this point."

"You and Lee can handle this."

"I can't get a response from the Louisville police chief. He won't take or return my calls. You used to work for him, so I thought you might get through."

Steven let out a long huff, thankful this was today's mess and not yesterday's. "Give me his phone numbers. I'll see what I can do."

Ending the call, he paced to think things through before phoning his old police sergeant. Eleven years, and he still dreaded talking to the old killjoy.

"You're gonna get cold out here." Gracie stepped out on the porch and into his arms. Her auburn hair smelled like strawberries, and her diamond and emerald engagement ring sparkled in the late afternoon sun.

Life was good.

"Not with you nearby to keep me warm." He kissed her forehead. "I need to make a few calls, and then I'll be back for another game. Is James doing okay?"

"He adores all the attention and is being wonderful as usual." She ran her hands over his arms. "Just don't make too many calls. I'm not ready to pack up and drive back to DC reality yet."

He nodded. Then he cupped her face in his hands and kissed her with a promise of more to come. He'd make it worth the interrupted vacations and all the FBI craziness.

Pulling back slowly, he rested his forehead against hers.

Smiling, she stepped out of his embrace. "I think it's a little too warm out here for me." Her tall, athletic form disappeared into the house.

Better to deal with Peter Hopkins sooner rather than later. He picked up on the third ring.

"Figured I'd get a call from you."

Off to a great start, just like old times. "Looks like we might be able to help each other out."

"This case is in my backyard. Right now, we're closing in on some promising local leads. We'd be happy to partner with you if our cases are connected, but we're not handing everything over for you Feds to get the glory."

Steven sat in the porch swing. He wouldn't let Chief Hopkins taint his vacation. "Not going to step on any toes. All I need is for your detectives to confer with my team so we can compare records."

"You think your FBI guys are better than my investigators?"

Some egos never changed. "Chief, it's not about who's better. But I have a priority investigation and need to know fast if your case is part of mine or not."

"Right."

"There was only one body found?"

"Yes. My hunch says this skeleton is our five-year-old missing boy from Shively. We're working on dental matches and will let your people know."

"Will you at least talk to my team?"

"Anything for you, Kessler. But my money's on my guys to bag this case."

Biting back a rebuttal, Steven closed his phone. No sense resurrecting trouble. Hopkins had applied to the Bureau too, about the time Steven did, but hadn't made the first cut.

He thought over his ViCAP cases. If this skeleton turned out to be Luke Davis from Lexington and not the missing Louisville boy, his face-to-face meeting with the Davis family would be a definite plus. But then again, local cops he'd met with would deliver the news to the family. He'd let them have it. Later, he'd send flowers and phone with personal condolences.

Having only the one skeleton presented a major problem though. A single body didn't support their serial kidnapper's profile. Quantico's analysis pointed to a dumping site with multiple bodies. Their suspect would do the same thing with each body and leave all of them in the same place.

Whether this case meshed with his others or not, this child, now a skeleton found at a construction site, belonged to somebody. Even if it didn't help him find his serial kidnapper, most likely a killer, positive identification would give some family closure.

And more pain than he could imagine.

But if this child became another of the CACU's cold cases they could tie to Edward Standish, they had little hope of finding Mattie Reynolds alive.

❋   ❋   ❋

Friday afternoon, his atrocious headache demanded a distraction from the incessant childish noise surrounding him. He desperately needed to tune out the slamming doors and constant chatter, so he flipped on the TV in his musty hotel room and watched *CNN Newsroom* with little interest.

"Sources report the skeleton found in Louisville, Kentucky, could be linked to untold numbers of other missing children cases." The attractive Hispanic reporter droned on. "The police have yet to release names in connection with this investigation."

In other words, the cops had no idea what they were dealing with. Bad for them. Good for him. Fascinating, though, how close the police were to his very first abduction.

He remembered that day with astounding clarity. Little Luke had been a relatively easy acquisition. After some logistical annoyances, they'd had a mostly pleasant drive back to his favorite park. But then the medication had worn off too quickly. A complication that had been corrected in subsequent years.

Luke had taught him so much.

The trouble had started when Luke began to fight. All those cries for Mommy ruined the entire experience. But a quick snap of Luke's neck ended the stress and made morphing back into normal life a rather uncomplicated affair.

Returning to the present, he focused back on the TV and listened with increasing interest to the reporter's interview with a spokesperson for the medical examiner's office.

Becoming more educated never lost its appeal. Knowledge was power. And he had more than the cops.

He'd keep it that way too. Especially when he returned home to deal with unfinished business.

❈   ❈   ❈

Sara's hands trembled with each navy blue button she fastened on her funeral dress.

"I'm sorry I can't make it today." Clint lay on their four-poster bed looking like he'd been hit with the flu a thousand times over.

She nodded. "I didn't think you'd be up to it the day after chemo. I'll be fine." Her hollow eyes in the full-length mirror told a different story. "Erica said she'd pick the kids up today and take them to her house for an after-school snack. I'll pick them up from there by dinnertime."

Clint winced as he rubbed his stubbled jaw. Her doctor's brain switched to alert.

"Have the mouth sores started? Are you rinsing well and getting enough fluids?" She walked into their bathroom. "You're using the soft bristle toothbrush. Is it helping?"

"I'm okay. Just exhausted."

Her body moved, and her mind focused on minor details without her approval. She wasn't Clint's doctor. But she couldn't help noticing everything.

"Come sit with me."

Robotlike, she crossed the room to her husband's side. Autopilot might be her only salvation today.

"Frank's last words to me were about remembering the truth. That God is good. Always. And that He has a good plan." Clint cleared his throat. "You need to believe that, Sara. Even in the face of death, God hasn't left us."

The lump in her throat kept her from talking. She nodded.

He took her hand. "I've apologized for my temper more times than I can count. And I'm truly sorry for the pain I've added to this time. But I'd like us to start praying together again. Both of us praying. We need this."

She took a deep breath. "I'm not ready for that, Clint. You pray, okay?"

Clint closed his eyes and leaned forward. "Lord, I know You had me read Psalm 116 this morning for a reason. You said the death of Your saints is precious in Your sight. And I believe that, even though I don't understand. I knew Frank for such a short time, but I miss him.

I can't imagine what June is going through. Or Sara. Father, all I know to do is ask that You wrap them in Your arms and comfort them as only You can."

She jumped up before the rushing tears could spill all over the place. "I'll call on my way home from the church." At the door, she paused and looked back to the bed. Her husband appeared to be changing right before her eyes. His pale face. His continued weight loss. She didn't have the emotional reserves to handle Clint's cancer and the funeral. Or life, for that matter.

"I love you, Sara."

She closed the door in response and rushed out to the Range Rover, grabbing her purse on the way. Pushing the garage opener, she fumbled for her keys. Anything to keep from feeling.

When the garage door opened, Marilynn's light blue Volvo blocked her way. Good. She had no idea how she'd drive anyway.

Marilynn stepped out of her car looking like sunshine in her bright yellow pantsuit. "You don't look well. Are you sure you're up for this?"

No.

Focusing on Marilynn's beautiful outfit didn't help. Sara couldn't imagine wearing such a cheery color to a funeral. Even if Frank would have approved.

"I'm fine. It's just my nerves. I can't seem to keep my food down." Her gaze met Marilynn's concerned eyes. "I checked my temp, and I'm fine. No signs of a cold or flu or anything else."

"Just tired?"

"That's probably it. All the things I'm juggling right now resemble the Cat in the Hat's balancing act. Soon it's going to come crashing down around me."

"Maybe your physical symptoms have another source." Marilynn touched her arm. "Could you be pregnant?"

Sara almost turned an ankle backing away. Her high-heeled mules were a poor choice, especially for today.

"Not likely. We managed to make Valentine's Day a decent evening, but I've never reacted to a pregnancy that fast." They walked toward the Volvo.

"It'd be quick and painless to find out."

"I'll look into it. Later." Subject closed.

Sara's mind whirled with possibilities as they pulled out of the driveway. She couldn't handle the thought of a pregnancy now. Not with Clint in chemo. Not with Frank's funeral minutes away. Her physical reaction to the world-altering events of the last few weeks was stress. Nothing more.

"Have you talked to June?"

Sara stared out the window and watched the cars speeding around them. "No."

They rode in silence a good while before Marilynn spoke again. "Why don't you talk to HR and take a leave of absence until Clint is done with chemo? It would be one less stress on your very full plate."

Sara opened her mouth to argue, but then shut it again. Could they manage it? Finances might get tight, especially with Clint's astronomical medical bills. But they'd saved well over the years. Maybe it would work.

They sat at a red light near the church for what felt like an hour. Marilynn said nothing as Sara mulled over the options. She hated that Clint and now her best friend so easily zeroed in on her lack of coping skills. But it wasn't worth the fight any longer.

She turned to Marilynn as the light changed. "I'll talk to them on Monday."

Marilynn turned off Russell Road and found a close spot despite the crowded parking area. Frank's church had moved into this little brick building with an imposing white steeple only two years ago. She'd been to visit once.

As they entered the packed sanctuary, Marilynn put a hand on her back. "There's June."

Sara took a worship program and looked straight into Frank's smiling face on the front. All their conversations over the past few years swirled through her mind, and her knees buckled. She forced herself to remain standing and concentrated on taking one step at a time. She'd get through this. She'd be strong for June. If she didn't think too much, it could work.

It had to work.

June stood as they neared. "I'm so glad you both came. Sara, Frank left a little something for you in his office. I'll take you there when the service is over."

Sara enveloped her in a tight hug. "I…I'm sorry I wasn't there for you on Tuesday."

"I'm doing okay. Really." June stepped back from the hug and held on to Sara's hands. "Frank was ready to go home. And I'm leaning on God like I've never done before. I—"

The soft music signaled the start of the service.

Sara and Marilynn quickly found their reserved seats behind June's family. Watching the scene in front of her, she had no tears left. She couldn't even think.

All she could see in her mind's eye were Clint's cowboy boots and Stetson sticking out of a huge brown coffin. Funny the things that stood out at moments like these.

She looked down at the program and into Frank's blue eyes again. Scripture verses and the dates of his birth and death started to swim in front of her.

She couldn't do this.

Everyone around her stood to sing and then sat, listening to special music. Sara followed along mindlessly. An assistant pastor stood to pray and spoke about Frank's life and his cancer, how he'd lost the battle but won the war. Frank was face to face with Jesus. No more pain. No more chemo.

No more muffins or conversations about the future either. Her heart felt ten sizes too big for her rib cage. So did her stomach. She took a deep breath and prayed she wouldn't throw up in the middle of the pastor's message. She missed Frank more than she wanted to admit out loud.

When would she sit in June's place?

As the choir sang, "My Life Is in Your Hands," Sara couldn't shake the impression that they were singing straight to June. Reminding her she wasn't alone. They would all stand with her and show her that Frank was right. Jesus hadn't left His throne.

After the music ended, the family was dismissed first. June caught her eyes in passing and paused. Sara couldn't look away. And she couldn't understand what she saw in the new widow's eyes.

Joy.

Joy?

Minutes later, an usher touched Sara's elbow. Whispering near her ear, he motioned away from the group walking outside. "June wanted to speak with you before going to the cemetery. If you'll follow me."

Marilynn waved her on.

When they arrived at Frank's office door, the man motioned for her to go in.

"June?" She forced herself to step over the threshold.

Turning from the window, the young widow smiled through her tears. "Frank left you and Clint a card he'd written a few days before he passed away." She held out a large off-white envelope. "Make your peace with God, Sara. The journey is so much better with Him."

What could she say to that?

Oh, God. Please don't make me stand in June's place. I can't.

"God's grace is sufficient. He's given me what I needed today, and I know He will continue. He'll do the same for you, Sara."

But she didn't want to experience June's peace. Not if it meant standing in a funeral home, looking at Clint's lifeless body.

"Your story is different from ours, but God is the same. You can trust Him. He won't abandon you."

June's words burrowed deep into Sara's heart. "Thank you. I don't know what else to say."

"I understand. Your being here was gift enough. Thank you for loving Frank and me and praying us through the journey from beginning to end."

They walked out to the parking lot in thoughtful silence. Marilynn met them, and they said tearful good-byes.

Her best friend pointed to the car. "You ready to go home?"

Yes. No. Only one way to find out. As they headed home, Sara watched more traffic fly past them. Trees. Kids on bikes. Schools.

Life continued.

So would she. Somehow.

12

Michael slapped the fax printout on his leg as he snaked his way through the nearly deserted CACU floor. Friday evening, and everyone else had plans.

Not him.

At least he hadn't had to buy some dumb Valentine's gift for a woman whose name he couldn't remember now. Still, being single in the city remained a highly overrated notion.

His desk chair squeaked as he flopped into it. After the stellar month he'd had so far, the information in his hands shouldn't have surprised him.

Louisville Metro police had positively identified their five-year-old skeleton before they'd deigned to return Michael's calls. Proof that you couldn't discount cop instinct, that following a hunch could mean all the difference between an unsolved crime and a successful investigation.

In this instance, the Louisville detectives solved the cold case because they ran with Hopkins's idea that the skeleton belonged to an old Baker District missing-persons case. Dental records proved Hopkins right. Not only that, but they also landed a full confession when questioning the boy's stepfather.

He skimmed the fax again. Reading between the lines, he could tell Hopkins enjoyed rubbing it in. The Louisville chief obviously believed he'd bested Kessler by nailing one of his cold cases before the CACU had any real leads on their three similar ones.

Michael dreaded telling his immediate supervisor the news. Coming on the heels of not finding Mattie and a multitude of other dead ends, the experience would be about as much fun as getting wisdom teeth out sans Novocain. He'd top Kessler's favorite list for sure. Not.

He tossed the fax on his desk.

"Hey, man." Lee leaned against Michael's stack of paperwork still requiring attention. "You gonna join the party at Kessler's tomorrow?"

"Nope."

"Why not? Seems like a perfect way to get him to chum up to you more. You've been gunning for his favor for a year now."

"Too bad you and Clint made the preferred circle long before I arrived."

Lee rubbed his ebony chin. "You're wrong, rookie. He likes you. Else he wouldn't be letting you do any fun stuff. Get on Kessler's bad side, and you'll be pushing paperwork in triplicate till you babble incoherently."

Michael stood, pulling on his suit jacket. "Then explain why I didn't make the guest list for this weekend?"

Tapping his finger on his lips, Lee tried to hide his grin. "That's easy. You're single. So's the sister we're moving in tomorrow."

"Figures."

"One thing Kessler keeps close to the vest is his family. If I was you, I'd steer clear of Miss Hanna Kessler."

"Thanks, Steven the Second. Already got that vibe loud and clear."

Lee chuckled. "Wanna grab dinner with me and Rashida? My lady is doing some serious cooking tonight. Mouth-watering steak with plenty of fancy fixings."

"If I bring some wine, will you call Kessler and tell him about this?" Michael handed over the fax.

Lee skimmed the papers and then slapped them down on the desk. "Not on your life. Steven's old boss has been a burr ever since I came here. But you can still bring the wine. Seven sharp. You know the way." Lee exited the floor chuckling.

Michael gathered up paperwork to deal with later tonight. Now he had plans and didn't have to eat takeout Chinese three nights in a row. Sweet.

Still had to call Kessler, though.

But maybe it'd turn out better than he hoped. Surely Kessler wouldn't let Hopkins's ego get the best of him. And even though the Louisville skeleton didn't give them any case leads, its not being one of theirs meant their investigation matrix continued to point strongly to Standish. And at last report, Standish still had Mattie with him. Alive.

That hope kept him slogging through masses of data, convinced they'd solve this case well. But what if, after all his work, Mattie still turned up dead?

Truth was, he'd gotten too close to this one.

Clint would say he should try praying. His mentor was right. But maybe Michael just wasn't cut out for CACU. Maybe it was time to take a step closer to his ultimate career goal and finally apply to the CIA. His computer skills and intelligence work in the Army would improve his chances of acceptance.

With a CIA job, he could travel the world as he'd done in his military days. Unattached. No Matties haunting his sleep.

Yeah. Maybe he'd dust off that high school dream.

After Mattie Reynolds came home.

❋   ❋   ❋

"We got Standish."

Steven snapped awake and nearly crushed the phone in his hand. "Mattie too?" He started pulling on work clothes.

Parker's silence stretched a beat too long. "No. Baltimore PD nabbed *Jim* Standish this morning, trying to snatch Wes."

"Don't ever pull that bait and switch on me again."

"Figured it'd get you up and at your door faster. We need to high-tail it to Baltimore."

Parker's knowing him that well grated on Steven's last nerve. The ploy had worked too. He'd managed to go from asleep to ready in under a minute. "What's your ETA?"

"Twenty minutes."

Ending the call with Parker, he punched the number-two speed dial. Dad would be reading his Bible at this hour, and Steven hated to interrupt. But he needed Dad to watch James. Good thing FBI families knew how to flex.

"Steven? You're up early for a Saturday."

"Parker's en route. One of our suspects is in custody, and we need to move before leads go cold. Can you get here in fifteen?"

Water running in the background indicated Dad would be on his way soon. "Not a problem. Is James asleep?"

"Yes."

"I'll start the chocolate-chip pancakes when I arrive. Want me to save you some?"

Steven paused by his son's door. "Sure. Thanks, Dad. I owe you."

"No you don't. Love you, son."

Closing his phone, he slipped into James's room. His son's rhythmic breathing said he was still sound asleep, the spaceship toy Angela had given him during her last visit resting at his feet. They'd had a good three days away, with James his constant companion.

Back-to-work stress had returned far too soon.

Once out of the room, he sped to the kitchen to scarf a Pop-Tart before Parker arrived.

Fifteen minutes later, both Parker and Dad pulled into the driveway. He loved on-time people. Passing his dad on the way out, Steven paused. "I'll meet you at your house as soon as I'm done."

"Go get 'em, you two." Andrew Kessler waved at Parker like they were old friends. Dad always made people feel like they were part of the family. And as long as Parker stayed clear of Hanna, that was fine with Steven.

Parker revved his Mustang, and soon they were flying northward on MD-295. "You still sore about the Louisville Metro PD thing?"

Yes. Chief Hopkins's one-upmanship rankled. But he shouldn't entangle himself in the same immaturity. "It's good someone gets closure. Just wish it was our cold cases too."

"Sergeant Moore took great pleasure in waking me up to say they were processing Jim Standish for attempted kidnapping. B and E too. All before sunrise. Said he'd send us a tape of the interrogation if we needed more beauty rest."

"Some people just enjoy pushing buttons. Between Moore and Hopkins, I'm about ready to leave this cop dance to someone else."

"Seriously?"

Steven laughed. "No." Not that he hadn't considered it. But even with obnoxious law-enforcement allies, Lord willing, he'd stay with the Bureau until retirement.

Parker kept his focus on the road. "What's the probability we're dealing with four unrelated cases?"

A pounding headache spread across Steven's forehead. "Behavioral analysis indicates the strong possibility we're dealing with a serial kidnapper. From what we've found on Standish, he remains our prime suspect. But without substantial forensic evidence, there's no ruling out multiple perps."

"Sure wish we'd find a dumping ground."

"Maybe Jim Standish will hand us a better lead. His brother, for one. And Mattie alive."

Fifty minutes later, they entered Baltimore PD's headquarters and were directed to the interrogation in progress.

"Our guy is going down hard and too stupid to realize it." Moore pointed through the two-way mirror at Jim Standish's wiry form decked out in all black. A stocky Asian detective leaned against the wall behind Standish, asking questions. "Standish is pretty spooked now that he knows Chief Dickson is dating his former sister-in-law."

Steven shook his head. Standish couldn't have picked a worse place to get busted. "What do you have so far?"

"Ed Standish phoned from the Inner Harbor to arrange a hand-off, which was supposed to have occurred right about now. Unfortunately, Jim is going to miss that appointment."

"Who's on it?"

"Three of our best detectives and two Feds from the Baltimore field office."

Michael pointed his chin toward the glass. "When can we get in there?"

Moore headed for the door. "I'll notify Detective Tang. The chief will be down shortly."

Steven and Michael entered the small white room minutes later, trading places with the detective. "Jim, tell me how your brother rooked you into his game, and maybe we can work a deal for you."

"No way. They done said I was getting the book thrown at me. Nothing you big FBI people can do."

Parker sat in the chair across from Jim. "Don't be too sure. You've messed with their chief's girlfriend, so it's personal with these guys. Not us. We just want to find Mattie alive."

"Mattie. That kid Ed's toting around?" He snorted. "Ed and that kid get along better than Ed and Wes ever done."

Steven squinted, not sure he wanted an answer to the next logical question. "How so?" He sat on the desk.

"Kid calls Ed 'Pops,' just like we called our dad. And he sat on the couch, busy with his new PlayStation thing the whole time me and Ed talked." Jim swallowed hard. "He ain't never tried to get away, neither."

"When did you meet with Ed?"

A look of defeat swept over Standish, pulling the corners of his mouth farther south. "Don't matter now. The plan is all ruined. I'll never get out of here in time."

"In time for what?"

"I was gonna take Wes to Ed, and then we was gonna disappear to Montana."

They had to keep Standish going while his lips were so loose. "After you got Wes, the four of you were going to hop a flight out to Montana?"

He nodded. "Always wanted to see that big-sky place. Go hunting with Ed again like we used to do with our pops. But Ed wouldn't go without Wes."

"Since the hand-off didn't happen, will Ed head out there with Mattie?"

"Naw. He wouldn't go without me and Wes. He's been holed up somewhere around here. Wouldn't say where, in case you Feds bugged my phone. Guess he'll lay low for a while and then try to get Wes hisself. Ed wanted to get his kid far away from that ex of his and start over."

"With what money? Neither of your bank accounts are all that hefty."

"Last week I gave Ed the rest of the money our folks had squirreled away. And I also gave him the cash I had from selling our parents' stuff. I stashed the money at my place so's Ed wouldn't gamble with it. That woulda took care of us for a year or so."

"Won't do you much good now. Aiding and abetting on top of attempted kidnapping could send you away for a long time."

Standish sat up straight in his chair. "Thought you said we'd make a deal."

Steven nodded to the door. "If you think of anything to help us find Ed and Mattie, then we'll talk about a deal."

Stepping out of the room, Steven noticed Moore's pinched face. His pulse thundered in his ears. "Tell me you have the other Standish in custody."

Moore shook his head. "No one showed at the drop site. We're scouring the harbor area for leads, and we'll saturate it with pictures of Standish and Mattie Reynolds. We'll find them."

So close once again. But close wasn't good enough. Not when he had a warm trail and a child to deliver home.

He turned to Michael. "Let's check out the Inner Harbor."

Standish was most likely long gone. Little chance of finding him now. But still they had to try.

❅   ❅   ❅

Hanna watched out her dad's front door, James plastered to her leg.

The little boy looked up. "Dad said he'd be here for dinner, right?"

She checked her watch just as a kicking black Mustang pulled into the driveway. Steven was nothing if not punctual. But he wasn't alone this time.

"Mr. Parker is here too! Cool." James opened the door. "Dad, you're here! Hey, Mr. Parker!" Jumping into Steven's arms, James wrapped himself around his dad.

Steven's stance shouted controlled anger. Until he returned James's hug.

The handsome stranger hung back, watching Steven and James. He walked like a military cadet. Blond buzz cut too. Nice build, even with a coat on.

She snapped her eyes to the floor. Old habits died hard. She'd left Louisville because of a guy and had no intention of messing things up like that again.

"Hey, big brother. Thought your buddy Lee and his wife were coming."

Steven harrumphed. "They got tied up at an art exhibit in Baltimore. If I'd known they were up there, I'd have traded afternoons with Lee."

James slid from Steven's arms. "I'll get Grammy and Gramps."

"Hanna, this is Michael Parker. We work together."

Michael stuck out his hand and smiled. Very cute. No wedding band. "Pleased to meet you." And old-fashioned manners.

"Same." She shook his hand, enjoying the controlled strength of his grip. Not wimpy or bone crushing. Just right.

No. No. No. Judging from her brother's cold glare, Michael Parker was off-limits. Not that it was any of Steven's business. But she should know better anyway.

Dad and Sue joined them in the foyer and welcomed Michael warmly. "Before we start hauling boxes over to Hanna's brownstone, why don't you all hang up your coats, and we'll go have some pizza?" Dad gave Steven a side hug. "Gracie called a few minutes ago and said she's on her way."

Everyone trooped toward the kitchen, but Dad hung back with Steven. "By your scowl, I can tell today didn't go as hoped." Helping Sue and James get out plates and cups, Hanna kept an ear tuned to their conversation, trying to ignore Michael's gentle brown eyes watching her.

"We worked with Baltimore PD and field agents all afternoon,"

Steven said. "Nothing. Any more of this close-but-nada could prove deadly for Mattie if too much time passes."

"We'll keep praying."

Steven nodded. Michael studied the floor. Not a believer? That could explain Steven's watchdog act.

"Mrs. Lang is redecorating our classroom," James informed his dad as he handed over a stack of white plates. "Said it's in celebration of spring coming soon."

"Wishful thinking." Michael's mumble caught everyone's attention. "No offense, but the rain and snow up here makes me homesick for Florida sometimes."

"Hang in there, Michael." Sue patted his shoulder. "Spring will come. Now, what can I get you to drink?" She opened the refrigerator and took out a pitcher of tea as everyone loaded up plates with pizza and breadsticks.

"Your sweet tea is the best. I'd love a glass."

Sue filled multiple cups with her famous sugar-shock tea. "Coming right up."

Michael stepped up behind Hanna and took one more slice than she had. "You're a runner, right?"

"I…um…yes." She considered putting a piece of pizza back. "But how did—?"

He grinned. "Your brother has a picture on his bookshelf of you winning some kind of race. I used to run track in college."

"It's the best exercise. I ran regularly before I started managing Dad's coffee shop in Kentucky and my photography work took off. Even did a couple of 10Ks." She looked down at her plate. "I need to get back to it after I'm settled."

"Not by yourself, I hope." Steven cocked an eyebrow.

"Whatever you say." She glanced toward the front door. "Is Clint coming too? I might as well get the lectures from my bothersome big brothers done in one fell swoop."

"Not this time, Sis. Clint's been sick. I was going to check up on him tonight, but after we get you moved in, I need to crash. I'll see him tomorrow." At the sound of a car door, Steven excused himself. "There's Gracie. I'll be back in a minute."

Hanna giggled. "He's a little overeager."

"You'd better tread carefully, Hanna-girl. Your brother has waited a long time for someone who makes his eyes light up like that." Sue placed glasses at everyone's place. "And it was well worth the wait."

If Sue only knew how much those words stabbed at Hanna's soul.

Steven and his fiancée joined them. "Gracie, you remember Michael Parker?"

She smiled at Michael. "You're looking better than you did on New Year's Eve."

"Blind dates rank up there with getting shot at."

"You've been shot too?" Hanna put down her glass. "I'm not sure this FBI stuff works for me anymore. Gracie, don't you think it's about time Steven retired?"

Gracie held up her hands. "You can take that up yourself and see how far you get."

After Gracie and Steven filled their plates, the conversation turned to Hope Ridge Academy news and Hanna's new place. Then her nephew's back-to-back jokes had everyone laughing. Hanna itched for her camera. Some freeze frames of everyone gathered around the dining room table would be perfect to hang in her brownstone. A daily reminder of the relationships that mattered most.

Michael helped her clear the table when they were finished. "Thanks for being here." She put glasses in the dishwasher. "There really aren't that many boxes to move, and all we're doing is dropping them off at my new place. I just need to get the U-Haul turned back in tonight."

"Not a problem." He dumped the empty pizza boxes into a large silver trash can by the back door, then leaned against the counter beside her. "Did you drive by yourself from Kentucky?"

"Dad and Sue followed me to Louisville after Steven's engagement party." She crossed the room and wiped the table with vigor, intensely aware of his presence. "Then they helped me load my things and head to Alexandria."

"You must have been looking for a place here long before you packed up."

She rinsed her hands and slipped a strand of hair behind her ear. "Actually, no. A friend of Steven's wanted to rent her brownstone near Old Town Alexandria. We talked about it on Valentine's Day, and she handed over the keys this morning."

He flashed another charming grin. "We'll be almost neighbors then."

Steven cleared his throat, frowning in the doorway.

Hanna let out a long sigh. No worries about Michael asking her out. Big brother would keep her dateless once again.

Good thing too. It was safer that way.

13

Tears splattered on the off-white card in Clint's hands. For the first time in months, his waterworks didn't send him flying into a rage. The meds had a wicked effect on his emotions. But Frank's message held an answer he'd missed until now.

Sunday's sunrise still an hour away, he took his prednisone and finished off his bagel and juice before looking again at the three pictures Frank had included with his note. One of Frank and June on their wedding day, another snapped shortly after Frank's second melanoma surgery, and a final one of Frank and June with Sara in her office two months ago.

He reread the note.

Clint and Sara,

If you're reading this, I'm already home with Jesus. But after meeting Clint, I sensed you two might need the words I'm about to write.

I'd be lying if I said I have no fear of death. But I remind myself where I'm going and that my God will welcome me into His arms. Then there's peace. Keep that in mind when things look their worst.

Cancer is the hardest battle I've ever fought. The first round, June and I stood together, praying all the way. Rejoicing when I went into remission. But the second round, two years later, tossed our faith around like a tornado.

We were so sure I'd beat the beast of cancer. The course

of the past year showed God had a different plan. One I won't
try to explain because I don't understand.

There were times I tried to make June leave so I could die
alone and not drag her down. But she refused. Many days the
wedding vows "for better or for worse" stretched us to the
breaking point. But we made it because we held on to love.
And we let our church family surround us with their prayers,
food, and practical help. Otherwise we might not have made
it through together.

Think about that. You saw mostly our good days.

My point is, don't lock people out of your battle. Let
them fight with you. Fight together.

And for better or for worse, hold on tight to the truth.
God is still on the throne. And He is good. Always.

Forever changed by love,
   Frank

Clint dropped his head in his hands, pierced by the Holy Spirit's
conviction. The chemo could be blamed for only so much. He'd kept
everyone, including Sara, outside of his pain. Protecting his pride had
mattered more than loving well.

Father, forgive me.

Peace like he hadn't experienced in a month flowed through him,
followed by a surge of hope.

Now to tell Sara and rally their friends around them.

They'd fight together.

And win.

※   ※   ※

"Everybody up! Rise and shine. We're going to church."

Sara jerked awake at Clint's booming voice. She pulled the covers over her head. The weekend had passed without much necessary input from her. Sunday could do the same.

"Mama, come on. It's time to go to Big Church. You don't want to miss Daddy's first time back, do you?" Susannah tugged at her comforter.

Yes, she did in fact want to miss church. And the next three months of chemo too.

"I told Susannah and Jonathan. They know about the cancer."

Sara sprang up and nearly lost her balance as she stood on the soft beige carpet. "Without me?" How could Clint tell their children he was going to die without her there to hold them and comfort them?

"Daddy said he's taking some yucky medicine, but soon he'll be done with it and be able to play with us again." Susannah's bright eyes held no tears. In fact, she and Jonathan looked incredible, all dressed in red and ready for church.

"Daddy pway, Mama. He bedder." Jonathan wrapped his pudgy little arms around her thigh.

"My arm's fine, I'm doing better than I did with the last chemo, and I'm ready to let our friends know so they can fight this battle with us." Clint sat on the bed, and Jonathan wiggled out of her arms to be near his daddy.

Clint was ready to let people help them? Maybe getting up wasn't such a bad idea.

Susannah jumped on the bed to join her little brother. "And I get to shave Daddy's head before we leave for church! Come on. Let's go get ready." Susannah tugged Jonathan out the door.

"What?" Sara's temples throbbed with her racing heart.

Clint pointed to his pillow. A little clump of dark brown hair poked up from the cotton sheets. "It started to come out on Friday, but I didn't have the heart to tell you." He shrugged. "The Web sites say it'll grow back after the last chemo, maybe before. I'll survive until then."

Survive.

For more than a decade now, she'd watched patients lose their hair. For many, the alopecia proved one of the most distressing side effects of chemotherapy. But only once had a patient asked for her help. Three years ago, she'd been the one to cut off Lucy Cohen's ten inches of thick blond hair for a Locks of Love donation. An experience more personal and painful than she ever expected. She had no desire to do that again. Any more than she wanted to watch Clint's whole appearance change before her eyes. He already looked like a different man. Without his hair, the transformation would be extreme.

"Sara?" Clint's gentle voice brought a wave of shame. How could she be so petty? This was her husband. And even if he looked like Clint's great-uncle, he was still the man she had married nine years ago. The man she loved with all her being.

Tears spilled onto her cheeks.

"Sara, honey, it's gonna be okay." Clint tucked her into his arms. "I need you with me today. Will you help?"

She nodded. "How…how are you dealing with all this so easily?"

"Follow me." He walked over to the closet and pulled something out of his robe pocket. Even with the physical changes, his navy slacks and white dress shirt looked good on him.

He held out an opened envelope. Frank's card. The one she'd tried to forget about. "We need to get moving to make it to church. But after we get home, please read this and remember I love you, Sara. For better and worse. And better again."

He nudged her toward the bathroom. "I'll get the kids eating, then I'll be ready for my buzz."

Fifteen long minutes later, Sara's hands shook as she helped Susannah with the clippers.

"See, Mama. Daddy looks like an Indian from those old movies." Susannah giggled as she stepped down from her stool and away from the dining room table. Clint didn't budge. The stripe of hair down the middle of his head stood on end.

Jonathan held up the mirror to Clint's chest.

Her husband tensed, then moved the mirror to his face with a quick jerk of his wrist. "Not a bad look, huh? What do you say we keep it this way?"

Susannah and Jonathan laughed.

Sara swallowed the lump in her throat as she stepped forward to finish the job. This wasn't about her. Clint wanted her involved in every part of this journey. And so she would be.

Even if a little piece of her heart died with each step.

"Sara, it's not the end of the world."

His voice made her jump. Turning the clippers back on, she finished shaving her husband's head. Every time she hit a clump of already-loose hair, her hands rebelled and shook worse. But she kept going until the job was done.

"Daddy, you look like a baseball star." Susannah rubbed his head.

"Perfect. We ready for church now?" Clint brushed some hair from his dress shirt.

Sara swallowed, then nodded. "Everybody out to the car."

The opportunity to share with friends at church had finally arrived. Maybe the time had come to let a little hope back in.

※　※　※

Steven stood frozen on the Rollinses' porch Sunday night, staring into the foyer at Clint's bald head.

"Come in, Steven. The kids are in bed, so you and Clint will have plenty of time to talk." Sara tugged off his overcoat and whispered. "Don't stare. He'll explain." She closed the door behind him and hurried out of the front hall.

"Like the new look?" Clint rubbed his head.

Visions of his mother swam in Steven's mind. He needed to sit down.

He followed Clint into the living room and sat near the blazing fireplace. "You don't have the flu, do you?"

"Nope."

"Did you ever?"

Clint shook his glossy head.

Steven pulled at the knees of his jeans. "Are you going to die?"

"Eventually."

Steven clenched his fist and fought the urge to punch his partner. "Don't be a jerk. You lied to me, and now you're...you're..."

Clint took a deep breath and held up a hand. "If I'd have told you a month ago when I found out, would you have gone to Georgia and proposed to Gracie on Valentine's Day?"

"Probably not."

"That's why I stretched the truth."

"Telling me you had the flu isn't stretching the truth. It's lying. It's not your style." Steven swallowed hard and stared at Clint. His partner hadn't just lost his hair. He'd lost weight, a lot of it. Twenty pounds or more. And he'd aged a decade in the last month. No wonder Clint hadn't taken his calls or let him come for a visit. He'd have instantly recognized the disease that had stolen his mother's life.

"What...what's the official diagnosis?"

Clint stood and walked over to the white fireplace. "Diffuse large B-cell lymphoma. Stage four. Best-case scenario, forty- to fifty-percent survival rate." Clint recited the statistics with practiced nonchalance, leaning against the mantel and staring into the fire before turning back to face Steven. "It's not a death sentence. Don't look at me like that."

Steven tried to dial back the fear gnawing through his gut. But the images of his mom's cancer assaulted him. For a time Steven had kept his head shaved to be like her. Not this time. He couldn't go through it again the same way.

"I'm sorry I lied, Steven." Clint sank down on the couch. "I didn't even tell my parent's till Valentine's Day, and the kids didn't know anything until this morning."

"Pride or fear?"

"Both."

"Sara?"

Clint grabbed a gray and maroon sweatshirt and pulled it over his head. "It's taking a toll. But today was good. We asked friends from church to pray with us, and a bunch offered to bring meals and run errands. That'll help Sara a lot."

"Is she going to keep working full time?"

"She's already cut back. And she'll talk to HR tomorrow about taking a leave of absence. Then we'll get to play house more often."

Steven nodded and tried to smile. He needed to see Gracie, needed to process the emotions swirling around his brain. But now wasn't the time. "So are you coming back to work?"

"First of March if I continue handling the chemo okay. And if Dr. Sara lets me come out to play. I'm getting stir-crazy with just books, TV, and the computer."

"Don't rush." Questions were piling up in Steven's head. "Are you having any weird dreams? Mom had a ton. Some were pretty intense and out there."

Clint cleared his throat and picked up his huge bottle of water. "Me and my big ol' water jug won't be parting anytime soon." Wiping his mouth, he leaned forward. "Yep, the dreams are something else. A weird mixture of case files, kids dying, and old memories of the Berlin Wall from my days in the service. It's all pretty confusing."

"If it helps to talk them out, I'm here."

"Thanks, but it's one of those chemo side effects I have to suck it up and deal with." Clint took another big drink. "Guess I should apologize for not taking your calls, huh? I'm sorry."

"I know. And I understand."

Silence hung between them for a long minute. Finally, Clint cleared his throat. "So what's up with you? I trust Gracie said yes."

"Of course. Hanna snapped tons of photos, and everyone's pulling out all stops to make this July wedding happen. Especially Hanna. She moved into Maria Grivens's brownstone in Alexandria this weekend."

"Life continues, doesn't it?" Clint laid his head back and stared at the ceiling. "Did you tell me Hanna was moving?"

"Left you a few messages about it. But there's been a lot going on." Steven studied his partner. His mom's memory had become a lot shakier the further the cancer progressed. It worried him to hear Clint start acting like that so soon.

"Am I gonna have to wear my Stetson to work?"

"Sorry. I'll go grab the Valentine's Day pictures." He got up and retrieved the photos from his coat in the hall closet. "Sorry about staring. I'm sure the novelty will wear off soon." He handed over the pictures.

Clint missed, and pictures scattered everywhere.

"My fault." Steven picked them up and handed the pile over a second time.

Clint's jaw muscles clenched. Best friends or not, it had to be hard on Clint to let anyone see his weakness.

"I think I'd better head out." He rose and wiped sweaty palms on his jeans. "Want me to keep the news to myself so you can share it at your party in two weeks?"

Clint stiffened. "You can tell whoever needs to know. I'd rather everyone hear before then. I'd prefer to celebrate on my birthday, you know?"

He did. "Gracie and Sara and I will take care of everything. We'll keep the guest list small. It's not worth the risk of infection."

"Don't start, Steven. I'm not gonna die if I get a cold."

"Then promise you'll play it straight with me from now on."

"Deal." Clint's voice was low. He looked like he'd be asleep in two seconds.

"I'll show myself out." But before Steven could slip into his coat, Clint was already fast asleep. He watched for a minute, until the walls started closing in.

Cancer.

No wonder God had him praying for Clint so hard.

14

C lint tossed and turned as sleep evaded him.
The Tuesday Bible study at church had worn him out. But every time he closed his eyes, the same dream darkened his mind.

He paced in front of the enormous gray Berlin Wall, his rifle ready. Back and forth. Then the scene shifted, and he stood near a tan stucco Army apartment building, watching an enlisted man yell at a little boy. The brown-haired child cried and screamed as the man hit him. The soldier's face became a twisted mask of anger. Then, in one sick, slow-motion move, the man's fingers closed around the little boy's neck. Clint ran and ran, trying to get to a car. Except the tubing attached to his port kept pulling him back...

He bolted up in the four-poster bed, struggling to catch his breath. Sweat drenched his T-shirt. Sara lay beneath the comforter sound asleep. Must be used to his crazy sleep patterns by now.

Slipping into the bathroom to rinse off, he replayed the dream. Few nightmares made sense, but why these particular events? Why now?

He'd been stationed in Berlin and worked Checkpoint Charlie with his MP unit until the Wall came down. But the incident with the enlisted man had happened much later. He'd put that situation out of his mind. Or tried to.

That night, he'd responded to a domestic call and noticed bruises on the arms of a young boy. Unable to forget or do nothing, he approached the stepfather's superiors. But no charges were filed until Clint found a pattern of abuse and a teacher at the base elementary school willing to speak out. By then it was too late.

He turned off the water. No use rehashing bad memories. He couldn't fix things now anyway.

Toweling off and looking into the bathroom mirror, Clint struggled to accept the image before him. Nine days with a bald head, and now he had no eyebrows or eyelashes either. Or nose hairs. Constantly wiping his nose was one more reminder of his powerlessness over the destruction of cancer.

He rubbed his forehead. How could he manage going back to work next week if he couldn't even make himself sleep? Or remember the important details of old cases? The dream supplied a perfect example. He had no clear picture of the little boy or man in his dreams. Not even a name.

He couldn't remember the status of the CACU's current cold cases either.

Fear about his forgetfulness and not measuring up must have sparked this strange series of dreams. That and the chemo. Even Steven said weird dreams were standard.

"Honey, you okay?" Sara padded into the bathroom, still half-asleep. Her mussed hair and silky skin caused an ache in his chest.

Dimming the light, he pulled her into his arms. Even half-asleep, the beauty pressed against him awakened every nerve ending. She snuggled deeper into his chest and wrapped her arms around his waist.

"Sara." He bent over and kissed her neck, moving up to her earlobe.

She jumped back with wide eyes. "I was… I thought I was dreaming. We were…" Sara inhaled as her face flushed red.

He stepped closer. "Making love?"

"Yes." She moved her hands over his biceps.

He longed to pick her up and carry her back to their bed, but he wasn't physically able. Before he could curse his circumstances, Sara stood on her tiptoes and pulled his head down to meet her lips.

He pulled back to look into her eyes.

"What are you waiting for, cowboy?" Her smile danced in front of him as she led them back into the bedroom.

For a second he wondered if his mind was playing tricks. If another, more pleasant dream had replaced the last set of nightmares.

As Sara kissed his forehead, his eyes, his chin, he realized he didn't care.

Dream or not, he didn't ever want to wake up.

❖ ❖ ❖

"So you're really going to do it?" Marilynn's voice teased from Sara's office doorway.

Sara smiled a response and kept packing her pictures and personal items. "Yes. I'm taking an indefinite leave of absence. Effective today, the last day of February."

Part of her hated to leave work. But Clint and Marilynn had been right. She couldn't do it all. The results of a home pregnancy test had clinched it. That and the prospect of spending more time with Jonathan and Susannah kept her from being consumed by the guilt of not measuring up to her own expectations.

Marilynn helped her pack shelves of medical texts and the most recent research findings. Laughter twinkled in her eyes. "Don't use these for bedtime reading."

Sara winked. "Who knows? With extra time on my hands, these might prove useful."

But she didn't anticipate spending a lot of time in her books. Clint had turned a corner emotionally, and they were all looking forward to the arrival of his parents next week. If she could keep her husband from pushing too hard and getting sick, they'd make it to May tenth, the date of his last chemo, stronger than ever. Following June's advice and Clint's request, she had even started talking to God again. That had accelerated the growth of hope.

"You look like you had a good night's sleep." Marilynn brushed dust from her hands. "That's a change." She smoothed her red and gold traditional African wrap as she sat in one of the maroon armchairs. "Anything you want to share?"

"Not at this time."

"Ah, there's mischief in those Irish green eyes."

"Maybe so, but that's classified information for now."

Shaking her head, Marilynn grinned. "I'll play along for the time being. But I have a question."

"Ask away." Sara took a seat next to her friend. "I'm here for another few hours."

"Are you depending on people or circumstances for your hope and happiness?"

The question hit Sara in the heart. She brushed a few red hairs from her denim wrap dress, buying time to construct an intelligent answer. "No. Of course not." She shrugged. "I don't think so."

Marilynn held up a hand. "I can't see into your heart, and I haven't watched my husband battle cancer. But I've observed many patients' families, and this is an issue I've seen a great deal. So I'm simply offering a caution from a friend. You talk it over with God and see what He says."

Sara nodded and returned to packing.

"What will you do with yourself when Clint goes back to work?"

Sara laughed. "Sleep. Clean. Catch up my scrapbooks." She put the last book in a box. "I'm going to cut back on Jonathan's hours at day care. I missed so much of Susannah's baby years, I don't want to miss his too."

Marilynn raised a perfectly sculptured eyebrow. "What about preparing a nursery?"

"I'm not saying a word." Sara placed the crystal waterfall prism that Frank and June had given her on top of her favorite afghan in the last box, then looked around the office to see if she'd missed anything.

"Do you have time for a quick consult before you leave?" Marilynn looked out the window.

"Sure. I'm about finished here."

"I have a new patient, admitted to the hospital via the ER. A five-year-old girl. She was successfully treated for neuroblastoma three years ago in Tennessee. Now it's recurred, and the parents have demanded a second opinion on treatment."

"Histology report?"

"Unfavorable. The prognosis is not good, even with a stem-cell transplant. And the parents are resistant to the treatment options I've outlined."

Sara rounded the desk and squeezed Marilynn's hand. "Can I review her charts for a few minutes first?"

"Yes. I'll go get them." Marilynn slipped out of the office.

Could she face another patient so close to death? She fingered the crystal prism with shaking hands as scenes from Frank's funeral flashed through her mind.

"Dr. Rollins?" A sweet voice and slight tap at her open door drew her attention back to the present.

"Lucy?" Sara smiled as the young woman stepped into her office. "Lucy Cohen. Come in. How are you doing?" She wrapped the short blonde in her arms. Lucy's hair had grown long again, as beautiful as ever, but Lucy's blue eyes were troubled. Sara motioned for her to sit. "I was thinking about you the other day. Tell me how you're doing."

Lucy sniffled.

Sara's stomach lurched.

"I wish I had better news, Dr. Rollins." Lucy gave a slight smile and sat down in the armchair. "I just got test results back. I'm here to see Dr. Holland because they said you weren't taking new cases."

"Dr. Holland is a bone-marrow specialist."

Lucy nodded. "The leukemia returned. It came back just before I'd reached the three-year mark. I'm here to schedule a transplant."

Sara sank back into her desk. An elephant had settled on her chest, and she couldn't think of what to say.

"I start chemo again next week. And then—"

"Lucy, wasn't your sister a perfect six out of six match?" That offered an excellent possibility of a successful transplant.

The young woman's face brightened. "Yes. I'm surprised you remember. That was a long time ago." Lucy moved to the edge of her chair. "Lindi's coming down to help with Joel and Jessica. Dale's just taking it one day at a time."

Lucy's children had to be about five and seven by now. Just babies. Cancer's indiscriminate destruction pounded on Sara's hope once again.

"Dr. Holland is wonderful. He'll take the best care of you." She reached out to take Lucy's hand. "You'll make it through this. You have fire in you. You'll beat this."

Lucy sniffed back her tears. "We beat it once, didn't we? We'll do it again. You always said God hears the prayers of His people and He still does miracles."

Sara handed her former patient a Kleenex, her own echoed words accusing her. She'd given up that hope so easily with Clint's diagnosis. Maybe circumstances did control her more than she wanted to admit.

"You still believe that, right?"

Sara met Lucy's eyes. "Yes. Yes I do." Even if she doubted, she'd find her way back to that belief.

"So…will you come and be at the hospital with me when they do the transplant? I'm hopeful we can do it March twenty-seventh. That's the day you put my name up on the 'off treatment' board. Remember?"

Sara did remember the celebration. But here they were again.

"Will you come, Dr. Rollins?"

For Lucy, she would do this. "I start a leave of absence today. But I'll come, on one condition."

The young woman tilted her head. "What?"

"That I come as Sara, your friend."

Lucy jumped up and hugged her. "It's a deal."

Marilynn knocked on her door and startled them both. "Sorry to interrupt. I can come back in a few minutes."

Lucy fumbled for her purse. "No. I need to get to my appointment anyway." She faced Sara. "Can I call the home number you gave me before?"

Sara nodded. "I'll be there, Lucy. And I'll be praying."

"Thank you." The young woman smiled and slipped past Marilynn.

Her best friend closed the door. "She was another of your favorites, wasn't she?"

"Yes." Sara extended her hand for the chart Marilynn held. "After this, I'm going home for a good soak in the tub."

Marilynn eyed her closely. "Good idea."

It took only a few minutes for Sara's practiced eye to scan the chart. "Says here that Megan Carter's first treatment was three years ago. Stage three. The tumor was not completely removed by surgery, but she went into remission after aggressive chemo." Sara looked up and met Marilynn's eyes. "Her labs say there are extra copies of the MYCN gene."

"Yes. Everything in Megan's chart places her in a high-risk, low cure-rate group."

"Why did they request a second opinion?"

"Megan's mother and father are in conflict about treatment. She's in serious denial. And she seemed confused when I asked why they hadn't come in when the symptoms first presented."

"The dad?"

"He says he moved them up here for business and to be near the best cancer center he'd found. He travels a good deal and had told his wife to bring her in. She apparently kept putting it off."

"They're both in Megan's room now?" Sara scooted her boxes behind her desk and then slipped on her lab coat. It'd be the last time she donned one of these for hospital rounds for who knew how long.

"Yes, they're expecting me."

"Maybe we should, um, pray before we go."

Marilynn nodded and waited, but Sara held back. Ever since Frank's funeral, she'd been open to Clint's leading them in prayer again. But praying out loud with someone else still felt awkward.

Finally Marilynn stepped in with a prayer for discernment and wise words. Sara added her amen, and they left the office together.

Minutes later, Marilynn knocked on the fourth-floor patient room door. "Come in," a deep male voice responded.

Sara followed Marilynn through the wooden door and surveyed the inhabitants while Marilynn greeted them. Megan Carter, a little five-year-old china doll, slept soundly in bed, flanked by a handsome blond man in a tailored suit and a woman near Sara's age.

Sara's heart constricted.

"This is Dr. Sara Rollins."

"Tim Kramer." The man extended a hand. "And this is Donna

Carter." Sara shook hands with Megan's mother and father. On closer inspection the dad appeared older than she'd first thought, maybe early forties.

"I'm here to discuss your reservations about Dr. Richards's treatment recommendations."

Ms. Carter returned to her seat and started to speak, but her partner cut her off. "We appreciate Dr. Richards's advice but had hoped for a less invasive and more positive option for Meg."

Marilynn nodded and spoke first. "I've also consulted with Dr. Holland, our most experienced bone-marrow specialist, and he agrees that the blood-forming stem-cell transplant is Megan's best and most promising option." Marilynn's voice was confident and compassionate, offering hope without overblown promises. Sara would miss working with her.

"But this procedure can't guarantee a higher cure rate."

"Given Megan's biopsy and blood-work results, the cure rate for this transplant can be anywhere from thirty to sixty percent. Definitely an improvement over the standard chemotherapy treatment options."

"And what's your opinion, Dr….um…" Mr. Kramer studied Sara's name badge. "Dr. Rollins?"

"I've also looked over the lab reports. Harvesting some of Megan's blood-forming stem cells and treating them with special antibodies while Megan undergoes high-intensity chemotherapy is a very good treatment option. Her own stem cells would be returned to her body, and then Megan would be in the hospital only until her white cell counts return to normal."

"How long would that be?" Ms. Carter's legs bounced up and down. An annoying gesture of nervousness. But understandable. Watching a child endure such treatment would make any mom struggle.

"She could be hospitalized at minimum three weeks, possibly up to six."

Tears welled in Ms. Carter's eyes. "And then Meg will be okay?"

Marilynn handed her a Kleenex. "We'll do everything in our power to make that happen."

Mr. Kramer squared his shoulders and faced them as if he were con-
cluding a particularly lucrative business deal. "I'll hold you to that.
Thank you both for meeting with us. We need to talk again before we
make a final decision." He walked over to where Ms. Carter sat looking
at Megan.

They exchanged a few parting words with Marilynn, then began a
quiet discussion.

Marilynn caught Sara's eye, lifted an eyebrow, and pointed them out
the door.

After a silent trip back to the safe haven of their offices, Marilynn
stepped into the break room and made herself a cup of Earl Grey tea.
"Aren't you glad today's your last day for a while?"

Sara sighed. "That poor little girl." She leaned against the break
counter and tore apart a cinnamon-raisin bagel. "I can't imagine being
in her mother's place. Makes me kind of ashamed."

"Ashamed? How so?"

"For being glad that Clint's odds are better."

Marilynn tilted her head. "Don't do that. It's difficult no matter
what the diagnosis. Be where you are. Pray for the other patients, but
don't compare. That does no good."

Her best friend was right again, but Sara still felt horrid. And at the
same time relieved that Clint's treatment wouldn't require another hospital stay.

As long as he steered clear of infection. That would be her challenge
for the next three months.

That...and holding on to hope.

15

Michael looked up from his case files and groaned.

Maxwell's barked orders only compounded the day's many annoyances. First the steady morning rain and then a slew of new cases. Sure didn't bode well for the rest of the week.

The whole floor fell silent ten minutes later, and he stood to see why. Watching over partitioned walls, he saw Kessler and some bald guy dressed in a dark suit walking across the floor. The sight didn't do anything for him. Certainly not move him to silence.

He returned to his chair and stared at the computer screen in front of him. The computer forensics labs were backed up just like all the lab units downstairs. It'd be ages before he could get a report on Standish's computer. The Virginia field office's first pass at Standish's high-end machine had yielded no leads. So the regional examiners in New Jersey were working their magic on the computer's entrails.

"Michael?"

He turned to stand at the sound of his name, but then fell back into the swivel chair, his mouth hanging open.

"It was a shock to my mirror too."

Clint stood his full six-foot-five height, but he looked smaller somehow. His totally hairless head must have triggered the silence a few minutes ago. Michael couldn't help but stare.

When Clint cleared his throat, Michael jumped and fumbled for something normal to say. "It's good to have you back."

"You might not be so glad when you hear the conditions." Clint pulled his gray-and-black desk chair across the floor and sat down. "I didn't make performance review."

The words hit like a fist blow. Why couldn't Clint handle the physical assessment?

"Steven didn't tell you?"

Michael clinched his jaw. "Tell me what?"

"Steven was supposed to let everyone know I have cancer."

Again Michael's head felt like a boxer had clocked his cheek. Maybe he should have guessed because of Clint's new look, but it never crossed his mind. An agent with cancer. The words didn't fit; they didn't make sense. Why would God let that happen? To Clint Rollins, of all people?

He couldn't form words to respond, but he had to say something. "But you're still able to work, right? And you'll beat the cancer?" He hated the crackling teenager sound of his voice.

"That's where you come in." At least Clint's smile seemed the same. "I get to come back on limited desk duty as long as you'll help me keep up with the donkeywork."

Michael looked over the senior agent in front of him. He wanted to say he'd pray, that he'd do anything to help. But he only nodded.

Clint ran his hand over his empty holster and forced a chuckle. "And watch my back if any terrorist charges the floor?"

Michael didn't see the humor in an agent without a gun.

"You two going to do any work today or what?" Even Kessler's voice sounded strained as he clasped Clint by the shoulder.

Michael struggled to assimilate the news.

The world spun the wrong way on this first Monday in March.

❈   ❈   ❈

Clint forced his eyes to focus on Lee as the younger agent diagramed cases on the conference room board.

"The first ViCAP case is Luke Davis, missing in January three years ago from a park in Lexington, Kentucky. No body and no leads from follow-up interviews." Lee stuck a red pin on a wall map of the United States.

Michael flipped through files. "Credit card statements place Standish and a guest at the Keeneland track kitchen for breakfast near the time of Luke's disappearance."

Taking a drink from his massive jug of water, Clint squinted as he tried to remember how the possible guest tied in. "Do we know who this guest was?"

"From Billy Raeford's confession, we can place him there with Standish."

"And who is Billy Raeford again?"

The three men around him stared. Steven jumped to answer first. "He's the man we apprehended in Blacksburg in connection with Wes Standish's kidnapping. The one who shot you, remember? He died in jail."

Clint didn't remember ever seeing the man who shot him or hearing his name. But judging from the looks, he'd been told this information already. Probably more than once. But he refused to prove Sara right about his needing to stay home longer, so he concentrated harder. Bad enough that he'd failed to make assessments.

Lee turned back to the board and wrote a series of new names. New to Clint, anyway. "Next we have John Reed, age six, missing in January two years ago from a park in Cincinnati, Ohio. Again, we have credit card and phone records placing Standish at a casino twenty minutes from Cincinnati."

Another red pin on the map.

"Third case is another boy, age five, Niles Shore." Lee added another pin, and Clint shifted in his seat, his muscles aching from all the walking this morning. "Missing in late January last year from Pittsburgh, Pennsylvania. This child deviates from the possible pattern. He was apparently abducted while on his way home from school. But according to an older brother's statement, they stopped at a park first, and he last saw Niles talking to an adult he'd never seen before."

"Could easily be that the parents didn't want the older brother blamed in any way, so they left the park out of their story." Steven stood and grabbed another pin. "It still showed up on our radar because Niles fits the brown-haired, blue-eyed physical description, and the kidnapping occurred in January. And I just received another cold case the Child Abduction Center in Quantico flagged."

"How old?" Michael's fingers flew over his keyboard.

"January, this year. Six-year-old Chuck Little from Atlantic City, New Jersey. No one reported him missing for days because he was a chronic runaway getting shuffled through the foster-care system. When he couldn't be found in any of his usual places, his caseworker finally filed a report. But it didn't get submitted to ViCAP until local investigators exhausted all leads and found nothing. He matches the physical profile and time of year missing."

Clint leaned his right arm on the table. "But if he's really part of our serial kidnapper's case, doesn't that rule out Standish?"

"Not necessarily." Michael studied the board. "We don't know the exact date in January Chuck disappeared. Say Standish spent time in Atlantic City feeding his gambling habit while waiting for news about Wes. He finds Chuck, does his deal, and then goes to Blacksburg to pick up his son. When that doesn't happen, he gets frustrated and goes trolling in Charleston and finds Mattie."

"That would make two kidnappings this January, not counting Wes." Clint thought he'd gotten that straight. "If he's a serial, that indicates he's beginning to decompensate."

"Exactly." Michael continued typing. "That's why we need to keep pushing and find the guy. Because even if he hasn't hurt Mattie yet, he's most likely going to."

Clint's head hurt. It was too much all at once on his first day back. He shouldn't have expected any less.

"We've verified Jim's story about the money his folks kept hidden at home and the cash sales of his parents' belongings. So Standish isn't hurting for money." Lee crossed his arms. "And we know Standish is involved in two kidnappings. Wes and Mattie. We have eyewitness statements, Jim Standish's confession and his missing truck, plus Ed Standish's fingerprints at the cabin."

Clint rubbed his temples. "So you think Standish killed some kids but kept Mattie alive? If he's been reported with one boy, why wouldn't he have Chuck with him too? Or the others?"

"Maybe Mattie's the only one who didn't fight." Lee shrugged. "It's happened before, you know. Pedophiles prefer victims who buy into their games."

"That's possible. One angle we need to discuss further." Steven checked his watch. "Let's take a break and revisit this issue after lunch. But first, Lee, I'd like you to go back over what we know on Standish and see if we can place him around Atlantic City in January."

"On it, boss." Lee left the room.

An administrative assistant stuck her head in the room. "Agent Kessler, you have a call on line one. Name's Samantha Reynolds. Says she has an update on her son's disappearance."

Steven hightailed it out of the room.

Enjoying the quiet, Clint laid his head back on the chair.

Michael broke the silence. "How'd you feel going through assessments again?"

"Like a spindly fifth-grader in the boy's locker room."

"That bad?"

"Worse."

Clint looked up to see Michael on his feet, studying the floor. The younger agent shrugged on his coat. "You want to come to Union Station and grab some Asian food with me?"

"No thanks. I'm not helping out much here, and my head is killing me." Clint stood and fought a wave of dizziness. "I should go home."

Steven returned, stony-faced. "Samantha Reynolds got a call this morning from an unidentified person. Some heavy breathing, but nothing said. She believes it was Mattie."

"What makes her think it was Mattie and not some pervert?"

"She said it sounded like her son." He shrugged. "I don't want to doubt a mother's intuition, but…"

"I'll start an inquiry into her phone records and see if we can pinpoint the location of the call." Michael flipped his laptop closed.

"No need. Virginia field office is on it. But you can follow up with them and see what they've learned." He held up a warning hand as Michael started out the door. "Don't even think of running with this yourself, Parker. You have plenty of other cases to keep you busy without chasing after long shots."

Michael lifted his jaw and sped out of the room.

"Lighten up on the kid. He's holding out hope that Mattie is still alive."

"At this point, it's unlikely. You know that."

Clint shook his head. "It's not like you to give up so soon." He leaned back and grimaced. "I know you and Maxwell are taking a chance having me back here. And I hate to do it, but I'm not gonna make it much past a half day."

Steven ran a hand through his hair. "I need you here as much as you can be. But I want you healthy too. Go home and rest."

"Thanks. See you tomorrow." Clint rubbed his left arm and made his way back to his desk. Struggling to stay awake, he gathered notes to review at one o'clock that morning when he couldn't sleep.

Michael joined him. "I'll be praying for you." He shuffled his black shoe. "I just wanted you to know that."

"It means a lot, Michael." Clint scanned the large room with tired eyes. "I'll see you both tomorrow."

He hoped.

✸ ✸ ✸

"So are you going to tell me what the distant look in your eyes is all about?" Gracie's gentle challenge startled Steven.

"For a kiss."

She obliged.

He grinned and then pulled her hand toward Union Station's bustling food court. "Let's get some food and get you back to school before your headmistress comes after me."

"I doubt Mrs. Hall will have anything unkind to say about my leaving an in-service day for a short time. In fact, she suggested we take an extended break. We're going over all the new security protocols, and it's a lot to process." Gracie stepped closer to his side and hugged him.

Everything in Steven begged for the memories from last November to disappear. Good thing Gracie taught in a school where high-ranking government officials brought their children. People with clout demanded the best security measures available.

"Where's Hanna?" He looked around, needing some relief from the specters that still popped up at the most inopportune times. He'd never wanted to kill a man as much as he had the one who'd kidnapped and tried to kill Gracie. And his current investigation didn't help matters. After a frustrating morning, maybe having his fiancée meet him for lunch wasn't the best idea, even if it was the only time he'd see her today.

"Hanna and James are shopping and riding the escalators. They'll be here in a minute."

He raised an eyebrow. "I thought Dad had James today."

Gracie linked arms with him. "Hanna had the day off, and she couldn't stand the thought of James being stuck in the house all day because it's still too cold and wet to play outside. So I thought it would be good for us all to do something fun together. Besides, James loves seeing his daddy any chance he gets."

His heart constricted. He knew Gracie meant his son adored him. But guilt over his long hours died hard. Maybe in a few years he'd step aside and give Clint or Parker a shot as the CACU's head coordinator. He'd even contemplated setting up as a private investigator.

Someday.

"Hey, big brother." He tensed as Hanna appeared at his side.

"You have to stop doing that. You're making me look bad." He grabbed her in a hug and lifted his son from her other arm. "How's my little man?"

James's blue eyes danced. "I'm good. I get to see you."

Only his little boy could make him feel so important.

Gracie scanned the food-court selections. "How does a gyro sound? And then some Ben & Jerry's Chunky Monkey."

Steven grinned. He'd rather just look at his fiancée. Her smile and wink did the same job on his heart as his son's words.

Well, different reason. Same fullness in his chest.

They ordered and found seats a few minutes later. James grabbed his hand. "Are you going to pray, Daddy?"

Steven nodded and bowed his head. "Lord, thank You for this day and for the amazing company of my favorite people. You are so good to me. Amen."

Everyone dug in.

"So why didn't you invite Michael to lunch?" With her black plastic fork, Hanna cut into the egg roll she'd ordered from the Asian restaurant. The greasy thing shot off her plate and onto the floor. Red-faced, she bent to retrieve it.

Stephen sipped his Coke. "I didn't want to invite Parker."

Gracie nudged him with her foot.

Hanna sat up and shook her head at him.

"I think Mr. Parker likes Aunt Hanna. Don't you, Daddy?" James attacked his rice and vegetables.

"Don't know." His little boy had no idea how on target his powers of perception were or how much the comment irked Steven. He hadn't wanted to introduce Parker and Hanna in the first place. But he and Parker had been working together in Baltimore the day of Hanna's moving party. It would've been beyond rude not to invite Parker when Lee couldn't make it. Neither Hanna nor Parker had mentioned the evening since, but Steven had seen the mutual interest. And knowing Parker's past, he didn't want Michael dating his sister.

Hanna's crystal blue eyes squinted with mischief. "I doubt the man would even ask for my number, what with you and Clint scrutinizing his every move."

"I intend to watch him like a hawk if he ever does ask you out."

"I bet you do. But—"

"Speaking of Michael." Gracie nodded her head toward the food counters behind him.

He turned. Sure enough, Parker stood waiting for his daily Asian fix at Panda's Rice Bowl.

"Why don't you ask him to join us?" Gracie's eyes challenged. Steven stifled an irritated response. They'd have to discuss her misguided matchmaking.

Walking over to Parker, he wondered what Clint would think about this situation. "I've been sent to ask you to join us."

Parker looked over to where Steven pointed and tried to hide a grin. "I don't want to impose."

Guilt over his recent conduct toward Parker, one of the best rookies he'd worked with, jabbed at Steven's conscience. "My family wouldn't see it as such."

"Really?" Parker cleared his throat. "I mean, sure, I'd like to join you."

Looking Michael straight in the eyes, Steven wanted to get his point across in no uncertain terms. "Hanna's special to me. Don't mess her over."

The twenty-eight-year-old stretched his neck and nodded. He'd gotten the message. They returned to the lunch table in silence.

"Hey, Mr. Parker!" James wiggled in his seat.

Parker gave James a high-five and smiled at the women. Then he pulled a chair over to sit next to Hanna.

Gracie smiled. "It's good to see you again, Michael."

"Thank you. It's good to see you all too." Parker took his beef and rice off the tray and bowed his head.

That scored points with Hanna. She smiled and studied her food.

Gracie wiped her hands on her napkin. "How was Clint's first day back to work?"

He'd known she would figure out his earlier distant look. "He's okay. Not himself yet. But he'll get back to full speed soon."

Parker made short work of his meal. "You sure? I mean, I don't know how he's going to work as much as he wants to. It looks like the chemo is really taking a toll."

James's eyes widened. "Daddy, you said Mr. Clint was going to be better soon, right?"

"Yes." Steven spoke through clenched teeth. "And he will be. We're all praying for that."

Parker closed his eyes. "Sorry. I didn't mean to imply..."

Steven scowled.

Gracie shot a warning glance his way but spoke to Parker with a soothing voice. "We know. The first time seeing Clint was hard on all of us."

Hanna caught Steven's gaze and narrowed her eyes, then quickly turned to Michael. "Are you coming to Clint's party Wednesday?"

"I'm planning to." Parker didn't look anyone in the eye.

"Maybe my big brother won't be such a bear then." Hanna crinkled her nose at him. "Did you know I can still sneak up on him?"

Everyone laughed. Steven forced a grin, then glanced at his watch. "Well, ladies and my little man." Steven squeezed his son's shoulder as he stood. "I've enjoyed lunch, but I need to head back to work."

"Me too." Parker stood and took his and Hanna's trays to the trash can. Her eyes followed him all the way. Steven bit his tongue.

"Will you be home before bedtime, Daddy?" James looked up at him with hopeful eyes.

"Yes. I'll read you a story when I get home."

"All right!"

Steven cleared the rest of the trays and then walked outside Union Station with his arm around Gracie.

"I still have some time before I need to head back to Hope Ridge, so the three of us are going to do a little shopping." Gracie pressed a quick peck to his cheek. Steven responded with a real kiss. He reluctantly pulled back and saw Hanna roll her eyes.

Too much PDA for his baby sister? Too bad.

After James and Hanna hugged him, Steven and Parker wove their way through tourists, heading back to the Hoover Building.

"Regardless of what you do or don't do in terms of asking my sister out, let's keep work and off-duty separate."

"Fine by me."

Steven held the door for Parker. "Ready to see if Standish was in Atlantic City?"

"That and drop kick him into jail."

On that at least, he and Parker agreed.

16

He scanned the packed playground Tuesday afternoon with practiced disinterest.

Once more, someone's incompetence had nearly cost him everything. That wouldn't happen again.

And someone would pay.

"Mommy, I need to go potty." A little blond girl skipped off by herself to the rest rooms on his left. Her bouncing curls and pink dress might attract a different type, but not him. Still, she shouldn't be out of her mother's sight.

One never knew what could happen.

Another child caught his attention. He lowered the hardback book he'd been busy highlighting moments ago like a college kid studying for an exam. Under most circumstances he could still pass for a student.

The little brown-haired boy looked about six. He walked to the water fountain and took a long drink. Beyond the boy and the gray stone rest room area, he could see children on swings and play gyms. The huge mass of children swarming the playground couldn't have been better cover. To his right side were baseball fields and a wooded lakefront. Within a short walking distance, more parking lots offered quick access to the park's entrance.

Easy escape.

Now all he had to do was get the needle in the little boy's arm and walk out of there, past the baseball fields as if his son had fallen asleep on his shoulder.

Piece of cake.

Rummaging in his dark blue backpack, he found some bubble

gum. The book and highlighter disappeared into the bottom of the sack, and he hoisted it over his shoulder.

"Afternoon. How'd you like some bubble gum?" He popped a piece in his mouth to curb any fear that the gum might be poisoned. The other piece he held out for the little boy to take.

The six-year-old stepped forward, eyebrows raised into his wild bangs.

Two more steps and he'd be close enough. He felt the tiny needle in his left hand, ready to inject. His heart hammered his chest and the rush of adrenaline charged him. The pressure starting to build inside would be quickly appeased.

"Mom!" the little boy screamed and ran off to his right.

Curses spilled out. But he forced himself to turn around and walk slowly past the rest rooms and past the ball fields. No need to arouse suspicion and make other people start looking. No need to get his license plate scribbled down. He'd learned well how to cover his tracks, but there was no need to tempt fate.

His hands started to sweat as he recapped the needle and replayed the past few seconds. Passing pine trees that swayed in the moderate breeze, he checked his watch. He cursed again as he spotted the blue rental car.

The boy had been just within reach. Then the stupid kid screamed.

No worried mother had looked up to see, though. And no footsteps followed him now.

He punched the unlock button on the key ring and threw his backpack into the passenger seat. The black hood and blanket in the back wouldn't be used today.

He started the engine and slipped out of the park without a backward glance.

Tomorrow.

There was always tomorrow.

※   ※   ※

Pastry bag in hand, Hanna put the finishing touches on Clint's birthday cake.

Steven entered the kitchen and poked her in the ribs. "It's looking good, little sister."

"Hey, lay off. You'll make me mess up the cake."

"Even dropped, that piece of sugar shock would look good. It's not as good as your photography, but it's close." He smiled and stood at her side watching her work.

"You think it's good enough?" She studied the green and gold cake. Maybe the end-of-the-rainbow design was a bit over the top. "It's definitely better than your over-the-hill theme."

"I had to put that one on hold for a little while. But I will do it for Clint's big four-o next year. And you can make that one too." Steven crossed the kitchen and pulled more plates and silverware from the cabinet and utensil drawer.

"Aren't those Gracie's dishes?"

Steven grinned. "She'll call this home soon too."

"The sooner the better." Gracie stood smiling in the kitchen doorway. Steven put down the plates and went over to her.

Her future sister-in-law looked like springtime in a peach sweater set and coordinating flower-print skirt. Hanna sighed. Gracie and Steven made a great couple, sickening sweetness and all.

Hanna touched up a few letters on the cake. "When will Clint and Sara be here?"

"Sara said they'd be about half an hour. Everyone else should follow shortly afterward, by seven." Steven turned to Gracie. "Erica's already upstairs with James, Susannah, and Jonathan, right? I want them in bed early. Sleepover or not, it's a school night."

"Yes. Clint's parents are with them too." Gracie added napkins to Steven's stack of white china on the counter. "James and Susannah are already worn out from decorating on top of a busy day at school. And Clint's parents spent the day at the park with Jonathan, so I'm sure he'll be ready to crash soon."

"It'll be good for Clint and Sara to have some alone time with his parents after the party." Steven grabbed a soda from the fridge. "As long as they don't talk about cancer all night. Seeing Clint was a shock for them. But I still don't want cancer to be tonight's focus."

"You could always do karaoke." Hanna smirked.

Steven almost spewed his soda. "And let Clint rib me about being an FBI singing telegram? Not on your life."

"Yeah, maybe not. You do have to work with these guys." They all laughed and returned to their tasks.

Hanna wiped her hands on her brother's silly "Kiss the Cook" apron and reached up to adjust her loose ponytail. Inspecting herself in the mirror this morning, knowing she'd be coming here directly after work, she'd tried hard to appear professional without being frumpy. Michael might not know she was thirty, and she had no intention of looking a day older than that.

The burgundy patterned skirt and simple cream shirt sticking out from under a tan jacket felt comfortable and in style. Or they had this morning anyway. Now she wasn't so sure.

The fact that she even cared made her insides quiver.

Steven and Gracie disappeared into the dining room with the stack of dishes and napkins. Picking up her piping tools, Hanna started to wash them in the sink. Why did she care if Michael Parker found her attractive?

Last time a man felt that way toward her...

She shook her head. She'd promised herself and God she wouldn't go there anymore.

"So how's the staff training coming along?" Her dad's calming presence filled the kitchen.

She dried her hands and returned his hug. "We're on track for our grand opening on Monday. Bakery accounts are all set up, and the storeroom is well stocked. We'll finish the training this week, and then I think we'll be ready. This venture into a mall environment will be good for your coffee business."

"I can't wait to come in and help out. As long as this store keeps you nearby, I'm content." Dad helped her remove the apron without damaging her very hair-sprayed ponytail. "I'm glad you moved, honey. I've missed having you live close."

Her heart settled down. Being around her dad did that to her.

"Are you planning to hang some of your prints in the store? You could even do a showing there one evening. That'd be great for the shop and should help your photography business too."

"I'm not quite ready for that." She dried the last of her decorating supplies. "But I will put up some of my landscapes and maybe a few black-and-white portraits."

"Whatever you're comfortable with. I won't push as long as you keep going with the photography. You have a gift, Hanna. And your eyes dance whenever you have a camera in your hand."

She reached over and gave him another hug. "Thanks, Dad. Your support means so much."

She stowed her decorating tools under the sink and grabbed her camera from the counter, enjoying its perfect fit in her hand. Capturing beautiful images on film made her come alive like nothing else.

No wonder she loved photography.

It was the one thing she knew without a doubt she did well.

❊   ❊   ❊

"You know, Clint, we've done some research online about detoxification and colon cleansing, also fasting and chelation." Clint's dad pointed to his wife. "We printed the articles for you. I'll pull them out of our luggage when we get back to the house."

Steven clenched his teeth to keep from saying something rude. He'd listened to their well-meaning friends talk about dandelions and teas and diets till he almost burst. None of it had helped his mom. He doubted whether any of it would help Clint either.

Sara tugged on his arm, and he followed her into the dining room. "You're a good friend, but Clint can hold his own, so stop scowling at the advice people give. This is an emotionally healthy bunch. A little shaken with his cancer, but nothing they've said yet is harmful." Sara glanced at the floor, then met his eyes. "We have a little announcement to make before we eat, okay?"

His stomach growled. The kids were getting antsy, and the finger-food appetizers had only left him hungry for real food. Clint had requested a simple meal of hamburgers, fries, and salad fixings. All organic. Hadn't been too hard to comply. Just expensive.

"Not a problem." He narrowed his eyes. "You're not moving or anything, are you?"

Sara brightened into her Irish princess smile. "Let's get this show on the road, and you'll find out." She put a hand on his arm. "It's nothing you'll hate. I promise."

They returned to the living room, where Sara rejoined Clint and his parents. Steven looked for Gracie amid the bright green streamers and balloons crowding his formal dining room. Only a few agents and their families stood around the Kentucky cherrywood table. They all looked as hungry as he felt.

He walked to the back of the house through the kitchen to see if Gracie had retreated onto the glass-enclosed back porch. He found her sitting in a light brown wicker love seat with her eyes closed and head bowed. Leaning against the door frame, he waited till she looked up.

"Hey, beautiful."

She smiled. "Did I miss the birthday song?"

"Were you trying to?" He crossed the room and pulled her into his arms. "I think you have a wonderful voice, so I can't imagine that's why you're back here."

She took a deep breath. "I was praying for Clint and the rest of the group."

He looked down into her hazel eyes. "Why?"

"I've been watching and listening since all the changes started. Clint's diagnosis, Hanna's move."

He nodded as they sat back down on the wicker love seat.

"I've seen how Clint's the leader in your group. Everyone depends on him. Even you."

"No argument there. He's always been light-years ahead of me spiritually and as a parent. Plus, he's a hulk. It's hard not to think of him as a rock of sorts."

"But now he needs to lean on Sara and you more, so those roles are reversing a little. Sara's staying home to support Clint and taking over more household responsibilities that Clint used to do, like yard work and such. She's also stepping in to help him remember little things he's forgetting. So are you. You're all protecting him, and that's good. It's part of God's provision, especially in times of crises." Gracie shrugged. "I was just praying that the adjustments continue smoothly and thanking Him for the growth I'm seeing in how everyone's handling this situation."

Except he didn't want this type of growth. Didn't want to trade places with his best friend.

"But you're not adapting where Hanna is concerned."

He disliked this turn of conversation more than the last part. "I don't understand."

"The way I see it, you've always been a third parent to her. And you moved even deeper into the protector role when you lost your mom."

"That's what big brothers do."

"I know. And I love that you care about her so much. But Hanna is a grown woman who needs to be free from living in your shadow and doing everything to please you." Gracie took his hand. "I'm not saying you should stop loving her. Just back off a little. And stop trying to scare Michael away. He's a good man, Steven. A lot like you. Give him a chance."

He opened his mouth to argue, then realized he couldn't. He didn't like what Gracie was saying, but he'd come to trust her gentle observations. He still felt responsible for Hanna. But maybe he should back off. A little.

Clint cleared his throat in the doorway. "I know I'm interrupting, but you'll get used to that." He chuckled. "Everyone's asking when we're gonna eat, so will you come get the meal started with a prayer? A nice, short one? And remember we have an announcement to make."

Steven nodded. "I'll be right there." He tugged Gracie's hand to follow Clint into the living room. "We'll talk more later."

A strange mix of emotions rocketed through him as he gathered everyone together for Sara and Clint's announcement. Relief that Clint was doing well enough to rib him a little. Unsure about what his friends had to share. And troubled by Gracie's words concerning his sister. They stirred something inside. He didn't know how to think differently about Hanna. She'd always accepted his big-brother protection.

Sara's dramatic pause captured his attention. "...And while we so appreciate your prayers for Clint's cancer, we'd also like to share some joyful news that we hope you'll pray about too."

He stood up straighter.

Clint pulled Sara tighter to his side. "We'd like to announce the arrival of another Rollins, scheduled for early October. Not too long after Steven's birthday."

Steven blinked. A few ladies squealed. Clint's parents practically squeezed Sara and Clint to death, while Gracie and Hanna and all the others crowded around the happy couple. He caught his partner's look over the excited bobbing heads and smiled.

A baby.

"So you gonna tell me I'm crazy to have another baby in my old age?" Clint asked a few minutes later.

"Not on your life, partner. I think it's great."

Clint sank into the dark brown leather couch near the stone fireplace. "Glad to hear it." He looked across the crowded room and smiled at his wife, who was still receiving well wishes. "I appreciate your postponing the all-black decorations till next year. The big four-o is when they're supposed to happen anyway."

"I'm going to do that one up even bigger. You can count on it."

"I know."

"Gracie and I were talking—"

But Clint had drifted off to sleep, right in the middle of all the loud chatter.

Sara appeared at Steven's side. "Would you be okay if the others went ahead and ate? I'll make a plate for him later."

"Does he fall asleep like that often? Right in the middle of things?"

"For a few days after chemo, yes. But going back to work has drained him too." She pulled Steven's red and black Louisville Cardinals throw over him. "He'll wake up before too long."

That didn't help at all.

It was too much like his mom. Way too much, in fact.

※   ※   ※

By ten o'clock everyone had eaten and said their good-nights. The kids were sound asleep too. All in all, it'd been a great party. Steven helped Gracie and Sara take down the decorations in the living room. Hanna and Parker were in the kitchen boxing up leftovers.

He was being good and staying away from them.

Clint took a swig of his ever-present water. "How were the hamburgers?"

Steven chuckled and sat down. "Gourmet quality, if I do say so myself. We saved you some."

"Did I snore?"

"No."

"How'd my parents handle me falling asleep?"

"They were a little startled, but Sara assured everyone you were okay." He rubbed his hands over his trousers. "You sure you'll be able to handle work after tomorrow's chemo?"

"Not till later next week. That draino they call medicine wipes me out worse than this. I think I need to take it a little slower."

"I agree."

"Good." Clint stood to stretch. "Any case news I missed yesterday afternoon?"

"We continued Monday's discussion on possible scenarios of what Standish might have done with the children. Then Tuesday's workload piled things higher on all our desks."

"What about that case in Louisville? I'm having trouble keeping it all straight. Remind me what happened."

"Louisville Metro's CSI folks examined the child's crushed skull and broken bones and concluded blunt-force trauma was the likely cause of death. When the mom saw her second husband beating their son on the head, she couldn't ignore the warning signs anymore and didn't want to lose another child. Once they got the husband in for questioning, it didn't take long to get a confession about the murder and burying the body five years ago."

"I'll never understand perps like that." Clint sat back down and wiped his nose. He'd done that all night. Without eyebrows, his expressions were different too. "I know it's crazy, but I had this dream about a thirteen-year-old situation from back in my military days. Won't leave me alone, so I'm thinking maybe it's related. I kept forgetting to mention it to you, but I finally wrote down what I remember about the case. No leads from the little Internet work I've been able to do yet. But if I can ever get caught up on work reading, I'll look into it further."

That didn't sound like a promising lead. Probably nothing more than the chemo messing with Clint's mind. What bothered Steven more was Clint's slipping memory. He just didn't forget details like that. Well, didn't used to forget anyway.

"Hey, guys." Hanna glided in from the kitchen with a smile. She bent down to hug Clint. "I wanted to say good night."

Steven stood. "If you'll hang on a minute, I can follow you home."

Hanna shook her head. "Not necessary. I am an adult, you know." She looked to Clint for some backup.

"Don't look at me like that. I'm not getting in between the two of you for any reason."

Steven pulled his sister to him in a sideways hug. "Humor me. I'm just concerned about your safety."

She snorted. "More like insanely overprotective."

He shoved his hands into his pockets. "Are you going out with Parker tonight?"

"No. What do you have against him anyway? He's a nice guy."

"Yeah, but things with Craig didn't go so well, and I don't want you rushing into another situation that could turn out the same way. I just don't think Michael is right for you. He—"

"Good night." Hanna stormed out and slammed the door.

Steven followed close behind. Talk about blowing it.

17

The bright lights of a Las Vegas casino glared throughout the College Park restaurant. One of the waitresses he'd met there earlier in the day had suggested he join her for her boss's gambling-themed birthday party.

How could he pass up such a pleasant Friday night diversion? It'd been awhile since he'd allowed himself a night on the town.

His reordered plans were unfolding more or less according to schedule. But the pressure continued growing. It demanded far more and far sooner than in years past. In the end, only one thing would appease it. But maybe this distraction would help him relax.

Maybe it'd be enough for the time being.

"Hey, babe. I see you made it back my way. Wanna start at the blackjack table or play some poker?"

He'd always fared well at casinos. And he'd visited some of the finest during his travels. Winning was a matter of discipline, self-control, knowing when to stop. And he enjoyed the challenge of matching wits with the house. But this little theme party couldn't possibly boast a real payoff. "What kind of prizes are here for the taking?"

"Mostly trinkets. Some bigger prizes for the high winners at the end of the night. A plasma screen TV and a trip to the real Vegas." The perky redhead sidled up closer to him. She wasn't family material or his usual, more sophisticated date, but she'd do for one evening of adult conversation. "What say we pool our winnings and see if we can't win that trip out west?"

The possibility of honing his skill and a free trip to Las Vegas became instantly more appealing. "Shall we?"

Several hours and some watered-down martinis later, the novelty of the party wore thin. No real smooth dealers to challenge him. Most other guests were too drunk to match wits verbally or at cards. Memories of Atlantic City increased his distaste for the evening's festivities.

This wasn't enough distraction either.

He needed more. Always more.

※　※　※

Clint woke with a jerk and looked around as Sara hunted for a parking place in downtown Alexandria early Monday afternoon. Gray skies and budding green trees mixed in a confusing blur. He hated falling asleep all the time. He hated the pity in people's eyes more. And the stranger in the mirror he hated most of all.

He'd begun second-guessing his decision to tell people at church about the cancer too.

"We gonna get some 'tuffs for my baby sister?" Jonathan bounced in his car seat, doting grandparents keeping him company in the backseat.

"Yes, we're going to look at some things for a nursery. But we don't know if it's a boy or a girl, so we probably won't buy much stuff today." Sara gently corrected Jonathan's almost-three-year-old verbal miscues.

"So your numbers were good when you went to the center on Thursday?" Dad wouldn't let up with the research and questions. Clint's increased fatigue after last week's chemo had revived a wealth of worries for his father. But Sara had handled everything so well during the first part of their two-week visit. He was trying to do the same.

"Not bad. My ANC was 910.23."

"So your blood work shows a moderate infection risk. Better keep up with your Neulasta shots."

"We've got it covered, Dad." Sara pulled the silver Range Rover into a front row parking place close to a specialty baby store.

"Ice c'eam, Grammy?"

"We'll see. Maybe later. First let's find a nice gift for the baby, okay?"

" 'Kay."

The five of them entered the large baby store and looked around. Mom and Sara oohed and aahed over every stitch of little girl things. He and Jonathan sat by a rack of kid's books and started reading. Dad listened close by, pretending to look at baby furniture. Struggling to keep his eyes open, Clint suggested a walk outside.

"Gramps, you comin'?" Jonathan started coughing and wiped his nose on his sleeve.

Dad hurried over. "You okay there, champ? Not getting sick, are you?"

"He's fine, Dad. Kids cough. Please. Can we just get through the rest of this outing without worrying about germs or cancer or all the rest of it?"

"I'm sorry, son. I just…well, I'm concerned."

"Join the club."

"Clint. Don't sass me. Let us help. I'll try to be more subtle about it, okay?"

Subtle like a sledgehammer.

He should be thankful for everyone's concern. And he would be, if all the attention didn't leave him feeling like a gigantic baby living in some stupid plastic bubble.

❋ ❋ ❋

Steven shut his cell phone with a little too much force.

The restaurant sounds behind him forced him to shove his welling emotions to the background, where they would stew until he was steady enough to deal with them.

Gracie's gentle touch on his shoulders startled him.

"You okay?"

He turned to face her. "No. But I'll get there." He returned his phone to its clip. "Clint completely forgot about dinner tonight. Sara said to go ahead with the planning and they'll set another time to catch up on details."

"He'll be okay, Steven. He'll make it to the wedding." Gracie took his hand and tugged him back toward the table.

All the Irish décor in the place reminded him again of Sara and Clint. Maybe coming to Bennigan's wasn't the best idea. They'd set it up in honor of Sara as a fun night out to talk wedding plans. Not her favorite Irish hangout, but close enough.

Some fun. The pain in his jaw muscles increased with every step through the restaurant. His best man should be here to help plan things.

He hated cancer. The way it changed people. The fear it generated. The anger that made him feel guilty and then more angry. Same emotions he'd cycled through countless times during his mom's slow decline.

Gracie's college roommate and her husband watched them return to the table. "Clint okay? We were hoping to see him again. It's been awhile."

Leah McDaniel was one of the few lawyers Steven liked. Good thing, because she was Gracie's closest friend and a major force behind the push to get wedding plans under way. They only had three and a half months to make it come together. Which was plenty as far as he was concerned, although Gracie assured him it was a very short time.

"Clint's not feeling well. His chemotherapy is really doing a number on him." When the waiter appeared, Steven handed his menu over and ordered without thinking. Everyone else followed his lead.

"That's rough." Kevin looked him square in the eyes. "All this has thrown a major kink in your wedding plans, hasn't it?"

Steven stared. Kevin made it sound like Clint's life-threatening illness was a scheduling glitch.

Gracie nodded. "It has been hard. But we're trusting Clint will be there, and we're planning for that."

They all watched basketball on the TV monitors for a few minutes before the waiter returned with their salads. Kevin said a quick blessing. Then Leah took up the business at hand while they ate. "So we're settled about having the ceremony at the school chapel?"

Gracie brightened. "It's the perfect place. We've both had big church weddings and would prefer to go smaller this time. Plus, Hope Ridge is where we first met."

"The chapel is one of the things I loved when we were first considering private schools for William." Leah took a bite of salad and swallowed before continuing. "All that high-tech security gets a little old, but after the shooting last year, I'm thankful for it."

Steven agreed. Though he didn't consider a discussion of last year's shooting a vast improvement over talking about Clint's cancer, he'd learned that Leah never minced words or considered any topic off-limits.

Kevin studied the green and white tablecloth. "I didn't mean to sound glib about Clint's cancer earlier." He rubbed the back of his neck. "I know it's a huge deal. But you've both gone through so much already, I just hope nothing has to alter your wedding plans."

Gracie reached across the table and squeezed Kevin's hand. "I appreciate your concern and your being real and honest, Kevin. We're praying Clint's chemo ends well and all our plans remain on track too."

Conversation turned to wedding colors and other details Steven wasn't too keen on debating. Instead, he and Kevin craned their necks to catch a few more snatches of March Madness basketball.

Until dessert time came. Then he gave his full attention to the decadent Death by Chocolate concoction he and Gracie had ordered to split. Gracie always said that chocolate, after God, was the most important part of any big decision or celebration.

That worked for him.

As long as Clint made it to the next round of planning.

18

M ama, my tummy hurts."
Jonathan's words caused Sara's stomach to flip. This Tuesday
morning hadn't started well at all. She was still throwing up
some and not getting enough sleep because of Clint's night waking.
They didn't need another illness on top of everything else.

At least Susannah had gotten off to school without incident, thanks
to Grandma and Grandpa.

"Let's check your temperature and then see if we can find something
to make that belly owie go away." She picked up her pint-sized Clint and
headed for the master bathroom. Clint was resting downstairs in the
family room, watching the end of a taped basketball game before he
went in to work. They'd agreed on his going in late and coming home
early, at least for the week after chemo.

"Why don't you tell me what Elmo is doing in your book while I
hold your arm?" She placed the white instrument under Jonathan's
skinny arm and held it in place.

"How beeg is Ehmoh?" Jonathan held his other arm high over his
full head of sleep-tangled brown hair.

She smiled. Lessening Jonathan's time in day care had been one of
her better ideas. The little digital beep commanded her attention, and
the results made her swallow hard. One hundred point two.

Not enough to head to the clinic. But enough to cause a readjust-
ment of her plans for Jonathan's nap time. While he slept, she'd scour
the house with antibacterial wipes and make sure everyone washed their
hands even more often.

She studied the dry and cracking skin on the back of her own hands. "Let's wash up before we go see Daddy."

The delicate scent of roses filled the air as she washed. The new soaps they'd found at the health-food store, rose petal, lavender, even mango, had become staples.

"How about some vanilla hand lotion?"

"Want Daddy's hand 'tuff." Jonathan hid his hands behind his back. No girly smells for him or his daddy.

She squirted a dab of the nongreasy, no-scent whiteness into his little palms without making contact. After rinsing off the bottle and returning it to Clint's sink, Sara scooped the excess from Jonathan's hands and slathered it on her elbows. No use wasting good moisturizer.

"Find me, Mama!" Jonathan took off down the hall.

Sara sighed. As her pregnancy progressed, keeping up with Jonathan wore her out more and more. How would she manage when the baby was born?

She glanced at the stack of ultrasound photos on her nightstand as she hurried out of the bedroom. They'd done an ultrasound earlier this time because of her "advanced gestational age." She was only thirty-seven, thirty-eight in October. But even though her OB insisted the age notations on her obstetrics chart only meant they needed to keep a closer eye on things, she still worried about possible complications.

So many things crowded her mind these days. Top of the list right now was finding her two-year-old and keeping him from spreading too many germs around.

Checking the book nook in each of Jonathan and Susannah's rooms produced no little brown-haired boy. She padded downstairs. No little hands smearing things about the kitchen. Then she heard giggles down in the basement family room.

"With seconds left on the shot clock, it looks like the Cardinals will advance to the Final Four." The widescreen TV blared through the room as she came down the stairs.

"That's Steven's team," Clint told Jonathan. "The University of Louisville Cardinals."

"Yay, 'Teven and James! They winned!" Jonathan gave Clint a high-five and hugged his neck.

She smiled at the tender scene.

Until Jonathan planted a huge, sloppy, little-boy kiss onto his daddy's lips.

"Jonathan, no!" She rushed to the sofa and grabbed Jonathan out of Clint's arms.

Clint looked up, confused. "Sara, what in the world?"

Jonathan's tears and the numbers on his thermometer battled for priority.

The numbers won.

"We need to not kiss Daddy right now." She held Jonathan close and looked at Clint. "He has a fever. We need to be careful."

Her husband's sad eyes nearly unraveled her resolve. He flipped the TV station and refused to respond.

Jonathan picked up his blanket and flopped back on the burgundy sofa, away from his daddy, pouting around the fingers stuck in his mouth.

She gazed at the ceiling and prayed her in-laws wouldn't return from their morning walk anytime soon.

I'm doing the best I can here, what I think is right. A little help would be good, God. Just a little?

※   ※   ※

He had to try something new. The pressure inside his head grew increasingly intense every time he thought about his child. March had not been kind to him thus far. Maybe that would change before the month ended.

He sat in the rented truck on Friday afternoon and watched the elementary school kids pass by. The frenzy of little girls with bouncing curls in the midst of a group caught his attention. The sickening memories sped around his mind.

He hated this. Hated his lack of self-control.

Hands clenched around the steering wheel, he inched forward when the crossing guard motioned for the cars to go.

All he needed to do was find one little brown-headed boy walking alone. But the only boys he'd seen were in groups. One more trip around the school, and maybe he'd get lucky. He couldn't do much worse than he'd managed last time.

He stopped for the crossing guard again and scanned the full playground.

A quick rap on his window startled him. "Sir? Do you need some help?"

Rolling down the window, he affected his best motivational-speaker voice. "I'm sorry to interrupt your important work. Not being from around here, I'm slightly turned around. If you could point me to the school office, I'll collect the information my wife requested about local elementary schools."

The woman pulled out a cell phone. "I'll get Officer Douglas over here to assist."

His hands moistened, and his mind blanked on what persona he'd just used.

Talking to a cop did not fit the plan. He'd hidden too much for too long to lose it all now.

"Uh, no, that's a very kind offer, but I'll just go back around and look for the main entrance again."

She tucked her phone away with a shrug and moved back to her post.

Now to drive away calmly so as not to arouse suspicion. Cruising a school had not been a brilliant idea. Better to find another park. Stick with what he knew. But it had to be a place he'd never visited before. Staying this close to home added to the adrenaline-rush challenge.

First stop, Wal-Mart. Gum hadn't been enough last time. He wouldn't make that mistake again.

19

"Happy Saint Patrick's Day!"

The entire staff of the Benefield Cancer Center shouted as Sara and Clint entered the Old Town Alexandria hotel ballroom. Tears stung Sara's eyes.

Happy tears this time.

The center's annual St. Patty's Day benefit celebration had been one of the many things she'd been sad about missing when she began her indefinite leave of absence. But her friends at the center had invited her anyway. And now the ornate ballroom's gold and green decorations swam before her eyes.

"I see you have donned the required colors." Marilynn smiled as she hugged them both. "You may enter without a pinch."

Sara smoothed her emerald green pantsuit. Its velvety feel comforted her while she and Clint looked around and listened to the Celtic band. Clint appeared paler than usual. But he also looked good. Tall and lean in his black dress pants and green silk shirt, his bald head reflecting the sparkling lights.

The shock of his physical changes hit her yet again. It was like dating another man. He was still handsome, still Clint. Just different.

"So to get that look from you, all I have to do is dress up a little more?" Clint's brown eyes widened and then narrowed mischievously. "And to think, I get your admiration even without my Stetson and jeans."

At least he hadn't mistaken her appraisal for doctoring. "I'm not the only one who's noticed you." She grinned and pointed her chin toward the older volunteers busying themselves with the punch and appetizers.

She'd caught them smiling and whispering among themselves as they looked in her direction a few minutes ago.

Clint chuckled and waved a greeting as they approached the drink table.

What a change from just days ago. Jonathan had recovered from his tummy trouble without much fanfare. But Clint had taken awhile to explain that her snatching away their son had registered like a slap in the face. All because of a little kiss.

It seemed silly now. But at the time it'd felt important, necessary to protect Clint. She brushed away the memory and scanned the crowd for Marilynn. She hadn't spoken to her much since leaving the cancer center two and a half weeks ago. A good gab session was definitely in order.

Marilynn waved, her green and yellow slip dress flowing gracefully around her as she walked toward them. "I'm so glad you both could come. Where are the little ones?"

"Home with grandparents. Clint's mom and dad arrived on the seventh and will have to head home next week. They've been wonderful." She tugged Marilynn toward a quieter place away from the food while Clint filled his plate. "Did I ever tell you the pregnancy test results?"

"No, but I knew. A month ago, in fact."

"I'm so sorry I didn't call."

Marilynn smiled and squeezed her hand. "I understand. But spill the details now. I want to hear all about it."

"I'm almost eleven weeks. We're going to find out the baby's sex the end of April. He or she already looks like a little gummy bear on the ultrasound. I can't believe I get to do this again." She smoothed her gently rounded abdomen. "And since our little one apparently joined us New Year's Eve, pre-chemo, we shouldn't have to worry about any side effects from the medicines."

Marilynn's grin reached her deep chocolate eyes. "I've missed you, my friend. A little more of Sara is shining through."

"Yes, and it's a beautiful sight, is it not?" Clint extended a plate in her direction. "Your favorite party mints, plus a healthy selection of bread and cheese."

Sara smiled her thanks.

"I won't interrupt the girl stuff." Clint nodded toward the ballroom entrance. "I see Steven and Michael. They didn't require too much convincing to come support the fund-raiser."

Clint weaved among the elegantly decorated tables and greeted their friends with a hug. Gracie accompanied Steven, of course, but seeing Hanna on Michael's arm was a pleasant surprise. Interesting.

Sara waved at the group across the room before turning back to Marilynn.

"Thank you for sending us staff tickets. I feel a little guilty because most of the people here will have paid good money for their meal."

"Even if the HR department had put up a fuss, the rest of us would have pitched in to see that you both spent the evening here. Working or not, Sara, you're still part of this family."

She didn't doubt her friend's words. With the mention of family, though, she missed her mom and dad a little more. She'd spoken to them by phone weekly since right after Valentine's Day. Once Clint relented about sharing their burden, she'd blubbered about the cancer and told her parents everything. Often they listened. Sometimes they prayed. But just hearing their voices helped so much. So did hearing about their escapades all over Ireland and the list of things they were bringing back for their three grandchildren. At her insistence, they'd agreed not to cut their dream vacation short. But she couldn't wait to see them when they returned in April.

"...past the worst, yes?"

Sara blinked and tried to formulate an intelligent answer. How much of the conversation had she missed? "Um, yes. Yes. We're over the hump, I guess." She wasn't sure if Marilynn meant Clint's chemo or the first trimester of throwing up.

A loud sound near the dance floor commanded their attention. The music stopped.

"You people should be ashamed, celebrating what you do." The young, dark-headed man waved his shot glass in front of him. "Killers. That's what you are. Killers. Putting poison in babies. My son died because of you."

Several men in dark suits escorted the raging man toward the door. He resisted but was too drunk to do much.

"I'll see you all rot—" His angry tirade ended with a loud slam of the ballroom doors.

Celtic music filled the room once more, but conversations were few and far between. Ice cubes clinked against Sara's glass, shaking in time with her thundering heart.

The man's violent words drained the room of joy. And she couldn't think beyond the memory of her patients who'd died. All because she'd failed to save them.

❈　❈　❈

Michael returned to the ballroom, his sidearm secured in its holster.

"That idiot's on his way to dry out in the county jail." He caught Gracie's widened eyes and regretted his bluntness.

"Were you part of the group that removed him from the room?" Sara held her glass with both shaking hands.

"No. I just went to make sure hotel security had things under control."

He looked over at Hanna. She stood with Kessler and Gracie, watching the other ballroom guests with rapt attention. Looking gorgeous in a simple, dark green dress, her blond hair piled on top of her head.

"The guy's little boy died of leukemia yesterday, and he's convinced the doctor's incompetence caused the death. He came here to—"

Kessler's glare stopped him cold.

Then it hit him. Sara Rollins was an oncologist. That man's words must have sliced her to the core. His explanation only served to deepen the wound.

"Why don't we all take a seat and get ready for dinner?" Kessler motioned toward their assigned table. Michael followed, mentally kicking himself. Why hadn't he just kept his mouth shut?

Sara put a hand on his arm. "It's all right. I'll be fine, Michael. People overwhelmed by grief often speak without thinking."

He couldn't use that excuse. "I'm sorry, Sara. I shouldn't have said anything."

"Let's move forward and enjoy the rest of the evening." Clint squeezed his shoulder as they headed to their table.

At least the guy's gun had stayed hidden, and he'd do no more damage tonight. Michael stepped aside to let an elderly couple pass. Now if he could stay quiet, he might avoid doing any more harm too.

Hanna slipped her arm through his. "Sara will be fine. She knows the truth. Don't let Steven get to you." Her soft whisper and warm breath on his neck made his boss's previous disapproval fade into insignificance.

He held out Hanna's chair and moved to the seat next to her, enjoying every bit of her dazzling smile directed at him. Discussion turned to Saint Patrick's Day history and celebrations. Light topics and laughter. And after a short blessing when their food arrived, Sara's smile gave no indication of the earlier trouble.

Michael relaxed. The beef melted in his mouth, and the warm bread smelled incredible. But nothing could hold a candle to Hanna's presence next to him.

If he'd had his way, they'd have been dining alone in a quiet restaurant near the river.

But that time would come.

Because when Clint asked him to support the cancer center and mentioned that Hanna would be there too, Michael had decided two things.

First, dinner with a group was better than not seeing her at all.

And second, it was time for a real date with Hanna Kessler.

※ ※ ※

Clint extended a hand to Sara and bowed.

"May I have the pleasure of this dance?" Her laugh made him feel less silly. Steven's smile helped too. Even with the earlier mess, their first real date in ages was turning out well.

On the dance floor, Sara wrapped her arms around him. "How's your energy holding up, cowboy?"

A slow smile spread across his face, and he nuzzled her neck in response. They needed to get out more often, especially when he felt human in between treatments. They were halfway through with chemo. Almost done.

"Think your parents will be waiting up for us?" Sara's voice tickled his ear as they danced. His parents had better be fast asleep.

"It won't matter if they are or not. Our bedroom door has a lock."

Sara shook her head and grinned.

"What's the joke, you two?" Steven and Gracie slow-danced close beside them.

"Nothing you won't figure out in a few months."

Sara swatted him.

Steven bit back a guffaw, and Gracie blushed deep red. Clint couldn't help but laugh.

"You need to rein it in a little, don't you think?" Sara's voice was soft in his ear as Steven and Gracie moved away. "They were both married before. Waiting for their wedding day can't be easy."

He hadn't thought of that. "You're right. I should've kept quiet." He pulled her close, and they danced awhile without speaking.

"What are you thinking?" Sara tilted her head. "You sort of disappeared for a minute there."

"I'm thinking that between my lousy memory and chronic exhaustion, I'm a miserable candidate for best man."

She kissed his cheek. "You're the only best man for Steven. He knows you've had a lot going on, honey. He understands."

"And how do you know what Steven's thinking?" Clint pulled back to stare into his wife's beautiful eyes. He knew she had amazing intuitive powers, but this was a bit much for her to just decode from body language.

"I have my sources."

He shook his head. "You ladies talk about far too much, you know."

"Be thankful I have friends. Or else I'd be talking your ears off nonstop."

He pulled her closer and bent down to kiss her earlobe. "Just be kind when you're discussing us males. We have fragile egos, you know."

"I wouldn't say anything unkind about you."

"You've talked to Gracie about my outbursts, haven't you?"

"A little. But it's not like I'm trashing you, Clint." Her eyes held his attention. "I love you, and I don't want to snap back. So, yes, I have called Gracie to help me get my feelings under control and to pray. She's an amazing pray-er."

He looked over Sara's head and found his partner and Gracie wrapped in their own intimate conversation. He had to agree with Sara's assessment. He'd heard Gracie pray for them and for her students and Steven.

A man about his age, a little shorter with a distinct military walk, caught his attention. *I used to walk like that.*

Sara snuggled against his chest away from his port. The deformity didn't cause him as much self-loathing anymore, but in some situations it still bugged him. Slow-dancing was one of those.

He noticed the man again as the guy pulled his date close. A little too roughly for Clint's taste. The man must have sensed Clint's glare because he released his date and looked up. When they locked eyes, the guy smiled in recognition.

Did they know each other?

Clint concentrated on placing him but came up with nothing. That realization seared his ego with a vengeance.

The man's tailored suit spoke of a healthy pocketbook. Not a current military man. A salesman maybe. Or a lobbyist. No matter how hard he tried, Clint just couldn't place him.

What kind of FBI agent forgot details like that?

Anger roiled at one more hit to his competence.

"Let's go find something chocolate for dessert." Sara broke into his thoughts. "I think our littlest one must be a girl. My chocolate craving has reached new heights."

She placed his hand on her abdomen and grinned. He grinned back. Chocolate actually sounded good to him too. Might taste like tin, but he hadn't forgotten the smooth, slightly bitter bite of his favorite dark chocolate. Or the fun of watching Sara enjoy it.

Maybe he couldn't remember an old acquaintance. But his wife would help him think of better things anyway.

Far better.

20

Monday came as Mondays always do.

But this day would be different. A good Monday. Because they were heading to Sara's second OB appointment.

Despite initial fears, she'd realized that her pregnancy was a gift. The nausea had faded, and she'd begun to embrace the excitement and enjoy the bubbles in her stomach. Plus, getting proper nutrition and medical care for herself had given them all something besides Clint's cancer to discuss when they went shopping at the health-food store or drove to doctor's appointments.

And soon there'd be a baby in their home again.

"Jonathan sure reveled in his grandparents' full attention this morning, didn't he? I hate that they're leaving Wednesday. This time with them has flown by." She changed lanes and kept talking. "Jonathan didn't even put up a fuss when we left to take Susannah to school."

When traffic slowed, she glanced over to the passenger seat and saw the reason for Clint's silence.

His closed eyes and heavy breathing twinged her with annoyance. She wanted him awake and listening to her nervous prattle, excited like he'd been with their other two babies. Not asleep and out of it with cancer fatigue.

I should be more understanding. But what about me? Guilt took her by the throat and threatened to shred her again. She couldn't keep it away for long.

"Sara? What's with the tears?" Clint's groggy voice shook through her.

She wiped her cheeks. "Nothing."

"I've been married too long to accept 'nothing' as an answer." He placed his hand on her thigh. "Tell me why you're crying."

His tenderness reminded her of their first-ever OB appointment. She'd been terrified about bringing a baby into the world and frantic about how to manage a full-time career and motherhood.

Supermom she was not.

And yet her children were loving, polite, and adorable inside and out. So she'd done something right. Well, God in her anyway. That reminder stirred a wave of gratitude. She wasn't by herself, even if Clint did sleep through the OB appointment.

"Sara?"

"Sorry. I…I was crying because I felt alone. It's hard going to the doctor with you sleeping and not talking to me like we did with Susannah and Jonathan." She took a deep breath and shoved the lying guilt thoughts away. "I started believing I was the worst wife ever for wishing you'd wake up."

At the traffic light near the doctor's office, Clint's understanding eyes held her attention.

"You know the truth, right?"

"Yes." She returned her gaze to the road. "I've never been alone as a parent. And even if you have to sleep and can't be here like the other times, God is with me."

"That's true. But I'm here—"

Clint's sudden burst of coughing startled her and set her mind whirling down a different path.

"Are you okay?"

"It's just allergies. No big deal."

His mood shifted back into sullen quietness. Maybe she shouldn't have said anything about his sleeping. She hated this cycle of drawing close and then, in seconds, having it all evaporate.

Cancer had long been a despised enemy. But now it was personal, amplified a million times over. This whole new side of the battle chipped away at her day after day, one draining challenge at a time.

"May tenth."

"What?" Clint's question smacked with irritation.

Her shoulders knotted. The light turned green, and she drove without comment for a minute before answering. "You'll be done May tenth, and then we'll have the rest of the pregnancy to enjoy."

He grunted.

God, where are You? How could her trust in Him ping-pong so out of control? Sometimes things seemed almost normal, and having Clint pray for them filled her with peace. But the next time Clint's exhaustion derailed the day's plans, she was back to exasperation with God, friends, and life in general.

"Are you depending on circumstances for your happiness?" Marilynn's words dredged up the guilt feelings again. How could she *not* do that? All the "just trust, just hope, just pray God's healing promises over Clint" stuff she'd heard again and again at church only added to the frustration.

Her cell phone blared "When the Saints Go Marching In," and she fumbled for her purse on the console. "Hello?" She hadn't checked the caller ID and prayed it wasn't Clint's parents. She couldn't handle a problem with Jonathan right now.

"Sara, it's Gracie. I had a quick break during music class and wanted to invite you to dinner tonight. Leah and I are going to look at wedding dresses, and we'd love to have you come too."

Gracie's excited voice turned Sara's thoughts back to better times. She remembered the excitement of her engagement, the fun of planning a wedding.

"We thought about meeting at four and then grabbing some dinner. Can you make it?"

Sara shoulders relaxed. Some positive girl-time would help salve her injured emotions. With grandparents there to watch the kids, Clint could sleep and she could have a guilt-free escape.

"Sure. It'd be wonderful to get away for a fun evening. Want me to pick you up at Hope Ridge when I get Susannah?"

"Thanks, but I have a few things to do before I head home." Gracie paused. "Would you mind if Leah picked you up? She's snagging her husband's convertible Beamer."

"That's so eighties." She smiled into the phone. "But I'm game. I'll look for her around four."

"We'll get you fitted too, if you don't mind. I'd like you and Leah to pick out your dresses. Something you can reuse for a fancy dinner party or special date."

"That sounds great." Bless her, in the most un-Southern use of that term. A dress to wear again and not some orange monstrosity like one of her former college friends had chosen. "Oh, but my dress will have to be a maternity one. Doubt I'll use that again."

"You never know. You'll have August and September for a big night on the town before baby arrives."

Good thinking. A few minutes later, she clicked her phone off and pulled into the doctor's parking lot. Clint woke up as she set the brake and came round to open her door.

As her husband always did, he offered his hand to help her out. "Hope y'all have fun tonight."

"We'll be trying on bridesmaids' dresses." Not knowing how much of the conversation he had followed, she couldn't gauge his reaction to it.

He nodded. "At least I have a few months to put some weight back on so I can fit into my high-class monkey suit again." A slight smile creased his face.

She lifted her eyes to the bright blue sky before stepping into the soothing cornflower and lemon décor of her favorite doctor's office.

Please, God. Let the real Clint stick around this time.

※　※　※

Clint cringed as Steven stepped around the partition and held out a hand. "You done with the Atlantic City case file yet? Michael needs it for his phone call with Chuck Little's caseworker."

Handing over the file he'd read and reread since coming in after Sara's appointment, Clint coughed so badly his ribs ached.

"When's your next appointment at the cancer center?"

"You gonna doctor me now that Sara's stopped?" He stood and glared at Steven.

"Not going to be bullied out of being concerned, partner." Steven raised an eyebrow. "Doubt your wife will be either."

Clint rubbed a hand over his bald head. "No. Sara won't be bullied." He exhaled long and slow. "I'm sorry. I...my temper flares all the time these days, and I'm not doing so well reining it in. I just hate being doctored. Okay?"

Steven held up his hands.

"My chemo is next Thursday. But Sara made an appointment for this Friday on account of this stupid cough. It's just allergies. I get it every spring. But she started talking about not wanting to bring a baby into this world without a father, so I'm going to see the doc early." He picked up Mattie Reynolds's file. "I've been doing some digging, and I have an alternate theory to Standish being involved in all these cases."

"I'm listening."

"We know Standish has Mattie, and that the boy was alive a month ago, so Standish remains a top priority to apprehend." Clint coughed again and struggled to recover.

"Need some water?"

He took a swig from his huge water jug and scowled.

Steven scowled back.

"Back to my theory." He straightened his scribbled notes. "I told you about that dream I had, the one from my MP days."

Steven narrowed his eyes. "The cancer-induced crazy dream? I thought we put that one to rest."

Clint didn't remember that. What else was new?

"I put in a call to the Department of Defense after you remembered the guy's name from your dream. Their files on John Miller end after his desertion and dishonorable discharge. Neither the child nor Miller were ever found. End of the line with that theory."

"You told me this when?"

"Last week."

Why couldn't he remember the simplest of things? "What if this guy reinvented himself? New birth certificate. New job history. It's not unheard of. And the thing is…I think maybe Miller is the guy I saw at the Benefield fund-raiser on Saturday. He could be here in DC."

"Or he could be dead." Michael joined them. "Sorry, Clint. I've done some digging and can't find anything recent on John Miller. No matter what's happened to him, after this much time, your theory will be nearly impossible to authenticate."

Clint slumped back into his chair.

"I'll look into it some more." Steven tapped the file on the desk. "Maybe someone else at the DOD will add a detail we can track down. But we can't put a lot of time into it."

"Fair enough."

Michael took the Atlantic City file from Steven. "The Virginia field office called. The phone used to contact Samantha Reynolds was a pre-paid cell purchased in a West Virginia Wal-Mart. It could have been Mattie."

Steven shook his head. "It could just as easily have been a prank. A bored kid with a disposable phone his parents gave him for an emergency."

"That's what the Virginia case agent said. He told me to toast the Reynolds kid with a beer tonight and move on to another case tomorrow."

Judging from the set of Michael's jaw, he'd do no such thing. Without a body, Michael would see this case to the end believing Mattie was still alive.

Steven ran a hand through his thick hair. Clint wished he could do the same. "Let's go back to the conference room and the map." His partner slipped around the partition. "We need to reevaluate our focus."

Lee joined them in the conference room a few minutes later and sat beside Michael. "Please tell me you have a good word. Among other things, I'm still pushing papers on the child-support recovery case the U.S. attorney dumped on me."

Michael shrugged. "Virginia agents reported a prepaid cell phone was used to call Samantha Reynolds. I think it could have been Mattie."

Clint chewed a piece of gum to abate the coughing. "But others believe it was more likely a prank call."

"And a dead end." Steven paced. "Phone was paid for in cash."

Lee's choice expletives filled the small conference room.

"But we can't rule out the possibility that Standish bought the phone and Mattie tried to use it."

No one challenged Michael's statement. But everyone knew the odds. If Mattie's case turned out badly, this child would haunt Michael like Ryan's death last year still plagued Steven. Every agent had one of those cases.

Steven stepped up to the whiteboard and pointed to the time line. "We have Standish missing since the week of January fifteenth. Mattie is snatched from Charleston, West Virginia, on January twenty-first. Next sighting is near Luray, Virginia, February ninth."

"And we have Standish meeting his brother somewhere close to Christiansburg to collect money. Then a week later he's in Baltimore hoping to retrieve his son and head out west." Michael opened a new document on his laptop to take more notes.

Lee drummed a finger on the table. "Every time eluding the long arm of the law. What's this guy doing? Wearing wigs and makeup and parading around in plain sight?"

"Isn't there another case in here somewhere?"

Steven looked him up and down. "Clint's right. We need to figure Chuck Little into this. He disappeared sometime around the middle of January from Atlantic City."

"No credit card trail places Standish in New Jersey. But he did make that huge withdrawal on January twelfth, right before he went off the radar."

Clint leaned forward and let loose with another coughing fit.

Steven scowled. "You need to go to the doctor sooner than Friday."

"You're an FBI agent, not a nurse. Knock it off."

Michael held up a handful of printed sheets, diverting attention back to the case. "The report from the New Jersey computer forensics lab gives us some insight into Standish's motive. Plus, it fits our violent pedophile profile. Another link to our cold cases."

"Go on."

Clint didn't want to hear details and prayed Michael wouldn't pull up any of the pictures retrieved from Standish's computer. He'd already seen far too much of that kind of thing.

"The computer forensic wonder agents found thousands of pictures buried on the hard drive. They range from simple ad-type pictures of young boys to serious bondage and torture stuff."

Clint was ready to call it a day. Another coughing fit, and Steven sent him packing with a strong suggestion to go to the doctor sooner than Friday.

Nothing doing. It was just a cold. He could survive a stupid cold on his own.

❀   ❀   ❀

Steven placed a call to Sara on his way home.

"I understand your concern, Steven. I'm not thrilled about Clint's bullheadedness, but I can't exactly hogtie him and take him in."

"I can."

She sighed. "Right now there's no fever, sweating, or shortness of breath. If it gets worse, I'll definitely call Dr. Silverman and get Clint in before Friday."

"I know you will. Sorry to butt in where you've got it under control." Turning onto Wagon Wheel Road, he longed to read a quick bedtime story with James and then collapse into bed. But that wouldn't happen. He needed to handle some administrative issues and review cases going up for trial that would require his testimony. And he'd promised to check into Clint's theory one more time.

"Sara, this might sound like a strange request, but can you remember any cases at the cancer center connected to a former military man, midforties?"

"You're looking for Clint's mystery man from the Saint Patrick's Day dinner?"

"Yes. I've never known Clint's hunches to be wrong."

"That was before cancer." Long pause. "Steven, I never even saw the man Clint talked about, so I can't be sure he was there. And none of my cases included anyone fitting your description. I'm sorry."

Steven pulled into his driveway and turned off the motor. "It's okay. I knew it wasn't likely. It's just hard to accept that cancer and chemo have done so much damage."

"Clint's pushing himself pretty hard. I catch him lifting weights until he's ready to collapse. Or on the computer all hours of the night. He's still praying, but he's not coping well with the reality of his limitations."

"Don't know that I would either."

"Keep praying for us, okay?"

"Always." Steven hung up the phone and let his head fall to the steering wheel. A stack of cases with no leads, long hours, and little time with Gracie and James, on top of watching Clint deteriorate like Mom—it all weighed him down like nothing he'd ever known.

Not to mention that Mattie's case looked more like Olivia Kensington's every day. Smart criminal, few leads, child missing for weeks with a slim possibility she was still alive. The memory of the British teen's body found at Memorial Hill Park last year still seared his mind.

Pulling out his phone, he placed another call. "Dad? How about I pick you all up in half an hour for ice cream?"

"Rough day?"

"Yep. I could use some distraction before I plunge back into it later tonight."

No doubt the rest of his team would be doing the same thing.

21

S taring at his computer Tuesday morning, Michael realized he needed a break.

Something besides paperwork. Maybe if he dug around Christiansburg, he'd find a lead the local cops missed. Was it too much to ask that God lead him right to Mattie Reynolds? Stranger things had happened.

He exhaled hard and walked over to Kessler. "I'd like to go back to Christiansburg and poke around a little more."

Kessler grunted. "Get the paperwork to me, and I'll authorize it."

"Will do."

His boss looked him in the eye. "You've exceeded my expectations, taking on Clint's share of work without complaint and keeping up with your stuff too. That says a lot about you, Michael. But like Clint, I'm concerned that this case is getting too personal. Like Ryan's case last year was to me. I hope this one turns out better for all of us, but you need to prepare for the possibility that it won't."

Michael didn't respond.

Kessler watched him a second longer, then turned to his computer. "Bring us back some good news."

Steven Kessler had called him by his first name again. Not since Hanna announced her plans to move had Steven treated him as anything more than a subordinate. Score one good thing for today.

Michael sped through travel plans and filling out the required forms. Maybe now that his boss was softening toward him, it was time to see if another Kessler welcomed his ideas.

He picked up his desk phone and dialed the number he'd memorized weeks ago, waiting for the right time to call. More like waiting for an opportunity when Kessler was too busy to pounce on him for calling Hanna. But maybe that wasn't going to be as much of a problem as he'd feared.

"Hey, big brother, calling to see if Michael's asked me out yet?" Hanna's voice was playful. "Thanks to you that hasn't happened."

He suppressed a grin. Her caller ID would have only shown a series of zeros, so she'd assumed he was Steven. And she sounded far more interested in him than he could have hoped.

"Um, this is Michael." He let the words sink in.

Silence.

He imagined her huge, beautiful blue eyes wide with shock.

"Michael, I'm glad you finally called. What took you so long?"

Okay, her playing it cool and calm defied his prediction. But it only served to intrigue him more. "Things have been a little busy around here."

"And then there's my big brother."

True. If Steven hadn't taken that "over my dead body" stance about dating Hanna, Michael would have called a lot sooner. "I was hoping you'd be free Friday night, maybe for a candlelight dinner on the river?" He'd have to make those arrangements before he left for Christiansburg in the morning.

A pause. "How about you meet me at Grounded this afternoon and we'll see how it goes?" He could hear a smile in her voice, a cautious one, but a smile nonetheless. "I'll be working, but I can take my lunch break when you arrive."

Another chance to see Hanna? No need to ask twice. "Grounded is your coffee shop, right?"

"My dad's shop. I manage it for him."

"I'll see you there this afternoon."

She was silent for a few seconds longer than he expected. "Okay. It's a date then." Her voice had lost its playfulness.

He shrugged the implications away and focused on his morning workload. Hanna had agreed to a lunch date today. An unexpected bonus.

"Daydreaming about my sister?" Kessler's voice surprised him.

Michael turned to meet his boss's intense stare. "Not exactly." He glanced at the paperwork on his desk. "But since you asked, I'd like to know why you seem so set against me asking her out."

Kessler pulled up a chair and sat down. "I've told you before that my sister means the world to me. And Kessler blood runs thick. She's been hurt recently, and I'm having a hard time forgetting all the dates you ran through last year."

"I'm not the same person I was before."

"True. But old habits die hard, even after you come to Christ. I don't want Hanna to be a casualty of your learning curve."

Michael shifted in his desk chair. Memories of past girlfriends he'd shared more than a date with sure didn't make things any easier. Kessler's concerns were understandable. But Michael was different now. That had to count for something.

As Steven walked away, Lee slid his desk chair past his office partition, a huge smirk on his face. "You know that saying, 'Big Brother is watching'? Mind it well, my friend. Mind it well."

"Not helpful, Lee."

What would Hanna think about his past? Maybe he shouldn't tell her. After all, with big brother watching, how serious could things get?

※ ※ ※

Hanna's nerves frayed more with each passing minute.

She'd dropped coffee cups, mishandled sandwiches for the lunch crowd, and given her employees conflicting orders. By now, the two young women working the deli counter and the tables out front probably hoped she'd take an extended lunch break.

It didn't help that both servers were drop-dead gorgeous. Once Michael saw them, she might have nothing to worry about.

Scrubbing the back counter and then scribbling a few notes about additional coffee flavors to run by her dad kept her attention focused. But her mind wandered back to this morning's phone call and how she'd wanted to sink through the floor when she mistook Michael for her brother.

Nothing like putting both feet in your mouth and swallowing. All in one bite.

She'd recovered well though. If her instincts were right, she'd also gained some respect in Michael's eyes with her quick comeback and return invitation.

A decision she'd begun to question. What if she wasn't ready for this?

"I'd like one of everything you have." A strong and familiar male voice registered.

Hanna turned in time to see Amber and Tiffany scramble to fulfill Michael's every wish. She couldn't help but giggle. One of everything? Not even Mr. Tall and Muscular FBI Guy could manage an order of five loaded sandwiches, chips, and some rather enormous pastries and cookies, along with four different coffees and an assortment of teas.

"Are you hungry today, Agent Parker?" She motioned for her employees to return to their duties without waiting on this new customer.

His brown eyes held a hint of mischief. "Hungry, yes. But not quite that hungry."

Her stomach growled. No wonder. The clock said ten before two.

"So what will it be?" She grabbed a small salad and half a sandwich for herself. "My treat, since I invited you."

He stiffened. Not accustomed to a lady buying him a meal? Could be a good sign.

"I'd like a roast beef on rye, no onions." He pointed to the little fancy sign in the glass showcase. "And one of those massive chocolate chip cookies. With a water."

She gathered the items and rang them up on the cash register, then slipped in the exact change from her purse. Amber and Tiffany watched her every move. "I'll be back in thirty minutes." She nodded toward the front door. "You can call my cell if you need something before then."

As she stepped from behind the counter and led the way out of

Grounded, Michael took the tray from her hands. After her first-time-asking-a-guy-out boldness, she couldn't think of a single thing to say, so they rode the escalator down to the busy food court in silence.

Michael set their tray down and pulled out a chair for her. What a novelty. It'd been a long time since she'd seen a guy do that on a date. When he'd arranged the food on the table, he bowed his head to pray.

She did the same. Then blurted out the first thing that popped into her head. "You must be pretty interested to ask me out when Steven's been so against it."

He smiled a disarming grin.

Danger, Will Robinson. Seriously.

"I'm not asking for your hand in marriage."

Her boldness tasted like Keds tennis shoes for the second time today. All with the same person.

Memories of what she'd hoped for with Craig pinched her heart. "Then you're just looking for a good time, huh?"

Her zinger connected, and Michael's grin disappeared. She should have kept her mouth closed. Not all men were like the guys she'd known in college. Life had given her the accelerated track in Growing Up 101. But she needed a refresher course in manners.

"Sorry. I shouldn't have said that. I guess I've been jilted a few times too many."

Did she just spill her life story or what?

Digging in to her salad, she refused to meet his eyes. A girlfriend would help her avoid this excess-of-words embarrassment. But last time she checked, her friends were all back in Louisville having babies and leaving her in the dust.

"Hanna? Where'd you disappear to there?" Michael leaned into her line of vision.

"Sorry." She sounded like a squeaky mouse. "I'm making a complete fool out of myself, and I wouldn't be surprised if you rescinded your invitation to dinner."

Michael reached over and took hold of her hand. Ignoring the jolt of attraction, she stared at a spot beyond his left shoulder. She'd gone down that starry-eyed road too many times to be stupid again. Always looking for something no man could provide.

"I like your honest, not-so-perfect self." His smile didn't soften the unglowing review she'd just received. "I mean, you're real. I like that. I'd like to play things straight from the start. Lay some ground rules, even." He looked down at the white floor, and something in his actions touched her deep inside.

"Like what?"

His face was a study in extremes, and she could almost guess what he would say next. Not a Christian for long, and way too handsome for his own good. Which probably meant his past and hers held some similarities.

"I'm going to be up front with you and hope it won't hurt my chances for Friday night." He took a deep breath and rubbed his thumb over the back of her hand. "I'd still like to take you out to a nice dinner, maybe a movie."

"I'd like that. Both the up front and the dinner." Words kept popping out of her mouth without permission. She did want to hear his story. And she didn't want to stay home alone another long Friday night. But maybe she should suggest a group date. With Steven and Gracie? She almost laughed. Wouldn't that be a relaxing evening? Michael acting like a stone pillar under the watchful eyes of her brother and soon-to-be sister-in-law.

Michael released her hand and finished off his sandwich.

"What did you mean by 'lay a few ground rules'?"

"For starters, we need to tread lightly when it comes to physical contact."

Kessler mischievousness kicked in. "So, like, no holding hands unless you ask Steven's permission?"

His eyes flamed with equal parts laughter and chagrin.

Why was it men couldn't talk about sex without coughing or dancing around the subject? Not that she wanted a list of which body parts would do what and how. But still. What did *up front* mean, anyway?

"I'm not about to ask your brother's permission for anything. But I do want to honor you and be truthful to my own weaknesses. I'm not a virgin. And as a Christian now, I'm trying to do things the right way. I don't want to disrespect you or even come close to it."

Whoa. Major up front.

"So by treading lightly I mean I don't want us to be alone at your place or mine." He looked her straight in the eyes. "And if, or when, I kiss you, I want you to be unafraid and sure of my future intentions."

Had she died and gone to dating heaven? Steven wouldn't believe this. No way would she tell him. But it was fun imagining his reaction.

"You certainly have my attention, Michael Parker. I don't think I've ever heard a man speak on this topic with such clarity and confidence. I'm impressed."

"Don't be. I'm not sure what percentage of that was for your sake and how much was pure self-protection."

"Even so, I get both. And I'm honored you care enough to say what you did."

If only other people in her past had been a tenth that honorable. She picked at her salad and forced down the remainder of her sandwich.

"Time for a subject change. Tell me about your photography. Clint said you had your own business in Louisville."

So he'd talked to Clint about her? "Before I graduated from the University of Louisville, I took as many photography courses as I could. I also tried working at a few of those mall-type stores. But at the time my passion was landscapes, and I just didn't fit the bubbly kid–photographer type."

"Is that how you got into working for your dad?"

"Yes. Offering to train me as a manager was his way of making sure I could support myself while I worked on my skills and later started a photography business." She smiled. "Dad has always believed in me."

"Those are your photographs on the walls in Grounded?"

"Yes."

"They're amazing. I loved the Cumberland Falls sunset. And the black-and-white portraits were beautiful. I'd enjoy seeing more of your work."

She nodded and swallowed the invitation to come over and see her portfolio tonight. No attractive male had ever shown this much interest in her compositions. Craig had called them a "nice hobby."

Sure, Dad and Steven raved about her work. And professors had called her "gifted." Her friends loved to have her take their pictures and then, later, pictures of their babies. But Michael's curiosity seemed deeper. That both excited and terrified her.

He checked his watch and then helped her clear the trash before they returned to the escalator. His not taking her hand made her wish he had all the more. But she needed to respect his boundaries as well as her own and not push anything, even if Michael's interest in her work touched a place inside that no one else had.

Regret washed though her like an unrelenting spring rain, complete with thunderheads and lightning. Michael didn't know her story. Maybe he never would. Either way, reality hit hard.

She still had a ton of work to do with God about her past.

22

The time for stupid mistakes had passed.

Tuesday, March twentieth, would be his day. Thinking of the myriad mistakes and thwarted plans since January, he let loose a string of curses that filled the rental car.

He'd gotten sloppy. Grown too soft. Let focusing on his child crumble his backbone and complicate what had once been a simple stress release.

But he couldn't walk away now. Not when everything continued to spiral downward. He was no longer in control. No, his compulsions were controlling him. That had to change.

Maybe one more time would be enough. Then he'd stop for good.

Pulling off I-95 and into the city of Richmond, he stopped to recheck the directions. It still took awhile to find the right park, one with dense trees and close interstate access. And a play area full of kids.

He circled the park in search of a target. March in the South provided good cover, with more people out enjoying sunny afternoons like this one. He'd chosen the perfect time of day. Parents were distracted with dinner plans and grocery lists while the kids were bored and wild.

He'd take a different tack this time. The new Game Boy would be a perfect enticement. A little more tempting than cookies or gum.

Watching from his car across the street, he waited for the ideal time to enter the park. A few minutes later, he flung his backpack over his shoulder and caught his reflection in the plastic window of a bus shelter. With his casual clothes and amiable grin, he could still pass for a twenty-something.

At a park bench a little ways from the main congregation of playground groupies, he took out the electronic toy and began to play. No one noticed. A slight breeze rustled the tall pines nearby. Once he found his mark, if he ducked into the trees after drugging the boy, he could make it up the block and double back to his car practically unnoticed.

Now for the wait.

Two or three possibilities presented themselves right away, especially with the number of park visitors today. None stayed long.

One boy drew near and took an interest in the mutant cartoonish things on his game screen. But the boy's articulate manners and nonstop chatter made him an unlikely candidate. He'd do well not to kill the kid before they left the park.

"Hey, do you play college basketball?" A little brown-haired boy approached.

Looking down at his orange and blue sweatshirt, he smiled. Nothing like appealing to Virginia pride. "I used to." He held up the game. "Want to try it? We can talk sports while you play."

The kid took the bait and flopped down on the bench. "My dad taught me all about basketball. Promised to take me to a game one day." The boy studied the grass at his feet. "But he left a few months ago, and I haven't sawn him since."

"You mean *seen*."

"Yeah. Anyway, my mom's pretty busy with work, so I get lots of time to play." He pointed to a woman fishing for something in her slate-gray Lincoln and talking on the phone clear across the playground. Lady must be doing all right for herself.

"Want to come catch a snipe with me?" The old high school trick might get this easygoing kid out of sight in the woods long enough to get him drugged. Then they could be on their way.

"A snipe?"

"It's small and furry and makes a great pet."

The boy's eyes grew as wide as his smile. "Sure. I've always wanted a pet."

They walked into the woods unnoticed as he explained to the boy how to hold his backpack and squat down.

"You know, I don't think I want to do this." The boy looked over his shoulder. "I better go back and find my mom."

"Let's just give it a try. I promise it'll be worth it." Surely this one wouldn't fight him like the others. Unfortunately, at some point most of them fought. He hated that. It ruined the experience for him.

"Okay. But just for a little bit." With his attention focused on the darkening woods in front of him, the boy barely noticed the needle prick.

He swiped at his arm. "I think something bit me."

"Keep watching the bag. We'll take care of the mosquito bite soon."

He watched the kid's eyes start to blink slowly.

"I'm not feeling so good."

"Here, I'll carry you." The boy slumped into his arms, and he quickened his pace out of the woods and across the busy street.

He loved it when a plan came together.

Looking to his left, he noticed the boy's mom still on the cell phone, unaware that her life had just changed forever.

Now all he had to do was make it back to his favorite park. Ten slow, sliding steps down the hill, fifty more to the east, then a straight shot south for about a mile. Picturing his favorite place heightened the rush of excitement.

A quick snap of the boy's neck and some midnight digging would appease the need and relieve his stress. It always had. Then he could settle back into his life and responsibilities as if nothing had ever happened.

Back in control.

Back to normal.

23

What a rotten way to end the week. One more child missing without so much as an eyewitness to the disappearance. Plus, Clint's Friday morning phone conversation with Michael held little positive info.

Pausing next to Clint's desk, Steven nodded toward the phone. "Has Michael checked in today?"

"Yep."

"Good thing he was already headed to Christiansburg on Wednesday. Diverting him to Richmond when the field office called made for less of a scramble here." Steven rolled his neck after his longer-than-expected meeting with the unit chief. "Tell me he's found something."

"Nothing. Danny Brower's mom was handling work calls while her son played at a busy park. They'd stopped there in between school and picking up dinner. She saw nothing, and neither Michael nor the Virginia field agents assigned to this case found anyone who reported a suspicious man hanging around without children."

"Is it possible he had Mattie with him?"

"Michael said no one recognized the pictures of either Mattie or Standish."

Steven's face went stone. "What if Standish is playing games with us like Lee suggested? Wearing disguises, hiding in plain sight. Staying close, but not close enough for us to handle things in our own backyard."

"Why?"

"Because he hates cops, especially us. After all, we interrogated his brother, who's now behind bars, and kept him from his son."

Lee stopped next to Steven and huffed. "Not to mention this dirt bag is getting his jollies while he keeps us running all over creation. Playin' cat and mouse fits a smart serial's profile. Ups the rush and feeds his ego when we don't find him before he can do his deal again."

Clint coughed until his lungs threatened to explode. Or implode.

Steven handed him the hoss jug of water he now toted everywhere. "When you going to the doctor?"

"Two o'clock."

"Is Sara taking you?"

"No. I'm fine." Clint stood and fell back down into his chair. Noodle legs and a Tilt-a-Whirl head didn't help prove his point. Rage flared. He had to manage all the physical requirements of a federal law enforcement officer before he could get away from a desk. But his stupid body wouldn't cooperate. In the meantime, kids kept disappearing. And he was powerless to do anything about it.

"Take it easy, Clint." Steven pulled his cell phone from its belt clip. "I'm calling Sara to come get you."

Clint pushed up from his chair. "Don't."

His partner closed the phone.

"I can get myself to the doctor." Good thing his parents had gone home Wednesday. He didn't need them, Steven, and Sara ganging up on him. Rubbing his bald head, he grimaced. Always something there to remind him. "I hate feeling like a ninety-pound weakling. I can drive. It's not that far."

"My mother was never this stubborn."

Steven didn't mention his mother's cancer often. When he did, it punched holes in Clint's ego. Cynthia Kessler hadn't made life this hard for the people around her. "If you want to follow me over there, you're welcome to. But I'm driving myself." With that, he sat down and straightened his jumble of notes.

The hogload of administrative garbage Maxwell piled on his desk kept him busy for the remainder of the morning. But elementary school busywork still beat sitting around the house watching bad reality TV. Or sleeping all day, only to stay awake studying ceiling patterns all night.

"Ready to go?" Steven leaned against the cubicle wall with a still-neat suit coat and keys in hand.

"You're really gonna follow me to the doctor."

"Yes."

"I'm not feeling the love."

"Better than you feeling the pavement, partner."

The ride to Alexandria proved noneventful. The only excitement came from a few swerves over the median after a monster coughing fit and the blaring from Steven's horn that followed. Clint signaled he had everything back under control, then turned up his stereo. A little kicking country kept him awake all the way to the cancer center.

He stepped out of his black, built-tough truck still humming. Too bad his Stetson and boots were at home. A suit and tie would have to do for the good Dr. Silverman.

Steven pulled up alongside. In one fluid move, he killed his engine and slammed the door of his Explorer. "You're calling Sara to pick you up, right?" His face looked pale.

"No."

"Wrong answer." Steven worked his jaw muscles back and forth. "Either you call Sara now, or I will."

"Fine, I'll call."

"Now."

"You don't think I'll keep my word?"

Steven crossed his arms. "You're a stubborn cuss if I've ever known one. Sure, you'll call. You'll call home when you know she's out, so she can't answer. That way you can keep your word and still drive your hard-headed self home."

His partner knew him all too well. And Clint didn't like the new picture either. He never used to compromise the truth. That realization and his inability to do his job reignited the rage.

He held back a string of the profanities he heard every day around the office. They wouldn't help or make him feel better. They'd only make Steven call Sara himself.

Clint pulled out his cell. "Sara. Hey, it's me. No, I'm fine. And, yes, I'm at the doctor." He looked up at the sky. She didn't make this easy. "Would you please come pick me up at the cancer center in about an hour?"

"Are you okay?" Her voice sounded pinched. "I'm on my way to get Susannah, but I can make it there before your appointment is over."

"No, don't bother. I'm fine, and it's no big deal. I can drive home myself." He shot a smug look in Steven's direction.

"Tell her the entire truth." Steven's loud voice ensured Sara heard him.

"What's that?"

"Steven is being an overprotective mother hen and thinks my driving is questionable. He followed me to Dr. Silverman's and insisted I call you." Clint hurried his words. "But you're busy, and I'm really okay. So I can drive myself home."

"If Steven's that concerned…"

He clenched his teeth so hard they could shatter. "Why don't you and the kids come pick me up after school then? You can follow me, and we'll grab something to eat on the way home."

He hung up the phone after a short good-bye. "Satisfied?"

"Yes." Steven moved back to his Explorer. "And you handled that with finesse, my friend. I'm taking notes for the next time I don't want to do something I know is right."

"Whatever."

Steven started his SUV. "See you at the office on Monday." His best friend drove away with a short wave.

The mother-hen bit showed Steven's concern and nothing else. No one was trying to control him or make him feel like an idiot.

Self-talk, no matter how truthful, failed to help.

Looking at his watch, Clint forced his feet forward and into the cancer center, his second home these days. Scans, shots, blood draws, and toxic chemicals had become a way of life. Tests and more tests made him feel like a pincushion. But maybe the doctor would help eliminate the cough so he could get back to the gym and step up his routine.

"It's good to see you, Clint." Laurie Denny greeted him in the main hallway. "But it doesn't look like you share the same sentiments."

"Nothing personal. I'm just tired of this place."

"Understandable." She nodded in the direction of the patient treatment lounge. "Why don't you get in on a chess game while you wait?"

"I'm here because Sara thinks I have an infection or something. I'd rather not expose anyone else in case I'm contagious."

"Your wife is usually right on the money." Laurie stepped into the main waiting room. "Why don't you find a good book, and I'll get you checked in and back to see Dr. Silverman." She pointed to a wall rack of paperbacks. "I hear there're some awesome suspense novels in there."

He grabbed one with a black cover sporting a spider's web. Fit his mood exactly. Trapped, with a dark outlook ahead.

Ten minutes later, he'd read only two pages. He should do better than that.

"Clint? Come on back." Laurie's voice jolted him.

He tossed the book onto the table in front of him and stood slowly.

"You can take the book with you."

"Nah. I'll let someone else enjoy it. I can pick one up at the store." He followed the tall administrator back to Dr. Silverman's office.

The oncologist looked up from his desk at Laurie's slight knock. "Come in." He waved to Laurie before she scooted away.

Clint almost pulled the old rocking chair over to Dr. Silverman's heavy oak desk. But sitting in the armchair across from Dr. Silverman meant less work. Easier was better right now.

His cough came on full force as he sank into the plush seat.

"So what brings you here today, besides that nasty sound?"

"My cough is getting worse, and I've been running some slight temps."

"Does Sara know about the temps?"

Clint shook his head.

"When did they start?"

"Monday night. I couldn't hide the coughs, so I started checking my temperatures then."

"And they've run…?"

Clint hated this Chinese water torture of questions. He couldn't risk another internment in the hospital. Time was critical. Lives were at stake, and he needed to stay in the game. Mattie Reynolds could still be alive. Maybe some of the others. The new case…what was the name?

"Your temperatures, Clint?"

"One hundred and one or lower." Except that right now he was sweating out of his shirt.

Dr. Silverman steepled his fingers in front of his face. "Let's run some tests today and see if we can't get an antibiotic to knock this out fast."

"It's just a cold."

"Not by the sound of it, Clint. Pneumonia can develop into sepsis quickly. If that's what we're dealing with, I'm going to hospitalize you. Kicking and screaming or not." The doctor's attempt at lighthearted didn't work.

God? Those miracles I've been asking for? I need 'em fast.

God owed him nothing, and he had no right to demand. But he asked anyway. Because right now it'd take a miracle for him to get back to work and find Mattie or any of the other missing kids alive. Michael wasn't the only one hanging on to that hope by a thread.

A few blood draws later, Clint walked out into the daylight. Sara would be here any minute, and he'd have to send her home because Dr. Silverman wanted him to stick around for the results. And possible hospital stay.

Everything in him wanted to get into his truck, ignore Dr. Silverman, and just call Sara on the way home. Not an option he'd face Steven with on Monday.

"Clint." A woman's voice derailed his train of thoughts. He turned to focus on the sound. Sara's red hair came into view. Why had he been so slow to recognize her voice? Susannah and Jonathan ran alongside her.

Fatigue like he'd never known suddenly threatened to push him over. "Hey, y'all." His mouth turned to cotton. Sweat dripped from every pore.

"Clint, you're not looking so well." Sara's voice sounded light and strained at the same time. "Let's get you back inside."

He focused on her emerald eyes. They had that cold, probing doctor's look. "Don't baby me."

She knelt in front of Jonathan and Susannah. "Would you two head right in those big doors and tell the receptionist at the desk you're Dr. Rollins's son and daughter? Ask if you can wait for me there."

They scampered to the door like this was a treat. They'd probably be given food that actually tasted good. Not like anything he'd tried since January twenty-fifth.

"I'm glad you made it to the doctor." Sara's voice sounded faraway. "But seeing you, I agree with Steven. He was right to have you call me."

"He didn't make me call."

"You can be so…"

His head started to swim. Clouds and pavement all swirled into a blur. Only his coughing reminded him of the pain in his chest. Pain like an anvil had smacked him right between his shoulders. He took a step and thought he'd connected with the white curb in front of the cancer center.

But he missed.

"Clint…"

He reached for Sara and felt nothing but rough, hard concrete.

Shouted syllables and unknown voices battered him from every side. All he could see and hear melted into one color.

Black.

24

What a wasted trip.

Michael shoved aside the thoughts of his futile expedition to Richmond and focused instead on the centerpiece of the elegant table. The soft flickering of the white candle did nothing to distract him or set a romantic mood. He checked his watch for the fiftieth time since he'd arrived.

Seven thirty. Hanna had agreed to meet him at seven o'clock.

No answer on her cell. No messages left on his. Where was she?

"Would you like another soda…or maybe something a little stronger?" The flirty brunette waitress bent down close. "I get off work in an hour."

His body responded, and he swallowed hard. "Thanks, Shelly. But I'll wait a little longer. My date's worth a lot more patience." He stiffened at the waitress's frosty stare. "But I will take another Coke. Thanks."

Shelly moved from his table like a runway model with a little extra sway. Male eyes followed her departure. Michael turned his head toward the window. No use adding fuel to the fire that was already making him second-guess his Friday plans.

Hanna was worth waiting for. But he was not a very patient man. One more thing he needed to work on.

That and finding missing kids. Especially Mattie Reynolds.

Michael wished he'd brought his briefcase into the restaurant with him. He'd left it in the car, figuring it would send the wrong message. No fear of that now, since it looked like Hanna wouldn't show. He should have chucked manners and gotten some work done.

He hated wasted minutes. Just like his dad.

"Time must be harnessed and used to its fullest potential."

His father's words returned to torment him at the oddest times. The man's demanding voice had never held a hint of pride, no matter what Michael accomplished. Track star. Baseball and soccer headliner in college. High school and college valedictorian. He would have done some extreme sports if his father hadn't vetoed it.

"I'm not footing the bill for your education to have you break your fool neck like some kind of adrenaline junkie."

That hadn't been his aim, but it didn't matter. His father's disapproval didn't bend to reason.

Not even high honors in Army Officer Training School had been enough to earn points with his father. Becoming an FBI agent had garnered a little respect though. But he would lose even that if the national news kept harping on law enforcement's supposed failures with missing children. Why couldn't they celebrate all the kids the FBI and police did bring home?

"Here's your soda." Shelly practically purred. "And my card. Call me soon." With that, she sauntered away.

He studied her business card, a classy gold-foil job that practically seared his hands. If she'd known he was a federal agent, she wouldn't have passed him a calling card for a flagged "personal dating" service. He'd pass it along the appropriate channels at work Monday.

If he didn't try to call her first.

Michael cursed under his breath. Hanna wasn't coming, and he wasn't getting more holy staying here with temptation begging to sit in his lap.

He needed a good run. Now.

Flipping a five and some change onto the table, he left the restaurant without a backward glance.

❉   ❉   ❉

Sara paced the halls of Alexandria Community Hospital on Saturday afternoon, kicking herself for not making Clint come in sooner. For not watching his temps. For failing as an oncologist once again. And as a wife.

Why'd she even get out of bed today?

"Sara, honey, we're here."

Sara fell into her mother's outstretched arms. Then guilt punched her in the stomach. "Mom, Dad, I'm so sorry. I was wrong to call and ask you to cut your trip short."

"Nonsense. It was only a few days early, and we were ready to come home." Mom showed no hint of her lie. "We should have come back last month when you finally told us about the cancer. No one really needs to spend all that time in a foreign country."

Except they'd saved up for years to take this sabbatical.

"But you're not home in Texas, you're here." Sara swiped at her eyes.

Her father's strong arms swept them into a deserted family waiting room. Dad's presence and powerful, silent direction hastened her undoing. She could only hold it together for so long. Now, sitting between her parents and wrapped in the safety of their arms, she couldn't stop the tears.

"My little lass." The lyrical Irish phrase, uttered in his East Texas twang, hit her as odd. He did that all the time. But growing up, she'd never noticed it.

Obviously, she'd been away too long. And become not only a rotten doctor and wife, but an inattentive daughter too.

Dad's soft touch on her hair sent guilt arrows zinging through her heart.

"You cannot do this to yourself, darlin'. We're here." He bent down in front of her and lifted her chin to look in his eyes. "We love you both, and the Lord does too. Our God is still a most powerful God."

Leave it to her father, the seminary theologian, to echo words that had grown hollow yet again. She nodded, yearning for the comfort of his faith while wanting to scream at his naiveté.

God might be powerful, but He still let people die. Or run a gauntlet of pain and exhaustion. Like Clint's second concussion in three months. And his pneumonia. Due to the chemo, this infection that a healthy person could easily fight off, might kill her husband.

Her sides ached from crying.

"Sara, this is not good for the baby." Her mother's appeal to maternal instincts failed. It just piled the guilt higher and heavier.

She was failing as a parent too.

She rubbed her abdomen, which would start ballooning any day now and serve as an even bigger reminder of her worst nightmare: losing Clint with a baby on the way.

Could her life get any worse?

Yes, she knew it could. She'd watched other families endure far more. Even so, her newfound hope was bruised, and she wanted to shake her fist at heaven and scream, "Enough!"

But not in front of her parents.

Not in front of other patients' families.

Not in front of her children.

She dried her eyes and straightened her back, taking deep breaths until she had her emotions back under control. "Why don't we go to the house so you can get settled?" She glanced at the waiting room clock. "Our babysitter couldn't come, so Steven's sister, Hanna, has been helping out. She should have the kids down for their naps by now. You'll be able to get at least a little rest before seeing them this evening."

Her parents exchanged one of their knowing looks as they started for the parking garage. Would she ever share that look with Clint again?

Another thought destined for the padded-cell place in her mind. The part of her that might explode soon if she didn't deal with all the issues piling one on top of the other.

No time now.

She had houseguests to care for and children whose frightened eyes still haunted her. She should have made sure they hadn't seen their father's collapse or the swarm of medical professionals working on him as they rushed him into the hospital.

Even she struggled with the images in her head from yesterday. A day she'd never forget.

A day when rage, terror, and defeat vied for first position in her heart. Failure had won.

⁂

"What day is it?"

Clint licked his lips and tried to make sense of all the wires and IV lines and beeping sounds. This wasn't a regular chemo day, was it?

"It's Saturday." A young Indian woman in a white coat shone a light into his eyes.

He tried to pull away and nearly yelped at the pain ricocheting through his head.

"Hold tight just a few more seconds for me."

He couldn't read her nametag. Blurry letters and a rectangle shape were as good as it got. He couldn't even answer all her bothersome questions.

"Who are you again?"

The mystery woman smiled. "I'm Dr. Mendonca, a neurologist. Dr. Rollins requested my evaluation because this is your second serious concussion in a little over two months."

This was not an answer to his prayers. Not the miracle he'd begged for. He now understood why Sara had such trouble praying these days.

"So you're my doctor while I'm in here." He hated the deadness in his voice. Looking at the plain white hospital walls, he wished he were in the Benefield Cancer Center again.

He tried to shake his head, but searing streaks of pain across his forehead stopped him. Then coughing threatened to make him pass out. What a wimp.

When he could get a steady breath, he slumped back into the bed. "Am I in ICU?"

"No. Not heading that way either, I hope."

That wasn't exactly encouraging.

Clint tried to stay awake for the rest of her assessment. Another concussion and pneumonia. Great. How this could be part of God's plan to get him back to work escaped him.

"I'll consult with your care team, and we'll discuss the results with you and Dr. Rollins when she arrives this evening." The doctor exited his room with a smile.

He had nothing to smile about.

A few minutes later, a man he didn't recognize strode into the room and stopped just inside the door. "Now what?" All he wanted to do was sleep and be left alone.

"I only need a minute of your time. See, I'm an old friend, and I have to leave for a business trip shortly." The man stepped closer and smiled.

The black jeans and white cable-knit sweater said he wasn't a doctor stopping by on rounds. Clint forced his brain to assimilate the details. On second glance, the man's face looked familiar, but his youthful features and condescending smirk didn't fit a recognizable acquaintance. Not that Clint could see it clearly. His head throbbed from trying to concentrate.

"Can't remember me, can you? I heard cancer was doing a number on you."

The taunt crawled over Clint's skin. "Care to tell me who you are?" His voice sounded like flint. Thank God for that little help.

Moving to the foot of the hospital bed, the man slipped his hands into his jeans pockets. "The medicines do that to you, don't they? They call it chemobrain, I think. Isn't that right? Or maybe you know it as declining neuropsychological function."

Clint swallowed the gall rising in his throat.

"I'll give you a little hint, Mister FBI Agent." The man moved a tan chair closer to Clint's bedside, just out of his reach. "You ruined my life with your meddling. I wouldn't really have hurt my son."

Clint pushed himself straight up with clenched fists.

"Since you're not quite up to snuff, I'll give you another hint. I've evaded the law for a long time now. But you people won't let the past alone. And your partner—Kessler, isn't it? His son looks so much like mine. And the others. The boy knows not to talk to strangers, right?"

The man leaned back in his chair and crossed his legs, way too smug and comfortable.

Focus. Years of Quantico training should make it easy to figure this guy out.

Who was he? Why was the creep targeting Steven?

"Ruined my life…hurt my son."

Standish?

"Where's the boy you kidnapped?" Clint fought to stay conscious. He might redeem himself and be of use to the case right here, right now.

The man sat forward. "You mean my son?"

"He's not your son."

"No matter. He's long dead, and you'll never find him. Wouldn't have turned out that way if you fools hadn't pushed me too far."

His visitor shoved the overstuffed tan chair back as he stood. "Well, I was simply in the neighborhood and wanted to check in on you. It's clear I'm ten steps ahead of you, anyway. And will remain so." He moved to the door.

Clint could hear the man's derisive chuckle as he disappeared down the hall. Hot barbed wires shoved into his chest.

He fought to stay awake. He needed to stand. Had to follow…

Grabbing the cold metal, he shoved the side rail down. The floor turned to Jell-O.

"Clint?" Sara crossed the room and put a hand on his chest. "What are you doing?"

Her terrified green eyes and the sweet smell of her vanilla perfume sent his mind reeling. Everything went blurry.

Sara nudged him back into the bed and clicked the rail into place.

"Visitor. Need to find him."

His wife's cold hands touched his forehead, then cupped his chin. "Who, Clint? There's no one here."

He couldn't force words through his cotton mouth.

Sara pushed the nurse's call button and paced.

"May I help you?" the nasal voice barked.

"This is Dr. Sara Rollins. I need Dr. Mendonca paged stat."

"Yes, Dr. Rollins."

He had to stay awake. Had to find that man. Sara might have seen him.

That thought compelled him to fight sleep, fight to stay conscious. "Tell Steven. Visitor."

The words disappeared as a coughing fit tore through him. Every fiber in every inch of his frame ached. Sleep. He needed sleep.

"Clint, who are you talking about? Tell Steven what? I didn't see anyone in your room." Sara's voice trailed off into the haze surrounding him.

"Tell Steven. Important. His son. Dead children…"

25

Sara's calendar blurred in front of her. The twenty-seventh of March. A Tuesday she'd dreaded for a month now.

She moved closer to her bathroom mirror. Maybe she could call Lucy and say she had a cold and it would be better if she didn't come. But she couldn't lie like that, not to Lucy. The red eyes and nasal congestion had nothing to do with germs and everything to do with her heart.

A weekend of wrestling with God didn't often yield any less.

Clint was still in the hospital. Still raging about seeing a man no one else had noticed. But his CT scan results were negative for hemorrhaging or contusion. And his pneumonia was finally under control.

Remembering the last few days hurt. She'd called Steven at Clint's demand even when she didn't know who the visitor was or why he was important. Before that, she'd watched her strong husband succumb to one more coughing spell and face a second concussion. Clint's hospitalization was one more proof of her incompetence.

Not only couldn't she do it all. She couldn't do even one thing well.

She should have been more careful when Jonathan got sick. She should have cleaned more, watched Clint closer, taken him to the doctor sooner. Something.

Anything.

She slid down the wall and rested on the soft beige carpet, her hand over her belly. Just out of the woods with morning sickness, and now stress upon stress had taken its place. She didn't have it in her to face this day.

"Hold on tight to the truth. God is still on His throne."

Frank's words penetrated the early morning haze in her mind. She tried to recall the truth God had shown her in bits and pieces over the weekend, the things Marilynn had said when she visited Clint's room.

Cancer was not her fault or Clint's. She could agree with that.

This dark path was not meant for evil, but good. That one she continued to struggle with at regular intervals. Like every ten minutes or so.

Fear was not God's way.

Neither was relying on circumstances…or depending on Clint to make her okay. God had shown her in no uncertain terms that Marilynn was on target with that statement.

The truth was, she'd always hidden behind Clint's strength. As a wife. As a parent. Even as a doctor. He'd always been the one to encourage her. To advise her. To remind her to pray.

What if Clint died?

She shouldn't keep going there. He was getting better. Clinging to that little shred of hope, she stood and brushed her teeth.

"Are you depending on circumstances?"

Marilynn's question chafed. How was she supposed to figure out how to depend on God alone instead of Clint?

"Sara, are you ready for today?" Her mom's melodic voice floated through the closed bedroom door.

Then little hands pounded the door. "Come in, Mama. Gammie an' me wanna see you." Jonathan giggled and continued to play the drum on her door.

She opened it with slow precision lest a little body come barreling through. Her almost-three-year-old stood and stared at her, still in her pajamas.

"You here, Mama." He pointed to her slightly rounded belly. "What's dat?"

"It's your baby brother or sister."

"Want a sister, like 'Sannah."

Her eyes stung with tears at his sweet declaration of love for his big sister. Susannah would beam when she heard later this afternoon.

"Why you crying?" Jonathan didn't miss much. He usually knew before anyone opened their mouth what the emotional climate of the room was. Her son might not be old enough to articulate his knowledge, but she could see it in his eyes.

She took him into her arms. "Mama has to go see a friend who's really sick, and I'm a little sad, honey." She waited for his response. No sense saying more than he wanted to know.

"Pway for her? Like me pway for Daddy?"

Tears threatened again. What a simple, beautiful faith. Jonathan hadn't picked that up from her. No, Clint had been the shining example of praying in all circumstances.

Maybe it'd be better for the children if she died instead of Clint.

Eyes closed, she tried to rein in her thoughts.

Lies were so hard to battle. Why did awful ideas slam into her at times like this?

Her mom stepped forward. "Jonathan, why don't we go fix your mama some good food before we go to the park?"

Jonathan took his grandmother's hand and led her away, rattling off all the things they could make for breakfast.

A deep sigh escaped. Jonathan was in good hands with Catherine O'Toole. She allowed him to be his sweet inquisitive self without trying to shut him down and hurry Sara into her day. Mom had always been that way. She listened without judgment. Encouraged without pushing. Prayed without fanfare. And guided without demanding.

She'd also shown Sara how to respect others without compromising truth. No icy arrogance toward anyone. No nagging wife or coy "feminine wiles" manipulation. Nothing but truth and gentle strength.

One more example Sara would never live up to.

She turned back to her mirror and finished her morning routine, focusing on anything but the battle raging within her.

Twenty minutes later, with a decent makeup job and her favorite blue capris, blue and white polo, and white jacket—she looked ready for the world.

Inside was another matter.

❊ ❊ ❊

Transported back in time, Sara watched through the window of Lucy Cohen's hospital door.

Here they were again. Because she had failed.

Logically, nothing in Lucy's case pointed to Sara's incompetence. But to her bruised heart, this procedure registered as yet another defeat.

Glad Lucy couldn't see her, she tried to compose herself. She considered turning around and leaving, but she promised. And since the full-body radiation was complete, the actual transplant today would be pretty anticlimactic.

Even so, the odds weren't in Lucy's favor, perfect six-out-of-six donor match or not.

Sara walked in.

"Dr. Rollins, I'm so glad you're here." Lucy looked up from her sterile steel-and-white hospital bed.

All her former patient's hair had disappeared with the recent massive doses of chemo. But Lucy maintained a cheerful attitude.

"It's Sara, remember?" She stepped forward, trying not to slip in the booties she'd tied around her shoes. The surgical mask and gown didn't improve her mood. And she sure wasn't sorry to have missed all the practical procedures necessary for preventing infection in bone-marrow transplant patients.

She prayed Clint would never see this point.

"Do you remember my Sinéad O'Connor look?" Lucy's smile invited Sara to relax. "Not quite as fashionable now, is it?"

"You have Sinéad beat any day." Sara leaned against the faded teal wall at the foot of Lucy's bed. "Did you donate to Locks of Love again?"

"Yes. The nurses kept telling me they'd pay triple for a wig made from my hair."

Sara almost kicked herself for encouraging this conversation thread. Nothing about cancer remained a clinical reality. It was all personal now. And swirled in the middle of everything were issues of vanity and symbols of defeat. Like hair loss.

She'd always known that alopecia registered as a crushing blow. But now she understood how intimate an assault it really was. And she hadn't even been able to help Clint. Since that first shave, he'd taken care of it himself.

"I thought the transplant would be a little more exciting than being hooked up to a blood-transfusion device."

"You wanted scalpels and staples?"

Lucy laughed. "No, guess not. A bald head and needle bruises are all the battle scars I can manage."

The room fell into uncomfortable silence.

"Has Dr. Holland given any indication of when you'll be discharged?" Sara bit her lip, hoping Lucy could stay out of the hospital as much as possible.

The young woman sniffled. Sara wanted to hug and comfort her, but she had to keep her distance. No physical contact. That was the rule.

"I'm staying only as long as I have to. Hopefully, no longer than forty-eight hours. Then my family and I will do everything possible to avoid a quick return visit." Lucy looked around the room at the medical equipment and sparse decorations. No plants or flowers were allowed, only a few balloons. That left a barren room, even with all the cancer center's pains to promote a nonhospital environment.

"Don't be a superpatient, Lucy. Come in quickly if the mouth and throat sores keep you from eating. Seeing you in that kind of pain won't help your family."

Lucy wiped her cheeks. "It's so hard to be here, though. The last few days, during the intensive chemo, I haven't been able to hug or kiss my children. My arms ache to hold them."

Sara closed her eyes. She had little to offer that didn't sound Pollyannaish.

"I'm not giving up, though." Lucy sat up straighter. "We beat it once. So I'm just going to believe we'll do it again. You always said God hears the prayers of His people and that He still does miracles."

Sara nodded. She knew Lucy's chances. Graft-versus-host disease attacked one-third to one-half of allogeneic transplant recipients. And serious GVHD could be life threatening, even with a successful transplant.

Lucy's hazel eyes blinked slower and slower.

Sara stepped toward the door. "I'm praying, Lucy, and I believe you're doing exactly what you're supposed to do. I remember all those newsletters you sent to family and friends the first time. Your faith in God came through every one."

"Thanks for your prayers. We'll win again. Right, Sara?"

Lucy drifted off to sleep as nurses came in to do their duties. Sara slipped out behind them and made her way to the hospital chapel.

What would she have said if Lucy had been awake to hear her response?

❋   ❋   ❋

Hanna hesitated before knocking on Michael's apartment door. Going through with her apology and explanation would take their relationship to another level.

But she needed a safe place to let herself cry, to feel. Being alone terrified her.

The worry over Clint's hospital stay, the terror in his children's eyes, and the memory of her mom's death pressed her into action. Maybe talking to Michael tonight would help silence the whispered taunts from her past. She didn't want to relive her twenty-second birthday, her first without her mom, when she'd wondered if the bottom of a bottle of pills might be her only escape.

Through the years, she and Steven had grieved together. Now Steven had Gracie. Dad would feel responsible for not helping her more if he saw how Mom's death still affected her. And Clint and Sara had their own problems.

Who else could she turn to but Michael?

She shivered and forced her hand to the buzzer.

Michael opened the door. His eyes flashed warmth, then turned guarded in a split second. "Hanna."

Everything in her wanted to run into his arms and prove she hadn't stood him up on purpose. But she stayed rooted in place. "I guess you know by now why I didn't make it to the restaurant on Friday."

Hurt showed all over his stoic face. "Steven passed along your apology."

"I'm truly sorry, Michael. I didn't mean to ruin your night. I wanted to be there. But when Clint passed out and ended up in the hospital, I had to help." She swallowed the tears threatening to spill. "Erica was away for the weekend, Steven was at the hospital and picking up Sara's parents from the airport, and Susannah and Jonathan needed me."

"You could've returned my calls."

She hung her head. "I was trying to help Susannah and Jonathan process seeing their daddy collapse and then be strapped to a stretcher. They thought he was dead." She couldn't hold back the tears any longer. "Clint's like a brother to me. And watching his children in pain was like looking into a mirror. I saw me years ago, watching my mom die all over again. I…I'm sorry I didn't call."

Michael wrapped her in a hug, and she cried harder. He maneuvered them into his apartment and closed the door. "When did your mom pass away?"

"In March. Nine years ago."

"I'm sorry."

She leaned out from Michael's arms, placing her hands on his solid chest. Before she could think of something to say, he nodded toward the living room and led her to a beige leather sofa.

His apartment resembled a European studio she'd seen in a magazine. Bamboo sculptures, strong earth tones, chrome accents. The kitchen beyond the breakfast bar looked spotless and very male. No cute potholders or fancy wall hangings, nothing but black, green, and shiny fixtures.

"You don't like my apartment?"

Could she do anything right around this man? "No. I mean that's not what I was thinking. I do like your apartment."

"But…"

"It's just very male. That's all."

He grinned. "And that's a bad thing?"

"It's not." The muscles under his white T-shirt held her attention. She swallowed hard. "Will you forgive me for standing you up and not calling to explain? I'm really sorry."

He scooted closer.

Her muscles tensed, but she stayed glued to her seat on the couch.

"I forgive you." He pointed his chin toward the door. "And I'm sorry for the icy reception earlier. You didn't deserve that."

"Thank you." His kindness sparked another rain of tears. As he pulled her closer, her mind screamed, "Flee." Her body didn't obey. And neither did her heart.

"Hanna." His breath warmed her hair. "I don't want you to be alone right now, but we can't stay here like this."

Tears slid down her cheek. No one but her father and brother had ever made her feel so safe and treasured.

Michael stood and pulled her up beside him, right outside his embrace.

"Let me call Gracie. Steven's bound to be at her house dealing with the same grief you are." He stepped away and grabbed the cordless phone by the kitchen. "It'd be good for all of you to be together."

She should have done that. If there was room in her heart for three important men, Steven had to have room in his for both her and Gracie.

A short phone conversation later, Michael took her hand again. "Steven said they'd be here in twenty minutes. He doesn't want you driving and crying at the same time." He led her to the other side of the room. "Let's take a walk. It'll do us both some good." After slipping on some high-end running shoes, he grabbed his keys and belt holster.

Hanna wrinkled her nose, looking at the gun. "It's not like we're in a high-crime area."

"No, we're not." He shrugged. "But this is part of who I am. And I think the Boy Scout motto applies at all times."

"Always be prepared?"

He nodded.

As they walked outside, she looked up into the night sky. Was she prepared for what was ahead?

Probably not. But maybe with Michael, this time she'd get it right.

26

C lint's got another chemo tomorrow, huh?"

Steven nodded at Lee's question, then focused on the Eutaw Place traffic passing in front of them. He hated talking about cancer. Especially Clint's. Still wished Hanna hadn't flung the door so wide open last night that he couldn't escape the topic.

Because now, thanks to the combined effects of the concussion, pneumonia, and chemo, Clint would be sidelined until the end of next week. Probably longer. No normal shoptalk. No seeing his partner in a suit instead of those awful hospital togs. No escape from the destruction of cancer.

Even with his partner's stubborn declaration that he was fine, the past few visits at the hospital had proven more depressing than Steven could handle. Especially when Clint kept insisting that Ed Standish had visited him in the hospital.

No one on duty Saturday could verify any visitor, let alone Standish.

Lee closed the file he was reviewing. "Chief Dickson's not thrilled about you interviewing his girlfriend, is he?"

"Nope."

"So why are we doing it?"

"Because Standish was sighted in his old Bolton Hill neighborhood. Baltimore PD looked into it and came up with zilch. I need more. Maybe Gloria Standish can give it to me."

"Good thing Standish's baby brother is still locked up."

"Yep." Steven maneuvered his Bucar into a tight parking space on the street.

Staring at the beautiful two-story tan house with its mature trees and low white picket fence, he shook his head at the irony.

Everything looked so normal.

But Wes Standish had endured a hell no child should ever face: being drugged, kidnapped, shot at, and surrounded by strangers when he woke up in the hospital. All that on top of having a dad who'd orchestrated his abduction and was wanted in multiple states for crimes still not cataloged.

They'd brought Wes home though. Alive. Which meant the boy still had a chance to heal.

Steven checked his watch. Ten minutes early. More like right on time.

"Chief Dickson gonna come supervise?" Lee stepped out of the Bucar and stretched.

"No. Too busy with administrative issues."

Lee huffed. "Join the crowd."

Wes's mom met them at the door, her dark brown pantsuit covered by a large apron. "Hello, Agent Kessler. Agent Branson. Ben told me to expect you." She wiped sculpting clay from her manicured fingernails. "Prep work for a group of elementary students I'm teaching tomorrow. New technique."

She held the door open for them.

"I need to run back to my studio for a moment. Please make yourselves comfortable in the living room." She disappeared down the front hallway.

Steven and Lee stepped into the formal room to their right. Lee whistled. "I've been in some nice homes, but this lady's got some serious art bling goin' on."

Marble sculptures of dolphins and a few ornate candles decorated the tables around the white leather chairs and sofa. The beige walls held impressionist beach paintings by an artist Steven didn't recognize.

He sat on the edge of the couch near Lee. "Not hurting in the finance department either."

Gloria Standish had a BFA from Virginia Tech, where she'd met her husband, and ran a lucrative art studio in Baltimore's cultural district. Even so, she must have acquired her décor long before the divorce. Or maybe Gloria and Chief Dickson shared a passion for collecting high-end art. But so far, the chief hadn't moved in or slipped an engagement ring on Gloria's finger.

"I'm glad you like my home." Gloria flipped her blond-and-black striped hair over her shoulder and perched on the love seat closest to them, long legs crossed at the ankles. No traces of art aprons or clay remained. "By your conspicuous assessment, I'm sure you're wondering how I can afford all this."

Dating a cop must have increased her powers of perception. "Yes, I was."

"My parents were the proprietors of an art gallery within walking distance of Bolton Hill. They were wise investors and took excellent care of the home that had been in my father's family for years. It became mine after my father died of a heart attack, and my mother followed soon after. Some say she died of a broken heart." She shrugged and flicked her hand in the air. "That's a little too sentimental for me."

Interesting.

"The point is, I don't need help from Ed. A good thing, because I haven't gotten a dime since the separation. But Wes and I will manage fine without him."

"How is Wes?"

She glanced at the gold clock on the end table, biting her lip until she turned back to speak. "My son is coping. Counseling has helped substantially." She touched her empty left ring finger. "What would help more is your putting my ex-husband behind bars."

Lee leaned forward. "That's why we're here. Hoping you can supply a little more information regarding his recent sighting in the neighborhood."

"I have no firsthand knowledge of that. Every officer in Baltimore is supposed to be on alert for his unwanted presence anywhere near

Wes. A neighbor claimed to have seen him and called the police before calling me."

"You don't believe your neighbor actually spotted Ed."

Gloria blew out a sharp breath. "I sincerely hope not. If I set eyes on him before his burial, it will be—"

"Mom!" The back door slammed, and a red-faced Wes Standish ran in the room, a worn soccer ball tucked under one arm. "Hey, Mom. Agent Kessler!" He looked at Lee.

Lee smiled. "Lee Branson."

"Hey, Agent Branson. Mom, I scored on Devon today! And he's the best goalie ever." He swiped a hand over his sweaty forehead. "Then after practice, Stu's mom took us out for ice cream."

"I'll have a talk with Stu's mom. She should have called before a change of plans." Her angled face pinched tighter. "Why don't you get a shower and start homework? I'll be up to help in a few minutes, and Ben should be here around seven to take us out for dinner."

"Is Agent Kessler coming with us?"

"No, Wes." Her voice hardened. "Agent Kessler will be leaving very soon. Now…shower."

"Yes ma'am." Wes hustled up the stairs.

Steven waited until Gloria tore her gaze from the stairway. "I have a few questions about your ex-husband's history."

"I'll have you know right now, I had no idea my ex-husband was such a despicable, perverted man. He never touched Wes, or I'd have thrown him out long before."

"You're sure about that."

She closed her eyes and clenched her hands together. "I assure you, if Ed had tried anything with Wes, I would have found out. And the counselor's confirmed that Wes shows no signs of…of being abused by Ed in that way."

"I know this whole matter is unsettling." Steven rested his clasped hands on his knees, leaning forward. "But any insight you can give could provide a lead."

"Please ask your questions so we can be finished."

"Did your ex-husband always travel a good deal?"

"He spent long weekends at various racetracks during the season. One of the perks of being a professor was his flexible schedule. Though, as you know, he abused the privilege and got himself fired."

"He only traveled for gambling?"

"No. When he was at the university, he frequented as many educational conferences as the department would bankroll. Presented a number of papers on things like human growth and development. He was an early childhood specialist."

Ugh. Not a pleasant thought in light of Ed Standish's revolting computer cache.

"Did the conferences usually fall in January?"

"Some. I have no idea what he did most Januaries though. After our anniversary in December, he'd just disappear for a week or two. The holidays were never a good time for us. Not that it was a great marriage to begin with." Gloria stood to gaze out her front window. "Looking back and adding in Ben's theories about my ex-husband, it stands to reason why Christmas was always miserable." She shuddered.

"Can you shed any light on Ed's computer habits?"

"Nothing beyond his obsession with technology. When Wes was awake and Ed wasn't working or traveling, they'd be together playing computer games. Even taking apart old computers. Sometimes he'd spend all night in his office. I thought he was avoiding me."

"But now?"

"Now it appears Ed used the computer to feed his mind with all manner of perversion."

The questions would only get worse. "Did you know about your husband's extramarital affairs?"

She snorted. "Of course I knew. He never bothered to hide it. But I couldn't understand why he'd go looking elsewhere when he wanted so little to do with me. Knowing that Ed's girlfriends all had sons, now it begins to make sense."

Lee cleared his throat. "Any anonymous callers or contact with Wes at school?"

"No. The patrols around the school have been increased, as have the ones in our neighborhood. School officials know the circumstances and will call the police if they spot Ed. Our carpool has been instructed to alert me about any suspicious activity or changes in routine." She turned to face them, and her lips tightened into a straight, thin line. "Or they're supposed to notify me."

"And here at home?"

"I've had the security system updated." Her eyes narrowed. "And I now know how to use the handgun Ben suggested I purchase."

Standish would be a fool to try anything at their house. Unless he didn't know about his ex-wife's new shooting skills.

For everyone's sake, Steven hoped Gloria would have no reason to use her firepower.

"Can we go back to your neighbor's report of seeing Ed a block from your house?"

Gloria seated herself with a little less aloofness. In fact, the fingering of her leather-and-silver choker indicated fear. "I've already made it clear that I didn't see anything."

"Discussing this bothers you more than the other questions I've asked."

"Agent Kessler, my son was kidnapped and drugged once. Almost kidnapped a second time. If there's one thing Ed Standish is, it's persistent. He's never failed to complete something he set his mind to. In school, with his research and with every hobby he's ever attempted, he never stopped until he'd mastered it. He won't give up." She took a shaky breath. "Talking about this yet again, knowing he's somewhere near us, watching and waiting, has me understandably upset."

"I can see that, ma'am."

Gloria waited a moment, then stood. "I think it's time for you both to go." She strode to the door, her stilettos clicking on the gleaming hardwood. "If you have any more questions concerning the investigation, please call Ben. I'm sure you have his number." She opened the door wide.

"Thank you for meeting with us today." He and Lee stopped in front of Gloria. "We appreciate your time."

Gloria nodded but stood next to the door in silence.

"Please let Wes know we said good-bye. He's a wonderful boy. I hope with counseling he continues to heal." Steven smiled. "And give him our best for his next soccer game."

She didn't return his smile. "Thank you for returning my son to me." She held the door handle with white knuckles. "Now please, help Ben and his officers make sure Wes stays safe. By putting his father away for the rest of his natural life."

27

Michael leaned on his boss's desk Thursday morning. "We have another Standish sighting."

Kessler continued typing and didn't even acknowledge him.

Straightening his shoulders, Michael cleared his throat and shoved his scribbled notes forward on Steven's desk.

The CACU coordinator turned ten shades of fury. Words that would never pass through his mouth no doubt scorched his mind.

"Why is Standish never apprehended? And why hasn't anyone seen Mattie in more than a month?" Kessler stood, nearly knocking over his chair. "Don't answer that."

"Is this all about Standish, or are other cases compounding things?"

Steven sagged back into his seat. "I had a consult with the Innocent Images Unit a few minutes ago on a domestic kidnapping. The father created videos of him with his daughter and uploaded them to the Internet. I also have an autopsy report to deal with on another missing child investigation."

Michael's stomach roiled. Innocent Images cases and pictures tormented even the most hardened agents.

"Where was Standish spotted this time?" Steven resumed typing.

"He wasn't seen exactly. One of the women he dated while working at the university contacted police after receiving a phone call from him this morning."

"Dickson and his people are on it?"

"Yes." Michael shifted from one foot to the other. "Want me to put in an appearance and see what else I can learn?"

"No. You have other cases that require your attention. Unless Baltimore PD gives us reason to believe it's not another dead end or ghost chase, I need you here."

Taking care of Clint's work too.

Michael returned to his desk, shoulders taut like a rubber band stretched to its limit. If Steven thought Mattie was still alive, they'd have been out the door, no questions asked.

❈ ❈ ❈

"I'm going back to work tomorrow."

Sara ignored her husband's ridiculous comment and looked around the Benefield Center's day-treatment facility. A number of patients milled about the area that resembled a hotel lobby. In the room where Clint sat, other patients were getting shots and hooking up to their chemo via PICC lines or ports. She said hello to a few she'd worked with before going on leave. But there were many she didn't recognize.

Only a month off work, and everything had changed. Life kept moving.

And death kept coming.

Clint had almost died for the second time this year. Not that he'd admit it. He'd say he'd only had a few minor concussions and a bullet "scratch."

She knew different.

"Did you hear me?" he asked.

She glanced over at the gloved nurse mixing Clint's chemo and snapped to attention. "I'll see you in a minute," she told Clint. "I shouldn't be in here with the chemicals. For the baby's sake."

She exited the room fast. Everything in her wanted to call her mom and run away from the treatment center, the cancer, and Clint's bullheaded insistence he could return to work. But Mom was at the zoo with Susannah and Jonathan. They'd talk later.

Finding herself in the hospital chapel yet again, Sara sat and studied the stained-glass windows. Before Clint's diagnosis, she'd spent time here every day she had worked, seeking wisdom and praying for her patients.

"It's good to find you in this place."

Sara turned at the sound of Marilynn's voice. Her best friend had been her mainstay during Clint's recent hospitalization, but now her eyes held trouble.

"Is something wrong with Clint?" The bile churning in her stomach hit her throat, scorching as she tried to find her footing.

Marilynn took her hand and gently tugged her to the front of the chapel. "No. Clint is fine."

Marilynn's bright patterned dress hung just to her ankles. Her beautiful mocha skin and curvy figure made every one of her outfits look stunning. Sara shook her head. Why did she keep focusing on such unimportant details?

"It's Lucy Cohen."

The words registered as a blow to her chest.

"Here. Sit down before you faint."

Sara molded into the oak bench and tried to still her shaking hands. "What happened?" Like she didn't already know.

"Lucy's on a morphine pump and being fed intravenously. She couldn't swallow due to the mouth and throat sores."

Tears spilled from Sara's tired eyes. How many more could she cry? But she'd known Lucy's chances of avoiding complications were slim to none. "Did she even get to go home?"

"No."

Sara leaned her head back against the pew.

"Don't go where your face says you're headed."

"It's not right, Marilynn. Lucy beat it once. For three years. She was almost out of the woods and moving on with her life. She has little ones who need her and a husband who adores her. She can't die."

Marilynn wrapped her in a hug. "Is this about Lucy or Clint?"

She didn't know. Both. Neither. She wiped her nose and dried her tears with the Kleenex Marilynn handed her.

"It's about God. I'm really struggling with how He fits into all this. It's hard to depend on God when I don't even want to talk to Him."

Marilynn stayed silent a minute. "Have you ever considered that praising Him instead of ignoring Him might be good for your heart?"

There were days when all she could manage was Martin Luther's desperate prayer, "Jesus, I'm Yours. Save me." Other times she just didn't know what to say.

Now she should praise Him? She didn't feel like singing or sending fake platitudes up to the heavens.

"God inhabits the praises of His people."

"I know. But hope hurts. So does praise." Not that she'd really tried it lately.

Marilynn raised her eyebrows.

"I can't, Marilynn. It's impossible to thank God for what's happening."

Marilynn didn't answer but reached in her pocket and handed Sara a white MP3 player with dangling earbuds. "As I was praying for you earlier, God put on my heart to give this to you. I've uploaded a number of songs I think might help. There's one by Matt Redmond I believe will speak to exactly where you are. If you'll let it."

"What's the song?" Sara stared at the small metal rectangle.

"'Blessed Be Your Name.'" Marilynn took her hand. "It's about praising God when things are as they should be and when the darkness closes in. When the Lord gives and when He takes away."

"But what if Clint…? I can't lose him."

"I know." Her friend pulled her close again and rocked ever so slightly. Just like a mama caring for a little baby whose needs were met but still wouldn't settle down to sleep.

Sara stayed that way, in the safety of her friend's arms, and waited for some sense of God's comfort. Nothing came.

"How do I praise God when life hurts so much?" The question came out in a whisper.

Marilynn leaned back. "Be honest about the pain even as you offer praise. That's how you draw close, find intimacy with Him." Marilynn tilted her head, tears glistening in her eyes. "Jesus understands your pain. He's not indifferent to it. Instead, He enters into it with you."

Sara sniffled. Praise Him when her emotions blew in the wind like a tattered rag?

Marilynn stood and straightened her dress. "Pray for Lucy. But don't go see her today. I'll let her know you were here."

Sara nodded, relieved. Facing Lucy wouldn't have made dealing with Clint any easier. She still had no idea how to handle his fool-hardy insistence on going back to work too soon. He would likely ignore Dr. Silverman's orders to stay home another week. But as tempting as it was, taking a sledgehammer to his thickheaded stubbornness wouldn't help.

What in the world would?

She rehearsed Marilynn's words as her friend exited the chapel.

"Praise God when things are as they should be and when the darkness closes in. When the Lord gives and when He takes away."

Could she really do that?

❋ ❋ ❋

Clint willed his stomach to stop churning as he buttoned his dress shirt.

"You are not going back to work today." Sara folded her arms over her chest.

Yesterday's argument continued. Still, Clint tugged on his shoes and fought the fatigue that dogged every move. "I can handle this. I'll go in for a few hours and come home. I need to track down Standish."

His co-workers could use all available help.

Because God and His miracles were way too slow in coming these days.

Not only that, Standish had made it personal. Even if no one believed the man had shown up at the hospital to taunt him, Clint had seen enough pictures to identify the perp.

"You were just released." Sara crossed their bedroom and picked up the cordless phone. "I'll call Steven and tell him exactly what the doctors said about your risk of infection and how crucial it is to rest after multiple concussions."

You're weak and worthless to everyone. The mental jab came more and more often since his last hospital stay.

Rage ripped through his chest, and he clenched his fists. His mind screamed at his feet to walk out of the house before he could say or do something he'd regret.

Jonathan ran down the hall and stopped in the open doorway. "Why Daddy mad?"

"Come here, honey." Sara held out her hands. "Daddy's just concerned about work."

The fear in her actions and eyes sent Clint racing out of the room, down the stairs, and out the front door.

Work. He needed to get in his truck and drive to work. His head throbbed.

He felt in the pockets of his black pants. No keys. Nothing. He tried the matching suit coat. Nothing. Turning to face the house again, he remembered his in-laws in the guest suite adjacent to the basement family room. They'd be awake soon, and his storming inside might make a scene.

He didn't want them involved.

Spring's morning chill motivated him into action. He tried the garage's side door. Locked. He kicked it with a fury that smarted his ego as badly as his foot.

A wave of fatigue almost knocked him to the ground, reminding him of Sara's valid caution.

Now he wanted to swear. But his elderly neighbors would more than likely hear him, and what an example that would be. Their local FBI agent all decked out for work and cussing like a drug dealer.

The backyard gate opened with a click.

"Forget your keys, did you, Son?"

Sara's father stood in front of him, probing eyes meeting Clint's foul mood with an unspoken challenge. This wasn't a man Clint wanted to battle today or any day. They were close in height, similar build. And heart to heart, Patrick O'Toole had enough faith and fire to run circles around him.

"Yes. I forgot my keys."

Patrick stepped aside. "Do you remember our first meeting?" The man motioned toward the floral patio furniture Sara and her mother had cleaned up days ago.

"Yes sir." Some of it anyway.

They both took a seat.

"I remember knowing you were the perfect match for my little girl."

"You didn't let on."

Patrick laughed. "No. Not for a good while, did I?"

How nice it would be to laugh and follow his father-in-law down memory lane. But Clint had a job to do and only a few waking hours of strength. He needed to head in to the office and get the latest update on Mattie's case. Help Michael hold on to hope that the child was still alive. Because Standish was a bad liar. No matter what the man had said in the hospital, Clint believed they could rescue Mattie yet.

"I will not lecture you. But this I will say." Patrick leaned forward and looked straight through Clint's heart. "Your work is vital. Important. On this we all agree. But my little girl and your children—all three of them—need their husband and father. Need him in health, not pushing to an early grave."

The fight in his bones drained out of him. "I know, Patrick."

His father-in-law stood and put his strong hand on Clint's shoulder. "You're a good man, Clint Rollins. You will do right. I know you will."

Minutes later, Clint stared into his empty backyard. The greening trees swayed in the morning breeze. Wet earth and grass scents stung his nose.

All signs of spring's new life.

He exhaled a long breath. Eyelids feeling like lead weights, he made his way through the unlocked basement door and still silent house to his first-floor study. He'd work from home today. Search the Net here. Apologize later to Sara and then to his father-in-law.

Sleep first. His sand-colored couch drew him with palpable force.

Beneath the fatigue, emotions still flared. Fear stalked. Rage ignited at all the things he couldn't do because of cancer and the necessary evil of chemo. He couldn't sleep at normal times. Couldn't handle work when every moment and every body working a case counted.

He'd have to deal with God about all that. Again.

But for now he'd rest.

Not like he had much choice in the matter.

※   ※   ※

"This is Crystal Hernandez with the National Center for Missing and Exploited Children."

Michael sat up straighter and hit the "save" icon for the file he was updating. The pretty Hispanic analyst didn't usually call to chat. Not since he'd turned down her invitation to dinner. "Do you have something for me?"

"Just completed an analysis of a CyberTipline report that might interest you. It'll be accessible shortly, but I figured you'd appreciate a call as well."

"Absolutely."

"Baltimore PD has been notified too. An anonymous poster reported a man fitting Edward Standish's description browsing a child-porn site at the new public library branch in central Baltimore. The poster believes it's our guy because of all the pictures he or she has seen around town lately."

Michael touched his holster and stood, barely holding on to the phone. This could be it. "Thanks, Crystal. I'll let Kessler know, and we'll get on this right away."

After securing his laptop for transport, he grabbed his suit coat and went to find Steven. They could review the tipline report on the way to central Baltimore. But for now they needed to move, racing the clock and praying the locals would have Standish in handcuffs before their arrival.

28

Good Friday came early this year. Too bad catching Standish didn't.

Steven tossed his keys on the foyer table and headed into the kitchen as he loosened his favorite basketball tie. At least one more perverted child-porn addict was off the street. Too bad the guy nabbed at the Baltimore library wasn't their perp. Not the one who could have revealed Mattie's whereabouts or led them to the others. Dead or alive.

Most likely dead.

Grabbing a Coke from the fridge, he noticed his son's school projects covering the door. Held side by side with Cardinal magnets were April shower collages and May flowers made by gluing paper basketballs inside baking cups. Gracie's art projects drew out a smile. A much-needed change from the place his thoughts had been headed.

He glanced at the clock over the sink. James and Dad would be here any minute, Gracie shortly after. Then he and Gracie would meet the Rollinses for dinner at the Morrison House, the first place he'd taken Gracie on a date.

A quick chug finished off his soda, and he sprinted upstairs. March had not been kind in terms of work, Clint's health, or one of his favorite distractions—U of L basketball. And planning a wedding with a best man who looked like the Grim Reaper's punching bag wouldn't be easy. He shrugged away the thoughts with his suit coat and moved to his walk-in closet.

Seeing Gracie and hearing her truth-filled words would help him focus on God instead of his best friend battling an enemy that had already stolen so much. He pulled some tan dress pants and a white button-up off the hangers.

"Think you'll be ready for dinner soon?"

The feminine voice in the hall made his senses come alive. So did the beautiful woman standing in the doorway, giving him a hundred-watt smile.

"I recognize that look." Gracie stayed in the hallway.

"Then why aren't you running the other way?" Tossing his outfit on the bed, he closed the distance between them and touched his lips to her soft auburn hair. She smelled of honey and strawberries.

"Because July seventh is only three months away, and I know you'll do the right thing."

"Not if you stay here." He cupped her cheeks in his hands and kissed her with years of pent-up longing.

Gracie steadied herself with outstretched palms on his chest. "Steven Kessler."

Her now-shaky voice snapped him out of the hazy, red-hot place his mind had gone. One look in her deep hazel eyes strengthened his resolve.

"I'm sorry."

She smiled again. "I'm not. But we have a wedding to plan tonight. And to wait for."

"Which is why you need to head downstairs. Fast." When her floral-print dress disappeared beyond his bedroom door, he exhaled and headed for the dresser.

She poked her head back through the wide-open doorway. "I knew you'd do the right thing." With a wink, she disappeared once more, her gentle giggle floating down the stairs.

She had more faith in him than he did.

Within fifteen minutes, he'd showered and dressed and forced his mind to safer places. Like their upcoming dinner with Clint and Sara. Tonight Gracie and Sara would talk about reception plans, music selections, and bouquet options. He and Clint would smile and nod and talk smack about favorite sports teams. Trivia, compared to work, but a far better place to dwell.

Steven slipped his wallet into his pocket. He'd take wedding details over the depressing shadows of cancer and serial profiles that dominated his nightmares.

Even discussing flower colors he honestly couldn't care less about.

Unless Gracie wore them on their honeymoon…minus the wedding dress.

❊ ❊ ❊

"Are you going to make it to church later tonight?"

Clint ignored Steven's question. It hammered at a raw topic. One he couldn't stop wrestling over with God.

He still wasn't back to work after his last hospital incarceration. In his current state, a simple evening out was a major production. Where were the answers to his prayers?

"You still with us, partner?"

Sara pursed her lips. And the look on Steven's face suggested Gracie had kicked him under the table.

Clint chuckled. Their protectiveness didn't scorch his ego this time. That showed a little progress. "Nothing like mother hens, huh?"

Steven rubbed his shin. "Nope. Nothing quite like 'em."

Sara and Gracie both huffed. Then they all four laughed.

"Enough dancing around the elephant in the room tonight, okay?" Clint kept his voice low. "It's been a rough week. I think I'll pass on attending the service tonight. I want to be there Sunday to celebrate Easter."

Sara squeezed his hand, and a wave of confidence surged through him. They'd make it through this battle. Together. Listening to all the stories on chemo days and hearing it from Sara as well, he knew many patients survived the disease but still lost their marriages.

Not them. He would never again keep Sara isolated from friends, shut down and hiding because of his bullheaded ego trip. Through Frank and again through Sara's dad, God had taught him the foolishness of his early way of handling things.

Now all he needed was for God to hurry up with the miracles.

"Well, let's order and then talk wedding stuff." Sara picked up her elegant menu. "You know, Gracie, you all could change the plans and get married right here in the Morrison House Hotel."

The twinkle in Sara's eyes left the rest of her thoughts unspoken.

Gracie blushed her answer to Sara's teasing.

"I think a *meal* at The Grille is about all I can afford." Steven's stomach growled as a waiter placed steaming plates of salmon and ribs on a nearby table.

The young waitress took their order with forced professionalism. She looked like she wanted to go home as badly as Clint longed to get back in the game.

Soon. He'd keep working out and stay focused on the goal. Fight the fatigue, return to his old life, and put Standish behind bars. Maybe even bring some missing kids safely home.

Steven's cell phone buzzed. "It's Lee. I'll be right back."

Clint followed as his partner stepped outside and flipped his phone open.

"Kessler." He listened to Steven's side of the conversation with increasing interest. "Any report on the victim's age?"

A body? Clint hated that possibility, but if it meant a crack in this steel case, he'd take it. Because if they caught Standish, they'd keep other kids out of his hands. They couldn't change what had already happened. But they could have an impact on the future.

"Stay on it and let me know. We could be in for a long night later if this pans out." Steven closed the phone. "Locals are digging in Rock Creek Park tonight. An old man and his dog found a human leg bone, and the crime scene guys are tearing up the place. Lee was working late and took the call."

"We need to head out?"

"Not yet. We should go back in and eat." But Steven just stood there, staring into the growing dusk.

"You're thinking about Olivia."

It wasn't a question. Neither one of them could forget being called out to Memorial Hill Park last summer. Seeing the decaying body of a British teenager they'd hoped to find alive had left an indelible mark.

When Steven later shot Olivia's killer, he'd saved another child. He'd done his job. But their job came with a price. The use of deadly force, no matter how necessary, ripped into the life of every agent it touched.

"You want to talk about it?

"No." Steven wouldn't meet his eyes.

Clint stepped closer. "I know that look. I've seen it plenty over the years. You shut down to protect the people you love. But it only makes things worse."

"I just don't want to discuss it."

"If you don't want to talk to me, at least let Gracie know what's going on. She can handle whatever it is you need to get out, even if it means rehashing the past." Clint bit back a yawn. "Sharing your dreams and your nightmares is the stuff of a good marriage. One that'll weather the storms."

"You taking your own advice this time?"

"Trying to." Clint studied the grayish stairs. "I shouldn't have kept my cancer from you or let pride keep me from sharing my fears with Sara. But I'm done with that now." He clasped his friend on the shoulder. "Come on. Let's go in."

They returned to the dining room in silence. Sara's eyes locked with his from the moment she spotted them. "I thought only women took so long primping in the rest room." Her lighthearted comment didn't ease the question in her eyes.

"We don't have to leave. Yet." Steven sat down.

Sara's features relaxed as Clint settled himself next to her. He squeezed her hand, thankful both she and Steven had refrained from stating the obvious. If Steven had to leave, Clint wouldn't be going. Not passing physical assessments meant he couldn't have his Glock. No sidearm meant no action. No matter how much they needed him.

The waitress placed onion soup topped with melted cheese in front of Gracie and a spinach salad in front of Steven. When she left a Caesar salad in front of him and more steaming soup in front of Sara, his curiosity trumped his manners. "Tell me she got this wrong."

"Nope." Sara bent to inhale the aroma of sweet onion and sharp cheese. "We thought you both needed more greens in your diets. I can eat your salad too if you don't want it." She smiled. "Eating for two and all."

Gracie giggled. "I'm not. But you keep saying I can eat like a horse and not gain weight. So I'm testing your theory tonight."

"The joke's on us, partner." Clint bowed his head and prayed out loud, refraining from any mention of the food not tasting good. They'd heard more than enough of his cancer complaints.

When they all looked up, everyone but Steven tore into their food. Gracie cocked her head and nudged Steven's shoulder. "You okay?"

"Work stuff. But I'll handle it."

"By discussing things with Gracie, right?"

"Thank you, Bulldog Clint. Yes, we'll talk later. But tonight's for focusing on the future." Steven motioned to Clint's empty salad plate. "Besides, right now I need to catch up with you so you won't be tempted to eat my dessert before I get to it."

Dinner passed with talk of basketball, flowers, and caterers. Clint enjoyed the playful banter. Almost like old times.

"Sara, you look like you'll explode if you don't say something." Steven took a sip of water and waited.

Sara narrowed her vibrant green eyes. "Women are supposed to be the only ones with those intuitive powers." She studied Steven. "Then again, you two are star federal agents. I shouldn't be surprised you can read minds."

"If you could read my mind, honey…" He winked at his wife and lengthened his Texas drawl to *Gone with the Wind* proportions. "…we wouldn't still be sitting in this restaurant."

Sara swatted his arm.

They all laughed.

"Getting back to what you wanted to say…" Gracie wiped a smear of maple-syrup ice cream from the corner of her mouth.

"It's more of a question." Sara shifted in her chair. "But maybe it's none of my business."

Gracie and Steven looked at each other. "If you don't ask, we'll never know."

"Well...okay." Sara studied Clint's face.

He had no idea what his wife wanted to know, so all he could do was shrug.

"I...well, I was wondering if you all had talked about having more children." Sara straightened the cloth napkin on her lap.

Gracie's eyes clouded. She took a long, deep breath. "We've talked about this a little in our premarital counseling. I really miss my babies."

Clint cringed. He couldn't imagine seeing his children under cold white sheets the way Gracie had seen hers. She bit her bottom lip. "I can still remember their newborn wails and their weight in my arms. Some nights I still cry."

"Gracie, I'm sorry." Sara looked ready to cry too. "I shouldn't have asked."

"No. I'm glad you did. Steven and I need to talk about it more."

"It can wait, honey."

Gracie sent him a coy half smile. "Considering that children are the natural result of the passion I've seen in your eyes recently, I'm not sure it's wise to wait for our next appointment with the pastor."

Clint coughed into his napkin to cover his laugh. "You have met your match, Steven Kessler."

They ended the meal with some corny jokes Susannah had shared earlier in the day. The others groaned over them, but Gracie agreed she should try them with her students. "First-graders love that kind of thing."

Shortly afterward, Clint helped Sara into her coat, and their party of four walked to their cars.

On the way, Steven checked his phone for messages.

"Any updates?" They paused at Steven's Explorer.

"Nothing yet. Let's pray this is the big break we've been looking for."

Clint nodded, frustration dampening his excitement.

Even if he couldn't get in on it, he could still pray. Maybe that would count for something.

29

Friday the thirteenth bothered Sara more than she cared to admit. Especially with Clint pushing so hard to get back into shape and another chemo day fast approaching that would lay him out again. It didn't help that the search for Ed Standish was going absolutely nowhere.

The grisly discovery that interrupted their dinner last week had turned out to be an adult skeleton, a college student. Nothing related to the case. She felt bad for the family of the dead girl and a bit guilty for being relieved it wasn't another boy too close to her son's age. Pushing those thoughts aside, she kissed a sleeping Clint good-bye and headed out to the garage.

She pointed the silver Range Rover toward the Beltway and the Benefield Cancer Center to meet Marilynn for lunch, thankful her mom and dad could stay with Jonathan. Tomorrow her parents would say good-bye and head home to Texas. And she'd miss them something awful.

Mom and Dad had provided necessary stability in a time filled with chaos. They'd been there for Susannah and Jonathan, and their presence and counsel had helped Clint manage his emotions a little better.

Marilynn had suggested praising God in the good and the bad. Well, she could wholeheartedly praise God for the support of their family and friends.

The cancer, fatigue, and uncertainty about the future? Not so much.

Butterflies floated inside her belly, and she smoothed a hand over her pink and yellow top. This pregnancy was another thing she praised God for. She smiled as she anticipated little baby kicks and seeing more ultrasounds. Soon they'd find out their baby's sex and could start using the name they'd chosen together.

That had been an interesting family discussion.

Jonathan had voted for Elmo.

Susannah, who had recently been introduced to C. S. Lewis's Narnia series, lobbied hard for Lucy. Not a reminder Sara could manage on a daily basis.

Clint's had been the suggestion that most pleased her parents, offering two Irish names: Kathleen and Conor. Her husband had even looked up their meanings on the computer. Kathleen meant "pure," and Conor meant "wise aid."

Jonathan and Susannah had okayed both names, and she liked them too. Mom and Dad had beamed.

Sara smiled, remembering. Again and again, this pregnancy gave her reasons for joy.

Except that feeling disappeared every time Clint paced the bedroom in the middle of the night or fell asleep before they could be intimate. Both of which left her tired and grumpy.

The radio announcer complained about today's soggy forecast. Another dreary day to match her mood.

She still kicked herself for bringing up the issue of babies with Gracie. Her friend had been through so much already. Now she was going to marry an FBI agent, and that would bring a whole new set of worries. Steven's sister, Hanna, had joined the club and started dating Michael, even if Steven wasn't thrilled about it.

Not a lot of fodder for praise in all that.

Sometimes she wondered why God put up with her pessimistic ramblings. She hadn't always been that way. A realist, yes. But afraid to hope? Yet another area of failure.

"So little makes sense to me anymore, Father." Sara sighed. It'd been a long time since she'd taken a few quiet moments to pray aloud. "I'm trying to follow Marilynn's advice and praise You. But it's hard to hope when so much could still go wrong."

She wanted desperately to hold on to her mother's oft-repeated words about trusting God in prayer. *"God often says, 'Wait.' Or He will say, 'I have something even better.' Because His goal is for us to grow in faith, to depend on Him more and more."*

In all her years as a physician, the "even better" part had continued to stump her. How could Lucy Cohen's second battle with cancer fall in the "something better" category? Or Frank's death? Or the heartache inherent in every fight against cancer?

Why did God let His children go through such pain when one touch from Him could obliterate cancer forever? What could be "better" than that?

Then she remembered Lucy's letters to her family and friends during her first round with leukemia. Lucy had talked so personally about how God held her close and walked with her through the fear and pain. She'd shared the deep lessons of faith her illness had taught her.

In many ways Lucy's dependence on God, like Frank's, humbled Sara. Clint's strong belief humbled her too. Though something had changed in him since his hospitalization. The strain on his face and the hollowness of his prayers weighed on her more than she liked to admit.

But maybe God's "better" plan for her included the tentacles of cancer squeezing and emptying her of dependence on others. Maybe that's how God was teaching her to put her hope in Him alone.

She wished there was another way.

After pulling into a visitor's parking place, she took a minute to practice her smile. She'd need more than that to convince Marilynn everything was fine. Her best friend would see right through her anyway, so she gave up and headed for the front doors. Cool air and the scent of pine and flowers greeted her at the entrance.

"Good afternoon, Dr. Rollins." Laurie Denny smiled, standing a head above most of the milling group of patients and family members.

"It's Sara. Remember?"

Laurie nodded and gave instructions to the new receptionist before heading toward the office doors. "You can come on back to Dr. Richards's office if you'd like. Or I can buzz her and let her know you're here."

"I'll follow you, if it's okay." They stepped into the office hallway together.

"Works for me. Marilynn's expecting you."

They passed Sara's old office, still unoccupied. "Why aren't they using that for something more than gathering dust?"

"Word from the doctors' lounge says you'll come back."

She stopped in her tracks. "Marilynn said that?"

"No." Laurie's voice dropped to a whisper. "She probably knows different, doesn't she?"

Sara nodded.

"The rest think that once your husband has returned to work full time, you'll get tired of your scrapbooks and diapers and beg to come back here."

"Not likely." How could anyone get bored with newborn coos and little boy hugs? Not to mention her daughter's cheerful after-school greeting. Hers now and not a babysitter's. With parents here to help, they hadn't seen Erica much, and Sara had found a great deal of joy in spending more time with her children. If they could manage it financially, she wanted to stay home, at least until their youngest started school.

Laurie gestured down the hall leading to Marilynn's office. "You two have a great lunch. See you soon."

She'd return soon indeed. The following week, in fact, for Clint's next-to-last chemo. The end was within reach. She only needed to convince Clint to take things slowly and work up to passing his physical assessment *after* treatment stopped.

Like he'd ever do that.

She knocked on Marilynn's door.

"Sara? Come on in."

She paused just inside the door when she noticed June Wells sitting beside Marilynn's desk. "Oh. June. I didn't know you'd be here. It's good to see you." She turned to exit. "I don't want to interrupt. I'll wait back in the reception area."

"Actually," June stood, straightening her lavender dress, "I brought some baked goods for the patients, but I was really hoping to talk to you and Marilynn. It's been awhile since I've visited, and I wanted to let everyone know I was doing okay."

Sara couldn't imagine coming back to a place so full of painful memories.

June extended a small leather-bound notebook. "I also wanted to leave this in case I didn't get to talk with you."

"What is it?" Sara wasn't sure she was ready for June's gift.

"It's my cancer journal. Something a friend suggested Frank do when he was first diagnosed. I hoped writing out my thoughts might help me too."

"Did it?"

Marilynn stood and looked at her watch. "I wish this weren't the case, but I have an appointment at one thirty and a few things to do before then, so I need to go to lunch now. Would you two like to find a nice restaurant where we could continue this conversation?"

"I don't want to intrude." June fingered her wedding band. "I can leave this, and you can call me later if you want to talk."

"We'd love it if you would join us." Marilynn pointed toward the door, and Sara nodded. Minutes later, all three settled into a booth at the steakhouse frequented by cancer-center physicians. A waiter quickly took their orders and left them to talk.

"How are you holding up, June?" Sara wasn't sure she wanted to hear the answer. It'd only reveal one more way she'd never measure up to June's strength.

"Do you want the answer I give to concerned church members? Or do you want the truth?"

Maybe the first answer. Sara hesitated. "The truth."

"The people in our church have been wonderful. The associate pastor is stepping into Frank's role, and no one is rushing me out of the parsonage. People have stopped crying when they see me. And our ladies' ministry hosted a beautiful evening of encouragement with a wonderful speaker who made us laugh and cry about life. No mention of cancer."

Marilynn inspected June's face as she talked. "But?"

The waiter returned with their drinks.

June waited until he left and then gave a sad chuckle. "But it's still hard. Awful, sometimes. I miss Frank every day, and many nights I cry myself to sleep." She took a sip of her soda. "One thing that keeps me going is remembering the life we shared. We loved each other, and we dreamed together. Some of those dreams are surfacing in my heart now. I didn't die with Frank, so I won't live as if I did."

"So what will you do?"

"Well, I've been teaching a quilting class at church. And I'm thinking about going back to school for a counseling degree. God has taught me too much these last four years to keep it all to myself. I want to help others in their cancer journeys."

That fit everything Sara had witnessed in Frank's and June's lives. Good for June. She'd be a wonderful support for others walking where she had once been.

Sara sighed. Not a chance she'd be doing that well if she were in June's place.

The waiter delivered their sizzling steaks and refilled soda glasses. After a quick prayer, June took out the book she'd shown Sara earlier and flipped a few pages.

"I want to share this quote that meant a lot to me. It's from someone named Samuel Rutherford. 'Christ chargeth me to believe His daylight at midnight.'"

Sara didn't want to think about any more days full of dark midnight. Surely God would let the last month of chemo finish without any more surprises. They'd been through so much already.

June read her face. "Sara, the words in here aren't all like that. Many of them detail my anger and frustration and the bargains I made with God about healing Frank. Our path was not as easy as it may have seemed from a doctor's point of view."

Sara could relate. Having experienced cancer from both sides of an oncologist's desk, she didn't think either side looked carefree.

"But I want you to know that even when the journey ends in a way you couldn't have imagined and didn't ask for, God is still there. Every step of the way. You can believe that, Sara. Lean on Him, and He'll hold you up. He'll show you how to say what Job did: 'The Lord gave, and the Lord hath taken away; blessed be the name of the Lord.' "

There were those words again, reminding her not to depend on circumstances but on the Lord. To praise Him no matter what.

"Fear doesn't have to win. It's truly your choice. Focus on Him, Sara."

Marilynn wiped her mouth with a maroon napkin. "Blessed be the name of the Lord. Ever hear anything like that? In a song maybe?"

Sara had to smile. Subtlety wasn't in Marilynn's vocabulary.

Or in God's. He was speaking to her through so many sources. It was time to listen and depend on Him.

Time to live without the shackles of doubt and guilt.

Time to praise Him in the storm as well as in the sunshine.

Time to stop being afraid of hope.

Okay, I'll try it Your way. For better or worse…and for better again. Lord willing.

❋   ❋   ❋

Unending paper trails and legal gridlock strangled Michael's few patient thoughts.

Whenever privacy rights and public safety concerns collided, the aftermath often paralyzed the investigative process and left him wanting to whale on the gym's punching bag. Something he'd already done earlier today. With Clint, of all people. The older agent had shown up before Michael finished his predawn workout. He hadn't lasted long, though. A few easy free-weight reps and some info gathering had nearly done him in.

That and trying hard to stay out of Kessler's and Maxwell's sight. Appearing at the gym before his oncologist even cleared him for desk duty wouldn't earn Clint points with either supervisor. Or his physician wife.

Michael couldn't fathom his mentor's push to return to work. Clint could barely stay awake, wore no sidearm, and struggled to remember basic case details. Why shortchange his family and risk his health? Especially when all they'd let him do was chase shadows in files while more and more kids were kidnapped and killed.

Kids like Mattie.

The Standish case harassed his conscience every time he sat down at his desk.

If only they'd made it to that cabin ten minutes sooner.

Or the Inner Harbor before Standish could disappear.

He clicked a few keys on his desktop and turned away from the case summary he'd been typing. A missing child's body had turned up in a neighbor's home, the residence of a convicted sexual predator who'd failed to update authorities on his whereabouts. Just one more victim among many.

Even their recent "successes" left an acid trail through his insides. For every "traveler" the Innocent Images Unit busted, there were untold more sexual deviants working chat rooms and enticing children to meet them in person. Only those young teens weren't meeting the soul mate they expected but running headfirst into hell on earth.

And too many of the missing kids they did bring home ended up so damaged by perverts, they had little hope of returning to a normal life.

So much for keeping kids safe and administering justice.

Maybe the time had come to get serious about his CIA aspirations. Before another year in the CACU ratcheted his cynicism beyond that of Bureau veterans.

Michael locked his hands behind his head and relived his teenage dream of being a superspy.

Espionage trumped tracking kid killers any day.

But what if it also meant saying good-bye to the one woman he might want to spend the rest of his life with?

The necessary and often prolonged separations, the secrets, and all the danger offered no captivating incentives to a wife. Not to mention never knowing when he'd be home and always wondering if the next time she saw him he'd be in a body bag. Or simply MIA and never heard from again.

He couldn't ask Hanna to live like that.

Was he really thinking about her that way? Already?

Talk about a 180-degree change from his previous dating experiences. But he didn't enjoy single life anymore. Not after spending so much time with Hanna's family, enjoying the support and companionship. And seeing her love for her nephew, her compassion for Clint's kids. She'd make a great mom someday.

Would he make a good dad? Given his background…

God, I could use a little direction here.

"I'm heading out, Parker. You might want to nix the daydreaming and wrap things up so you can too." Lee sauntered over and sat on Michael's desk. "Bet you got big plans tonight with Kessler's sister, huh?"

"Hanna and I have a date, yes."

"What? A movie and some serious lip lock?"

Michael grimaced. "Go home to your wife, Lee. And stop projecting your love life on mine. I'm far more boring than you can imagine."

"So the playboy's met his mate?"

Tossing a brick at Lee would have been too kind. Instead, he lobbed a Nerf football at Lee's head and growled a good-bye.

Lee kept the football and walked away chuckling. "See you Monday, Parker. Remember Big Brother is watching while you're being boring this weekend."

Whatever.

He shoved his laptop into its carrying case and straightened his minimalist desk. He'd deal with case updates tomorrow.

Leaving the Hoover Building didn't take long. Most support staff were gone from the office by now, anyway. But it took him awhile to maneuver his Mustang through streets crowded with commuters and tourists and past all the trendy hangouts he used to frequent a year ago. On George Washington Parkway, traffic continued to crawl.

The vacuum that once drove him into all the voguish clubs gnawed at him still. What he wouldn't give to have Hanna meet him at the door and help him forget his day's load. That being an impossibility, he parked his car and climbed the stairs to an empty apartment.

Tugging off shoes and suit coat in the living room, he left everything on the couch and went to watch the darkening sky from his balcony.

How did Hanna unwind after a long day? Beneath the dazzling blue of her gentle eyes were so many things he wanted to know. Favorite childhood memories. Why she loved photography so much. How she'd gotten so good at it.

Why she was real and vulnerable one minute but then disappeared into herself so quickly.

They'd talked about family, college, and work, but he wanted to know more.

He wanted to know *her.*

That his interest in Hanna went way beyond sex surprised him. He'd come a long way from grabbing a beer with his buddies or engaging in a one-night stand for distraction.

Guess You are guiding me, God. Now if You could make Steven see that...

Michael took a quick shower and then slipped into jeans and a white polo. In the past two weeks, he'd managed a little time off and taken Hanna to some fancy restaurants. But tonight he wanted to go casual. Maybe the old-fashioned ice-cream store in Old Town Alexandria where they could sit outside at the sidewalk café.

A knock at the door startled him. He brushed his hair fast and went to see who would be bugging him on a Friday night. Lee or Steven would have called.

He opened the door with a frown. There stood Hanna. She wasn't crying like last time, but still. "What's wrong? I was just on my way to pick you up."

Her bright smile disappeared. "I called and left a message about a surprise I wanted to bring over. When you didn't answer, I took my chances, hoping I'd catch you." She stepped back. "I didn't mean to upset you."

"You didn't. Hanna, come in. I'm sorry." He held out his hand and drew her into a quick hug.

"If you keep growling at me every time I change the plans, then I think I'll refrain next time and keep your surprise for myself." Her smile returned.

He loved her ability to roll with his moods. On more than one occasion he'd done the same thing on the phone, answering in a foul mood, only to have her make him laugh before she said good-bye. This lady was a keeper if he'd ever met one.

"Will your surprise ruin a trip to the ice-cream place?"

"Um, maybe. That depends."

"On what?"

"On whether you like canine company with your chocolate ripple."

"Come again?"

She tugged on his hand and pulled him down the stairs before her words registered. At the passenger side of her blue Equinox, little yelps and a hyper dog tail greeted them.

His neighbor's dogs answered back.

"You bought a dog?"

"Not exactly." Hanna reached in the car and pulled out a wriggling yellow Lab pup. The dog gave her face a bath. "His name is Champ." She motioned toward a jumble of supplies in the backseat. "He's housebroken. And I bought him a bed and enough food to last a good while."

"Why?"

She hugged Champ tight. "It was the pound or us sharing the responsibility and becoming his new family. One of my employees had an emergency. Her mother just had a stroke, and she has to move back home to take care of her. She was taking Champ to the pound tonight because she didn't know what else to do on such short notice."

"Did you just say we were going to become his new family?"

"If you'll help me take care of him."

Champ looked him over and licked his outstretched hand. How could he not take a pup that looked exactly like the important sidekick of his boyhood fantasies?

"Does that mean you'll be moving in too?" Michael regretted the words as soon as they left his lips. The whole situation had him more than a little off balance. But Hanna didn't comment, so he put his arm around her as they walked up to his apartment.

Champ growled.

"That's his way of saying I'm not moving anywhere until we're legal, buster."

Watching Hanna play with Champ on his kitchen floor made him laugh. Her words hadn't clicked in her brain yet, or she'd be embarrassed. After all, she'd pretty much declared they were going to be a family in the near future.

No matter. Michael had heard.

And he kind of liked the picture playing out in his apartment. A beautiful girl and a frisky pup. Family.

Maybe his dream job could wait another decade.

Or forever.

30

One more child dead.

More would die if circumstances didn't change fast with his own child.

Wednesday night, he wiped soil from his hands and looked around the dark, forested park. No sense burying the body six feet deep this time. He had to get back. And no one had discovered his special place for more than three years.

The FBI was certainly none the wiser. His recent contacts had proven that. They had nothing. Neither did the Charlottesville police.

All he had to do was keep his secret hidden. And find a way besides this to silence the voices. Stop the pressure.

He trudged back to his rental car and slipped out of the park unnoticed. Ditching the shovel out the window in a back alley made his blood pressure skyrocket. Would they find it? Scrape off some DNA and trace the missing boy from Richmond or Charlottesville to him?

Not likely. But who knew the extent of their forensic resources. The terrifying thought of capture hounded him more each passing day.

He chided himself for such paranoid notions but kept a sharp eye on his rearview mirror.

Watching *America's Most Wanted* and regularly perusing the FBI's Top Ten list had provided a measure of reassurance. No mention of him. Nothing. And the stupidity that got most criminals caught wouldn't be his undoing. No, not him. He knew better.

Teaching no-brain collegiates how to survive in the real world supplied plenty of fodder for alibis and new destinations to explore. He'd learned the best backwoods places and big-city haunts to score everything he needed. And he knew what made little boys tick.

Nothing could stop him.

Nothing but death.

※ ※ ※

"Come to bed, honey."

Clint glanced up from his computer and stopped typing. Sara's sleepy eyes, cute pink pj's, and clear invitation weakened his resolve.

"I'm working on a composite of John Miller. I remembered more of his facial details in my last dream, and I'm almost positive he's the man I saw at the Saint Patrick's Day shindig for the cancer center. Maybe this will give Michael something to circulate at the hospital. Someone's bound to recognize Miller from my drawing."

She slumped into the tan couch. "Chemo is tomorrow. Last time it laid you out hard. Going back to work next week may not happen like you hope."

He inhaled fast and deep. The rage flickered in his chest, but he slammed those thought pathways shut. Truth was, Sara wanted him healthy, and she wanted him back to work too. Just not too soon. He tried to accept that.

But he couldn't wait forever. Not when the CACU count was up to six missing boys fitting their serial kidnapper's profile. Or was it seven? Yes, they'd received notification about another missing child earlier today. The boy had disappeared from Charlottesville, Virginia, this morning.

Seven children, all most likely dead. And Michael, Lee, and Steven worn out from carrying his load. This perp had to be stopped. Both perps, if his hunch proved correct. And the sooner he could get to work, the better shot they had at finding these guys.

"Did your Department of Defense contact get back to you today?"

"Yes. But his help didn't yield any more information than what Steven received."

He started fiddling with the facial composite software again. The forensic artist they'd worked with on past cases had been very willing to give him a bit of tutorial help. Along with the caution that Clint not give up his day job.

"Could John Miller be using an alias?"

He held out a hand to his wife and chuckled. "You've been watching too much CIA stuff on TV."

She sat on his lap and snuggled into his chest.

"But it's a valid question. Miller had to find a way to survive after his dishonorable discharge. So unless he's living in another country or dead, we have to assume he's established another identity."

"So how do you track him down?"

"Michael's helping with that. Right now we're working next-of-kin information the DOD sent. A fast check verified Miller's parents are deceased. Any other relatives have long since changed residences. But there has to be a lead somewhere in the DOD files. All I need is a small clue as to who Miller became. Then I'll find him and bring him in for questioning."

"Can you do that?"

Clint stiffened. "Personally? Not without passing physical assessment."

"Soon." She kissed his neck. "I know you'll do it soon, cowboy."

His cell phone danced on the desk. He should have remembered to take it off manners mode.

Sara pouted. Picking up the phone, he winked. "I'll be up to bed soon."

"Wake me if I fall asleep?" She sauntered across the room and stopped in the doorway, watching him.

He considered letting the caller go to voice mail. "I will. Promise."

Blowing him a kiss, she slipped out of the room.

He jerked the phone to his ear. "Michael, what do you have for me?"

"Partner, you'd better check caller ID." Steven's voice.

He didn't need Steven's lecture on wasting his or Michael's time with a theory about two perps. Especially not a hunch based solely on

Clint's recurring dreams. Steven was convinced the whole thing was some cancer-induced hallucination.

"Care to fill me in on why Parker would be calling you at ten o'clock on a Wednesday night?"

"No."

"Not good enough." Steven exhaled with a sharp breath. "I warned you about working overtime on that theory of yours. But what I need right now is to get a hold of Parker."

"Call his cell."

"Like I wouldn't have tried that. He's not returning my calls, and I can't reach Hanna either. I don't think this relationship is a good idea."

Clint leaned back in his desk chair. "Hanna's a grown woman. If she and Michael are gonna have a snowball's chance, you have to stop playing Secret Agent Big Brother."

"I don't want her hurt."

"Michael's not gonna take anything from her."

"But if my hunch about her past is right, she might not say no either."

"And that's her choice."

A loud thump sounded through the phone. Steven slamming into his punching bag no doubt. "She wouldn't do that."

"They've been dating for almost a month now. What's the rush to find them tonight?"

"I didn't know they've been caring for a puppy at one of their apartments every night. Not until Lee said something about it at the office today. Did you know about that?"

Clint shot up a quick prayer for wisdom. "Michael told me and asked me to keep him accountable to the boundaries he's set with Hanna. They'd originally agreed to not being alone at their homes, but that's a little hard with a shared dog. So they set new rules." He yawned and hoped Michael wouldn't be too steamed at him for sharing this with Steven. "They really care about each other, Steven. And Michael's a different man than when he came to the CACU. I don't think you have to worry about him hurting her."

"He's human."

"Aren't we all?"

"Not funny."

Standing to stretch, Clint hated his rubber legs and the tingling that still plagued him when he'd been sitting for a long spell. "All I'm saying is they both walk with God and have good sense."

"That doesn't stand up to damaged emotions and heated opportunity."

No. His partner was right about that. And sharing a dog sure sounded like the beginning of something serious. But while Michael admitted there'd been temptation, he'd also shown he was committed to not repeating his past. Clint believed him.

"Why are you being so controlling? What you're doing is way beyond brotherly protection. Just because Hanna moved to Alexandria doesn't give you the right to act like she's still in high school and you're her parent."

Steven was silent for a moment. "I think someone in Louisville raped her."

A baseball bat to his back would have felt better. *"What?"*

"I've talked to some of her friends, and none of them have much good to say about her last boyfriend."

"Steven, she's an adult. You can't go snooping into her past like that."

"If you had a sister, you'd understand."

"I have a daughter."

"She's not a teenager yet."

For that Clint was glad. Maybe Steven was right. "How much time have you put into this violation of Hanna's privacy?"

Steven practically growled.

"Have you talked to Hanna about it?"

Background noise indicated Steven had walked outside on his deck. Silence stretched thin.

"Steven?"

"We've talked about Mom a lot. But every time I try to discuss why

Hanna was so ready to leave Louisville, she shuts the conversation down. And now she won't return my calls."

Clint's eyes started to close, and he yawned again.

"I'm sorry to keep you awake. This isn't your problem."

"Yeah, it is. You're my best friend. And Hanna's like a sister to me." The heat from his cell phone scorched his ear. "How 'bout I talk to both of them. Then maybe we can all get together and sort some things out."

"Hanna will love that."

"She knew what she was getting into when she moved close to both of us."

Steven chuckled. "That she did."

"Go call Gracie. That'll help."

His partner blew out a long breath. "Maybe I should have prayed before talking to Hanna's friends. But something's wrong, and Hanna won't explain what happened in Louisville. Fixing things is still my knee-jerk response."

"You mean you're not perfect yet?"

"Whatever. Don't you need to go to bed or something?"

Yep. And it was the "or something" he intended to do as soon as he hung up the phone.

A few minutes later, he slipped past the kids' bedrooms and into his own. Losing his jeans and T-shirt, he slipped into bed and wrapped his arm around Sara's waist. Her smooth skin and little abdominal bulge ignited a fire.

"Hey, cowboy." She turned over slowly and ran a hand down his chest.

Then she bolted to the bathroom.

Pregnancy had its drawbacks.

His eyes closed against his will. He had to stay awake. Just a few more minutes, and Sara's nearness would trump this blasted fatigue.

Or not.

31

"About last night…"

Sara checked her watch and maneuvered the Range Rover up Richmond Highway. "You don't have to explain. Really. Just being in bed at the same time was a nice change."

He shook his head and huffed.

"We're almost done, Clint. Less than a month."

He leaned his head back onto the seat and closed his eyes. "I still hate cancer and everything it's stolen the past four months."

She did too. More than she would ever say out loud. But this Thursday's chemo would be the next to last one. They'd celebrate Clint's becoming a cancer survivor and Gracie turning thirty-three the second Saturday in May. Right before Mother's Day.

And soon she'd snuggle her newborn close and inhale his or her fresh baby scent.

Waiting at the stoplight near the cancer center, she imagined what her baby would look like. She could practically feel the wiggly pressure in her arms.

Hear the sweet little snuffles.

Smell the newness and joy.

And see Clint cradling another baby in his strong arms. What a picture. One she would hold on to fiercely.

"You seem pretty happy about going to talk to Dr. Silverman. Could be bad news." Clint's words dissolved her daydream.

"It'll be good news. You'll see."

"Okay, Pollyanna." He stared out the window at the drizzle making streams down the glass.

Pollyanna? Not quite. But she had grown more hopeful after meeting with June and Marilynn last week. Interesting how Clint's spirits sagged just about the time she turned a corner.

Or maybe that was one of God's gifts. A way they could help each other when one of them forgot to look to Christ.

She didn't know how to be strong for Clint this morning, though. Last night may have been less than they'd hoped, but his melancholy mood couldn't be just about that. They'd handled far worse in the past three months.

"Any reason you're being exceptionally like a donkey today?"

Clint locked eyes with her. "Because I'm sick of forgetting so much. Not being able to do my work. Not being able to make love to my wife."

Heat crept up her neck. Not one for mincing words, she still reddened at Clint's forthrightness. "Why are you so angry about that today?" She turned into the cancer center and parked.

"Because coming here is a rotten reminder of the pathetic image in my mirror." Clint slammed the car door and stalked toward the center without her.

His words hit her with the force of a bubble-popping needle. And she had nothing to offer but some Bible verses and bits of advice that felt good when she read or heard them but quickly disappeared into the shifting sands of her life.

Funny how knowing the truth and believing it were two very different things.

Clint turned back and came to her open door, extending a hand. "I'm sorry. Last night hit me harder than I wanted to admit." He pulled her close. "I love you, Sara. I want to share your hope."

She managed a weak smile and nodded toward the big glass doors. "Let's go hear what Dr. Silverman has to say."

Thirty minutes later they were seated on Paul's couch, watching him riffle though Clint's medical file after some small talk. How many years had she sat in her colleague's place, not truly understanding the deep emotional scars cancer inflicted? If she came back, she hoped to never forget the patient's side of this relationship.

And to be sure she didn't, she'd started keeping a cancer journal like June's. It helped to have a safe place where she could unleash her emotions without the worry of hurting someone else.

She searched Paul's features from the top of his bald head to his silly Looney Tunes socks. Nothing hinted at the information he was waiting to share.

"You gonna play the suspense for all it's worth there, Dr. Silverman?" Clint pulled at his khaki pants and recrossed his long legs.

Paul startled. "Oh. Sorry, Clint. Sara. I'm just going over the numbers in my head again." He looked up and smiled. "Your ANC is 1671.39. Excellent. I'd say the Neulasta injections are working, wouldn't you?"

Good blood counts.

She waited for the rest of the news, the proverbial other shoe to drop, just as she'd waited since the first blow of the cancer diagnosis. Every test, every chemo, every sniffle felt like the thump of a military boot, with the other one poised to come crashing down any second.

"The scans show extensive lymph node shrinkage, and your lungs are clear." Paul beamed.

Clint smiled. "That's good news, right? I'm close to done, to complete remission." He took Sara's hand. "That's great news!"

She nodded but kept her eyes fixed on Paul's. There was more. She sensed more than saw it. "What aren't you saying, Paul?"

Her colleague smiled. "It's double the difficulty having an oncologist's spouse as my patient."

"Try being married to her." Clint grinned.

Paul's smile brightened.

"Paul?" Her hands moistened.

Dr. Silverman smoothed his Tweety Bird tie and leaned forward. "I want you both to celebrate today's news. It's good." His deep blue eyes locked with hers.

"But?" She knew better than to let the appointment stop there and go pop open the champagne bottle.

Paul steepled his fingers. "You know the cautions, Sara. Clint, I'm sure you do too. Keep in mind that even though the cancer is respond-ing to treatment and you're in partial remission—not complete remission yet—this type of lymphoma can be aggressive, returning about half the time."

"How soon?" Clint sat up straighter.

"Within two years."

She took a deep breath. She knew the stats. Clint's blood work looked good, but she'd seen similar numbers on many patients whose cancer returned. Like Lucy. Her ANCs near the completion of chemo had been excellent, just like Clint's. And now, three years later, she was back in the hospital.

But even as Sara's thoughts spiraled downward, she remembered Lucy's eyes the last time they'd talked. Her former patient was nearing the one month mark after the bone-marrow transplant, and her whole face glowed with hope. The young mom felt sure she'd make it to transplant plus thirty days with no graft-versus-host disease and be out of the woods.

Sara prayed Lucy was right. She knew at least one patient whose GVHD had flared like a fire-breathing dragon well past the one month mark. But Renee had valiantly beat the odds and survived with a radi-ant smile to match her unconquerable determination.

"Sara." Paul's voice jerked her back to the present. "I really think, despite that doubting look of yours, that we're close to full remission. In fact, I'd say with this chemo and how Clint's body has responded to it, we've almost hit a home run."

Almost.

That one word and its depressing heaviness stood out from the rest of today's good news. Clint's earlier melancholy had now become hers.

They all three smiled, though, and shortly after went their separate ways. Clint to have his chemo administered. Dr. Silverman to meet with other patients. And Sara to the car to find some distracting errand until time to pick up the kids.

Even the little baby movements inside couldn't help her shake the only discouraging word Dr. Silverman had spoken.

Almost.

She took a deep breath as she stepped outside and walked to her car under clearing skies.

Hope was still there, hiding like the sun behind clouds. Waiting on her belief to clear the doubt away.

God is still on the throne. And He is good. Always.

The truth that Frank often quoted and June had written over and over in her journal ran through her mind.

Always. A good replacement for *almost.*

Remembering Frank's declaration gave her the push to do as he had done and refuse to focus on the circumstances. She'd follow Marilynn's wise counsel to hold on to hope and praise God no matter what.

She was almost there.

Almost.

※   ※   ※

Hanna paced in front of the informal dinner she'd prepared. Steven had called an hour ago and, in his short and clipped way, practically commanded her to wait at her brownstone for him.

She'd briefly considered being gone when he arrived. After all, she didn't have to jump when he gave orders.

But continuing to elude Steven would only make things worse.

She'd avoided him all week, ever since the night she took Champ to Michael. That had been a good decision, and she and Michael had enjoyed time together every evening since. But with the late hours and a few too many close calls...

Maybe they ought to go back to the original ground rules.

A knock on the front door made her jump and back into the cluttered kitchen countertop.

Then the safety chain jangled.

Her heartbeat kicked into high gear and sweat beaded her forehead, but she remained frozen in her warm kitchen.

"Hanna?" A man's voice filled her brownstone. "What's going on?"

Steven. Her brother. Not some deranged killer. Or former boyfriend.

She forced her feet forward and unfastened the metal chain.

Jaw muscles jumping, her brother stepped into her brownstone and slammed the door. "You need to engage the deadbolt, you know. The security chain isn't enough."

"And hello to you too."

He ignored her sarcasm. "I've left more than a dozen messages this week. Why haven't you called me back?"

"I've been busy." She matched the raging set of his jaw and shoved her shoulders back, standing to her full height. Compared to her brother, it wasn't enough to give her much confidence. "I'm an adult. I don't have to check in with you."

He ran a hand through his thick brown hair. "You don't return my calls all week, and now I find out you're sharing a dog with Parker."

She stalked into the kitchen. Mom's special spaghetti recipe wasn't going to be wasted on her big brother's temper tantrum. "I'm planning to have dinner while the food is still hot. You said you wanted to eat at six sharp." She looked at her stove's digital clock. "And it's six. I'm eating."

Sitting at the table, they bowed their heads together. He kept his down several seconds after she looked up.

They ate in silence a few minutes, but she couldn't win this game. Not with Steven. She smoothed the pink sweater set she hadn't had time to change out of and looked her brother in the eye. "Tell me why you're so mad that I brought Michael a puppy."

"Because you're not home before midnight, you're not answering my calls, and—"

"Am I under surveillance? What business is it of yours what time I get home?"

He lowered his fork. "You *are* coming home, right?"

That did it. She wouldn't be grilled and accused like a teenager breaking curfew. Not in her own home. Not by her big brother. She stood and pointed to the door. "Get out, Steven."

"No."

Her limbs shook with fury. A tear slipped down her cheek, and she tried to wipe it away.

"Come here." Steven wrapped her in his strong arms. "I love you, Hanna. Talk to me. Tell me what's going on. I can't get out of my head that Craig hurt you more than you've explained."

Something broke inside. Her defiance dissolved as she recognized the love behind her brother's stubbornness. The kind of love that wanted only the best for her. That sought to protect, not exploit.

But Steven wanted to protect her from Michael. When Michael was the only man she'd ever met who was anything like her dad or brother.

At least he seemed to be. So far.

She dampened the front of Steven's suit before she could rein in her tears. "I...I don't know where to start."

He led her into the living room, which was decorated with some of her favorite enlarged landscape prints. Photos Michael had suggested she look into getting published.

She and Steven settled on the comfortable navy love seat.

"Start from the beginning."

She wiped her drenched cheeks and closed her eyes. There was no way she'd go back and reveal everything she'd kept hidden from her FBI brother. "There's not much to tell."

"Did Craig rape you?"

His quiet question stole the air from her lungs. It'd be easier to lie and say yes.

"No."

"Then what's going on, Hanna? Talk to me." He shifted away from her slightly. "You left Louisville in a hurry and then jumped right into a relationship with Michael."

Shame heated her face. "I didn't jump. Michael asked me out. I thought he'd be safe since he worked with you, and I knew you'd keep your eagle eye on him."

"I have."

"I know."

"Then why won't you tell me what happened in Louisville?" Her brother's deep blue eyes searched her face. He studied her for a long time, saying nothing.

She waited for Steven's shoulders to relax. It'd be good to come clean. Or partially clean. "I slept with Craig by choice. It's not something I'm proud of, and I didn't want you to know, ever. But you'll keep digging until you find out, and I'd rather be the one to tell you about it."

"I'm listening." She couldn't read her brother's monotone comment.

"I'm embarrassed by how easily I gave in, but I really thought he'd propose before Christmas last year. I figured he was the one, and letting him have what he asked would keep him interested. Instead, he spent the holidays with some other girl and told our mutual friends he was never very serious about me."

"I'm so sorry." He pulled her into his arms. "The guy's a jerk. But I wish you'd have told me all this sooner. Is there more?"

She didn't respond. Of course there was more, but she wouldn't go there. Not after already tarnishing what Steven thought of her.

No way would she admit Craig hadn't been the only one.

"I was wrong to come blazing in here earlier." He ran a hand through his hair again. "I'm sorry. My gut said something was wrong, and when I couldn't get ahold of you… I guess I just let it get out of hand."

She hugged her brother but offered no answer to his earlier question. "You're still trying to live up to Mom's request, aren't you?"

Steven stood and walked to her balcony. "This isn't about Mom."

"You sure?" She stepped up beside him and nudged him with her arm.

"I don't know. I had this crazy idea that you'd been raped and I hadn't protected you like Mom asked me to before she died. That's been eating me alive this past week. And having to face every day what Clint's chemo has done to him."

"Not to mention planning a wedding and shouldering the stress of too many big cases."

"Yeah."

They stared out into the lingering storm clouds in silence. Good thing Steven's attention had drifted away from her experiences in Louisville. She loved her brother and trusted him. But he didn't need to know everything.

"Be my friend and a less meddlesome brother, not my keeper. Okay?"

"I'll try."

For Steven, that was a good start.

32

M ichael didn't need this distraction late Friday afternoon. "Replay that for me, Clint."

"I finished Miller's composite, and I have a hunch about where he is."

Scribbling a few notes on a yellow pad, Michael kept his voice even. "Something else from your dreams?"

"You too? Steven's doubt is enough. This isn't some cancer-induced hallucination. Besides, I thought we agreed this angle was worth pursuing."

"We did. But I don't have a lot of extra time to chase down unverifiable information. We're up to seven missing children that fit our serial's MO and the strong possibility this guy's becoming disorganized and more deadly by the hour. Two cases haven't gone completely cold yet." He took a breath and continued. Clint needed some perspective. "Virginia field agents are doing all they can in Charlottesville to find Thomas Lee, and we're doing all we can on our end. And that's just the tip of my caseload this week."

"Needless to say, you're swamped."

Michael hated the deadness in his mentor's voice. Maybe if he listened one more time, Clint would get it out of his system. "Tell me again what you heard at the cancer center."

"Yesterday, the nurses were talking about a recently discharged cancer patient, a little girl with neuroblastoma. She'd undergone a stem-cell transplant in March and spent weeks in the hospital. The doctors did all they could, but the child's body shut down. She was released into home hospice care on Monday, and they doubt she'll make it through the weekend."

"What does this have to do with John Miller?"

Clint's volume rose. "Details about the dad and the timing of the child's diagnosis make me think he could be our perp."

"So you want me to do what?"

"Talk to the doctor. Her name is Marilynn Richards. See if the father matches my composite for John Miller. I'd do it myself if it wasn't for the chemo drain."

"And the fact that this doesn't qualify as deskwork."

"That too. Will you help? If this is our perp and his child dies, there's no telling what he could do."

Michael weighed the cost-benefit ratio of helping out his friend. Clint wanted back in the game so badly he'd keep pushing himself no matter what Michael did. Maybe stopping by the hospital before he went home would put Clint's suspicions to rest. If this guy wasn't Clint's elusive John Miller, no harm done. But if Clint was right…

"I'll see what I can do."

After ending the call with Clint, Michael made an appointment with Dr. Marilynn Richards and straightened his desk. If he hurried, he could do his good deed for the day and still make it home in plenty of time to get ready for his date with Hanna. Minutes later, he slipped behind the wheel of his black Mustang and revved the engine.

He loved doing that. A prideful holdover from his wilder years, but it still felt good to experience the power of his sports car. And right now he needed all the powerful feelings he could muster.

Work stress continued to escalate. Clint still wasn't able to handle even a minimal workload. He'd fixated on a lead that would likely go nowhere and enlisted Michael in his investigation. And Steven was close to fed up with the search for John Miller.

Which left Michael smack-dab in the middle of trouble. And worn out from all the extra work. But he'd promised Clint he'd help, so he pointed his Mustang toward the Benefield Cancer Center.

Driving south on I-395, he reviewed the information Clint had faxed and settled into the flow of traffic. He drummed his fingers to the steady flow of tunes he'd downloaded to his new iPod last night. Some

Christian alternative, some '90s rock. Clint could have his country and Steven his James Taylor, but he'd stick with what made his fingers air guitar with the best of them.

The windshield wipers kept time with his favorite U2 songs. Maybe the recent rains would wash up another clue in Rock Creek Park. Or the planets would line up, or God would handwrite the answer in the clouds.

Something.

Three years running, there had been one missing child fitting the same pattern. Male, brown hair, blue eyes, missing in mid-January from a busy city park. Luke, John, and Niles. This January, three had gone missing. Chuck, Wes, and Mattie. Then Danny in March and Thomas Lee this week.

Why had Standish broken the pattern? The divorce? Not being able to see his son?

And what had Standish done with all of them?

Michael didn't want to accept the most likely scenario. Didn't need "one of those" cases haunting him like so many of the agents he knew.

His dark speculations almost caused him to miss the entrance to Alexandria Community Hospital. Checking his watch, he hotfooted it toward the cancer center. Good thing the receptionist escorted him right back to Dr. Richards's office, or he'd have crawled the waiting room walls.

"Come in, Agent Parker. It's good to meet you." Dr. Richards extended a manicured hand. The woman's bright-patterned African-print dress matched her warm smile and comfortable office. He prayed her relaxed demeanor would make his crazy errand as painless as possible.

"Thank you for agreeing to see me on such short notice." As they sat, Michael extended the composite and list of background information Clint had invested so many hours in creating. "Is there any possibility this picture resembles the father of a patient recently released after a stem-cell transplant? A little girl with neuroblastoma?"

Marilynn studied the papers, a deep frown creasing her forehead.

"It's possible, but I can't be positive. Megan's father is Timothy Kramer. He's much older and isn't bald. He has very short blond hair. And I don't recall any military background." She pulled a document up on her computer. "Is this part of an investigation?"

"Yes ma'am. If you can give me Kramer's contact information, I'd appreciate it."

"By law, I can release that to you, but I hope Mr. Kramer isn't the man you're seeking. He's been through so much recently." She wrote an Annandale address and phone number on a piece of stationery. "Mr. Kramer is a training consultant who works with HR management software for large corporations. He travels extensively, so I doubt you'll find him at home."

Michael took the note. "What else can you tell me about Mr. Kramer?"

"Not much. His reaction to Megan's treatment struck me as very odd. He insisted on knowing every minute detail of our protocol recommendations. But he seldom visited after Megan's transplant. I had expected him to cut back on his travel to be with her."

Puzzle pieces of information began to click into place. "When's the last time you saw Mr. Kramer at the hospital?"

"I believe he was here once in late March. And then again the day Megan was released." Her brown eyes saddened. "Unfortunately, Megan passed away earlier this morning."

"I'm sorry to hear that, Dr. Richards." She nodded and took a shaky breath. Michael didn't know what else to say, so he stood to leave. "Thank you again for your help."

Walking outside, Michael folded Tim Kramer's contact information and flipped it through his fingers like Iceman in *Top Gun*.

Maybe Clint's hunch had been right all along.

If so, he had one more very important stop to make.

❈   ❈   ❈

Friday's gray skies seemed fitting. A little girl had died today.

Michael pulled into the driveway of the mother's attractive two-story brick in Annandale, a fifteen-minute drive from Alexandria Community Hospital. It appeared normal by all indications. But its walls might have housed a killer.

At the front door, he straightened his suit coat.

A petite blond woman opened the dark green front door. "Yes?"

"I'm Michael Parker. We spoke on the phone a short while ago."

Her washed-out eyes looked dead. But she stepped back and motioned for him to come in. The front door slammed shut behind him, the sound echoing through the silent house.

"Meg's laugh used to fill the room." She sat on a drab khaki sectional, back straight as a ruler, and folded her hands in her lap.

He sat across the formal living room on a coordinating love seat. Not the way he would have spent his furniture money, but to each his own.

"You said on the phone you were with the FBI. I'd like to keep this short." She glanced past him toward the front door. "I have a great deal of work to do in preparation for the funeral."

"I'm very sorry about your loss, Ms. Carter. Megan's doctor said she was a wonderful little girl."

"She was." Donna Carter kept her eyes fixed on the front door.

"Are you expecting someone?"

She snapped her gaze to her lap and studied her chipped nail polish. "I have no family here, so my neighbors are helping with the arrangements. They're supposed to come over this evening."

Surveying the immaculate sitting area, Michael noticed a picture on the mantel. "Is that Megan with her father?"

Ms. Carter's eyes watered as she stared at the silver framed photo. "Yes. It was taken when Meg was twenty months old, right before her diagnosis." She returned to studying her fingernails. "We'd gone camping at Memorial Hill Park for the first time that October. We've never been back there. Not together as a family."

That time line information meshed with what Dr. Richards had shared. Megan Kramer had been diagnosed with neuroblastoma in December four years ago. A recurrence had landed her in the hospital in late February of this year. More puzzle pieces clicked together. "When will John be home?"

"Who?" Donna sniffled. "You still haven't said why you needed to see me today."

"I have a few questions for Megan's father, John."

"You mean Tim? John is his first name, but he doesn't go by that. Never has as far as I know." Her weary eyes narrowed. "Why do you need to talk to him?"

"I believe he has some information that might be helpful in a current investigation." He sat forward, gauging her response.

Donna tugged at the hem of her white blouse. "I...I haven't seen Tim since Meg was released Monday. After driving us home from the hospital, he left. I haven't heard from him since. He loved her so much. I guess he couldn't handle watching her..." She put her hands over her face and sobbed.

Michael handed her a Kleenex from the box on the coffee table.

"Thank you." She dried her eyes and looked up. "I'm sorry. I really need to get ready for my neighbors' arrival."

"I just have a few more questions. I'll make them quick. Did Tim live here?"

"Yes. He lives here. But he travels a lot in his consulting business. Is he in some kind of trouble?"

"Ms. Carter, if I can speak with Tim, we should be able to clear things up quickly."

"What sort of investigation is this where you need Tim's help? He's totally honest with his taxes and has never even gotten a speeding ticket. He's an upstanding citizen. He even served his country in the Army years ago."

Bingo. "Do you know anyone with the last name Miller?"

"Miller?" She frowned, but then the tension on her face eased a little. "I don't know any Millers." She stood. "I think you might have the wrong person in mind for your questions, Agent Parker." She walked toward the door with more relaxed shoulders.

"That could be. But I'd still like to talk to Tim."

She opened the front door and moved the mat with her toe. "If you'll leave me a number where you can be reached, I'll let Tim know when he returns home. But I think you're looking for someone else. Sorry I couldn't be of more help."

"I appreciate your talking with me." He handed her a business card. "Any idea where Tim would go to deal with his grief? I'm sure he's in a lot of pain."

"Yes, he is. When Meg was healthy, she was his life. They always went to Memorial Hill Park to fly kites. They loved that place. Maybe he's there trying to remember the good times…"

"Thank you, Ms. Carter." Michael took a step away from the door. "I'm truly sorry about Megan."

"Thank you." She closed the door quickly.

He felt sorry for Donna Carter, losing her daughter and about to find out her boyfriend wasn't the man she'd thought he was. Because no matter what she'd said, he had a strong hunch they'd found Miller. And if Kramer was the John Miller that Clint reported thirteen years ago, this guy had motive, extensive travel, and a history of violence. Plus a major stressor that could explain the recent change in his behavior. So much of this new information fit with their case.

Now all they had to do was get their hands on Kramer.

As he pulled out of Ms. Carter's driveway, he phoned Steven and filled him in on the interviews. "This looks like the lead we've been digging for."

Steven was less than thrilled. "Sounds like another a rabbit trail to me. We know that Standish arranged one kidnapping. We have forensic evidence linking him to another and paper trails that put him in the vicinity of two more."

"But what I discovered about Kramer is strong too." Michael headed his Mustang toward home. "We can't just ignore it."

"I'll grant that Clint's hunch is more credible now. But we still have little beyond conjecture and hearsay. Until you can give me some solid evidence, I can't allocate federal dollars for surveillance or even secure a search warrant."

Great.

His good deed for the day had just earned him a weekend or more of mind-numbing grunt work. But if Clint was right, they might put an end to the string of missing brown-haired boys. And if Standish made another attempt to kidnap Wes, surely they'd nab him soon as well.

But would finding Kramer and Standish mean finding Mattie alive as well?

Michael could only hope.

33

Sara sat in the obstetrician's office sweating like it was August, not the last Monday afternoon in April. Clint, Jonathan, and Susannah played with blocks in the kids' area.

Dread and excitement duked it out in her stomach, accompanied by the little kicks she could faintly detect from the baby.

Today was the day. They'd soon find out if she was carrying Conor or Kathleen.

Verses she'd read in Isaiah this morning came to mind.

"Fear not, for I have redeemed you; I have summoned you by name; you are mine. When you pass through the waters, I will be with you; and when you pass through the rivers, they will not sweep over you. When you walk through the fire, you will not be burned."

The promise would have been comforting had she stopped at verse one. But she could do without the reminder that life included sweeping rivers and scorching fire. Not that she didn't want to be rescued. She'd just prefer not needing rescue in the first place.

Today, at least, held hope for a little peace.

Following the ultrasound, Clint would put in his first day at the office this month. A week later than he'd hoped. Even so, after the hospitalization and two tough rounds of chemo, he'd handled the forced rest pretty well. Better than at the beginning.

She had a full day ahead too, helping out with Susannah's class at Hope Ridge later this afternoon. Gracie eagerly awaited their news about the baby.

"Mama, I need to use the bathroom." The panic in Susannah's green eyes matched her tugging insistence.

Sara needed to go too, but she had to wait for the special cup. She stood with practiced slowness and led Susannah beyond the waiting room doors, into the first available bathroom.

Susannah finished quickly and washed her hands. "We're going to see the baby this time, right?"

"As soon as they call us back."

Before Sara could settle back down next to Clint on the plush blue couch, the waiting room door opened. "Sara, you ready to come see this baby?"

Tess, her favorite nurse, extended her dark, grandmotherly arms and hugged Susannah and Jonathan. "Staying home from school so you can see your baby sister or brother?"

"Yes ma'am." Susannah skipped through the door.

Jonathan wrapped his arm around Clint's leg as they passed the reception area door. Popping his thumb in his mouth, he looked up at Clint. "Baby okay?"

His little crinkled face made Sara smile. "Yes, honey. The baby is fine. We're just going to find out if it's a boy or a girl." Sara rubbed his back until he unstuck his thumb.

Stepping toward the scale, she scowled. "No looking." She pointed to Clint. He only studied the ceiling with a smile.

They walked into exam room three, and Tess handed each of the kids a cup full of crayons and a small coloring book.

"Thanks!" Susannah and Jonathan said together.

After all her vitals were taken, Tess helped her stand. "Dad, you settle in here with the kids for a few more minutes. I'll be right back to get you when we have Mom ready for the show."

Sara followed Tess to the ultrasound room down the hall. Her nerves tightened with every step. Was the baby okay? Would Jonathan be scared of all the medical equipment? Did she want a boy or a girl?

Not that it mattered. That outcome had already been determined seventeen weeks ago.

Tess opened the door and pointed to the adjoining bathroom. "Go ahead and empty your bladder into the fancy cup you like so much. I'll get Dawn, and she can do some of her assessment before we bring in the cavalry for the unveiling."

❋ ❋ ❋

Clint held the phone, trying to measure his words carefully in front of his coloring children. "He was a no-show at the funeral?" His first day back at work could be a week too late. "Any clue where he could be hiding?"

"Nada." Michael yawned between words. "I'm doing as much as I can in between other responsibilities." None of them had slept much these past few weeks. He had chemo to blame, but Lee, Steven, and Michael could all blame Clint for their lack of shuteye.

He'd make it up to them somehow.

"I'm still tracking down credit card and phone data, but there's a mountain of information to sort through. Multiple phones and tons of business accounts. Saying this guy travels a lot is a monumental understatement. Based on what I've already seen, if Kramer's our guy, he's not likely sitting around somewhere waiting for things to blow over. He's disappeared again."

If it were up to Clint, Michael would receive an award for service over and above the call of duty, plus a nice long vacation. He'd pulled both their weights for way too long.

"Hey, Clint, hang on a second." In the background he could hear loud voices and movement. "Looks like we're heading to Baltimore. A man matching Standish's description was spotted at a Home Depot in Middle River, Maryland, buying rope and duct tape. Surveillance cameras picked up his car and tags. Everyone's on alert. Let's hope they catch him and we find Mattie. Pray hard."

Pray and wait. The story of his life these days. A pounding pulse and the image of slapping handcuffs on Standish made Clint wish he could jump in his truck and race for Baltimore.

Then again, there was no telling what awaited Michael and Steven if they did find Standish's hideout.

❖ ❖ ❖

Sara took a deep breath and stared into Clint's eyes. "You ready?"

The overhead light in the ultrasound room reflected off his bald head. A twinge of sadness rushed through her at the unpleasant reminder that this wasn't like Susannah's or Jonathan's ultrasounds. But Clint was here. Awake, even. And their children were wiggling with excitement.

Maybe this wasn't like last time. But it was still good.

"Ready."

She turned to Dawn, the technician. "And the verdict is…?"

Dawn moved the ultrasound wand over Sara's belly. "Well, little one's flipped and is giving us a clear view of his…or her…sunny side."

She held her breath. "Come on, little gummy bear, let us know if you're Kathleen or Conor."

The baby wiggled and popped a thumb in its tiny mouth. Susannah and Jonathan stared transfixed at the little screen. Clint too.

Dawn pointed out baby features on the monitor. "There's a foot. Here's the baby's backbone."

Sara's eyes filled with tears. She always got this way during an ultrasound. Seeing her baby healthy and moving around did wonders for her heart and made the weeks of sickness and forgetful tiredness worth it.

"Everything is fine with the baby, right?" Clint's voice sounded tight.

"Baby is doing great. Healthy and growing." Dawn studied the screen. "I think…yep." She turned to smile at them. "Got a great view now. Ready?"

They all nodded.

"You are going to have a bouncing baby…" Dawn paused dramatically. Neither Sara nor Clint could be sure what they were seeing on the grainy monitor.

"Girl, right?" Susannah bit her pointer finger.

Jonathan crumpled his eyebrows. "Boy. Is a boy. Wight?"

"I thought you wanted another sister, big guy." Clint tickled Jonathan and winked at Sara.

She squinted into the screen, glad the decision wasn't up to her. "Dawn, tell us. I can't wait any longer, and I also can't see a thing."

Dawn chuckled. "You all are having another little boy."

Jonathan whooped.

Susannah stuck out her lip, then looked back to the screen. "I guess another brother is okay." She hugged Jonathan and Clint.

Clint planted a kiss on Susannah's forehead. Then he leaned over to give Sara a kiss too.

"Hello, little Conor." She stared at the moving black-and-white form. "Welcome to our family."

Sara hoped he'd grow tall and strong like her husband, maybe with her curly hair and his gorgeous brown eyes.

"Another boy," Clint whispered to himself. His pinched face made it clear he was thinking about the case.

No, Clint. Not now.

Memories of Clint's recent phone calls with Steven and Michael about a breakthrough intruded on her thoughts. She pulled Jonathan closer and shoved the images away. Pregnancy hormones and a mom's greatest fears were a dangerous combination, one she had no intention of feeding with her imagination right now.

She fixed her eyes on the monitor. Their Conor.

Please, God, protect my children.

The song Marilynn had shared with her ran through her mind. *"Blessed Be Your Name."*

Well, the Lord had given them another boy.

She could definitely praise Him today.

※　※　※

Michael kept the scanner blaring in his Bucar and pushed well beyond the speed limit. Standish hadn't been spotted anywhere near Wes's house, so they rerouted toward the boy's elementary school.

Officials had been notified.

"We're looking for a gray four-door Honda Civic." Steven called out the description as they neared the three-story stone elementary school. Cop cars circled the perimeter.

"And why do they think today of all days he's going to try to snatch Wes?"

"The clerk at the store said he wouldn't have thought anything of the guy except he kept talking crazy about finally getting his son and all the things they were going to do together. Clerk figured the guy was high, but then he remembered seeing a notice in the break room about Standish and Mattie."

"Was Mattie with him?"

"No."

"Suspect's car spotted north side of school." The scanner crackled with every word.

Steven pointed. "Turn right here, and let's see what we can see."

Michael drove slow and steady, the school on his right. Children scurried along the sidewalk, and parents picked up their kids. Everything seemed normal.

But this wasn't a normal day. He'd spotted three cruisers so far, but no gray Civic. Everyone kept police lights off and eyes vigilant.

"There. Up ahead." Steven radioed in their coordinates as they stopped for a crossing guard. A cruiser pulled in behind the Civic.

Tires squealed, and children rushed out of the road. Standish turned right down a residential street before Michael could reach him.

Watching the cruiser take off after Standish, Michael's hands clamped the steering wheel. As soon as the road cleared, he followed, listening to the scanner and trying to keep his bearings through the grid of unfamiliar streets.

"There he is." Standish whizzed by right in front of them. "Turn left here."

Michael just missed the Civic's bumper. Standish skidded to a halt and bolted from the car.

"Suspect on foot. In pursuit."

Michael shoved the gearshift into park and took off, Steven right behind him. Two cops blocked Standish's way far in front. No side streets between them and the Baltimore PD.

Standish stopped, panting hard, and wheeled around, looking for an escape. "Okay." He threw up his arms in surrender. Michael and Steven unholstered their Glocks. "I'm unarmed. I give up. Don't shoot."

The two cops advanced, guns drawn. He and Steven kept theirs trained on Standish's balding head.

Standish didn't move.

A young cop whipped Standish's hands behind his back and cuffed him. "You have the right to remain silent. Anything you say can and will be used against you in a court of law…"

Securing his weapon, Michael closed the remaining distance and stood toe to toe with a man he wanted to beat senseless. "Where's Mattie? What did you do with him?"

"He's at home." Standish blinked rapidly. "Waiting for us."

Steven's eyes narrowed with rage. "Where are the others?"

"What others?" The cop jerked Standish's arms. "I…I don't understand what you're asking me. Mattie is the only one I've ever asked to come with me. He…he's looking forward to meeting Wes, and then we're going—"

"Where is he?" No time to process the implications of what Standish was babbling. They needed to verify Mattie was really alive. No telling what part of Standish's insanity held any shred of truth.

"My townhome in Middle River. Mattie should be there playing video games and fixing a snack."

As the cops led Standish back to the cruiser, Michael caught the full address amid the perp's pleas of innocence. He never intended to hurt Wes. He hadn't hurt Mattie. It was all a big misunderstanding.

Right.

Michael and Steven hurried back to the Bucar, lungs still raw from gulping in air during their last sprint.

So close. Mattie had been so close the entire time.

Hiding in plain sight.

Thirty minutes later, Michael pulled into a small townhouse community and parked near the unit matching Standish's description.

Steven knocked on the door.

No answer.

The living room curtain moved. Michael forced his voice to sound normal. "Mattie? This is the FBI. We're here to take you home."

Silence.

"Mattie, please open the door."

"Pops said to never let strangers in here. I'll get in a lot of trouble when he comes home."

Michael clenched his jaw. "He's not coming home, Mattie. We're here to take you back to your real home with your mom in Charleston. She misses you."

"He said my mom told him to take care of me." Mattie's whimpery voice came closer to the door.

Steven inhaled and exhaled with eyes closed.

A lock clicked, and the door gradually opened. Mattie Reynolds, alive and matching Samantha's last picture of him, stood blinking slowly, his clothes dirty and disheveled.

Alive. Mattie was alive. *Thank You, God.*

Michael knelt down. "Thank you for opening the door. My name is Michael, and this is my friend Steven."

"Where's my mom?"

Steven pulled out his cell. "I'll get her on the phone now."

Mattie watched them with dull blue eyes, showing no emotion. What had this kid endured?

"Kessler. Put me through to Samantha Reynolds. I'll hold." Seconds later, Steven knelt down too. "Yes. I'm standing right next to him. Here he is."

Mattie took the phone. "Mommy? Can I come home now?"

Samantha's cries carried through the receiver.

Mattie was going home.

34

G ood job, you two." Clint loved celebrating a child's return
home. The smiles on Michael's and Steven's faces said they
did too.

Steven clicked a pen at his desk. "You deserve a dose of congratula-
tions too, Clint. You followed your instincts and kept after the hunch
you had in the beginning."

Too bad cancer had knocked him from the top of his game, or he'd
have pointed them in Kramer's direction earlier. Thankfully, Michael's
bulldozing through credit card data had paid off, and they had probable
cause to deepen their investigation of Timothy Kramer. But they still
needed Kramer himself. And finding him could prove as easy as catching a greased pig.

Kramer's credit card use had ceased after a large cash withdrawal
from his bank. Which meant he'd been in the DC area at that time. But
in the eleven days since, there had been no sign of him.

Steven tapped a few keys on his computer. "Based on Michael's
interviews and research into Kramer's past, we've coordinated efforts
with the local police and are searching Memorial Hill Park. So far,
nothing."

"With nine hundred wooded acres, that could take awhile."
Michael leaned against Steven's desk. "Ms. Carter's house still under surveillance?"

"Our guys have made themselves comfortable."

Jan, one of their favorite support professionals, joined their group,
handing out coffee and free advice. Both of which she did with flair. "You
gonna use those cadaver dogs to speed up the search at Memorial Hill?"

Steven grinned. "Most likely. The team out there now is set to work all night."

Clint could barely keep his eyes open. Usually by the second week after chemo he was better. But all the late nights helping Michael from home had fatigue dogging his heels again. He had to push through and keep working. If they uncovered bodies soon, they might still find DNA or fiber evidence to definitively link Kramer to the six missing children.

Removing Wes, Mattie, and Standish's computer files from their investigation matrix left a clear profile of a serial killer. Gone was the hope that they were dealing with a man who kept his victims alive for a time.

Clint took a swig from his water jug, then toasted, "Here's to Kramer's fatal mistake of showing up at the cancer center's benefit party." Too bad he hadn't realized earlier that it was Kramer and not Standish who'd visited his hospital room in March.

Michael folded his arms across his chest. "Let's hope he makes another error real soon."

"Agreed." All Clint needed was release from desk duty, and he'd be ready to bring the guy down.

That would require a minimum assessment score of twelve on his performance review. Something he'd blown out of the water at Quantico. But now? Last time he'd tried, back in March, he'd probably set the record for the most dismal failure.

Not again. He'd continue working out hard and spend more time at the firing range. Keep Timothy Kramer's arrogant face as his focus too. Along with the photos of missing children.

The way the man he'd thought was Standish had taunted him in the hospital still infuriated Clint. That description of dead little boys looking just like Steven's son…

He clenched his fist in justified rage.

He needed back out there, so he could see the end of this case with his own eyes.

❈   ❈   ❈

Memorial Hill Park looked like an archaeological dig.

Steven took a swig of his double espresso early Wednesday morning and watched the methodical commotion below. The spring rains that made trees full and forests smell fresh hadn't created an easy working environment for the Evidence Response Team. They'd been slaving in mud since midnight under glaring lights and time pressure.

Maybe paperwork wasn't that bad after all.

Philip Walters, a longtime professional friend and ERT leader, joined him near the southern boundary of the park. "You forgot my grande mocha lite. Slipping in your old age, huh?"

"Philip, you make this case wow a jury like the Kensington forensics did, and I'll buy you a year's worth of coffee." He pointed his cup down the steep incline, just now catching the morning rays. "What can you tell me?"

"I'll take you up on that coffee." Walters grinned. Turning back to the excavations, his expression sobered. "Sad stuff down there, Steven. I'm getting way too old to look at little kids dumped six feet under."

"How many?"

"We've uncovered a fairly fresh body, not more than two weeks old at my guess, and two skeletons close by." Walters rubbed his bald head. "Your guy got sloppy with the last one, didn't bury the boy well at all. That helped the dogs find him, and now we're in the process of digging up however many others are down there."

"There should be at least six total, maybe more."

Walters met his eyes. "Less is better."

"I wish there weren't any. But if these match my cold cases, it'll provide the families some form of closure."

"We'll bag and tag all we find." Philip yawned. "And we'll put in as much overtime as we can manage. Just for you, my friend."

He clasped Walters's shoulder. "I appreciate it, Philip. Really. You're the best. With you on this case, I'm sure it'll be watertight come court time." They walked down the ravine.

"Hope you remembered not to use Vicks."

"No sticky stuff opening my sinuses, thanks to your sage advice."

Even so, the smell of decay hit him full force, and his coffee didn't sit well anymore. "Got anything specific that might point me to this guy?"

"From the two skeletons, I can tell you he was definitely organized. But given the last burial, I'd say he's grown desperate and descended into complete disorganization. Which means he's likely to leave us some good clues. Hopefully fiber samples." Walters nodded to a few of the techs taking pictures and doing sketches of the body. "Course he could be like many of his type, playing a forensic game and obliterating all possible clues. But let's hope not."

"How long till I see your reports?"

"I'll call and let you know anything that will expedite your putting this guy out of work and behind bars." Philip stopped walking and faced him. "Hug that boy of yours a little tighter tonight when you get home."

"Will do." Steven ignored the acids burning his rib cage. "There's an APB out with all we've gathered on Timothy Kramer. It shouldn't be too long before we get a bite."

"My bet is this guy will hang around and watch the appraisal of his handiwork. You have that in your favor." Philip pointed his chin to the body. "Snapped the boy's neck, looks like."

"We'll get him."

"Fast, Steven. I don't want to see this guy's signature ever again."

35

So the federal termites had found his stomping grounds.

Yellow tape and FBI jackets, plus all the local boys in blue, decorated Tim's favorite park. They'd brought the dogs too, pulling out all the stops. Pride and pleasure shot through him, overshadowing the fear.

They wouldn't find him, though, no matter how much they uncovered. He was part of the forest, and they were too close to see the trees.

He smiled and leaned against a damp evergreen, fresh with dew that sparkled in the early morning sunlight. Mingling with the crowd of gawking neighbors and concerned citizens across the street from the park, he assured himself that no one would notice him. Not since he'd done a little physical altering of his persona.

Now he looked like Meg.

His child. His only daughter.

Fury and loss had long ago shriveled any remorse he'd had in the beginning. Meg was gone, and with her any reason to stop what Clint Rollins had begun thirteen years ago.

Rollins was to blame for his stepson's death. He wouldn't have killed the boy if Rollins hadn't interfered.

And now Dr. Sara Rollins, with her pathetic cancer diagnoses and reassurances about Meg's transplant, shared culpability for his daughter's death.

They'd forced him to this. Pushed him too far. Stolen too much.

"I heard there's twenty bodies down by that stream." An elderly man pointed his dark cane toward the teeming forest.

Twenty? His renown grew with every idiot's exaggeration.

A slight breeze moved the overhead clouds along. Ah, the second day of May. Birds crowding the sky and fools of all ages coming out for a gulp of fresh air. And fresh gossip.

"It's getting creepier to live around here all the time." A housewife with a tight ponytail held a baby on her hip. "This is the second time in the last year a body was found at this park. Nine months ago it was some British teenager." The woman shivered.

"Considering the national crime rate, I'd say that's not too terrible." Tim smiled down at the woman. "Just imagine all the places in Rock Creek that haven't been explored yet."

She looked him over from the top of his shaved head to the last pair of expensive dress shoes he'd purchased. "And who are you? Some undercover reporter checking out the locals' reactions?"

"No ma'am. Just a concerned homeowner making sure my tax dollars are well spent."

The old man nodded his head vigorously.

Him, a reporter? That was laughable. He'd have preferred her pegging him a cop. Even so, she'd obviously ingested far too many bonbons and watched too much investigative television. Or maybe the *CSI*-type shows made her skittish. Those people never got it right anyway. Hollywood hype. He was sure Agent Walters agreed.

Too bad Rollins and Kessler hadn't left well enough alone. But they had to continue searching for him. Keeping him from Meg's funeral with their infernal do-good snooping.

Meg's blond curls came to mind, how she looked before chemo. His little princess, the one good thing in his miserable life. Gone.

The FBI had likely poisoned Donna against him too. But because of their stupid surveillance, he'd never know for sure. Too much of a risk to go back.

So he had nothing left.

The crowd around him shuffled and twittered as a uniformed cop approached.

"You all go on home now. We have things under control."

"How many bodies have they found, officer?" The older man leaned on his cane, cemented to his spot, begging for some juicy tidbits to share at some senior citizens function.

"There'll be a press release soon enough. You all head on home and watch the news to keep up with the latest." The officer shooed the crowd like an old-fashioned cowboy herding cattle.

How quaint.

"Why can't we watch from here when the TV crews are allowed into the park, officer?" The housewife's baby let out a squall. All the men in the crowd, old and young, flinched. How he hated that sound. He much preferred older children. Though he'd rather not hear them either.

The young officer grimaced. "If I could make them go home too, I would, ma'am."

And keep them from showcasing his fifteen minutes of exhilarating fame?

Good thing cops didn't control the media. But they nevertheless exerted far too much power over his life.

That would soon change.

Tim moved en masse with the rest of the herd, feeling the distinct urge to moo. But he refrained. No use calling attention to himself at this time.

He had more surveillance work to do. Watching them while they searched for him.

Too bad they wouldn't find him until his last hurrah on this wretched soil.

Then he'd show them.

Meg's image kept filling his mind, along with the infernal pressure that wouldn't release him. He rubbed his temples with vigor, trying to abate what kept building inside. He couldn't act yet. He needed more time to plan.

If only Meg had survived.

His little girl had fought so well against the cancer that took her life. Scratch that. She'd almost survived the doctors who had destroyed her.

They'd pay.

Walking out of the neighborhood alone, he crossed the street and slipped into the upscale rental he'd obtained under an assumed name. The cops could have his regular credit cards. He'd slipped away from the law once. Doing it again was just as easy.

Where to next? Maybe he'd drive to Mount Vernon or up to Alexandria. He'd already scoped out the highfalutin school where the Kessler and Rollins children spent their days.

No. He'd settle his score with the FBI more creatively than that.

Show them how it felt to watch a child die.

This time he was playing with the big boys.

Well, maybe not.

More like their little men.

36

Chemo or not, Clint would pass today's test. He had to. There was no other way to get out from behind a desk and be part of Timothy Kramer's takedown.

Walking into the gym early Thursday morning threw him back over a decade in time.

"You're not an agent until you walk across the stage at Quantico."

Back then, his head had been full of dreams and enough ego to think he could not only walk across that stage, but do it having made the top assessment score to win the fifty-point award.

Which he'd done.

Now chemobrain caused his head to swim, and every muscle ached with a fatigue resembling quicksand.

"It's too soon, Clint. Don't." Steven stood in the locker room doorway dressed in sweat shorts and an old academy T-shirt.

"You sound like Sara." Clint tied his running shoes tighter than they needed to be.

"Always said she was a wise woman."

He grunted. Thinking over his wife's curt words from this morning didn't help. She'd voiced the same concerns Steven was sure to start any minute. Except she'd used a bunch of doctor terms. Steven wouldn't go there.

"You're not at a good place, partner."

"So you're a shrink now?"

Steven walked over to the bench and sat next to him. "Even if you could physically do this and pass review, you're not ready to go back into the field."

Knots formed in Clint's neck and stomach. "Is this Steven the CACU head coordinator speaking, or Steven my best friend?"

"Both."

"I have to try."

They stood and walked to the track in silence. Weights clanged below them, and the smell of sweat already filled the early morning air.

Clint stretched his legs and then headed for the start line. "Will you time my practice?"

"No."

The steel in his partner's eyes froze him to the floor for a second. Then the gnawing in his gut took over. Storming back to the stairs, he invaded Steven's personal space with clenched fists. "Why can't you understand I need to do this?"

"I do understand."

"Then time me."

Steven stepped back. "Why? So you can land yourself in the hospital again?"

"I won't."

"Or get your gun back and do what?"

"Bring Kramer in." Kramer had attacked him at a point of weakness and given Clint something to prove. Both to Kramer and to himself.

He turned from Steven and stared into the gym below. Young and old, agents slammed through their workout routines without a thought of losing the muscles and fitness they gloried in.

Looking down at his still feeble frame, he wanted to punch something.

It could happen at any time. An illness or a gunshot that ended a career even if it spared a life. Critical incidents could leave agents with failed marriages and free-falling personal lives. Even with support and counseling, men and women who once thought themselves invincible sometimes found they couldn't make it back.

Not him. No cancer or GSW would keep him out of the game.

"You've done more on this case than anyone could have asked."

But not enough.

Weak and worthless. That thought ate at him through Steven's words. "I want in on the takedown."

"You're too close to this case."

Standing to his full height, Clint turned and glowered at Steven. "Without me, you wouldn't have anything on Kramer. I'd say I was indispensable."

"I agree. But that's beside the point."

"And the point is?"

"Have you worked a full day since chemo started?"

Low blow. His eyes narrowed.

"Have you worked out or gone to the range at all?"

"Some."

"Why? Because you can't stand the man in the mirror?"

Rage distorted everything, made it hard to think. No. This was about Kramer. That's why he needed to pass assessments. What was wrong with keeping his focus on taking down a perp who killed kids? That was his job.

Snapshots of Sara, Susannah, and Jonathan filled his mind, along with the ultrasound of his littlest one. Conor.

"Not this time, Clint. Wait."

"No." He stared at the still empty track. "Time me."

Steven nodded, but the look on his face was one of resignation. "You need less than thirteen-thirty on the mile and a half." Not a shred of belief in him. Whatever.

Clint had come in at ten minutes or under plenty of times. And he'd take today's time and shove it down his partner's throat.

The first laps flew by without a problem. He pushed his legs as hard and as fast as they'd go, feeling the burn. Savoring the assurance that his muscles would cooperate, he knew he'd be back on top in no time.

Images of Kramer at his hospital bedside made the fire in his gut flame higher.

On the last lap he pushed with everything in him. Sweat poured down his back. Fatigue blackened the finish line.

But he crossed it.

Steven's silence as he walked off the agonizing kinks in his calves didn't help his already-racing heart. But his partner had never been good at being proven wrong. Too bad. This time he'd have to take his lumps.

"How's that for just a warmup?" He wasn't sure he could do more than one run at the moment, but it didn't matter. If he beat the failing time this morning, he could do it for real this afternoon. After a hot shower and a long nap.

Steven walked up to him, stopwatch in hand.

He stared at it. "Fourteen minutes?" The words came out more growl than question.

"Yeah."

He fought the urge to grab the offending timepiece and hurl it against the gym wall. He'd done the mile and a half at Quantico in right under nine minutes. How could he fail it by so much now?

When it counted the most.

Grabbing his towel, he ignored Steven's calling after him. He'd deal with his partner later. Right now, before he collapsed, he needed to get home and unlock his personal backup to make sure it was clean and fully loaded.

He wouldn't face Timothy Kramer unarmed. But he would face him.

And make sure the man spent the rest of his life in a cell, without parole.

※　※　※

Hanna passed through the magnetometer at Hope Ridge Academy Friday afternoon with sweaty palms.

Regardless of how many times she'd done that in the last two months, it still made her insides turn to rubber. Not that she had anything to hide. She didn't even own a weapon. Steven's collection was about as much as she could stomach, and it was kept under lock and key in his basement gun safe.

Walking through the halls toward Gracie's classroom, Hanna took a few deep breaths and brushed the wrinkles from her peach capris. With

Steven gone so much the past few days, James was already out of sorts. She didn't want to make things worse by adding her stress to the mix.

The door to the first grade classroom opened after her first knock. Gracie's flower print skirt and coordinating lilac top looked crisp and unbelievably clean after a full day with finger-painting first-graders.

"Hey, Gracie. How are you?"

Her brother's fiancée smiled, but her eyes looked like they'd close any minute. "It's been a long week."

"Will you get to see my way-too-busy brother tonight?"

Gracie's smile faded. "Doubt it. Talking to him for only a few minutes yesterday was difficult enough. I guess I'm getting a crash course in life as an FBI wife."

"Clint's cancer and his push to get back in the field are still hitting Steven hard."

"That's the understatement of the year." Gracie glanced over her shoulder. "Let me go get our little man. I'm sure he'll be happy to see you."

Little man. Steven's nickname for James.

Hanna studied the closed classroom door and hated how Gracie's comment made her defenses snap to attention. Gracie had every right to speak like she was part of the family. She was. The wedding in July would only make it official. That and maybe temper Steven and Gracie's goofy grins.

Okay, well, maybe not.

"Hey, Aunt Hanna!" James exploded through the door and into her arms just as she bent down to greet him. "We're going to get ice cream, right? It's Friday family night, and Dad said he'd meet us there after school for a snack."

She met Gracie's sad eyes. "James, honey, I think it'll be you and me tonight."

"But…"

Gracie stepped into the hall and closed the door. "Susannah and Akemi will be fine with Mrs. Theresa for a few minutes." She knelt by James. "I know your dad's work schedule is sometimes really hard.

Would it help if we called your grandpa and grandma and all met at the ice-cream shop in a little while?"

James's face brightened, and then he hugged Gracie for a long time. Hanna fought the green-eyed monster creeping up on her. Next to Sue, she'd been James's favorite lady since he was born, and it was hard to share her nephew's affection with someone new.

She stood and tried to focus on the fact that one more set of eyes to keep watch over James would be a very good thing, especially with all the news warnings.

"Can you bring Jake?"

Gracie laughed and ruffled James's brown hair. "I'm sure my big ol' moose of a golden retriever would be happy to hang out with us." She looked up at Hanna. "As long as that's okay with you."

"Sure. No problem. Champ will love playing with Jake." Her voice sounded less than convincing, even to her.

"I'm sorry, Hanna. I should have asked first before inserting myself into your plans." Gracie bit her lip. "Guess I'm a little too quick to make myself at home with you all."

Hanna could have kicked herself for being so obvious. "It's not a problem. At home with us is where you belong."

Gracie stood and flashed a grateful smile. "Thank you."

"Want to pick us up at Dad's around four?"

James nudged her leg. "You like Gracie's Jeep too, don't you?" His smiling blue eyes made her feel like a million bucks. And sufficiently guilty over her jealousy. She had nothing to worry about. Her nephew's heart could include Gracie without knocking her out of her special spot.

"James! Nanna! I see you." Jonathan galloped down the hallway, his mom fast on his heels. He plowed into Hanna's leg and grabbed James's arm, then looked up at Gracie and smiled even bigger. "Hi, Mrs. Gracie. I see you too."

They all laughed.

"Hey, Jonathan, check this out." James pulled a paper-airplane book from his backpack and showed Jonathan while Sara caught up and joined them, just a little winded.

"Nothing like charging after an almost-three-year-old when I'm as big as a whale." Sara tugged her long white maternity top in place over light blue shorts.

"You are so not." Gracie shook her head.

"I could take some maternity pictures like I did for friends back home." Hanna tilted her head, thinking of the possibilities. "Then you'd see just how beautiful you are."

Sara beamed. "That's a great idea. Clint would love it. And I'm sure if you take the photos, I'll love them too. Why don't we set that up soon?"

"Awesome. We'll do it."

"How about you and the kids joining us at Pop's on King Street?" Gracie's invitation set Hanna's mind whirling with possibilities. She could snap a few practice shots at Pop's. That would be fun. And Dad and Michael would be thrilled she'd taken another step toward building a new clientele in Alexandria. "Hanna and I can entertain Susannah and Jonathan while you kick back and relax a little."

"I'm very tempted. Pregnancy and ice cream go together, you know." Sara yawned, looking way overdue for a nap. "And I would enjoy the girl talk."

Hanna would too. With all the kids around, conversation would definitely stay light. No discussion of cancer or FBI investigations either. And that was good. They could all use a break from serious stuff.

"Come on." Hanna ruffled Jonathan's brown hair and grinned at Sara. "We'll have a great time, and I'll capture it all with my camera."

Sara blew her red bangs out of her eyes. "Methinks I'm out-numbered."

Gracie opened her classroom door. "I'll get Susannah and see what she says."

"Like that'll tilt the balance." Sara smiled and shook her head.

"You know you want to." Hanna nudged her friend. "Besides, I haven't seen you outside the house much since I moved." Given that Michael would be tied up with work, hanging out with Sara and Gracie beat brooding alone. Even if being around Gracie's annoying perfection made her wish for a life do-over.

She finally had a serious relationship with a great guy, though. Last night she'd gone over to Michael's apartment to visit Champ and hear about his day. After only a few minutes, she'd wished he and Steven had a different career. People who killed kids didn't rank high on her list of favorite discussion topics.

Especially when her nephew fit the deranged man's victim profile. What kind of monster preyed on six-year-old boys and took them to a place like Memorial Hill Park to bury them?

She pushed those thoughts aside and listened to Sara. "You're right. The kids and I don't get out enough, and a trip to Pop's will be fun. And if you're taking a few photos for my scrapbook, it'll be even better."

"Always happy to support your creative indulgences. They keep folks like me in business."

Sara smiled. "You're an artist, Hanna. Pretty soon you'll have more photo shoots than you can keep up with."

Unsolicited compliments sure made the day brighter.

And even if she hadn't planned for that much company, her ice-cream-shop date with her nephew was shaping up to be a blast.

37

Sara's exhaustion had her reconsidering her list of errands.

But they needed to be done. The cupboards were bare, so the grocery had to be visited, and Clint needed his new, smaller suits from the dry cleaner. He'd need more when he started back to work full time.

Soon. Unless he believed his own brooding and ranting after not doing well on his mile and a half. He shouldn't expect so much of himself before completing chemo.

"Care to share those depressing thoughts, big sis?"

Hanna's sweet voice from the passenger seat pulled Sara out of a potential downward spiral. "I think I'm all talked out after our trip to the wonderful ice-cream shop."

"Yummy ice c'eam, Mama! Get more?" Jonathan's cute words from the backseat made her smile. Conor's kicks caused that same smile to grow bigger. Soon they'd have two little boy voices filling up their home.

"We'll see, honey. There's a lot of good, nutritious food we need to buy and take home for dinner before we eat any more sweets."

Susannah groaned but kept her nose in a new library book. Just like James. Those two would rather read than do anything else.

"Sorry, Hanna. Kids are wonderful. But along with their sweet attitudes…" She glanced into the rearview mirror. Susannah didn't look up. "…come unnumbered distractions."

"No problem."

"Thanks for agreeing to help me with the groceries. I'm forever grateful."

Hanna looked her way and grinned. "How could I pass up a trip to the grocery store?"

She nudged Hanna. "Sarcasm doesn't become you."

"Okay. Well, the grocery might not be my favorite place, but I could tell you were too tired to do it on your own." She paused and turned down the *Veggie Tales* CD. "And Gracie knew it too. Why else would she volunteer to watch Champ for me? Caring for that wild puppy is a total labor of love."

"Hmm…maybe she offered because she's going to marry your brother and wants to build a closer friendship with you?"

Hanna shrugged. "She doesn't have to take my dog to do that."

"That's Gracie, though. Kind and thoughtful and—"

"Enough, please. I hear it from Steven all the time."

They both giggled. "I'm sure you do."

Sara slipped into a front parking place and sighed. Long walks weren't on her agenda today. Thankfully, the previous grocery store patrons had been kind enough to leave her a premium spot. And she hadn't even had to fight a little sports car to snag the space.

Minutes later, she grabbed a silver buggy and reached for Jonathan. Corralled kiddos meant an easier shopping experience.

He backed away. "I want to walk wif 'Sannah an' James. I a big kid too." Jonathan planted his hands on his hips in an adorable pout.

So much like her. So much like Clint too.

But it wouldn't help world peace if she let Jonathan get away with that. Cute at two wasn't cute at sixteen. She plopped Jonathan and his pout into the buggy.

"I'm going to head back to the deli for tonight's dinner." Hanna picked up a small shopping basket and took James's hand. "What say we meet you at the bakery in a few minutes?"

"See you then."

James waved at Susannah and hopped down the aisle at Hanna's side.

Susannah and Jonathan were too busy squabbling over which type of cookies to get to put up much of a fuss.

Thank God for small miracles.

But watching Hanna glide away, blond ponytail swishing side to side, without a care in the world, she sighed. Oh, the ease of shopping for one. Or two, since Hanna was keeping James tonight.

Sara shook her head. Truth be told, she'd never really missed that part of singleness. Or any other part, besides solitary trips to the bathroom. Give her a large kitchen and a good-sized family to feed, and she was in heaven. As long as Clint did the dishes afterward.

They maneuvered around some displays and into the produce section.

Susannah tugged at her shorts. "I need to go to the bathroom, Mama."

Sara looked at her son unhappily secured in the cart and then back down at her little mini-me. "Let's go meet Hanna. Maybe she can watch Jonathan while we find the rest room."

They caught up with Hanna at the deli counter. "Sure, I'll keep an eye on the little guy."

"Want to walk. Pease?" Jonathan's wide eyes begged for a little taste of freedom.

Sara lifted him from the buggy. "Stay with Hanna and James."

" 'Kay."

"We'll be fine." Hanna took Jonathan's hand in hers. "Meet you by the phones in a few minutes?"

Sara nodded.

The three of them turned toward the bakery for a cookie.

Her stomach turned queasy as she watched them go. From the news reports and Clint's case, she knew that too many little brown-haired boys had disappeared in the last few months and ended up dead in a park way too close to her home.

Shaking her head at her own paranoia, she steered Susannah toward the rest rooms.

Being an agent's wife challenged her sanity on so many levels.

No use giving in to today's round of crazy thoughts.

❀ ❀ ❀

Tim parked his rented SUV in the alleyway behind the grocery store.

Two weeks of watching the Rollins family while the FBI was spying on his house had provided exactly the information he needed.

He'd also discovered that late afternoon was the perfect time to slip into the back of the grocery through the employee entrance. He'd already done a very successful trial run. At this time of day, with no deliveries, most employees stayed busy at the registers out front. And all of them grew antsy for the weekend and weren't paying attention to much besides the time clock.

Self-absorbed teens served him well.

So did the fact that Friday was grocery day for the Rollins clan.

He waltzed into the delivery area and made a beeline for the place where he'd spotted the work aprons last time. Straightening his tan pants and white button-up, he relaxed his shoulders and grabbed one of the blue uniform pieces.

Too bad things hadn't worked out at the ice-cream shop. It would have been easier to do what he'd planned at King Street and then hop on George Washington Parkway toward Rock Creek Park.

But he had gotten another good look at Dr. Rollins. Close enough to see the fatigue of her pregnancy showing. And he'd watched her long enough to know she'd do her weekly grocery run regardless…and take both the children with her.

Acid in his gut crawled upward. The good doctor was going to have a baby. That fact alone sent ice slivers through his veins. Because of her and her colleague's incompetence, his child was dead. And yet here she was, free to have more and more of her own flesh and blood. With the man who had ruined his life thirteen years ago.

Today he'd put an end to all that.

Tying his blue apron behind him, he looked up just in time to see the redheaded doctor approaching with her daughter in tow. Why was she back here? His hands grew clammy.

No time now to lose it.

He forced his mind to concentrate. He'd adapt to the circumstances. In only a short while, they'd remember him forever. The incompetent doctor. The man who'd started it all. Those FBI agents who couldn't leave well enough alone.

All of them.

"Excuse me. Could you tell me where the bathrooms are? I must have missed them." The woman looked down at her fidgeting little girl and stopped. "Just a second, Susannah. We're almost there."

Perfect.

Tim smiled. "Um, sorry. I'm new." He shrugged and pointed to his right, toward the storage area. "You might check that way."

"Thanks."

His system kicked into military mode. Slow, controlled breathing, no matter how erratically his heart beat. All he had to do was find what he wanted and slip out the back.

Fast.

Stepping out from the back area and turning right, he decided to walk the perimeter of the store first. In the dairy section, he spotted an attractive blonde with two small boys dancing around her legs while she tried to decide on which creamer to purchase.

His targets.

Grabbing an armful of milk jugs, he swapped them with an adjoining group.

"Sweetie," said an old woman, stepping between him and the blonde and touching her arm. "Could you tell me what your favorite brand of yogurt is? I just read how good yogurt is for your digestion, and…"

"I wanna find my mama." Rollins's little boy darted past the bottled-water aisle, his brown-headed friend in pursuit.

A brown-headed, blue-eyed boy.

Just his type.

Tim followed. Just past the aisle, he laid his hand on the older boy's shoulder. "You all shouldn't be running around. Didn't your parents teach you not to race inside?"

Kessler's boy stared at his shoes and held tightly to his friend. "Come on, Jonathan, let's go back to Aunt Hanna."

"I just saw your mommy over by the rest room. She looked like she was searching for you."

"My mama?"

"Here." Tim held out his hand. "I'll take you to her." The three of them started walking toward the middle of the store.

Perfect.

"James?" A panicked woman's voice the next aisle over made him bite back a curse.

The older boy tried to pull Jonathan back. "I think we'd better go get my aunt."

Tim jerked the boys' hands apart. He could only manage one of them.

"Why don't you go get your aunt?" He shoved Kessler's boy away and hurried toward the bathrooms. "Look, here's the rest room now."

"Mama!" The little boy tried to pull free. Out of the corner of his eye, Tim could see a redhead running his way.

"Jonathan!"

He pulled the boy into his arms like a football and turned with an upraised fist, just as she drew close. Connecting with her jaw, he spun clear around and took off. Behind him, he heard the little girl scream as Dr. Rollins smacked hard against the floor.

"Mama! Let me go. I wan' my mama!" Jonathan struggled against his arm.

Behind him, he could hear loud calls and stampeding footsteps.

He ran through the storage area and right past stunned employees. No one even got close enough to lay a hand on him.

Grabbing the keys out of his pocket, he unlocked the doors of his SUV with the remote, shoved the boy onto the passenger side floorboard, and climbed in.

The engine roared to life as a stupid teen slammed his fist into the driver's side window.

Tim floored it and left the punk flat on the ground.

Mission accomplished.

Jonathan cowered on the floor, whimpering. At the stoplight, Kramer slipped a small syringe out of his pants pocket and leaned over.

"Don' touch me!"

He reached past the flailing hands and jabbed the needle into the boy's thigh.

Tossing the syringe in the backseat, he counted seconds until the pathetic wailing ceased.

Silence.

That was more like it. Now all he had to do was get to the pre-arranged spot and wait. The cavalry wouldn't be too far behind. Then the real fun would begin.

38

"Slow down, Hanna, and tell me where you are." Steven threaded in and out of freeway traffic on his way toward Alexandria.

They'd been notified of Sara's attack and Jonathan's disappearance and were closing the distance between them and the grocery store where Kramer was last sighted.

Clint white-knuckled the door handle, his jaw set like stone.

Hanna's sniffles over the phone tore at his heart. "We're on our way to Alexandria Community." Her voice trembled. "Sara's bleeding. The EMTs say she'll be—"

Call waiting beeped, blotting out the last word.

"Hanna, you stick with Sara and Susannah and James." He switched lines and adjusted his earpiece. "Kessler."

"This is headquarters, Agent Kessler. I'm patching you through to a caller who's being taped and traced."

"Go ahead."

"Agent Kessler, so good of you to take my call."

Steven gripped the steering wheel and wanted to rip it off its base. "Where are you? What do you want?" Keeping an eye on Clint, he fought to maintain a calm tone.

"I thought you'd never ask." Kramer's slithering voice crawled through the phone line. "Tell the Rollinses this is payback for ruining my life. Twice. Now they'll see how it feels."

Kramer's words grew louder every syllable. "Since you've destroyed my favorite park, you'll find us in Rock Creek. The Western Ridge trail north of Military Road. Right where the trail intersects the Pinehurst Branch tributary. I'm sure you can find me. The question is, will you be in time?"

The line went dead. Steven pulled a U-turn and headed north.

"Is Jonathan still alive?"

Clint's question didn't surprise him. "I believe he is. I don't have time to drop you off at the hospital like we planned, so I'll leave you at head-quarters. You go see your family and sit tight while we find Jonathan and take Kramer down."

"Nothing doing. I'm going with you."

"That's exactly what Kramer wants. He'll get a bead on you and kill Jonathan too." He hated blasting Clint this way with the most likely scenario.

"You'll waste time dropping me off, and my son could be dead before you get there."

True. The loss of time might prove fatal. Steven changed lanes and sped past a dawdling Lincoln, letting his mind readjust. He'd have to take his chances with Clint there. And try to convince him to stay out of the fray.

His phone buzzed. "Kessler."

"I'm almost to the park now, boss." Michael's voice sounded harder than granite. "Locals are on-site and heading to the north side now. When are you due?"

"ETA twenty minutes."

"Where's Clint?"

"With me."

Michael's low growl spoke volumes. "You gonna handcuff him to the car?"

"We'll see when we get there."

❈   ❈   ❈

Hanna paced the waiting room like a caged tiger.

Sara and Susannah were probably terrified back in the ER, waiting for news about Conor and Jonathan.

Hanna had called Steven, who assured her they'd find Jonathan and meet them at the hospital soon. But how could he know they'd find him?

This is all my fault. If Jonathan doesn't come home…

She replayed the whole nightmare for the hundredth time. The boys disappearing around the aisle. The sound of James's panicked voice. The tall, bald man with Jonathan tucked under his arms. Sara running. A fist connecting. Susannah's screams.

Sara's blood everywhere.

With each memory, her insides threatened to explode.

James wrapped his arms around her legs. "When can we see Susannah and her mommy? Will Mrs. Sara be okay? Does Daddy have Jonathan?"

She picked up her nephew and hugged him close. No honest answer formed in her mind.

A middle-aged male nurse cleared his throat. "Miss Kessler? Dr. Rollins is asking for you. If you'll follow me." He led them back to a treatment room and opened the sliding glass door, moving the curtains as they entered.

"Sara." Her friend looked as white as the hospital sheets beneath her.

"Are you okay, 'Sannah?" James wriggled out of her arms and hurried to Susannah's side.

Tears filled Sara's green eyes. A screaming red mark streaked one side of her face, and a white bandage stood out against the other side.

Sara held out a shaky hand. "Please make them tell me what's happened to Jonathan. And Conor. They won't say whether my boys are all right or not. Please, Hanna, I need to know my babies are okay."

Another wave of unbearable guilt. If only she'd kept a closer watch on Jonathan.

"I'll see what I can do." She hurried from the room.

Walking up to the nurse's station, she steadied her voice. "Who's taking care of Sara Rollins? I need to speak with Sara's doctor."

"That would be me." A strong male voice spoke behind her. "Dr. Peter Greer."

She turned. "Is Sara's baby still alive? She needs to know. Now."

The doctor drew in a deep breath, but his gray blue eyes never left hers. "Let's go into the treatment room. I'll talk to Sara."

She followed the doctor, not knowing what else to ask.

Sara's eyes grew wide and then snapped closed when the doctor stepped in. "Peter, tell me what's happened."

Susannah buried her face in Sara's side. "Where's my J.J., Mama? I want my brother!"

"Sara." Dr. Greer stuffed Sara's chart under his arm and shoved his hands into his white coat. He hesitated, then brought them out again and reached for her hand.

Hanna hadn't thought Sara could get any paler, but she did. "Peter, I want answers right now. Where is Jonathan, and what's going on with my baby?"

"We don't have any word yet on Jonathan." He swallowed hard. "And the nurse couldn't find a heartbeat with the fetoscope."

Hanna's hands shook. *God, You can't let this happen. Not Jonathan and Conor too.*

Sara's grabbed her stomach. "No. He has to be okay. Fetoscopes aren't always reliable. You have to do an ultrasound. Conor has to be okay."

"Sara, calm down. We're waiting on the portable now. They should be here any minute." Dr. Greer examined the bandages. "Your external bleeding is under control. No broken jawbone either. And only a few stitches on the bottom lip."

"You'll tell me if you hear anything about Jonathan."

Dr. Greer didn't respond.

"Peter, I need to know." Her eyes flashed fury. "If you've heard something…"

"We haven't, Sara." He stepped toward the door. "I'll go see what's happening with that ultrasound." Dr. Greer and his white coat disappeared.

Hanna's mind searched for some way to help. "I'll call Steven again." It was all she could think of.

The first thing she heard over the phone line was tree branches snapping and male voices yelling in the background. "Make it quick, Hanna. What's wrong?"

"They can't hear Conor's heartbeat."

Silence.

"Where are you, and where is Jonathan?"

"We're at Rock Creek Park. Tell Sara we have the situation under control. Clint and Jonathan are safe."

"Really?" More silence. She tightened her grip on the cell phone. "Steven, is that the truth?"

"With God's help, it will be."

※　※　※

Michael looked over his shoulder toward the trail.

They were deep in the park, surrounded by green trees. And thanks to DC's finest, well away from curious civilians. Across a small clearing, members of the SWAT team sighted through their scopes and locked in on Timothy Kramer.

But no one could take a shot. Not when Kramer used Jonathan as an effective shield and stayed glued to the steep bank of trees rising behind him. He kept moving, his gun pressed into Jonathan's temple. It wasn't worth the risk.

Yet.

Michael had managed to find a spot where the natural terrain, a slight slope with dense trees, provided cover and denied Kramer an easy sight line.

He glanced at his watch and wiped sweat from his forehead.

Steven stayed locked in place next to him, not moving his eyes from Kramer or Jonathan's limp form dangling in front of their perp. They were close enough to hear Kramer's taunts.

Forcing his mind to concentrate, Michael kept his rifle trained on Kramer's forehead. He'd make the shot as soon as one came open.

"Where's your star FBI agent, Kessler? Your partner? I know you're both out there."

Steven's teeth ground together so loudly, Michael thought they'd break. He wasn't too far behind his boss.

"It's all his fault this ever started."

"What's that guy babbling about?" DC's top SWAT commander barked through the earpiece.

"He's talking about Clint Rollins."

"The boy's dad? Tell me you're not letting Rollins anywhere near here."

"He's staying put in my car." Steven voice was pure steel.

"Bad call, Agent Kessler."

"My call, Major."

Michael wanted to knock their heads together. Letting Clint anywhere near Kramer would be nothing short of a disaster. Clint had no agency-issued gun and no authority to use whatever backup he had. If Clint discharged a firearm under these circumstances, disobeying a direct order to remain in Steven's car, he'd likely be stripped of his badge. And judging from the ire in the SWAT commander's voice, he might even face jail time.

Michael wouldn't let that happen.

Standoff minutes raked his nerves raw. Then his earpiece crackled with SWAT warnings directed at Clint. "Agent Rollins, stay in the car."

As if that would deter Clint.

Michael allowed himself a quick glance. Enough to see Clint stalking toward them, Glock in hand.

Steven secured his rifle and body-blocked Clint from plowing into the small clearing in front of Kramer. "Clint, no. You are not walking into a massacre."

"He's gonna kill Jonathan." Clint shoved Steven into the tree roots. "Sara said he's already killed Conor."

Steven recovered fast and slammed into Clint's knees, bringing him down and kicking Clint's weapon out of reach before he could retrieve it. "No, Clint. He's not going to win this. I won't let you walk into his trap."

"I've gotta do something." Clint's voice sounded like sandpaper, but he would push until the very end. Michael couldn't blame him.

"Kramer has nothing to lose here." Steven kept a restraining hand on Clint's crouching form. "He knows he won't make it out alive. And he wants to take us all with him. You walk out there, you make it easy for him."

A small noise made them look up. Jonathan whimpered and started to stir. Kramer kept an arm tight around the little boy, while silver duct tape bound his hands and feet.

Michael refocused his sights. This looked like a bad replay of last year's standoff with Ryan's abductor.

"He's waking up, Rollins," Kramer shouted. "Don't you want the last thing your boy sees to be you?"

Clint's growl exploded through the forest.

Steven tackled him again. "No. Not this way."

"Oh, come on now, Rollins. Cancer can't possibly have made you this much of a wimp." Kramer kept moving in a crouched position with his back against an old picnic table. "Meg's dead. But you already knew that. Your wife lied, said they'd help Meg. They killed her instead. But I paid your wife back for that. Now it's your turn."

Michael wanted to land a bullet right in this fool's mouth. He shifted toward the right and reframed the rifle's scope.

"I'm here, Kramer." Clint's yell silenced Kramer for a beat. But Clint stayed hidden.

"So good of you to join us, Agent Rollins. Remember me? The one whose life you ruined thirteen years ago? Well, thanks to your wife's bumbling and the FBI's meddling, it's ruined once again."

Steven spoke low and directly into his body mic. "Hold your fire."

"Affirmative." The SWAT commander's terse reply sounded like gravel.

Michael forced his hands to freeze with his index finger curled around the trigger. Sweat beads trailed down his spine.

Steven's boot nudged against his leg. "Give me three beats after I speak."

Michael didn't move.

"We're coming out, Kramer. Let the boy go." Steven and Clint stepped from behind a clump of trees.

"Daddy!" Jonathan struggled harder and bent in half to get free.

"Well, look how the mighty—"

Michael pulled the trigger. The explosion pierced the forest and echoed.

"—have fallen," Michael finished.

Steven and Clint rushed to pick up Jonathan.

Adrenaline coursed through every nerve ending as Michael secured his rifle. Then he leaned over and puked into the bushes.

"Good shot, Parker. Didn't think a CACU rookie had it in 'im." The SWAT commander stopped next to him. Together they watched Kramer's little clearing swarm with law enforcement.

Wiping his face on his coveralls, Michael stood on wobbly legs.

He'd done it.

"I lub you, Daddy!" Jonathan's voice carried over the police shuffle. "You saveded me."

Michael's eyes filled with tears. Even the weathered SWAT commander nodded in silence.

This was what mattered most.

Returning children to their parents' arms.

Helping the good guys win.

39

Sara stared at her cell phone, willing it to ring.

Minutes ago, right after she'd told Clint her fears about Conor, he'd done something he'd never done before.

"I can't believe Clint hung up on me." When she needed him the most.

"Mama, I'm hungry." Susannah's confused eyes made it clear she couldn't possibly grasp all that was happening around her. And it had to be getting late. Why hadn't she thought about that?

"C'mon, guys." Hanna pulled Susannah and James to her side. "Let's go find something to eat." Looking at the floor, she continued. "I'll make sure the kids stay safe this time, Sara."

Hanna's sad eyes said she was blaming herself for everything. But Sara had no words of comfort to give. She had nothing left. So she let Hanna walk out bearing blame that wasn't hers.

It's not yours either.

The quiet thought startled her. But that was right. Some crazy man had taken her son. He'd hurt her and Conor too.

But maybe if she'd kept a better watch or kicked the man. Something. The lack of movement inside her abdomen pushed her beyond reason. She'd failed again. Failed to protect her children.

"The Lord gave, and the Lord hath taken away; blessed be the name of the Lord."

June Wells had quoted that verse to her. And Marilynn had given her that stupid song, which kept crashing through her thoughts. She'd listened to it again and again in the past few weeks, but now the words sounded cruel. And impossible.

She leaned back in the ER bed. So many thoughts and emotions swirled through her brain. Nothing made sense. Least of all praising the Lord who had let so many awful things happen.

Praise Him in everything? In cancer. In the hospital. When she'd failed. When people died. When there was nothing good in the circumstances. Or in her future.

"I know the plans I have for you...plans to give you hope and a future."

That verse from Jeremiah came out of nowhere. But it connected with her heart. "You have a hope and a future for me? What about for Jonathan and Conor too? How can I believe Your promises when nothing is going right?"

Are you depending on circumstances and people?

Marilynn's question laid Sara bare before God. That was what it all came down to. If she could only praise God in good times, then her dependence was on circumstances and people. But what if she praised God when it made no sense, when believing His promises seemed foolish? When her baby could still die? Or her husband?

Then what?

Then she was truly depending on God. The only One who knew all things and knew what was best, even if she didn't understand or want it.

Could she praise Him now, no matter what happened next?

"Yes." Tears fell as her defenses broke. She couldn't keep up the way she'd been going. This was the only right choice.

"You give." Touching her stomach, more tears came. "And You sometimes take away. Blessed be Your name."

❄   ❄   ❄

Clint stood transfixed, watching the paramedics examine Jonathan.

His son was alive. So was he.

Eyes burning with unshed tears, he concentrated on the sight of Jonathan picking at the green grass and sucking his thumb. His little boy smiled when one of the medics handed him a new teddy bear.

God had heard. And given him one of the miracles he'd begged for months ago. To help him catch a killer. Not only that, but he'd received a second miracle in the form of Jonathan's warm hug and laughing eyes.

But he hadn't really captured Kramer.

And the cancer remained.

And now Conor...

"Why do you look like you're at a funeral?" Steven's hand clamped his shoulder. Hard. Then he motioned toward the edge of the clearing and walked over, waiting for Clint to follow.

He didn't know how to respond. Any answer to his partner's question would sound ungrateful, given that Steven and Michael had been the ones to save Jonathan and keep him from walking into Kramer's bullets.

Jonathan was telling the paramedic some kind of story, his arms stretched high over his head. He would be safe with the paramedic for a few minutes. Clint joined Steven at the edge of the clearing.

He took a deep breath. It didn't help. Forcing himself to meet his partner's eyes, he explained. "When you left me in your Explorer, I called Sara. She told me that when Kramer hit her, he killed Conor."

Steven held up a hand. "Wait a minute. Did Sara actually say Conor died? Hanna said they couldn't get a heartbeat. That's not the same as dead."

"The doctor hadn't done the ultrasound when I talked to her last. But they couldn't detect a heartbeat on the fetal monitor, and Sara said she'd been cramping. Which means my son is most likely dead." He rubbed his bald head. "I'm sorry. You and Michael just saved Jonathan and me. I shouldn't be acting like this."

"Be where you are, Clint."

Steven's quiet words gave him the permission he'd denied himself.

No show. No tough cop. Just be.

Sinking to the ground, he pressed his forehead against his knees.

"I could quote you a bunch of scriptures."

"Don't." Clint looked up.

His partner's half smile fit. "You know them better than I do, anyway."

"Yeah." Forcing any more words past his raw vocal cords proved impossible.

"Daddy, I ride in the am'b'lance!" Jonathan beamed at them. He acted like his old self. But after an experience like this, even the most resilient kid would have scars.

Clint waved. "I'm coming, son."

Michael joined them. "They're ready to take him to the hospital. There'll be a crisis counselor from headquarters meeting you there."

The young agent's eyes had aged in the last few minutes. Using deadly force did that faster and harder than almost anything else in life.

"If you want, I can bring your truck over there." Michael swallowed hard.

Steven raised his eyebrows. "And pick up my sister and James?"

Michael studied his shoes. "I hadn't thought of that. But I'd be happy to take them home."

Michael not thinking of Hanna? That didn't sound good.

"Agent Rollins?" A paramedic called from a few feet away. "You ready?"

He stood and walked to the middle of the clearing, Steven by his side.

"Four words, Clint." Steven held up his fingers.

"That's it? After all the long-winded lectures I've given you?" The two paramedics and Steven smiled at that.

"In weakness there's strength."

He didn't want to think about that.

Steven stepped away and then stopped and turned back. "Talk to the counselor. Make sure your whole family does too."

Watching his partner walk away and slip back into full FBI mode left Clint aching and alone to face the four words he'd refused to accept.

In weakness there's strength.

He hated weakness.

Jonathan gripped his hand and held tight as they climbed into the ambulance and sped toward a situation he didn't want to face.

"Pway, Daddy. You know to pway." Jonathan's words rang through the ambulance's white and silver interior.

Pray. Jonathan's little-boy faith held the mirror in front of him and reflected what he'd tried to ignore.

God was God. He was not.

He'd fought the cancer. Fought his emotions. Fought the people who loved him.

And kept fighting to take care of things himself when God didn't answer the way he'd demanded.

Because he hated his weakness.

In the process, he'd missed the only thing worth holding on to.

"God is still on the throne. And He is good. Always." Frank's words echoed loud in his heart. Frank was right.

Clint squeezed his little boy's hand. "Yes, Jonathan. Daddy needs to pray." He looked at the paramedic, expecting scorn. But in the man's understanding eyes he found hope and a silent nod that asked and reassured at the same time.

"Father. Forgive me. I've been so stubborn and fought You every step. Fought everyone. But You saved us today. You answered my prayers Your way. I don't understand it all. But I do see that I'm not as strong as I thought I was. In my weakness, You were strong. And You are good…"

He couldn't finish for the tears clogging his throat. But he needed to say the words. Hear the words. "I hate cancer. I hate death. I hate being weak. But I am. And You are not. Forgive me for not believing You'd come through for me. Please—"

Tears splattered on the white sheet covering Jonathan. "It's 'kay, Daddy. Jesus lubs us."

Simple faith. No wonder Jesus said to come like little children.

"Please let Steven be right about Conor. Save our baby, Father. Let him live. And take this cancer away for good."

"Amen, Daddy." Jonathan smiled. "We see Mama and 'Sannah now? An' my brudder too?"

Clint couldn't speak.

The paramedic looked out the window. "We're pulling into Alexandria Community Hospital right now. We'll go directly to the ER."

Clint nodded his thanks.

A few minutes later, just inside the ER, he stopped. He wasn't ready to face Sara. *In my weakness, You are strong.* He repeated the words again and took a step forward.

Then another.

He was weak, but God was strong. God was God. God was in control.

And like Frank...like his little Jonathan...Clint would choose to believe that God was good.

Always.

❋ ❋ ❋

Sara studied the maroon and white balloons filling the special meeting room of the Benefield Cancer Center and smiled through her tears.

May tenth had arrived.

They would do Clint's off-treatment celebration today after chemo, and then they had an important July wedding to look forward to. In between, there would be numerous counseling appointments to attend as well.

Busy days.

They'd be looking ahead even as they talked about painful things.

And they'd be praising God in it all.

Conor was alive. And Clint was in remission.

But the last five months had shaken everything and left her still quivering on her knees with so many pieces to pick up.

A soft click of the door behind her stilled the memories.

"Hey, stranger. It's good to see you." Marilynn's bright yellow sundress swayed as she joined Sara. Leave it to Marilynn to dress in the color of hope. "Are you in here to hide?"

"No. Just thinking. Getting it out of the way so I can enjoy when Clint's finished with chemo and everyone arrives for the big celebration."

"Are both sets of parents here?"

"Yes." Sara placed a final balloon right by the place where Clint's picture would go. "They're all staying in a hotel this time to give us some space and still be close by."

Marilynn nodded. "You know it wasn't your fault, don't you?"

"I know that evil man did an evil thing. It's still hard not to look at what I should have done differently. Hard not to just stay in the house and try to keep anything else bad from happening."

"And suffocate in a bubble? That's not life. And even if you could do that, it wouldn't stop the reality of living in a fallen world."

"I know. Still…" Marilynn was right. But it didn't make her feel better.

"God protected them, remember." Her best friend's words struck a tender place inside.

"Jonathan and Conor, yes. But not…" She forced the words out. "Not the six other little boys."

Marilynn rubbed her arms. "That is a question you and Clint and the rest of humanity will have to wrestle with until we see things clearly. Not dimly, with the warped mirrors of human understanding, but face to face."

"You mean in heaven."

"Yes." Her best friend wrapped her in a gentle spring hug, one full of life and promise. Pointing to the off-treatment board, Marilynn added, "You made it. Survivors. Each one of you."

Sara studied the faces. Names she didn't recognize and pictures of people she'd never seen covered the large wall of cork. Next to it hung the tribute quilt June Wells had created and dedicated in Frank's honor. A starburst of colors embellished with photos, like the Ground Zero quilt. Except these photos depicted those who hadn't made it to the off-treatment board.

None forgotten. Only celebrated differently.

"I wish I had believed Frank's words earlier." Sara wiped her face with the Kleenex Marilynn pressed into her hand, then sagged into her friend's solid embrace.

"Sometimes we have to walk through the fire before we believe God can be trusted. Experience has a way of pressing head knowledge into our heart."

"If we turn to God, that is."

"You are. So is Clint. You're learning to bless God's name in all circumstances." Marilynn touched her gently rounded abdomen. "And so will Conor, come October."

New tears traced worn paths down Sara's cheeks. "But the cancer could come back. You and I know that better than most." She held up a hand to Marilynn's protest. "And Conor still might not survive. His heartbeat was barely detectable and much too slow when they did the ultrasound in the hospital."

"What was Frank's dying wish for you and Clint, Sara?"

She sighed. "That we hold tight to the truth, for better or for worse. That we remember God is to be praised all the time because He is good. That was Frank's legacy."

"What he wanted you to not only know, but believe."

Words wouldn't come, so she just closed her eyes.

"You and Clint are survivors, Sara. Frank is one too. Only he made it into Jesus's arms first."

Marilynn gave her one last squeeze and then slipped out of the room.

Sara glanced at June's quilt one more time. "Blessed be Your name. In death and suffering. In life and hope. You give and take away. Blessed be Your name."

40

Steven had survived to see July seventh.

Clint smiled and rubbed the military-cut peach fuzz on top of his head. He'd even bulked up enough to fill out his fancy monkey suit once more.

His smile grew to laughter as Steven paced the altar area of Hope Ridge Academy's chapel. Up the four marble steps leading to the platform, then back down and into the small room where they'd tangled with their tuxes.

Back out and down the aisle to the front doorway.

"Nothing doing, Steven Kessler." Clint shooed the groom away from the double doors. "You are not going out there to find Gracie."

"I should have eloped."

"And miss all this fun?"

Steven paced again. But when he grabbed a broom from the changing room and started sweeping the marble stairs, Clint had to step in. He snatched the broom and secured it far away from the nervous groom, whose butterfingers could send the wood flying through a stained-glass window.

"Is it eleven o'clock yet? Please tell me it's eleven."

Checking his watch yet again, Clint shook his head. "Not even close, partner." Leave it to FBI agents to be on time. At minimum, ten minutes early. But they still had a lot longer than that to go.

He walked to the front pews and pulled out an order of service. Steven had insisted on a short and to-the-point ceremony. *"Because the kids won't be able to sit that long."*

Right.

More like Steven had waited long enough and would boil over if he and his bride weren't sent off soon.

Michael slipped in through a side door along with a young man carrying video equipment.

"Is Hanna here?" Steven stopped pacing. "She'll get things moving, right?"

"She's downstairs taking prewedding pictures of the ladies and probably giving the wedding photographer last-minute tips." Michael studied his shiny black shoes.

The videographer started setting up as the pianist began her long list of songs to play.

Hoping a change of scenery would distract Steven, Clint herded both men out the side door into the small adjoining courtyard, where the florists and caterers were assembling their flower-and-food magic. His stomach growled. He'd been waiting for this day ever since his ability to taste had returned.

Michael's hand came down hard on his shoulder. "Packing heat again?"

"Every day but today." Sara had always hated watching him strap on his weapon as he dressed for work. But she'd smiled the first time he headed out, gun in place, after passing assessments and being reinstated to full duty. So today he'd honored her and left it at home, even if he'd rather have his Glock right where it belonged.

Michael joined Steven in wearing a path along the small walkway next to the chapel.

Clint leaned against the chapel's gray stone wall. "Your pacing is not gonna make time move any faster."

Michael shot a look at him. "Were you this crazy when you tied the knot?"

"Crazy doesn't begin to describe it." He grinned. "But the honeymoon and nine years of loving Sara was worth enduring the wedding ceremony and reception."

"If we could ever get this show on the road, I'd like to enjoy my turn." Steven stopped and quirked a grin that would have made Gracie blush.

"A few more hours till you're outta here, that's all."

"Hours?" Steven adjusted his cummerbund and started pacing again.

Clint laughed and then nudged Michael, who was studying the ground. "What's up with you? Already nervous about popping the question to Hanna?"

Steven scowled.

Missing the big-brother grimace, Michael leaned against the wall. "Hanna's not letting it go. You know, what happened in May. She hasn't wanted to talk about it or even go out except for wedding-related things or taking care of Champ. What can I do?"

"Maybe watching Steven marry the love of his life will help her see that things are getting better. We're all still walking through the healing one step at a time."

The younger agent shook his head. "I don't think the wedding will help. If Steven hadn't made her swear she'd be here today, I think she would have left for Louisville already and never looked back."

Raw pain filled Michael's eyes. So did fear. And love.

Clint stared at the caterers while he tried to think of a way to help. "How 'bout if Sara and I talk to her? She let herself cry when we told her we never blamed her."

"But now she cries all the time."

"You know all too well how hard the shooting was." He faced Michael. "But we trained for this. We busted our tails at Quantico to learn how to deal with deadly force situations. And we have counselors to help us walk through it without losing our minds."

"Hanna wasn't prepared."

"No. Being an FBI sibling isn't the same as being an agent or an FBI spouse."

Michael startled at that thought. "We're not talking marriage yet. Maybe not ever."

"You have Champ. That's a start."

"Champ's a great dog, but sharing him isn't like having a child. There's nothing to keep Hanna here if she believes running away will fix it all."

"Then you wait. And pray." He gripped Michael's bicep and let go quickly. "We're praying too."

"Thanks."

The perky wedding planner Gracie had hired poked her head out the side door. "Okay, FBI tough guys, conquer your butterflies, and let's get the party started."

"Finally." Steven looked up into the clear blue sky. "Thank You, God!"

Michael managed a chuckle.

He'd learn too. Like Clint and Steven had. God was still on His throne. And love not only covered a multitude of sins, but it never failed.

Ever.

❊   ❊   ❊

The church doors opened, and the familiar notes of the wedding march filled the chapel.

Gracie floated down the aisle on her dad's arm, her pink-tinged cheeks setting off a beautiful smile. Sara had described Gracie's gown as an "elegant, off-white, floor-length sheath with a sleeveless princess bodice."

That was total Greek to Clint. He only knew she made a stunning bride. And Steven stood transfixed.

As did the entire wedding party. Hanna, Leah, and Gracie's sister, Beth, stood with Sara, dabbing eyes and smiling big. Even Steven's dad, Michael, and Lee had their fair share of emotions showing.

Whispers and sniffles from family and friends filled the chapel. Gracie's students were all in attendance and behaving well. Susannah was the proudest of them all. Well, maybe second to James. Steven's little boy made a debonair ring bearer. And Susannah had been a beautiful flower girl, showering the aisle with yellow and white rose petals and making the chapel ready for Gracie's big walk.

He smiled across the altar at his stunning bride of nine years, visibly pregnant and all decked out in pastel blue. She looked even better than she had on their wedding day. And that was saying a lot, because she'd been the most beautiful bride ever.

Gracie kissed her dad and whispered, just loudly enough for Clint to catch it. "I love you, Daddy. I'll always be your little girl."

Her father sniffled. And Clint couldn't help but do the same.

This was part of having a daughter. And he wouldn't miss it for the world. Even if having a baby girl meant he'd walk her down an aisle and into somebody else's home one day.

For now, he loved being close enough to hear all the little things that wouldn't make it onto the wedding video. Like the sweet words from Gracie to her father. Words he hoped Susannah would whisper into his ear on her big day.

A day far, far away.

The videographer zoomed in, and the photographer snapped pictures as Robert Thompson clasped Steven on the shoulder and then moved Gracie's hand from his own to Steven's.

Clint's smile grew. This day had been so long in coming, and he and Sara had prayed for it as hard as they could pray.

Glancing into the congregation, he made sure Jonathan was safe with Mom. No worries there. His little boy sat beaming between his grandmas, getting a fair share of happy attention.

Even the presence of Steven's ex-wife had been a reminder of healing instead of pain. Steven and Gracie had agreed to invite Angela and her husband. That was a bold step forward in reconciling the past and present for all of them.

Beth sang a song that Gracie had written. While the bride and groom lit their tall white unity candle, Beth's clear soprano echoed the look shining from Gracie's eyes as she formed the words, "I hold you in my heart. My love to you I give. He holds us together as three in One we live."

Pastor Bowden stood in front of Gracie and Steven as he prayed for their future together and their shared commitment to purity, trust, hope, and love.

At the signal from the wedding planner, Clint stepped forward with James and placed the wedding rings on the pillow James held.

Gracie and Steven's pastor smiled like Christmas morning and cleared his throat.

This was the moment they'd all been waiting for.

"Do you, Steven Andrew Kessler, take Gracie Ann Lang to be your wife—to love and cherish even as Christ loved the Church and gave Himself for it? To lead her with gentle strength from this day forward, for better or worse, for richer or poorer, in sickness and in health, until you are face to face with Jesus?"

"I do."

Had it not been for the reverence of the occasion, Clint would have jumped up and given a whoop. The "I do" was his favorite part of a wedding. Well, besides the kiss. Those two little words held a lifetime of promise and hope.

As Gracie and Steven exchanged rings and whispered through their husky emotions, "With this ring, I thee wed," Clint wasn't sure how to stop the tears that trailed down his face.

They'd made it.

Five months ago, he hadn't thought he'd ever see this day healthy and ready for all the promises wrapped up in "I do."

The pastor's deep and solemn voice drew his attention back to the bride and groom. "What, therefore, God has joined together, let no man put asunder. And now, by the power vested in me by the Commonwealth of Virginia and Almighty God, I now pronounce you man and wife."

The clergyman paused and, at Gracie's raised eyebrows, chuckled before continuing.

"You may *now* kiss the bride."

Steven didn't have to be told twice. He smiled down on his blushing bride and bent to kiss her with controlled passion in front of God and the whole world.

Then he lowered her down into a lip-locked dip.

Laughter filled the chapel.

Sara winked at Clint from her perch on the second marble step. He smiled back. Then his wife's full peach-colored lips mouthed words that rooted deep into his soul.

"I still do."

He swallowed past the mass of emotions in his throat and whispered a reply. "Me too. Forever."

Lord willing, they'd live each day of that forever as a gift.

Steven and Gracie turned and faced the audience, both breathless, Gracie glowing.

Pastor Bowden's grin spread across his face. "It is my distinct privilege and pleasure to present to you Mr. and Mrs. Steven Kessler."

Clint chuckled as the newlyweds beat a hasty retreat down the aisle. He could relate.

They'd made it, all of them. From better to worse to better again.

And just like Steven and Gracie, he and Sara would keep walking back into life. Toward the open arms that held the future.

Toward trust. Into belief.

One small step at a time.

Dear Reader,

Thank you for taking this emotional and adrenaline-filled journey with me through the pages of *Healing Promises*. As I wrote this book, Sara and Clint's story became mine in many ways. Struggling with physical pain and fighting the "I can do it all" myth as well as lies about my worth, my weakness, and who I depend on shook me to my core. I've known the truth and taught it to others. But when life implodes, it's so hard to find solid footing and remember the truth.

One thing I learned in writing this story was that no matter how profoundly our lives and faith get shaken, God never lets go. He has a future and hope for each of us. No matter what.

Two memories played over and over in my mind as I worked on Clint and Sara's story. One morning more than ten years ago, I sat in my Sunday school class excitedly awaiting my chance to share the happy announcement of my first pregnancy. Everyone celebrated and congratulated. Then a couple sitting to my right quietly shared about their recent miscarriage. The silence in the room stole my breath and heartbeat. But the husband turned to me, looked me straight in the eyes, and said, "The Lord gives and takes away. Blessed be His name." The grace he gave with tear-filled eyes and a heart tuned to God allowed us to celebrate and grieve together, as well as praise the Lord in both situations.

That moment in time will stay with me forever. Over the years, I've had a turn in my friends' shoes. And it's taken time wrestling with God to say from my heart, with the image of my three children here on earth and one in heaven, "The Lord has given and taken away. Blessed be His name."

The other moment seared in my memory that *Healing Promises* brought back with painful clarity was the day of my friend Ken's funeral. At the end of a bittersweet but beautiful ceremony, I stood with my hand in my husband's, tears streaming down my face. Gayla, Ken's widow, stopped, looked at my hand in David's, and smiled at me on her way out with her family of three young sons. I marveled at her peaceful faith and tear-stained joy while I was still struggling to talk to God after three years of pleas for healing and then watching my friend die. Later, in answer to my questions, Gayla said these words: "God gave me exactly the grace I needed during this time. It was not the same as what you needed. But you have to keep looking to Him."

Most if not all of us have similar stories imprinted on our hearts. Different circumstances. Same wrestling with God. Pain. Broken bodies and hearts. Maybe even the strong desire to run from hope because it hurts. Or to turn away from God and never look back. When that happens, I hope you'll consider Peter's words in John 6:68: "Lord, to whom shall we go? You have the words of eternal life." I pray you'll remember He's the only best place to run.

God alone has the comfort your heart seeks. My prayer is that you'll cling to His hand, trust His promises, and rest in His perfect care. For better or for worse, believe the truth. God is good. And He is for you. Always.

Because of His grace,
Amy

Please visit me online at the Heart Chocolate (www.amywallace.com) and Defenders of Hope (www.defendersofhope.com) Web sites. As always, I'd love to hear from you!

Please look for the next installment in the

Defenders of Hope series—Michael and Hanna's story.

Coming Spring 2009!

DISCUSSION QUESTIONS

Healing Promises

1. Clint and Sara struggled to believe God's promises of protection and healing when life gave them a multitude of reasons to stop hoping. Can you relate? What scriptures do you cling to when life grows dark and painful?

2. What about when things don't go the way we prayed? Or when it seems like God hasn't protected and healed? I love the book of Job because Job's example gives us the freedom to ask God why and also to be reminded of the truth that we don't see the big picture God sees. When you read Job 1:8–12; 38:1–7; 42:1–3; 1 Corinthians 13:12; and 1 John 4:16, what thoughts come to mind? How can these verses strengthen our hearts when life hurts?

3. In the daily battles we face, internal and external, sometimes it appears that evil is winning. Like Clint and Sara, we're tempted to harden our hearts against hope because we're weary and just want to escape the pain. But what do Psalm 62:5; Jeremiah 29:11; Romans 8:28; and 1 John 5:4 say is the foundation of our hope? How do you stay open to hope and to God?

4. Think of a time when you've been wounded in the battles of life or prayed for others who have been wounded. What do Psalm 103:1–5 and Romans 5:3–5 say about hope, God's healing, and our response to difficult times?

5. What provision and promise has God given to each of us in Ephesians 6:10–18; 1 Timothy 6:12; and Hebrews 11:1 that will enable us to fight the fight of faith with hope…and win?

6. Frank's dying wish was that, for better or for worse, those he loved

would hold tight to the truth that God is on His throne and always good. If you've lost a loved one, how did God comfort you? What legacy of hope do you want to leave your loved ones?

7. In the face of death, what does it mean to grieve with hope? Read 1 Thessalonians 4:13–18. How does Paul tell us to deal with death and encourage one another?

8. When you read in Job 1:21 about blessing the name of the Lord when He gives and takes away, what does that stir up in you? If we lived like we believed this verse, how would our actions show it?

9. In what ways do we praise God? Are some methods of praise easier for you than others? Why or why not?

10. At the end of the story, Sara says she wishes she'd believed Frank's words earlier. But her best friend says, "Sometimes we have to walk through the fire before we believe God can be trusted. Experience has a way of pressing head knowledge into our heart." How have you found this to be true in your life?

11. John 6:29 says, "The work of God is this: to believe in the one he has sent." What does this mean to you? What about 1 John 3:23? Is belief something that comes easily to you? Why or why not?

12. One huge issue Clint struggled with throughout the book was body image. He hated all the physical and emotional changes cancer thrust upon him. He hated his own weakness. And how he viewed himself affected his faith, his marriage, and his job performance. Even without a major illness, most of us struggle with liking the view in our mirrors. Why do you think that is? And what do Genesis 1:27, 31; Psalm 45:11; 139:14; Zephaniah 3:17; and 2 Corinthians 12:9 have to say about what God thinks when He looks at us, His image-bearers?

13. Why do you think it took Sara a long time to stop depending on people and circumstances? Have you ever struggled with that? How did Sara begin to depend on God, and what part did praising Him play in that change?

14. Sara believed she was a failure when circumstances turned out badly or when she didn't measure up to her expectations. Fear of

failure is a common struggle that drives many of us to do better and to try harder instead of depending on the Lord. Take a look at Isaiah 41:10; 43:1–2; and John 16:33. How can these verses help us move from fear to faith?

15. Clint, Steven, and Michael exemplify the real-life FBI agents and other law-enforcement officers who are committed to protecting our children. If you have children in your life, how have you taught them about staying safe? Here are some possible scriptures to pray with your children, nieces and nephews, or other young people you care about to help them (and you) remember that God is our protector: Psalm 18:2; 23:4–6; 59:16–17; and 91:1–2.
16. If you don't already, will you please consider praying with the children in your life for the law-enforcement officers who serve us, daily working to keep us all safe? What other ways can you think of to encourage these men and women?
17. First Corinthians 13:8 says that love never fails. But many Christians experience broken or painful relationships. What do Mark 12:30–32; 1 Peter 1:22; and 1 John 4:16–19 say about God's love and how we are to love one another?

✱ ✱ ✱

I pray you'll know how abundantly, extravagantly, and completely you are loved by the God who fashioned you by His hand and who smiles as He looks at His beloved child—you.

Resources Used in Writing Healing Promises
Kay Marshall Strom, *The Cancer Survival Guide* (Beacon Hill Press, 2002).
www.cancer.org
www.clevelandclinic.org/cancer/scottcares
www.chemocare.com

Resources from Cancer Survivors
American Cancer Society—www.cancer.org
Leukemia Society—www.leukemia.org
National Cancer Institute—www.cancer.gov

Words of Wisdom from Cancer Survivors
"I think a patient is wise to get some basic information about the disease and treatments. However, too much information is not good. It is easy to get depressed looking at statistics. Each person is an individual case in God's hands. God will control the outcome of that person's illness! It is so important to place your faith in God to work through doctors.

"On a spiritual note, while I was sick I really enjoyed reading stories of people who truly put it all on the line for God and others—*J. Hudson Taylor: A Man in Christ* by Roger Steer, *Through Gates of Splendor* by Elisabeth Elliot, *The Hiding Place* by Corrie Ten Boom. These books reminded me how I actually had it easy compared to some of these people. They also reminded me to focus on using opportunities to share my faith—wherever that was—at the hospital, at the doctor's office, in e-mails. Sometimes when I wasn't feeling well, the most I could read was a daily devotional. I liked Billy Graham's *Unto These Hills*."
—Renee Koster

"The joy of the Lord was our strength, and our constant declaration was, 'When we come out on the other side of this, we're going to be better not worse.' We let the MD handle treatment, the Lord handle healing, and we focused on joy. It wasn't head in the sand; it was a time of great faith and trust in God's goodness."

—Chris and Tiffany Colter

CAN DREAMS BE REDEEMED?

GRACIE LANG lost her family and her faith all in one tragic moment. Now she gets through the days with nothing but the drive for justice propelling her forward.

STEVEN KESSLER is an FBI agent with an important job - rescuing other people's children during the day and caring for his son during the night.

Now a very real threat to a child dangerously intersects Steven and Gracie's worlds—a collision that demands a decision. One thing is certain…neither one of them will ever be the same again.